TREASON KEEP

TREASON KEEP

Book two of the Hythrun Chronicles

JENNIFER FALLON

A TOM DOHERTY ASSOCIATES BOOK • NEW YORK

TREASON KEEP: BOOK TWO OF THE HYTHRUN CHRONICLES

Copyright © 2001 by Jennifer Fallon

Originally published in 2001 by Voyager, an imprint of HarperCollins*Publishers*, Australia.

This book is printed on acid-free paper.

Map by Ellisa Mitchell

A Tor Book
Published by Tom Doherty Associates, LLC
175 Fifth Avenue
New York, NY 10010

www.tor.com

Tor® is a registered trademark of Tom Doherty Associates, LLC.

Library of Congress Cataloging-in-Publication Data

Fallon, Jennifer.
    Treason keep / Jennifer Fallon.—1st ed.
      p.   cm. — (The Hythrun chronicles ; bk. 2)
    "A Tom Doherty Associates book."
    ISBN 0-765-30987-4 (acid-free paper)
    EAN 978-0765-30987-7
    I. Title.

 PR9619.4.F35T74 2004
 823'.92—dc22

                                       2004051741

First Tor Edition: November 2004

Printed in the United States of America

0 9 8 7 6 5 4 3 2 1

For Dace Mikel O'Brien,
the original God of Thieves,
and as always, Adele Robinson

ACKNOWLEDGMENTS

My life is many things, but boring isn't one of them. Despite a wedding, a birth, a book launch, two house moves, a new business and a few other rather traumatic incidents that I would rather not relive, this book was written in considerably less time than *Medalon*.

As always, there are the usual suspects who deserve my thanks for their unswerving faith and their high tolerance levels in putting up with me during the creation of this work. In particular, I would like to thank my children, Amanda, TJ and David, for their support and for filling my life with so many distractions that I have, though sheer necessity, mastered the art of focusing on writing to the exclusion of all else. They will readily attest to this fact, although they may be surprised at how often I've heard them lament to each other, "Don't bother asking her anything, she's writing."

I would like to thank Stephanie Smith, Darian Causby and Midge McCall, and all the other people at HarperCollins whom I have never met but who have contributed to this series, along with Lyn Tranter and Cathy Perkins at Australian Literary Management and also Sarah Endacott.

With my dying breath, I will be thanking Harshini Bhoola for her never-ending enthusiasm and her constant re-reading of the manuscripts, and it still won't repay her. Thanks also to my good friend Peter Jackson for encouraging me to take a step into the unknown and my favorite sycophants, Toni-Maree and John Elferink MLA for helping me keep my feet on the ground while my head was in the clouds.

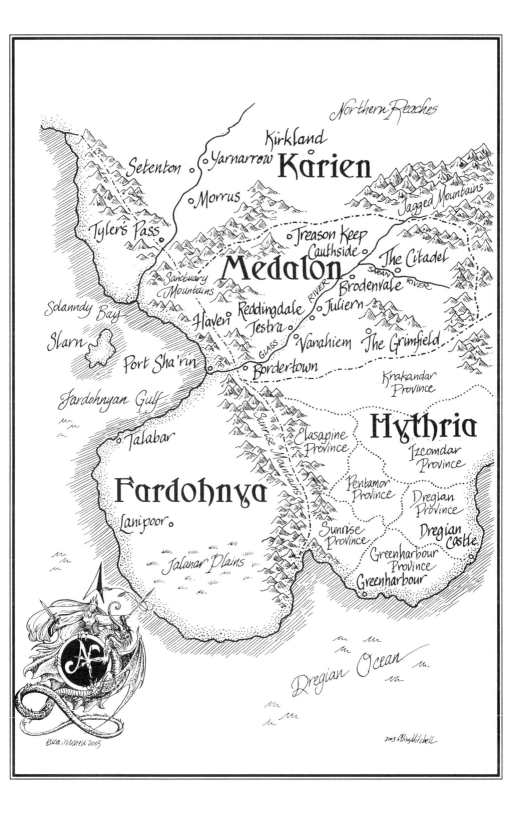

part one

POLITICS AND POWER GAMES

chapter 1

I took a conscious effort of will for Brak to take the final step across the threshold of Sanctuary.

The gates stood wide open, tall and impossibly white in the thin, chill mountain air. Sanctuary's tall spires reached elegantly for the scudding clouds, shadowing the Gateway and offering him one last moment of anonymity.

He had turned his back on this place more than two decades ago and, despite the loneliness, the guilt, and the hunger for his own kind, he still found it harder than he thought possible to return.

He was not unexpected. That would have been too much to hope for. As he trekked through the mountains he had clung to the idle hope that the demons would not betray his approach. It was the reason he had come on foot—this journey of months could have been accomplished in hours had he asked the demons for help.

As he contemplated that final, irrevocable step, a figure appeared on the other side of the Gateway. Tall, white-robed and smiling, Jerandenan had been the Gatekeeper for as long as Brak could remember—and that was almost a millennium. The Harshini's totally black eyes were moist, and his whole being radiated the warmth of his welcome.

The Gatekeeper opened his arms wide. "Welcome home, Brakandaran."

Still Brak hesitated. "You remember me then?"

Jerandenan laughed softly. "I remember every soul who has entered my Gate, as well you know. And you, more than most, I would not forget. Come, Brakandaran. Your family awaits you. The demons miss you, and . . ." The Gatekeeper's voice trailed off with a shrug, and he smiled that infuriating, calm smile that was already beginning to annoy Brak. And he had not even crossed Sanctuary's threshold yet.

"And Korandellan wants to see me?" Brak guessed.

Jerandenan nodded. "Did you expect anything less from your King?"

Before Brak could answer, several gray missiles launched at him through the tingling barrier of the Gateway. The demons jumped on him gleefully, chattering to each other incomprehensibly, so delighted by his return that they almost knocked him off his feet. He recognized a few of the creatures as he tried to shake free of them, but there were youngsters in the group he did not know. They knew him, though. His blood called to them more clearly than any words were capable of.

Jerandenan smiled indulgently as the demons pushed and pulled Brak until he was through the Gateway, ignoring both his protests and his greetings, which he seemed to be handing out in equal measure.

"You can deny yourself, Brak, but you cannot deny the brethren. They are as glad to see you as we all are."

Brak frowned, and peeled a little demon from around his neck who was hugging him so tightly he could barely breathe. No sooner had he removed one, than another tried to take its place. He pushed it away sternly.

"Begone!"

The demons fell back at his sharp tone, looking mightily offended. He immediately felt guilty for being so abrupt, a fact which the demons were probably counting on. At the first sign of his resolve wavering they were on him again, although this time they gave him room to breathe. Brak turned to Jerandenan helplessly.

"And you wonder why I haven't been back in more than twenty years."

"You are as hungry for the demons as they are for you, Brakandaran," the Gatekeeper said with an indulgent smile. "Don't deny them, or us, the joy of your return."

By the time Brak had disentangled himself from the demons a second time, other white robed figures had appeared, attracted to the Gateway by the unusual commotion. The Harshini rarely, if ever, left Sanctuary these days—not since the Sisterhood had come to power two centuries ago—and few had entered the magical Gateway in that time. The Keep was outside of normal time and space, in a dimension uniquely its own. No one but a Harshini, or those born within the walls of Sanctuary, could find it when it was warded.

The curious arrived first, to see what all the fuss was about, wandering toward the Gateway with a leisurely stride. Behind those came others, some at a run. These Harshini were té Carn, *his* family, alerted by the demons' joy at the return of their lost cousin.

He almost fled at that point. Seeing the faces of his family made him shrivel up a little inside. They had done nothing but try to make him feel as if he belonged here; and he had repaid their kindness with blood . . . this shame, this unbearable remorse, was the reason he had never come home.

"Brakandaran!"

A fair-haired woman pushed through the crowd and ran to him, twisting the knife of his guilt even harder into his soul.

"Samaranan."

She stopped a few paces from him and examined him with a critical eye.

"You're too thin."

Brak was expecting almost anything but that. Trust Samaranan to say the one thing guaranteed to ease his tension. He smiled at her blunt criticism.

"I've been living on nothing but . . ." he stopped himself before he could upset the Harshini with his carnivorous diet. "I've been living off the land. It's a long walk."

"It was also an unnecessary one," she scolded. "The demons would have brought you home. All you had to do was ask."

"I like walking."

"Actually, I think you like suffering. But you got here. Finally. Welcome home, brother." She hugged him tightly, pushing demons out of the way to reach him. He had almost forgotten how forgiving the Harshini were—how incapable of anger or resentment. His elder half-sister did not seem to care that he had not contacted her for two decades. Nor did she seem to hold against him the crime that had driven him from this place. "Come, you must pay your respects to Korandellan. He knew you would come."

Brak nodded, but did not bother to add that the King had left him little choice in the matter. Samaranan took his hand and led him forward, the demons skipping in his wake. The Harshini parted for them, some

simply smiling their welcome, others nodding to him with genuine pleasure at his return. Some even reached out to touch his travel-stained
clothes, to assure themselves that he was real. Brak tried to return the
warmth of their welcome, but his guilt and his human blood, as always,
made him feel like an outsider.

Sanctuary was like no other place on this world, and at first glance,
seemed unchanged since Brak had last walked these halls. The Harshini
settlement sat within a valley; the Keep tunnelled into the hills, its
broad, open archways looking down to the valley floor. The air was sweet
and moist from the constant mist created by the rainbow-tinted cascade
that supplied the settlement with water and tumbled down toward the
pool on the western edge of the valley. Although autumn was beginning
to turn the mountains red, here in Sanctuary the temperature never varied a great deal. The God of Storms was solicitous of Harshini comfort.

The long, tiled walkways echoed his booted footsteps as Samaranan
led Brak toward Korandellan's apartments. Everywhere they went people turned and waved to him, delighted to see him. It was as though he
brought them hope rather than pain, and the reaction puzzled him a little. It was true that the Harshini were incapable of anger or violence, but
even that could not explain their obvious joy. Many of them would have
been glad to see the back of him, he thought. Then another thought
occurred to him as he realized what else seemed strange.

"Where are the children?"

"There are none, Brak."

"Why?"

Samaranan slowed her pace and glanced at him. "It's the wards on
Sanctuary. They remove us from the real world. We do not age, but neither do we conceive."

"But you don't stay out of time constantly. Korandellan used to bring
Sanctuary back every spring to allow time to catch up." As far as Brak
remembered, the settlement had reappeared every spring for the past
two centuries. Such a return was vital for their survival.

"We've been warded now for nearly twenty years, brother," she
told him. "After you left, after the demon child was born, Xaphista
redoubled his efforts to find us. We could not risk exposing ourselves,
and Sanctuary would flare like a beacon to a Karien priest. Every time
we return to real time, Death is waiting to claim those who have

cheated him. There are no children to replace those who are lost." She seemed to understand his confusion. "In case you're wondering, that's why everyone is so happy to see you. You will aid the demon child and she will remove the threat of Xaphista. Then we will be free once more."

"Remove the threat of Xaphista? You mean kill him."

Samaranan frowned. "Please don't say it like that, Brak."

"Why not? It's the truth."

"You know what I mean. You've been back for little more than a heartbeat. You could at least *try* to be sensitive."

"Forgive me," he snapped. "I'll try very hard not to mention the fact that Korandellan has brought me back to train Zegarnald's pet assassin."

She stopped and glared at him, her black eyes as close to anger as they were capable of getting. "Stop it! This is not easy for any of us. There is no need for you to make it even harder."

"You think this is easy for me?"

Samaranan's eyes softened and she reached out to touch his face. "I'm sorry, little brother. I forget sometimes what it must be like for you."

"Don't apologize, Sam. I shouldn't be heaping all my anger on you. There's a god or two I'd like to throttle, but it's not your fault." Brak smiled wanly. "I promise I'll try to be as Harshini as I can while I'm here."

Her relief was evident. "Thank you."

They resumed their slow pace through the broad halls. Brak listened idly as Samaranan filled him in on the family happenings, which, considering how much time Sanctuary had spent removed from reality, was a fairly short list. There were no new nieces or nephews or cousins to celebrate. Only the demons, who could flit between dimensions at will, were able to reproduce—but even their numbers were starting to dwindle in the face of the Harshini's prolonged withdrawal. The Harshini and the demons were interdependent, and the creatures could not sustain an increase in their numbers that the Harshini were unable to match. It occurred to Brak that if something were not done soon, the Harshini would no longer be simply hiding. Their current state of limbo would eventually prove fatal. The knowledge was an added burden he did not want or need.

They reached Korandellan's chambers eventually, and the tall, delicately carved doors swung open at their approach. The King was waiting for them, his smile benign, his arms outstretched in welcome. The resemblance between him and the demon child took Brak by surprise. Korandellan was tall and lean and impossibly beautiful, as all the Harshini were. With the demons clustered behind Samaranan's long skirts, Brak fell to his knees and lowered his head, surprised at his need for Korandellan's benediction.

"You have no need to kneel before me, Brakandaran. It is I who should bow to you. You have suffered much on our behalf."

"Don't be ridiculous," he retorted without thinking.

"Brak!" Samaranan gasped. Even the demons seemed appalled by his disrespect.

But the King laughed. "Oh, how I've missed you, Brakandaran! You are like a breath of fresh air. Come, get off your knees and let us talk as friends. Samaranan, tell your family to prepare a feast. Tonight we will welcome your lost brother home."

"There's really no need . . ." Brak began as he climbed to his feet. The King ignored his objections.

"Leave us now. Your brother and I have much to discuss."

Samaranan bowed gracefully and backed out of the room. The demons followed her, subdued in the presence of the King. The doors swung shut silently as they departed. The King turned to Brak and his smile faded.

"What news have you of the outside world?"

"Nothing that is likely to bring you joy," Brak warned. "The Defenders were in Testra when I left. They were making plans to move north, to protect their border from the Kariens."

"Shananara tells me you went to Hythria."

"I indulged in a bit of theatrics, I'm afraid," he admitted. "The Defenders needed help and I had to stop them killing the demon child. I made a rather dramatic appearance in Krakandar and convinced Damin Wolfblade to form an alliance with them."

"The High Prince's heir?" Korandellan shook his head with a faint smile. "You never did listen to me when I told you about the dangers of interfering with mortal politics. But . . . perhaps such an alliance might eventually bring peace between Medalon and Hythria, so in this case, I will forgive you."

"You always forgive me, your Majesty. It's your one fault."

"I have more than one, I fear. And what news of the Kariens?"

"As soon as word reaches them about the death of their Envoy, they'll have the excuse they've been looking for to invade Medalon."

"Then war is unavoidable?" The King looked pained even contemplating such an idea.

"I'm afraid so."

"And Fardohnya? What is Hablet doing? It is unlike him to let such momentous events take shape without him trying to turn it to his advantage."

"I wish I knew," Brak told him with a shrug. "A couple of years ago he was making overtures toward Hythria. He sent one of his daughters to meet with Lernen Wolfblade, but I don't know that anything came of it. It's hard to tell with Hablet. He makes and breaks treaties as if they were piecrusts. You should think about sending someone to his court, now that the word is out that the Harshini still live."

The King shook his head. "I risked much in letting Shananara aid you, and I cannot sleep for fear of the danger Glenanaran and the few others who have returned to the outside might be in. The High Arrion has promised me that the Sorcerer's Collective will protect our people in Greenharbour, but we are not revered in the manner we once were. Our seclusion appears to have left us unprepared for the human world. Her assistance will come with a price, I suspect. Besides, Fardohnya is too close to Karien. I would not put it past Hablet to see some advantage in dealing with the Kariens, and I would not willingly give him a hostage." Korandellan walked to the balcony that overlooked the broad, sun-kissed valley. He studied it for a long moment before he spoke again. "A part of me rejoices to see you again, Brakandaran. Another part of me fears what your appearance heralds."

"And just exactly what does my appearance herald?"

Korandellan did not answer immediately. When he did, he completely changed the subject. "The demon child lives."

"Cheltaran healed her, then?" It was a relief to learn that his journey had not been in vain.

"Yes . . . and no."

The vague reply surprised Brak, and worried him. "What do you mean?"

"When the demons brought R'shiel here she was on the brink of death. No, even more than that, Death had her by the hand and was leading her away. Cheltaran healed her wounds, but Death does not like to be cheated, particularly by the God of Healing. They are having something of a . . . disagreement . . . over the demon child's fate."

"That sounds ominous. Where does that leave R'shiel?"

"She lives, but only just. Death holds one hand, Cheltaran the other."

Brak sagged against the balcony. "But it's been months!"

"I know. But now that you are here, we should be able to resolve the conflict."

"You want me to step into an argument between Death and a god? Thanks for the vote of confidence, your Majesty, but I think you vastly overrate my powers of persuasion."

The King turned to him, his expression serious. "I overrate nothing, Brakandaran. A compromise of sorts has been worked out to solve the problem. Unfortunately, none of us is capable of carrying it out."

"Compromise? What compromise?"

"A life for a life," Korandellan told him heavily. "Death will relinquish his claim on R'shiel, if another life is given in her place."

Brak closed his eyes for a moment as the weight of the task Korandellan asked of him pressed on him like a falling building.

"You want *me* to choose?"

"I do not ask this of you lightly, Brakandaran, but I have no choice. I cannot take a life, even indirectly. You are the only one who can make the decision."

"And to think I used to imagine my human blood would never be an asset to the Harshini," Brak remarked sourly. "Fine. I'll go out and pick some helpless, worthless human. That should satisfy Death."

Korandellan's golden skin paled at his callousness. "It is not that simple. Death demands a soul of equal value."

"Then I'll make sure I pick an obnoxious brat. That should even things up."

"A soul of equal value, Brakandaran. Death drives a hard bargain. He wants a soul whose loss will mean as much to the demon child as her loss will mean to us."

"Is there a time limit on this absurd bargain, or will the poor sod drop dead the moment I name him?"

Korandellan shook his head in despair. "I cannot comprehend your ability to make light of this, Brakandaran."

"I'm not making light of anything. I might be capable of making such a decision, Korandellan, but I certainly don't find it easy. It's an eminently reasonable question."

"And one I cannot answer. You will have to ask Death yourself. I'm sure he will be reasonable."

"Oh! You *think* so?"

"Please, Brakandaran! Do not think to approach Death with such an attitude."

As a race, the Harshini were a bridge between the gods and mortal man, but it was Korandellan who carried the full weight of that bridge on his shoulders. Brak appreciated his predicament, but found it hard to sympathize, given the burden the King had just handed him.

"Don't worry. Even I am not *that* stupid. Can I see R'shiel?"

"Of course." The King smiled faintly and placed his hand on Brak's shoulder. "You did well to find her, Brak. I know the remorse that fills you seems hard to live with, but ultimately, if she succeeds, R'shiel will free the Harshini. Your actions will have saved your people."

"All but one," Brak reminded him grimly.

R'shiel té Ortyn, the demon child who had caused Brak so much anguish—even before she was born—lay not far from Korandellan's chambers. The room was large and airy, filled with flowers and scented candles, as if the cheery atmosphere could somehow compensate for the battle being waged over her life. Two Harshini sat with her, watching the faint rise and fall of her chest, as if waiting for something to happen. As Brak approached they bowed silently and withdrew, the expectant joy in their black eyes at his coming making him feel unworthy.

She lay on the crisp white sheets wearing a simple robe of pale blue. Her dark red hair had been braided with care and lay coiled on the pillow. She appeared whole and unmarked. As unnaturally perfect as any Harshini.

She was breathing, but barely. Brak watched her for a time then turned to Korandellan.

"You've not spoken to her yet?"

"She's been unconscious since she arrived. Once the . . . decision is made, Death will release her."

Brak considered his next words carefully before he spoke. "Korandellan, have you considered the possibility that it might be better if you let Death have her?"

The King's head snapped up in shock. "Of course not! Why would I do that?"

"She may look Harshini, your Majesty, but this girl is not what she seems. She was raised by the Sisterhood. She is spoilt, manipulative and can be utterly ruthless when she's in the mood. And those are her good points."

"If Xaphista prevails, the Harshini will be destroyed."

"You've no guarantee that won't happen, even if she lives. You don't know her like I do. Believe me, she's not the stuff saviours are made of."

"You don't like her?"

"I don't trust her," he corrected.

The King studied R'shiel for a moment and then looked at Brak. His expression was troubled. "Be that as it may, I cannot let her die. We will not survive long enough for another demon child to reach maturity, even if such a child was born tomorrow. I have no choice."

"Then the gods help us all," Brak muttered to himself.

chapter 2

Her Most Serene Highness, Princess Adrina of Fardohnya, took special care with her appearance this morning. There wasn't much she could do about the black eye, but she could disguise the rest of her bruises. Her slaves fussed over her nervously, as wary of her foul mood as they were of their uncertain future. Their mistress had done many things in the past to incur the wrath of the King, but last night's escapade was spectacular, even for Adrina.

"Has anybody seen Tristan?" she snapped, pushing away the young, dark-haired slave who was trying to fix a diaphanous veil to her head with jeweled pins and trembling fingers.

"No, your Highness," Tamylan replied calmly, relieving the girl of the task. With a firm hand she pinned on the veil. Adrina yelped impatiently.

"Be careful! Where in the Seven Hells is he? I'll be damned if I'll take the blame for this alone."

"I believe Tristan was last seen beating a hasty retreat toward the South Gate, your Highness," the slave told her, barely able to conceal her amusement. Adrina glared at her in the mirror. Tamylan had been her constant companion since they were children. She had a bad habit of forgetting her place. "I imagine your brother was seized by an overwhelming desire to rejoin his regiment at Lander's Crossing."

"Coward," Adrina muttered. "When I get my hands on him . . ." She pushed Tamylan away, stood up and glanced at her reflection, satisfied that she had done her best under the circumstances. Her skirt was green, Hablet's favorite color, and the deep emerald shade brought out the green in her kohl-darkened eyes, even with the unbecoming bruise. The bodice was a shade or two lighter and edged with delicate pearls, exactly matching the larger pearl that nested in her bare navel. She could do little about her pounding head but she had gargled half a bottle of cologne to rid herself of the sour aftertaste of mead. She smoothed down the skirts nervously and turned to Tamylan. "How do I look?"

"As lovely as ever, your Highness," the slave assured her. "I'm sure the King will be so overcome by your radiant beauty that he'll completely overlook the fact that you ran his flagship into the main wharf last night."

"Tamylan, have I told you that you're dangerously close to pushing me too far?" She was no mood for Tamylan's eternal good humour. She wasn't in the mood for much of anything. She just wanted to crawl back into her bed and hide under the covers until her father forgot about her.

"Not for an hour, at least, your Highness."

A knock at the door saved Tamylan from a tongue-lashing. Gretta, the slave who had been so carefully trying to fix her hair, answered it hastily. The young girl bowed low as Lecter Turon, the King's Chamberlain, entered, scurrying out of his way as he waddled into the room.

The Chamberlain mopped his perpetually sweating bald head and bowed to Adrina. "The King is waiting for you, your Highness," the eunuch announced in his gratingly high-pitched voice. "I have come to escort you."

"I know the way, Turon. I hardly need an obsequious little toad like you to guide me."

"Your Serene Highness, I speak the truth when I say that never have I looked forward to a duty more." He was positively beaming at the prospect of her trying to explain her way out of this one.

Adrina decided not to dignify his jibe with a reply. She flounced past him in a swirl of emerald skirts and marched into the hall, snapping her head up haughtily. That was a mistake. The hangover she was trying to ignore objected violently to the sudden movement and sent a wave of blinding pain across her forehead. She strode ahead; not waiting for Turon, deliberately taking long strides, knowing the tubby little eunuch would have to run to catch up. It was petty, but he deserved it for taking so much pleasure in her misfortune. Servants and slaves scurried out of her path as she marched through the long black and white tiled halls of the Summer Palace.

It took nearly twenty minutes to reach her father's reception room, and Turon panted heavily in her wake. There were a disconcerting number of lords and ladies in attendance in the vast outer chamber, standing around the tall, potted palms in jeweled clusters like beetles around scattered honey drops. They stared at her as she strode past, their expressions ranging from smug humour to simmering anger. Even the slaves wore expressions of intense interest, as they manned the large fans that moved the humid air around, but did little to cool the oppressive heat.

She did not wait for permission to enter, but marched straight up to the delicately carved sandalwood doors of her father's office. The guards opened them as she approached. Turon was forced into an undignified run to catch her so that he could enter the chamber first to announce her arrival. Two steps ahead of the Chamberlain, she ordered the guards to close the doors behind her, and was gratified to hear Turon's indignant yelp as the obliging guards slammed the doors in his face.

Hablet looked up as she entered and smiled. That was not a good sign. The King was prone to violent outbursts when enraged, which usually dissipated as quickly as they started. But he was beyond anger now and into a quiet rage that manifested itself in a deceptively calm demeanor.

She had only ever seen him this angry once before. That time, her bastard half-brothers Tristan and Gaffen had stolen the statue of Jelanna, the Goddess of Fertility, from the Goddess' Temple and mounted it on the roof of the most notorious brothel in Talabar. She had half-expected Hablet to kill them when he learnt of their escapade. Her father was sly, dishonest and opportunistic, but he was very devout. He was also desperate for a legitimate son, certain that his baseborn sons' jests would make Jelanna strike him impotent as a punishment for their disrespect. He need not have worried. Hablet had sired another half-dozen or more children since then, although he still did not have the legitimate son he craved. Maybe *that* was Jelanna's revenge.

"Adrina," Hablet said through his dangerous smile.

"Daddy . . ."

"Don't you 'daddy' me, young lady." This was worse than she thought.

"I can explain . . ."

"You can explain, can you?" Hablet asked, picking up a sheath of parchment from his gilded desk. The sunlight streamed in from the tall open windows, catching the gilt and reflecting it painfully back in her eyes. There were no chairs in the room other than the seat that the King occupied, so she had no choice but to stand in front of him like an errant slave. "Explain what exactly, my dear? How do you explain this bill I have from Lord Hergelat for seven hundred gold lucats? It seems you sank his yacht. Or this one?" he added, holding up another leaf from the pile on the desk in front of him. "Lord Brendle claims you ran his dhow aground, too. He wants twelve hundred lucats. And then of course, Lady Pralton wants compensation because Lord Brendle's dhow was carrying a load of her vintage wine, which is now sitting at the bottom of the harbor, making a lot of fish rather happy, I imagine. Not to mention the twenty-eight injured slaves manning the oars of the *Wave Warrior* when you rammed the dock. Captain Wendele estimates the damage to the *Wave Warrior* to be between five and six thousand lucats."

He threw the bills on the desk. "As for the dock, it will take the engineers a *week* or more to work out what *that* will cost to repair, assuming they can find a way to get the *Wave Warrior* off it, without dismantling the whole damned structure! Would you care to hear what the Merchant Guilds are claiming they'll lose with the main wharf out of commission?" Hablet's voice had been growing steadily louder as he spoke, until he was shouting at her. She cringed, although more from the effect it had on her hangover, than for fear of him.

"But Daddy—"

"A party!" he yelled. "*It's the Feast of Kaelarn, Daddy, and we want to have a party!* I said you could have a damned *party*, Adrina. I didn't say you could *ruin* me!"

Now he was exaggerating. Even the staggering cost of her escapade would not dent Hablet's enormous wealth. "I haven't ruined you, Father, I—"

"As if I don't have enough problems! I've got the damned Hythrun allying with Medalon. I'm at an extremely delicate point in my negotiations with the Karien Crown Prince . . ."

Now that's a lie, Adrina thought impatiently. The Kariens wanted Hablet's cannon, and access to the Fardohnyan Gulf through the port at Solanndy Bay, which her father controlled. They were prepared to put up with quite a bit to get what they wanted. What Hablet really meant was that he had just raised the price again.

With the unexpected alliance of Hythria and Medalon, and the certain invasion of Medalon by the Kariens to avenge the death of their Envoy, Hablet's eyes had lit up with glee, thinking of the profit to be made. The Karien army was vast and even with the aid of the Warlord of Krakandar, the Defenders were sadly outnumbered. With the promise of the new weapons from Fardohnya—Adrina doubted her father had any intention of actually delivering them—Karien would be invincible. That left Hablet with two almost unheard-of opportunities. Not only could he demand vast amounts of timber from the Kariens to sustain his fleets, but while Medalon was occupied with the Kariens, Hythria lay open—all but undefended along its northern border.

Hablet cared nothing for Medalon, but the prospect of taking on the Hythrun was very tempting. The origins of the feud between Fardohnya and Hythria were lost in antiquity, but in recent years had much to do with the fact that the vast majority of the Fardohnyan fleet was engaged in acts of piracy, and the rich Hythrun traders were their favorite targets.

This latest, ill-advised deal with the Kariens was doomed to failure, Adrina thought. No amount of tall timber, iron ore, gold, or anything else the resource-rich Kariens could offer made it worth dealing with a nation of mindless fanatics. The Hythrun might be arrogant and belligerent, their High Prince might be a degenerate old pervert, but at least they believed in the same gods.

". . . and now, thanks to your irresponsible recklessness, I have half the nobles in Talabar asking for your head! What possessed you to think you knew how to sail my flagship!"

Adrina realized with a start that she had not been listening to him.

"I didn't think . . ."

"Well that's pretty bloody obvious!" Hablet sagged back in his chair, as if his tirade had exhausted him. He scratched at his beard and glared at her. "Who else was involved in this fiasco?"

For a moment, Adrina nobly considered taking the entire blame for this disaster upon her own shoulders. It had been her idea, after all. She quickly decided against it. From his expression, she could tell that her father probably knew everything and lying would simply make things worse.

"Tristan," she admitted, albeit reluctantly, even though the miserable coward deserved to be implicated for abandoning her.

"And . . . ?" Hablet prompted impatiently.

"And Cassandra."

"Ah, Cassandra," Hablet repeated with a dangerous smile. "I was wondering when we'd get around to her."

"She wasn't on the boat when it . . . when the accident occurred," Adrina pointed out cautiously. Cassie had been a reluctant accomplice to the caper, and Adrina felt honor bound to defend her younger sister.

"I'm aware of that," Hablet said evenly. "Do you know *where* she was?"

"She came back to the Palace." Adrina wondered if Cassie had actually done what she promised, or had found further mischief out of sight of her older siblings.

"Oh, Cassandra came back to the Palace, all right," Hablet agreed. "In fact, Cassandra was so drunk that she decided it would be a good idea to find out what sort of lover her fiancé was. She sneaked into his rooms and tried to seduce him like an alley whore and now the whole damned Karien delegation is threatening to call off the deal. How could you *do* this to me?"

The news did not surprise Adrina. Cassandra was a passionate young woman who had been talking about nothing else but the visiting Karien Prince all week.

"Cassie didn't mean any harm . . ."

"I don't care if she was on a mission from the gods!" Hablet shouted. "The Kariens are mortified. They think I'm trying to foist a whore on them. I offered them my most beautiful daughter as a bride and now they think I'm trying to get rid of a wanton hussy. They're ready to set sail on the next tide."

Adrina glared at her father impatiently. "Well, what did you expect, Father? Cassie was never cut out to be the bride of a Karien Prince. She doesn't have any interest in politics; she's far too self-indulgent. You should have thought about that before you arranged the marriage."

"Oh, you think so?"

"You know as well as I do that Cassie would have gotten herself into serious trouble within months of marrying Craytn. She doesn't think beyond her next meal, most of the time. I can't believe you were fool enough to think such an arrangement would work in the first place."

"Is that right?"

Deciding attack was the best form of defense, Adrina carried on recklessly. "Of course, I'm right. Whoever you send north has to have their wits about them. Cassie wouldn't seal a treaty, she'd cause a war."

"I'm glad you feel that way," Hablet said, his eyes narrowed. "Because the only way to redeem this situation was to offer another daughter as a bride and hope the Kariens would accept her."

"Well, Lissie is probably the prettiest," Adrina noted thoughtfully. "But Herena has the better head on her shoulders, although she's still quite young . . ."

"So I offered them you."

"You *what?*"

"As you so rightly pointed out, my petal, whoever I send to the Kariens needs to have their wits about them. They are mightily offended at the moment. The only way to appease them was to offer them the jewel in my crown. My eldest legitimate daughter."

"You wouldn't dare!"

"Would dare and have dared," Hablet announced with an evil grin. "I offered the Kariens a bride, and a bride they shall have. Fortunately, Craytn has only met you once and he doesn't speak Fardohnyan, so I can still hope your reputation hasn't preceded you. I can blame Tristan for the fiasco at the wharf easily enough." He chuckled softly. "Seems they thought I should have offered them my eldest daughter in the first place. It may even work out better than my original plan."

"You can't do this to me!"

"Care to wager on that?"

"I won't do it!"

"Oh yes you will! You'll marry the Karien Crown Prince and make him as happy as a pig in a wallow."

"I refuse!"

"Suit yourself," her father said, his voice dangerously calm. "In that case, I'll be forced to deduct the cost of your little escapade from your allowance. And while I'm at it, I'll see that your half-brother is demoted to a common foot soldier and I'll transfer him to watching the eastern passes, where he'll more than likely be killed fighting bandits in the Sunrise Mountains. Of course, should you *agree* to marry Craytn, then I could probably force myself to assign him to the regiment I'm sending north to King Jasnoff. That would get him out of my sight while I recover from this disaster . . ."

"That's blackmail!"

Hablet sighed happily. "It is, isn't it?"

"Daddy . . ." she pleaded, hoping to appeal to his softer side. Hablet was a scoundrel, but he loved his children, all thirty-seven of them. He made no distinction, normally, between his legitimate daughters and the sons he had fathered on countless *court'esa*. "You don't want to send me away . . ."

"I can't afford to *keep* you," Hablet snapped. "If I didn't love you more than life itself, I'd have you whipped."

"I'd *rather* be whipped than marry that pious idiot!" Realizing anger would get her nowhere she smiled sweetly. "I'm sorry, daddy. I promise never to . . ."

"Promise! Hah!" Hablet scoffed. "You promised me you'd marry well and you've rejected every suitor I've ever proposed."

"Well, what did you expect? All you've ever offered me were simpering boys or scabby old men!"

"That's beside the point!" he retorted. Then he sighed heavily, as if he could not understand where he went wrong. "Haven't I given you everything you ever wanted, Adrina? Haven't I indulged your every whim?"

"Yes, but . . ."

"There are no buts, this time," Hablet announced decisively. "This time you have gone too far and you can only redeem yourself by doing as I wish. And I *wish* you to marry the Karien Prince."

"But he's a child . . ."

"He's twenty-three," Hablet pointed out, unconcerned. "And at twenty-*seven*, you're an old maid. Just be grateful you still have your looks, otherwise I'd have no hope of pulling this off."

"Daddy . . ." she tried, one more time.

"Don't bother, Adrina. Your charms won't work on me. You are going to marry the Karien Prince and that is final. They're leaving in a few days so you'd better get packing."

If appealing to his better nature wasn't going to work, then she might as well try appealing to the politician.

"I can't marry him. It's far too dangerous."

"What nonsense! How could it be dangerous?"

"I might have a son. The Kariens might expect you to name him your heir."

"Bah! I've got plenty of sons. I don't need any whelp of yours."

"They're bastards, father."

"Then I'll legitimize one of them!"

"Which one?"

"Whichever one I choose!" he snapped. "Stop trying to defy me! You're going to marry Cratyn and that's final!"

Adrina scowled at her father. "I'll find a way out of this, I swear. I'm not going to spend my life bowing and scraping to that obnoxious little Karien worm."

"You do that. In the meantime, you have a trousseau to pack."

Adrina turned on her heel and left the room in a rage. As she stepped into the outer chamber, she passed Lecter Turon, and suddenly knew who had planted the absurd idea that she should marry the Karien Prince in her father's head. The little toad would pay for that one day, she decided.

As for the boy prince of Karien, he'd live to regret the day he ever set foot in Fardohnya.

chapter 3

er Most Serene Highness took the news well?" Lecter inquired cautiously of the King as he slipped through the door.

Hablet glared at the eunuch. "Of course she didn't take it well. She's livid."

"In time she will adjust to the idea."

"She'd better," the King grumbled. He pushed himself to his feet and walked to the window. The gardens below were a riot of color and the faint sounds of children's laughter drifted up from the fountain in the center court. The sound soothed him. He wondered what it was about his children that meant he only seemed to like them before they reached puberty. Once they grew up, they were no fun at all. They learnt to manipulate and grew greedy and caused him no end of trouble. But the little ones—ah, now they were his true joy in life. He had adored Adrina when she was ten. Now he was almost frightened of her.

"Might I suggest you place a guard on the princess? She could decide to defy you."

"She won't defy me," Hablet assured him. "It will occur to her soon enough that she'll be the Karien Queen one day. Adrina isn't stupid, Lecter. She'll do what I want, but not because it pleases me. She'll do it because it pleases her."

"I hope your trust in her is not misplaced, your Majesty."

"Trust has nothing to do with it. She's been dying to escape the palace, and I've just given her a crown."

"A crown she could turn on you one day?" Lecter suggested tentatively.

"Hah! Adrina? And that simpering Karien Prince? I don't think so! Adrina might have it in her to commit such treachery, but Cratyn is as spineless as a jellyfish. Did you see what they've agreed to? How much timber they're willing to part with, just to get access to Solanndy Bay and the Gulf? They're idiots!"

"You control the only access to their holiest shrine, your Majesty, not to mention any chance they have of sea-going trade. You didn't really leave them much choice."

"They want the secret of my cannon," Hablet added. "They want that even more than they want trade or access to that miserable Isle of Slarn. What sort of god chooses a lump of rock like Slarn to make his home, anyway?"

"The same sort of god who will demand your daughter convert to his worship. Your grandchildren will be followers of Xaphista."

"Adrina pointed out the same thing," the King mused, walking back to his desk. "Odd to hear you two in agreement on any point. Still, Laryssa is due to whelp any day now. She'll give me a son and it won't matter how many Karien bastards Adrina has."

"Of course, your Majesty." It was clear Lecter was as doubtful of the possibility as everyone else was. But surely Jelanna would not deny him again. Laryssa, the eighth woman he had taken to wife, had proved her fertility. She'd already given him two healthy bastard sons. Hablet had decided he would not marry any woman who could not produce sons and it was perfectly reasonable to assume that she would not let him down this time. The thought warmed him, almost making him forget his anger at Adrina. A legitimate son. Nothing would make him happier.

It wasn't that Hablet didn't love his baseborn sons. On the contrary, he adored them. But naming one his heir would cause problems. The throne needed a clear line of succession, and the law was clear, although not well known: either he sired a son himself, or the crown would go to Hythria, thanks to an almost forgotten twelve hundred-year-old agreement that Hablet had been trying to find a way around for thirty years. As he would rather fall on a rusty blade than see that happen, the only solution, if he did not have a legitimate son of his own, was to name one of his bastards heir. But he could not do that until he had removed the threat of any Hythrun heirs to his throne, a situation he planned to see to personally once he was across the border into Hythria. Then, if Laryssa failed to whelp a boy, he could legitimise one of his baseborn sons, probably Tristan, and not just because he was the eldest. Tristan was the brightest, the most personable, and the least likely to allow Adrina to control him. Although, given last night's disastrous escapade, Hablet was beginning to wonder about that. Perhaps it wasn't a good idea to send him north with Adrina . . .

Hablet sighed. It was a moot point. Laryssa *would* give him a son. Adrina would be off his hands, out of sight and out of mind in Karien. Let her play Queen of the Realm in the north. He had their timber, their gold and their iron. In return they were getting his most troublesome daughter and a promise he had no intention of keeping.

All in all, Hablet decided, looking down at the pile of debts Adrina had accumulated last night, it was a good bargain.

"So how are our Karien guests this morning?" he asked, pushing the pile to one side of the gilded desk. "Have they calmed down?"

"The prince was somewhat mollified by your generous offer."

"So he damned well should be!"

"I noted," Lecter continued, mopping his brow, "that the Kariens showed an unnatural interest in your offer to send a regiment with Adrina as her personal guard."

"I trust Adrina to keep them out of harm's way. She was right about one thing. I'd never have risked sending them with Cassandra."

"If I may be so bold as to offer my opinion, your Majesty, one wonders if it is a good idea to send any troops north at all."

"What do you mean? If I don't send her to Karien in a manner befitting her station, they'll know something is going on."

"I agree, your Majesty, but I have received more than one report that the Harshini have returned. There have been sightings in Greenharbour, at the Sorcerer's Collective, and even as far away as Testra, in Medalon."

"So? What has that got to do with us?"

"The Kariens are dedicated to the destruction of the Harshini, your Majesty. Marrying your daughter to their Crown Prince, and sending her north with your soldiers might be . . . misconstrued."

"You mean I might offend the Harshini?" Hablet scratched his beard as he sank down into his chair. "If the Harshini have returned, Lecter, and I seriously doubt they have, then why are they not here? I am the King of Fardohnya! If they *were* back the first thing they would do is send an Emissary to my court. Instead, all you can offer me are unfounded rumors about Harshini in Hythria. I have served the gods faithfully. Why would they send their people to that degenerate in Greenharbour, when they could come here?"

"High Prince Lernen has always supported the Sorcerer's Collective and the temples most generously."

"Lernen doesn't support anyone but himself," Hablet scoffed. "If the Harshini had returned, I would know about it. They are dead and gone, Lecter, so we will just have to stumble on without them as we have done for the past two hundred years."

"Of course, your Majesty."

Lecter mopped his brow again, looking rather uncomfortable. On days like this he annoyed Hablet. His grovelling manner was intolerable at times, but he had a sharp political mind and no scruples at all, that Hablet could discern. It made him an excellent chamberlain, if a tiresome one.

"What else, Lecter? I can tell there's something bothering you."

"It's a small matter, your Majesty. One that hardly needs your attention."

"Out with it, Lecter! I don't have time for your games this morning. Cratyn will be here at any moment."

"There have been other rumors, Sire, particularly in Medalon. About the demon child."

"Lorandranek's legendary half-human child? Those rumors have been around ever since the Harshini disappeared. Surely you don't believe them?"

"I don't believe anything, your Majesty, until I have proof. However, I feel they might be worthy of investigation. I could send . . ."

"No," Hablet declared bluntly. "I'll not have you wasting time and money chasing fairytales. The Harshini are extinct and there is no fabled demon child. I would much rather you spent your time fruitfully. Like finding out why the High Prince of Hythria sent his nephew to Medalon to fight with the Defenders."

"My sources tell me Lernen has little or no control over his nephew. I doubt he sent him anywhere."

"Then find out why young Wolfblade went north. I want a free path into Hythria, Lecter. I don't want a battalion of Defenders on my back, and Wolfblade needs to die."

"The Kariens will keep the Defenders off your back, Sire, and I am sure they can be prevailed upon to dispose of the Hythrun Prince. Why else would we support their coming war with Medalon?"

"I hope you're right, Lecter, because I'll be very put out if this doesn't work."

Before Lecter could offer another obsequious reply, the doors opened and the Karien Prince strode in, accompanied by his retinue. Hablet greeted them expansively and ordered the guards to bring chairs for the new arrivals.

Lecter bowed low, mopped his brow and backed out of the room, leaving the King to his guests.

chapter 4

Everyone's eyes were on Adrina as she strode down the long hall. As if to mock her, at the end of the hall, the princeling in question was heading toward her, with his gaggle of priests in tow.

Except for the ball held in his honor the day of his arrival a week ago, Adrina had not seen the young Prince, and counted herself lucky. He had spent the entire ball blushing an interesting shade of pink every time he caught sight of a Fardohnyan woman's bare midriff. As every one of the two hundred or so women present had been dressed in a similar fashion, he was damned near apoplectic by the end of the evening. For a fleeting moment, she debated doing something truly outrageous, right here in the Hall, which would ensure the Kariens would reject her as a potential bride. But she had caught the expectant look on Lecter Turon's smug, fat face as he slipped through the door to attend the King, and thought better of it. He would keep.

She stopped and waited as the young prince approached. Tall, serious and boring did not particularly appeal to Adrina, but he was civilised enough, she supposed. He was a little taller than her, with unremarkable brown hair, and eyes the color of dried mud. At least he knew how to chew with his mouth closed.

"Prince Cretin," she said, offering him her hand. The older man on Cratyn's right looked a little put out that she had greeted his prince as an equal, but Cratyn did not appear to notice. He was too busy staring at the pearl in her navel. "My father has just informed me that we are to be married."

Cratyn dropped her hand, jerked his head up and met her eye. He looked at her black eye curiously for a moment, but made no comment about it. Instead, he nodded—rather miserably, she noted with interest.

"Karien welcomes Fardohnya's favorite daughter, your Serene Highness," he said in his clipped Karien. "We look forward to a new era of prosperity and friendship between our two great nations."

Someone sniggered in the background at the idea. Adrina looked at Cratyn curiously, wondering if he was really as naive as he sounded.

"I look forward to serving Fardohnya *and* Karien, your Highness," she replied graciously, in heavily accented Karien. Two could play this game, and Adrina could mouth meaningless platitudes in any number of languages, when the mood took her. "Now, if you will excuse me, I have arrangements to make for my journey."

Cratyn stepped aside for her, forcing the rest of his party to do the same.

Adrina continued regally on through the hall. Until she came up with a way to escape her father's decree, she had no choice but to play along with it.

At least the meeting with the young Karien Prince had not gone too badly. She had made it clear to the Kariens that she held a rank equal to their prince, and Cratyn had been rather overawed by her, she decided with satisfaction. But he wasn't very happy with the idea of an arranged marriage. That much was obvious. It could simply be his distaste for a foreign bride—or perhaps he was smarter than he looked, and had some idea of how treacherous and unreliable her father was. She was almost back to her rooms, and still trying to puzzle it out, when a rather shamefaced Tristan caught up with her.

"The last I heard, you were running away like a cur with its tail between its legs," she snapped as he fell into step beside her.

Tristan was younger than Adrina by two days, and until an hour ago, she had considered him her best friend. Tristan's mother was a Hythrun *court'esa*, one of Hablet's favorites, who still lived in the palace harem, even though she no longer took the King's fancy. She had been a beautiful woman in her youth and Tristan had inherited most of her charm, as well as her fair hair and golden eyes. He turned all of that charm on his half-sister now, to absolutely no effect.

"Would I desert you in your hour of need?"

"I didn't happen to notice you helping me when I needed you, just now."

"I was busy," he shrugged, with an apologetic smile.

"Do you know what he's done?" There was no need to elaborate on who *he* was.

"Married you off to the Karien Prince and ordered me north with the regiment?"

She turned on him furiously. "You knew!"

"My orders were waiting for me at the South Gate. The ink wasn't even dry. You really pushed him too far this time, Adrina."

"You were there, too! I only tried docking the damned boat because you dared me . . ."

"It's a ship, not a boat," he corrected. "Anyway, this might be fun."

"*Fun?* I have to marry that snivelling, pious little cretin."

"And one day that snivelling, pious little cretin will be the Karien King. That's more than you'll ever get here, Adrina. You might be the eldest legitimate child, but Hablet will turn atheist before he lets a woman inherit the Fardohnyan crown. You've always known he'd sell you to the highest bidder. At least, this way, you get to be a queen."

Adrina listened to her brother thoughtfully, as she considered possibilities that had not had time to register.

"And what about you?" she asked. "He's banished you north as well."

Tristan shrugged. "I've got fourteen half-brothers, Adrina. When Hablet tires of trying to get a legitimate son on one of his wives, there'll be a rather spirited competition for our father's favor. That's a bloodbath I'll be more than happy to miss."

"This does present some interesting opportunities, doesn't it?" she agreed.

Tristan laughed. "You know, sometimes, you're so like Hablet it's scary."

Adrina stopped and looked up at him. "The regiment that's going north, what's its function?"

"They'll be the Princess's Guard," Tristan told her. "Under your command, to use as you see fit."

"And you are the Captain of the Guard?"

"Naturally," he said with a smug grin.

"Is Father sending any cannon with you?"

Tristan's grin vanished. He glanced up and down the hall before answering in a low voice. "No, and I'm not certain the Kariens will ever see any artillery."

"But he's promised them!"

"You know as well as I do how much Father's promises are worth. He'll take their gold and their timber and happily send his daughter to Karien as a bride to prove his good intentions, but he really doesn't want to hand the Kariens anything as dangerous as a cannon. He's had every man in Talabar who even thinks he knows how to make gunpowder taken into custody."

"He could be doing that just to drive up the price."

"I suppose."

"So the regiment going north are just light cavalry then?"

Tristan nodded warily. "For the most part. What are you up to, Adrina?"

"Nothing," she replied. "Not yet, anyway. Can you get me that list? Before we sail? And I want to know who Hablet arrested, too."

"Why?"

She ignored the question. "And I want you to do something else for me. Find out why Cratyn is so unhappy about this marriage."

"He's probably heard about *you*," Tristan suggested.

Adrina frowned at him, but did not rise to the bait. "Maybe, but I've got a feeling there's more to it than that. I want to know what it is."

"As you command, your Serene Highness," Tristan said with a mocking bow.

"One other thing," she added as she turned to walk away. "Do any of the regiment speak Karien?"

"Most of them, as far I as know," Tristan said.

"Then the first order you are to give them is to conceal that knowledge," Adrina told him. "The men are to act dumb. I want the Kariens to think they don't understand any orders but mine. Including you. If I have to go through with this, I'll do it on *my* terms."

Tristan was as good as his word, and by early afternoon Adrina had the names of every man in her regiment, and every man and woman rounded up by Hablet prior to the arrival of the Karien Prince, to prevent the secret of gunpowder falling into the wrong hands. She studied both lists carefully. The names on the first list, for the most part, meant nothing to her. She was not permitted to socialize with Tristan's fellow officers, although a few of the names she had heard spoken in court. The second list was much more interesting. She studied it carefully, delighted when one name appeared that she knew—by reputation at least.

Adrina spent the rest of the day driving her slaves mad as she made them drag the entire contents of her wardrobe out, so that she could decide what she should take with her on her journey north. By the end of the afternoon, the floor of her chamber was littered with discarded outfits. At that point, Adrina loudly announced that she simply had nothing to wear, and certainly nothing suitable for a future queen. She threw a rather impressive tantrum that had the entire palace scurrying out of her way. Just on dusk, Hablet sent word that she could send for the tailor of her choice and order whatever she liked.

The following morning Mhergon, the palace tailor, arrived, nervously clutching a bundle of cloth swatches. Adrina refused to see him and demanded to see Japinel instead. He was the only tailor in Talabar worthy of such a task, she declared. Nobody else would do. She threw another tantrum, just to make her point, and then sat back and waited.

She did not have to wait long. Less than an hour after Mhergon had fled her chambers, Lecter Turon arrived. Adrina, draped over the chaise in her morning room, graciously granted him an audience.

"Where is Japinel?"

"He is unavailable, your Highness. Your father, his Majesty the King—"

"I know who my father is, Turon. Get to the point."

"Mhergon is eminently qualified as a master tailor, your Highness."

"Mhergon couldn't make a sack out of homespun," Adrina scoffed. "My father said the tailor of my choice. I want Japinel."

"Japinel dabbles, your Highness, in tailoring as he does in everything else. The last I heard he was calling himself an alchemist. I cannot see why—"

"You don't have to, Turon. Get me Japinel or I will come to dinner tonight naked. We'll see what his Royal Highness, the Crown Prince of Karien thinks of that!"

Lecter Turon waddled off in a foul mood, but Adrina knew she had won. Just on sunset a very pale and confused-looking Japinel was ushered into her chambers. He seemed stunned that the Princess Adrina had even heard of him, let alone wanted him to design her trousseau. Adrina ordered her slaves out and waited until they were alone, before she allowed him to speak.

"Your Serene Highness!" Japinel cried as he prostrated himself at her feet.

"Oh, do get up! I don't have time for that!"

Japinel was a weedy little man with eyes set too close together. He scrambled to his feet, managing to bow at least half a dozen times on the way up.

"I am honoured, your Highness. I will design you a trousseau that the gods will envy. I will create—"

"Shut up, fool! I wouldn't wear something designed by you if my life depended on it."

"But your Highness! Chamberlain Turon said—"

"I have gowns enough to sink my father's flagship," she told him. It was a poor analogy under the circumstances. "I want something else from you, Japinel. If you do as I say, you'll be rewarded as if you really did create my trousseau. If you don't, I'll make sure you never see the light of day again."

Japinel might have been a scoundrel, but he wasn't stupid. His eyes narrowed greedily.

"What is it you want, your Highness?"

"I want to know how to make gunpowder,"

Japinel's eyes widened. "But I'm a tailor, your Highness. What would I know about such things?"

"My father is currently holding you in custody because you claimed you *did* know."

Japinel wrung his hands and shrugged helplessly. "A mistake, your Highness. I had thought to try a different career . . . I boasted unwisely . . ."

Adrina could have strangled the little worm. "Where are they holding you and the others?"

"In the slave quarters, your Highness."

"Then that's where you will return. I will see you again tomorrow. I suggest you get the formula from one of your cell mates. I leave Talabar in three days, Japinel. If I don't have what I want by then, I will have you sent to the salt mines in Parkinoor and you won't see Talabar until your grandsons are old men."

After he left, Adrina cursed for a full ten minutes. She was still cursing when Tamylan arrived to help her dress for dinner.

chapter 5

aptain Wain Loclon was forced to wait for almost an hour outside the Lord Defender's office before Garet Warner arrived. In that hour he had rehearsed, over and over again, what he planned to say. It sounded reasonable and logical and he was certain of success—right up until the moment the commandant appeared.

The commandant glanced at him briefly as he opened the door, his expression more put-upon than welcoming. Loclon followed him into the office, taking a deep breath. Although of lesser rank than the Lord Defender, Loclon wished it were Jenga, not Garet Warner, that he was forced to confront. The Lord Defender was predictable, and much easier to read than the enigmatic commander of Defender Intelligence.

"I see you've recovered," Garet remarked as Loclon closed the door behind them.

Garet lit the lantern on the Lord Defender's desk and studied the younger man in the flickering light for a moment, before seating himself in the padded leather chair behind the heavy wooden desk.

"I was released from the infirmary this morning," Loclon confirmed.

Garet nodded. "And you are ready to return to your duties?"

"Yes, sir."

"Good. Report to Commandant Arkin. He'll find you something useful to do. Sergeant Jocan will arrange for you to be accommodated in the Officers' Barracks, unless you prefer to make your own arrangements."

"I have rooms near the main gate, sir. I was planning to return there."

"As you wish. Was there anything else?"

Loclon swallowed before answering. "Actually, I was hoping I could request an assignment, sir."

Garet looked up curiously. "Request away, Captain, although I've no guarantee you'll get what you ask for."

"I want to be part of the detail assigned to hunting down Tarja Tenragan."

Garet Warner smiled briefly. "Is that so?"

"Yes, sir."

"Well, I hate to be the bearer of bad news, Captain, but there *are* no details hunting Tarja down. The First Sister has pardoned him."

"Sir?" Loclon thought he was hearing things. He had been out of touch for the past few months as he recovered from the wounds inflicted on him by R'shiel and Tarja, but he could not imagine any circumstance that could have arisen in that time that would give the First Sister reason to pardon her wayward son.

"You heard correctly, Captain. Tarja has been pardoned and restored to the Defenders."

"But after all that he's done . . ."

"All of which has been forgiven. Was there anything else?"

"Sir, I cannot believe that the First Sister would simply pardon him! What of the Defenders he killed? The heathen rebellion he led? What of his desertion? And what of his sister?"

"R'shiel? She has also been the recipient of the First Sister's mercy."

"I don't believe it."

"Believe what you will, Captain. The fact is they have been pardoned. While I can understand your distress, considering the circumstances, there is nothing you or I can do about it."

Loclon refused to accept Garet Warner's calm assurances. "Sir, I believe I have the right to insist that charges be pressed. After what they did to me . . ."

"Ah, yes, I read your report. You allege R'shiel used heathen magic on you."

"I do not allege, sir, I *know* she did. It was she who gave me this." Loclon pulled down the collar of his high-necked red Defender's jacket to reveal a savage pink scar that ran from one side of his throat to the other. It made an interesting counterpoint to the puckered scar that ran from the corner of his left eye to his mouth. His misshapen nose was the final touch on his ruined—but once handsome—face.

"Quite an impressive collection of scars," Garet noted. "But hardly proof that R'shiel is a heathen."

"I know what I saw, sir," he insisted. *They can't do this to me, not now.* Not when he was finally ready to seek revenge.

"Just exactly what were you doing when R'shiel revealed this unexpected talent for wielding heathen magic, Captain? Your report was rather vague on that point."

Loclon hesitated as images filled his mind of R'shiel, naked to the waist, her pale breasts stark in the jagged lightning, her eyes glittering and totally black, filled with forbidden heathen power. He could still taste her lips and the raindrops on her skin. He could still feel the blade she had used to cut his throat. Hatred burned through his veins like acid.

"She was attempting to escape, sir."

"And succeeded, as I understand it," Garet pointed out. "This entire episode is something of a blemish on your record, Captain. I would have thought you'd be anxious to let the matter drop."

"She is dangerous, sir, and so is Tarja. They must be punished."

Garet shook his head. "Unfortunately, the First Sister does not agree with you. Report to Commandant Arkin for reassignment and let the matter drop."

"May I ask where they are now?" It took all he had to ask the question calmly.

"Tarja is with the Lord Defender and the First Sister is on the northern border. As for R'shiel, I assume she is with them, although I cannot say for certain. I'm leaving for the northern border in the morning. I'll give Tarja your regards, shall I?"

Garet Warner was mocking him, but there was nothing he could do about it. "Permission to accompany you, Commandant!"

"Denied. Arkin will be in charge until the Lord Defender or I return. You are dismissed."

"But sir—"

"I said you are dismissed, Captain."

Loclon saluted sharply, rage burning in the depths of his blue eyes, the scar on his face a livid reflection of his mood. He slammed the door behind him, thinking that if Garet Warner thought that he would so easily forget the pair who had tried to destroy him, then he was sadly mistaken.

Later that evening, after he had reclaimed his rooms in Mistress Longeaves' Boarding House, Loclon made his way through the torchlit streets of the Citadel to the eastern side of the city. An earlier shower of rain made the cobbles glisten and the footing treacherous as he neared the seedier part of town. Passersby became more rare, then stopped completely, as he walked through the darkened warehouse district. Only the sudden harsh bark of an alert watchdog and the scurrying feet of rats disturbed the night. He had not been here in almost a year, but the route was familiar enough that he walked with assurance; unafraid of anything he might meet, as the streets narrowed into shadowed pockets of darkness. The cutpurses of the Citadel would be plying their trade along Tavern Street, where the pickings were more fruitful.

When he reached his destination, he knocked on the dilapidated door that was squeezed into a laneway between two warehouses. When he received no response to his summons, he pounded louder and was rewarded by a metallic screech, as the spy-hole in the door was forced open. A pair of suspicious dark eyes glared at him, taking in his red uniform with a frown.

"What d'ya want?"

"I want to come in. Mistress Heaner knows me."

"Yeah? What's her cat's name then?"

"Fluffy," he replied, hoping the scabby creature had not died in the past year. Mistress Heaner was fond of her cat and it amused her to use his name as a password.

"Hang on."

Loclon tapped his foot impatiently as the locks were drawn back. The door opened just enough for him to squeeze through. He waited as the man pushed the door shut and bolted it after them. The narrow alley was littered with garbage, and Loclon covered his nose against the smell as the hunched little man led him forward toward a square of light at the end of the lane. When they reached it, the man stepped back to let Loclon enter, then turned and disappeared into the darkness, presumably back to his post by the door.

The main room was sumptuous and belied the paltriness of the exterior. Cut crystal lanterns lit the soft draperies, and carpet thick enough to hide in stretched the full length of the room. Comfortable sofas were scattered through the room, each in its own private alcove, separated by diaphanous curtains that revealed as much as they concealed. Mistress Heaner's House was exclusive; known only to a few and only those who could afford the unique entertainments she provided. A captain's pay was not usually enough to allow one the funds to patronize Mistress Heaner's, but Loclon had just received several months' backpay and he intended to treat himself, this one night at least. Back in the days when he had been the champion of the Arena, his winnings had assured him a place here any time he wanted it.

"Captain."

Mistress Heaner glided toward him with a smile. Her gown was simple, black and plainly cut, although the material was expensive and the emerald necklace that circled her wrinkled throat was worth more than he could earn in a lifetime as an officer.

"Mistress," Loclon replied, with a low bow. She insisted on courtesy. One could do whatever they wished to the young men and women she employed, but the slightest hint of bad manners would see one banned for life.

"We've not had the pleasure of your company for some time, sir."

"I've been away."

"Then you must be looking for some . . . special . . . entertainment?" she suggested, with an elegantly raised brow. "I've several new girls that might interest you. Even a young man or two that might tempt a jaded palate."

"I've no interest in your fancy boys, Mistress. I want a woman. A redhead."

"Not an easy request, Captain." Mistress Heaner appeared to think for a moment, as if she did not know the physical characteristics of every soul in her employ. "Red is an unusual color. Is there anything else that might tempt you?"

"No. She must be a redhead. And tall. Preferably slim."

"Such specific requirements can be expensive, Captain."

"How much?"

"Fifty rivets."

Loclon almost baulked at that point. Fifty rivets would leave him almost penniless until his next pay. It would mean eating in the barracks and avoiding his landlady.

"Fifty rivets, then."

Mistress Heaner watched carefully as he counted out the coins into her arthritic hand.

"You may use the Blue Room," she said, as her claw-like fingers closed over the money. "I will send Peny to you."

Loclon nodded and pushed his way past a flimsy curtain hanging over a couch, where a middle-aged man was fondling the breast of a girl young enough to be his granddaughter. He stepped into the hall and walked the short distance to the Blue Room, named for the color of its door. The Red Room beside it was reserved for those whose tastes ran to multiple partners and boasted a bed large enough for six. The Green Room, further down the hall, housed a bath the size of a large pool. The Yellow Room at the end was the domain of those who got pleasure from their own pain, and was better equipped than the cell where the Defenders carried out their more "persuasive" interrogations. The Blue Room was reserved for less exotic pleasures, and Loclon was not surprised to find it unchanged since his last visit.

The room was lavishly furnished, with a carved four-poster, whose woodwork glowed softly in the lamplight. White sheets peeked out from under the blue quilt on the bed, and a pitcher of chilled wine with two glasses waited on the side table. Satisfied with the room, Loclon turned as the door opened and a woman stepped through. She was older than he would have liked, thirty-five perhaps—or maybe the life she led had aged her faster than normal. Her hair was carrot-red, obviously dyed and her body was too full under the thin shift she wore. Disappointed, Loclon ignored her welcoming smile and turned to the wine pitcher. He poured himself a good measure and swallowed it in a gulp.

"My name is Peny," she said.

Loclon turned to her, his eyes cold. "No. Tonight your name is R'shiel."

The woman shrugged. "If you wish."

"Come here."

She complied willingly enough, and began to unlace her shift as she approached.

"No. Leave it."

"What would you like me to do, then?" she asked.

"Beg for mercy," he replied and then he hit her. She cried out, but nobody would come to her rescue. Fifty rivets bought silence along with Mistress Heaner's whores. He hit her again, in the face this time, throwing her back against the carved bedpost. She cracked her head and slumped on the expensive blue quilt, too stunned to protect herself from his blows.

"Beg for mercy, R'shiel!"

If she replied he didn't notice. His rage consumed him as he took out his frustration on the hapless *court'esa*. The desire to beat her into submission left no room for any other thought.

chapter 6

amin Wolfblade was drunk. He knew he was drunk because the walls of the tent were starting to spin, and he could no longer feel his toes. Tarja Tenragan was even drunker. He had been at this longer, and was drinking to drown his sorrows. Damin, on the other hand, was simply drinking to be sociable.

"A toast," he declared, as Tarja uncorked another bottle. The floor of the tent was littered with empty flagons—an impressive testament to the amount of alcohol they had consumed. "To . . . to your horse. What's his name?"

"*Her* name is Shadow," Tarja corrected. He wasn't even slurring his words. Damin was impressed. The man must have a stomach lined with lead.

"To Shadow, then," Damin declared, raising his cup. "May she carry you safely into battle."

"I'd be happier if she carried me safely *out* of it," Tarja remarked, taking a long swig from the newly uncorked flagon.

Damin laughed and downed the contents of his cup in a swallow. He held out his cup and Tarja refilled it with a surprisingly steady hand.

"I'll drink to that, too! May she see you safely home again."

"You'll drink to anything. I'm surprised you haven't started toasting the gods."

"The night is young, my friend," Damin laughed, relieved to see that Tarja appeared to be coming out of the deep melancholy that had possessed him all day. The Medalonian captain had good days and bad days. Today had been particularly bad. "And when we run out of gods, we can always start on my brothers and sisters."

"Thanks, but I'd rather we stuck to the gods," Tarja said, taking another mouthful. "You've enough of them to keep us going for days."

"True, true," Damin agreed, silently cursing himself for bringing up the topic of brothers and sisters. Tarja's grief was centred on the woman he once believed was his sister. Reminding him of that was the last thing Damin wanted at this point. "To the gods, then!"

He downed his cup and glanced at Tarja in concern. The man had not touched the flagon, but was staring at him thoughtfully.

"What?"

"Your gods. They'd know if she's still alive, wouldn't they?"

Damin shrugged uncomfortably. "I suppose."

"How do we ask them?" Tarja demanded.

He shook his head. "It's not so simple, my friend. The gods do not speak directly to the likes of you and me. Perhaps, if Brak were here . . ."

"Well, he's not here!"

Brak had vanished only days after the Hythrun had ridden into Testra, some five months ago. Nobody had seen or heard of him since.

"Hey, isn't Dace a god? He spoke to us. Hell, he *traveled* with us. Can't we contact him?"

"If you have a reliable way of contacting the gods, then enlighten me, Tarja. Dacendaran appears when the mood takes him, as does any other god. I doubt if putting the mind of a non-believer at ease about whether the demon child lives or dies is enough to warrant even the fleeting attention of the God of Thieves." He placed his cup on the small table next to the guttering candle. "If R'shiel is still alive, she'll be back some day. If not, do your grieving and be done with it. Either way, you can't spend the rest of your life moping about the girl."

"When I need sanctimonious advice from you, I'll let you know. In the meantime, mind your own damned business."

"It is my business," Damin replied, "when your misery affects the decisions you make. Particularly when it concerns the safety of my Raiders."

"*Your* Raiders?" Damin could see the anger, the pain in the other man's eyes. "Your damned Raiders are nothing but a bunch of cutthroat mercenaries. And I've done nothing to endanger anybody."

"That's for certain," Damin retorted, deliberately goading him. "You've done nothing at all but sit here on the border and lament your great and tragic loss. Well, I have news for you, Captain. There's a Karien army heading this way and they don't give a pinch of pig-shit about your tender sensibilities. Dead or alive, R'shiel is gone, and you can't afford to sit here wallowing in self-pity."

The punch came out of nowhere as Tarja threw himself across the table, sending Damin backward off his stool. He rolled to the side as Tarja lunged for him, tangling himself in the tent as their brawl spilled outside. The candle fell from the overturned table and landed in a puddle of spilled wine, where it quickly caught and began lapping at the canvas tent walls. By the time they staggered to their feet in the clearing, the blazing tent provided a ruddy backdrop to their fight.

They were both drunk, so the blows they traded lacked the strength or accuracy of sobriety, but Damin was still surprised at the force behind Tarja's fist. Damin had time to wonder if it was guilt, even more than grief, which was eating up Tarja, before the Medalonian charged him with a wordless cry.

By now their altercation had drawn the attention of the other men occupying the surrounding tents, who quickly formed a cheering circle of red-coated Defenders, brown-shirted rebels, and leather-clad Hythrun Raiders, cheering on their officers as they brawled liked a couple of drunken sailors.

Damin didn't know who was getting the better of the fight. Tarja was a professional soldier, but he was operating on instinct as much as anything. Damin knew his own battle-trained reflexes were the only thing saving him from serious injury. His mind was too wine-muddled to think anything through, other than trading hit-and-miss blows with his equally inebriated adversary. He felt his bottom lip split as Tarja's fist connected with his face, snapping his head back, but he blocked the next blow with his left arm and slammed his fist into Tarja's gut. The other man grunted in pain, but kept his feet and came at him again, a feral grin on his face that looked all the more evil for being blood-streaked and illuminated by the blazing firelight from the tent. He ducked another blow and landed a glancing hit on Tarja's jaw, as the breathtaking shock of icy water brought the conflict to an abrupt halt.

Damin staggered backwards, shaking the water from his drenched fair hair, as Tarja did the same, looking about for the source of the interruption. Mahina Cortanen stood not two paces from them, empty bucket in hand, her expression thunderous. Lord Jenga stood just behind her, and a pace or so behind Jenga stood the suddenly quiet spectators, their faces ruddy in the flickering light of the burning tent.

"Is this something you gentlemen need to discuss privately?" she asked, with a voice that was colder than the water she had thrown on them.

Damin glanced at Tarja, whose grin was now rather more sheepish than feral. Both of his eyes were beginning to blacken, and blood streamed from his nose and the corner of his mouth. His normally immaculate uniform was torn and muddied. Damin had no doubt that he looked just as bad.

"We were discussing . . . the differences in Medalonian and Hythrun . . . hand-to-hand combat, my Lady," Damin explained, as he gasped for air, with a quick grin in Tarja's direction. "We had just moved . . . from a theoretical discussion to a more . . . practical demonstration of the techniques involved. A . . . most useful exercise, I must say." With the back of his tender hand, he wiped the blood from his mouth, and smiled ingenuously at Mahina. The spectators, Defender, rebel and Hythrun alike, nodded their agreement.

Mahina glared at him then turned on Tarja. "And what do you have to say for yourself?"

Tarja hesitated for a moment, his chest heaving, before he straightened up and smiled through his split lip at the former First Sister. "I'd say . . . both techniques were useful, given . . . the right circumstances, however—"

"Oh, spare me!" Mahina cried. "Perhaps now that you've finished your *discussion*, you might attend me and the Lord Defender in the Keep? A matter of some urgency has arisen that requires your attention, gentlemen. If you can find the time, of course."

Damin rubbed his tender jaw and glanced at Tarja, who seemed the better for their fight, despite his physical condition. Damin made a mental note to make certain that the next time Tarja felt the need to hit something, he arranged for somebody else to be the target.

"I believe we can accommodate you, my Lady," Damin said, as if accepting a dinner invitation. "Shall we, Captain?"

"Certainly." He looked around at the gathered spectators, suddenly noticing them for the first time. "Did you men want something to do?"

Several Defenders had taken it upon themselves to douse the blazing tent. The rest of the Defenders and rebels faded into the darkness with impressive speed. One look in the direction of his Raiders was enough to have the same effect on them. Looking idle was a thing to be avoided at all costs; every soldier in the camp knew that. Lord Jenga stood behind Mahina, a rare smile on his contour-map face as he watched the troops vanish back into their tents. Mahina glanced over her shoulder at him. He quickly wiped the smile off his face.

"Something amuses you, my Lord?"

"Youthful high spirits always amuse me, my Lady," he replied evenly.

"Is that what you call it? I can think of a better description." She turned back to the two combatants with a frown. "Clean yourselves up, then meet me in the Keep." She turned on her heel, still clutching the wooden bucket, and stormed off into the darkness.

"Has something happened?" Damin asked the Lord Defender. Mahina was fairly even tempered as a rule. Anger seemed strange in a woman who looked like somebody's grandmother.

"We have a visitor from the Citadel," Jenga told them.

"Who?" Tarja asked. The shock from Mahina's bucket of water seemed to have sobered him. Damin wished he could recover so quickly.

"Garet Warner."

Damin turned to him, trying to think of an intelligent question. It was quite depressing to be drunk under the table by a Medalonian. He had to at least give the impression that he could think straight. "Is he on our side, this Garet Warner?"

Tarja shrugged. "That remains to be seen."

Garet Warner proved to be a nondescript-looking man of average height, who wore the red jacket of a Defender and the rank insignia of a commandant. He had a balding head, a deceptively quiet voice and a piercing mind. The Warlord studied him by the torchlight of the hastily reconstructed great hall of Treason Keep. Damin was unsure where the name had come from. It certainly wasn't officially named that, and one referred to the ruin as "Treason Keep" in the Lord Defender's hearing at their peril. It seemed fitting, though. The Defenders were here to protect their nation from invasion, but they had broken any number of oaths to get here.

The ruin was deserted when they arrived some months ago, and a much sturdier and strategically more useful keep, closer to the northern border, would soon replace it. In the interim, Treason Keep was the closest thing to a permanent structure on the open, grassy plains of northern Medalon.

The commandant's expression gave away nothing as Tarja and Damin entered the hall. Garet Warner stood in front of the huge fireplace, his hands clasped behind his back as they walked toward him. Mahina sat in a chair on his right; Jenga in another chair opposite the former First Sister.

Tarja nodded warily to Garet when they reached the hearth. "Garet."

"Tarja," Garet acknowledged. "You've a knack for keeping your head on your shoulders, I'll grant you that."

Tarja smiled faintly, which made Damin rest a little easier. There was something about this visitor that marked him as dangerous, although Damin wasn't thinking clearly enough to define the feeling exactly. He hoped this man was on their side. He would be a bad enemy.

"I can't help being hard to kill. Commandant Warner, this is the Warlord of Krakandar, Damin Wolfblade."

"Our new and somewhat unexpected ally. My Lord."

"Commandant," Damin greeted him. "You come from the Citadel, I hear. Do you have news?"

"Questions, more than news," Garet replied, his glance taking in all of them. "The Quorum is understandably suspicious about the First Sister's extended absence from the Citadel. The orders arriving at the Citadel, under her seal, seem rather at odds with her . . . previous decisions."

"The First Sister has had a change of heart in recent months," Tarja said.

"Is she still alive?"

"Of course, she's alive," Jenga declared. "Do you think I would be a party to murder?"

"I'm not here to give my opinion, my Lord," Garet told him with a shrug. "I am here to investigate the issues raised by the Quorum. And there is plenty of reason to be suspicious. You left the Citadel with an army to capture and execute an escaped convict. Six months later, here you are, sitting on the northern border with that same escaped convict pardoned and a member of your staff, a foreign warlord, as your ally, preparing to fight a nation we very recently considered our friend. All with the approval of the First Sister, who, it is widely acknowledged, was in complete disagreement with you on all of those matters. The remarkable thing about all this is that they haven't sent someone to investigate sooner."

"There's a perfectly logical explanation," Damin offered helpfully.

"And I look forward to hearing it," Garet told him. "It will be fascinating, I'm sure. But first, I must insist on seeing Sister Joyhinia."

"You doubt my word, Garet?" Jenga asked.

"Not at all, my Lord. But I have my orders."

"Very well," Jenga agreed, with some reluctance. "You shall see her. Perhaps once you have, things will make a little more sense."

"I hope so, my Lord."

"Sister Mahina? Would you be so kind as escort Commandant Warner to the First Sister's quarters?"

Mahina frowned. "I don't like to disturb her this late at night."

"It cannot be avoided, I fear. I doubt the commandant wants to wait until morning."

"Very well," Mahina agreed. She stood up and pointed toward the narrow staircase that led to the upper level. "If you will follow me, Commandant."

Damin and Tarja stood back to let them pass, watching the old woman and the Defender until they vanished into the gloom. Once he was certain they were out of earshot, Tarja turned to Jenga with concern.

"This could be awkward," Tarja said, leaning on the long table for support. The movement heartened Damin. Tarja was not nearly as sober as he pretended.

"Awkward? This is bloody impossible! I have never been happy with this subterfuge! Something like this was bound to happen, sooner or later."

"Do you have a better alternative?"

"But to send orders to the Citadel? Under Joyhinia's seal? Orders that anybody in their right mind would know did not come from her?"

Damin found himself stepping between the two men, and between an argument that had been unresolved for months. "With all due respect, my Lord, the orders *have* come from Joyhinia. She has signed and sealed every one of them."

"She has the mind of a child," Jenga retorted. "You could place an order for her own hanging in front of her and she'd sign it with a giggle. I'm not as adept as you and Tarja at twisting the truth to placate my honor, Lord Wolfblade. What we have done is tantamount to treason."

"Refusing to slaughter three hundred innocent men was treason, Jenga," Tarja pointed out. "Everything flowing from that action is merely consequences. The treason is done and past. Our duty now is to protect Medalon."

"And the end justifies the means?" Jenga asked bitterly. "I wish I had your ability to see the world so . . . conveniently."

"I wish I had your ability to argue the same point endlessly," Damin added impatiently. "You Medalonians have a bad habit of not knowing when it's time to let a matter rest. What I want to know is who this Garet Warner is, and why you're all so afraid of him?"

Both Tarja and Jenga looked at him in surprise.

"Afraid of him?" Jenga asked.

"Afraid is not the right word, but it pays to be wary of him," Tarja said. "Garet Warner is the head of Defender Intelligence. And a loyal officer."

"Loyal to whom, exactly?"

"We'll find that out soon enough," Jenga predicted grimly.

chapter 7

Consciousness was a long time coming to R'shiel, but it pulled at her relentlessly, forcing her to acknowledge her existence. She did not want to awaken. She was perfectly content where she was, lost in a warm nothingness where no pain, no misery, no fear could intrude. The silence was complete, the darkness total. Were it not for the annoying, insistent voice calling her name, she could happily have stayed here forever. She had no sense of time in this place, no way to judge how long she had been here. All she knew was that she had no great desire to leave.

Yet the voice called to her and she was unable to resist it.

"Welcome back."

She stared at the man who spoke for a long time before she remembered who he was. His faded blue eyes were full of concern. And something else. Suspicion, perhaps?

"Brak."

"No, don't try to sit up. You've been unconscious for quite a while. It'll take a little time to get your strength back."

R'shiel let her head flop back onto the pillow, and contented herself with simply moving her head to study her surroundings. The room was large and lit by streaming sunlight; the air was heavy with the scent of wildflowers.

"Where am I?"

"Sanctuary."

She turned her head to look at him. "How did I get here? I don't remember anything. We were in Testra, I think . . ."

"Don't worry, it'll come back to you, and sooner than you want. You've been very sick, R'shiel. Cheltaran himself had to heal you."

"Who's Cheltaran?"

"The God of Healing. You should feel honoured. He doesn't often interfere directly with anyone, human or Harshini."

She closed her eyes for a moment, wondering why the knowledge did not surprise or frighten her. They seemed to be emotions that for the moment were out of reach.

"Tarja . . . ?"

"He's fine. He's up north, on the border."

Even that news failed to ignite much more than a small sense of relief in her. She wondered if she should feel something more. Perhaps she was simply too lethargic to care. Later, when she gained her strength, she could worry about such things.

"What are you doing here?"

"This is my home, R'shiel. It's your home too."

"Is it?"

Brak smiled, as if her vagueness amused him. "Go back to sleep, R'shiel. When you wake up the Harshini will attend you. They are a gentle people, so mind your manners. And try not to scream when you see their eyes. I didn't bring you all this way so you could embarrass me."

R'shiel smiled vacantly. "I'll be a good girl."

He nodded and moved away from the bed.

"Brak."

"What?"

"I owe you my life, don't I?"

"In ways you can't imagine," he replied.

When R'shiel woke the next time, she felt much better. The weakness that had gripped her was replaced with a sort of restless energy that did not take well to being bedridden. Her Harshini attendants, who introduced themselves as Boborderen and Janarerek, smiled at her constantly while they firmly refused to let her out of bed. She found it too difficult to pronounce their names, so she called them Bob and Jan, which made them laugh delightedly. Her one attempt to defy them was met with even more smiles, as they simply pushed her back down using magic.

R'shiel felt the now-familiar prickle against her skin and could not move a muscle. The Harshini fussed over her and scolded her gently, but they were not to be denied. She gave up and did as she was told.

Brak visited her again the following day, and brought with him a tall Harshini with hair almost as red as her own. He wore a simple white robe, the same as the other Harshini, but his bearing set him apart. He was regal, in a manner that R'shiel had rarely before encountered, and too perfectly handsome to be human—even if his black-on-black eyes had not betrayed his true race.

Freed from the magical bondage of her attendants, who had finally believed her when she agreed to behave, it was all R'shiel could do not to bow in his presence.

"Your Majesty, may I present your cousin, R'shiel té Ortyn," Brak said with uncharacteristic formality.

So this was the Harshini King. "Your Majesty."

"It fills my heart with joy to see you recovered, R'shiel," Korandellan said. He meant it, too. R'shiel had never met any group of people so free of guile; so genuine in their concern for her well-being. "But please, we are cousins. There is no need for such formality. You may call me Korandellan."

Mindful of her promise to watch her manners, she politely thanked the King. Brak gave her a small nod, and she amused herself with the thought that this was probably the first time in her life she had done something he approved of.

"When you are fully recovered, I will be delighted to show you Sanctuary," Korandellan added. "And we must see to your education. There is much for you to learn, young cousin. Shananara tells me you have some minor control over your power, but you have missed a great deal being raised among humans."

"I'll look forward to that," R'shiel replied, a little surprised to discover that she really *was* looking forward to it.

The King smiled at her—these people seemed to smile at everything—then withdrew, leaving Brak and R'shiel alone. Once the door had closed behind him, Brak turned to her.

"See, you can be civil when you try."

"Why would I be rude to your king? He seems very . . . nice."

"He is, so watch yourself. I brought you here to help you, R'shiel, but if I think for a moment that you might hurt these people, I'll throw you out of Sanctuary myself."

"Why do you always assume the worst about me?"

He shrugged and sat down beside her on the bed. "I've seen what you're capable of. Remember the rebels?"

She remembered, but only just. "I suppose I was rather . . . difficult. But it all seems so distant. I remember things sometimes that seem like they happened to somebody else. Other times it's as if I never even existed until I woke up in this place."

"Sanctuary is a magical place, R'shiel. You're bound to feel different here. The strangeness will pass."

It was then that she noticed he was dressed in leather trousers and a linen shirt—human attire rather than the Harshini robe he had worn the last time she saw him. "Are you going somewhere?"

"Yes. Back out into the big bad world, I'm afraid. Between you and Tarja, you managed to turn the whole damned world on its ear. I have to find out what's happening."

The thought of Tarja left R'shiel with a warm glow of affection, but little else. "Will you see Tarja?"

"No, I'm heading south. I want to see what the Fardohnyans are up to."

"Oh."

He smiled at her expression. Even Brak smiled in this place. "Is there anything you want?"

"Meat," she said, without hesitation. "I would kill for a haunch of venison *this big*, smothered in gravy."

Brak's smile faded. "Don't use that word in Sanctuary, R'shiel."

"What? Venison?"

"Kill. The Harshini cannot abide violence. Even the thought distresses them. As for the meat, I'll see what I can do, but don't go asking for it. The Harshini don't eat meat and it upsets them to be reminded that humans do. It will also upset them if they think you're not happy. Besides, it won't hurt you to eat like a Harshini for a while."

"They eat like rabbits," she complained, but her smile took the sting from her words.

"Then you'll just have to learn to like rabbit food."

Another thought occurred to her then. "So if they can't kill anything, where does all the leather come from?"

"It's a gift."

"From whom?"

"The animals who inhabit the mountains. When they die, they allow the Harshini to take their skins."

"How do the Harshini know that?" she scoffed.

"They are Harshini, R'shiel. They communicate with animals just as easily as they do with humans. In fact they prefer it, I think. Animals haven't invented war yet."

"You know, I almost like you here, Brak. Why did you ever leave?"

But he refused to answer her and something about his eyes warned her not to inquire too closely.

chapter 8

ow long has she been like this?" Garet asked.

They had settled in around the fire in the crumbling great hall, Garet in the chair that had been occupied by Mahina the previous evening. Tarja sat on the edge of the hearth near Jenga, who had taken the only other chair.

"Since Testra," Jenga told him, staring into the flames, not meeting the eye of the other officer.

Damin stood leaning against the mantle, stoking the inadequate fire with an iron poker. Fuel was a major problem on this treeless plain, and a sizeable number of their force had been occupied gathering enough wood to see them through the coming winter. Were it not for the vast number of horses here, many of the camp's fires would be sorry affairs indeed. It was a small extravagance to burn the wood, but Damin was grateful to be spared the sting of burning dung in the Hall.

"How did it happen?"

"I'm not certain."

Damin laughed softly at the Lord Defender's discomfort. "Dacendaran, the God of Thieves, stole her intellect, Commandant. The Lord Defender has some difficulty dealing with the concept."

"A difficulty I share, my Lord. We do not believe in your gods."

"Believe in them or not," Damin shrugged. "It's the truth. Ask Tarja."

Garet turned his gaze on the younger man. "Tarja?"

"Somebody told me once that he believed in the gods, he just didn't know if they were worthy of adoration. That sums it up fairly well, I think. The gods exist, Garet, and they took a hand in our conflict, as Joyhinia's condition proves."

"And you've been issuing orders in her name ever since?" It was impossible to tell what the man was thinking. He was a master in the art of inscrutability, Damin decided. He would have made a brilliant Fardohnyan merchant.

"Once the Karien Envoy was murdered on Medalon soil, the threat of a Karien invasion moved from a theory to a certainty," Tarja explained. "Had Jenga returned to the Citadel with Joyhinia, the Quorum would *still* be in session, arguing about what to do next. At least this way preparations could be made."

"Did you kill him?" he asked.

"No, but I led the raid. I suppose I'm responsible."

Garet shook his head wearily and turned his attention back to Jenga. "I've known you a long time, Jenga. I'm trying to imagine what finally pushed you into this. By any definition, this is treason."

The Lord Defender nodded heavily. "We discussed this once, you and I. I asked you what you would do if faced with an order you found morally reprehensible. I recall you said you would refuse it, and the consequences be damned. I find myself in that position now."

Garet leaned back in his seat and studied the three men before him. "Knowing Joyhinia, I find that easy enough to believe, but how long do you think you can get away with this? The First Sister's absence from the Citadel is causing a great deal of unrest. And the orders she's sending are too strange to be accepted without question. You've pardoned Tarja. You've ordered an end to the Purge and freed half the prisoners in the Grimfield. You've ordered troops north. You're spending money like the treasury is a bottomless pit and you've signed a treaty with a Hythrun Warlord. Joyhinia would never be a willing party to any of these actions."

"The next Gathering is only months away," Tarja pointed out. "Joyhinia will send a letter to the Quorum announcing her retirement and nominating Mahina in her place. With her vote, and the votes of Jacomina and Louhina, who will automatically vote for anything Joyhinia suggests, we should be safe."

Garet shook his head. "It will never work, Tarja."

"It has to work," he insisted. "The alternative is a civil war, and that would leave us wide open to a Karien invasion."

"We're not trying to bring down the Sisterhood, Garet," Jenga added, a little defensively. "Merely bring some sanity to it."

"Sanity? That's a strange word coming from men who think they can fool the world into believing that Joyhinia Tenragan is alive and well, when in fact she's a babbling idiot."

Damin listened to the discussion with interest. He was a Warlord and therefore absolute ruler of his province. He never had to justify anything he did to anybody, and it fascinated him, watching the Medalonians trying to convince themselves and each other that their actions were either honorable or necessary, or both.

"The fact is, my friends, you can argue the rights and wrongs of this until you're old men," he interjected. "What I'd really like to know is what *you* are planning to do about it, Commandant?"

Garet Warner looked up at him. "I have two choices that I can see. I can go along with this farce, or I can return to the Citadel and tell the Quorum what's really going on up here."

"No, you have one choice, Commandant. You can go along with this farce, or I'll kill you."

"Damin!"

"Be realistic, Tarja. If you let him go, he'll be back here in a month with a full force of Defenders, and you'll have the very civil war you're trying so hard to avoid. Killing one Defender now may save you from having to kill a damn sight more of them later on. I'll do it, if it bothers you."

Garet stared at the Warlord for a moment. "A pragmatist, I see. Not a quality I expected to find in a heathen who believes in the Primal gods."

"Then you sorely underestimate me, Commandant," Damin warned.

"I fear I've sorely underestimated a lot of things in my life, but I manage to get by." He turned back to Tarja, giving no indication that Damin's threat bothered him. "The Quorum will not accept Joyhinia's resignation without seeing her. How, in the name of the Founders, do you expect to pull this off?"

"I have no idea, Garet," Tarja admitted. "But we have to. Somehow."

"Who else knows of her true condition?"

"The three of us," Jenga told him. "Draco, of course. Mahina and Affiana know for certain. The Defenders and the heathens who were in

Testra when it happened don't fully comprehend the full extent of her . . . condition, and we've kept up the illusion that she is in command, so far."

"Who is this Affiana?"

"A friend," Tarja said. "She takes care of Joyhinia most of the time."

"I see," Garet said. He steepled his fingers under his chin and stared into the fire for a long moment. Damin wondered what he was thinking, his hand resting on the hilt of his dagger. Garet Warner would not leave this room alive if Damin doubted him for a moment. "Let's put aside the issue of Joyhinia, for the moment. What of the rumors that the Harshini have returned? You've made no mention of them."

"They, at least, are true. We've seen a few of them," Tarja told him. "But not for months. I've no idea what they're planning, or where they are. Believe me, if I could find them, I would have."

"To what purpose?" Garet asked. "You've acquired enough strange allies as it is," he added, looking pointedly at Damin.

"They have R'shiel," Tarja explained, his voice remarkably unemotional under the circumstances. "The Harshini believe she is the demon child."

Even Garet Warner could not hide his surprise at the news. "R'shiel? The demon child? Why in the name of the Founders would they think that?"

"They don't *think* she's the demon child, Commandant, they *know* she is. If she is still alive, the Harshini have her and I imagine they won't let her go until she has performed the task for which she was created."

"What task?"

"They want her to destroy Xaphista," Tarja said.

"The Karien god?" Garet shook his head in disbelief. "If this is some sort of joke, then you have me, Tarja. I'm afraid I—"

"My Lords?" the urgent voice rang out from the shadows near the door. "I seek Lord Wolfblade."

"Come in, Almodavar," Damin called, recognizing the voice of his captain. "What is it?"

"You'd better come see, my Lord," Almodavar said in Hythrun, as he materialized out of the shadows. "The western patrol is bringing in two spies they captured."

There had been a number of forays across the border by the half-a-thousand knights camped north of the border for most of the summer, although rarely did a knight sully his hands with anything so demeaning as reconnaissance. It was always some hapless page or squire, attempting to breach the border. It was an ambitious undertaking, particularly for city-bred youths who thought Xaphista's blessing was all the protection they needed on their journey. It had taken Damin quite some time to accept that the forays were genuine, not merely a feint to disguise a more effective attack. He had trouble believing that anybody could be that stupid.

"Can't you deal with it, Captain?" he asked in Hythrun. It was an advantage, sometimes, speaking a language his allies did not understand. Tarja was attempting to learn Hythrun, but he could not follow such a rapid exchange yet.

"They have news, my Lord."

Damin frowned and turned to the Defenders. "I'd better see to this," he told them. "I'll be back in a while." He followed Almodavar out of the Hall and into the night, to the curious stares of his companions.

The two spies proved to be boys, frightened and defiant. Both had mousy brown hair and freckled skin, and they were enough alike to be brothers. The older of the two wore a sullen expression and the evidence of a beating. The younger was more defiant, angry and belligerent. He wore a pendant with the five-pointed star and lightning bolt of Xaphista, and leapt to his feet when Damin entered the tent. The older brother did not rise from the floor. Perhaps he could not. Almodavar was not renowned for his tender interrogation techniques.

"*Hythrun dog*!" the younger boy cried, spitting on the ground in front of Damin. Almodavar stepped forward and slapped the boy down with the back of his gauntleted hand. The lad fell backwards, landing on his backside.

"That's *Lord* Hythrun Dog, to you boy," Damin told him, placing his hands on his hips and glaring at the youth. The boy cowered under his gaze.

"They are Jaymes and Mikel of Kirkland," Almodavar told him. "From Lord Laetho's duchy in Northern Karien."

Duke Laetho's banner had been identified months ago. He was a rich man with a large retinue, but rumor had it he was more bluster than bravery, a fact borne out by the presence of these two boys. Who but a fool would send children to do his reconnaissance for him?

"Almodavar says you have interesting news, boy. Tell me now, and I might let you live."

"We would give our lives for the Overlord," the older brother snarled from the floor. "Tell him nothing, Mikel."

"No, I'll tell him, Jaymes. I want to see the Hythrun quivering in their boots when they learn what is coming."

"Then out with it, boy," Damin said. "It would be most unfortunate if I have you put to death for the glory of the Overlord before you get the chance to see me quivering, won't it?"

"Your day of reckoning is coming. Even now, the Karien knights advance on you."

"They've been doing that for months. I'm scared witless at the mere thought."

"You should be," Mikel spat. "When our Fardohnyan allies join with us to overrun this pitiful nation of atheists, we will descend on Hythria and you will be knee-deep in pagan blood."

Damin glanced at Almodavar questioningly before turning his attention back to the boy. "Fardohnyan allies?"

"Prince Cratyn is to marry Princess Cassandra of Fardohnya," Mikel announced triumphantly. "You cannot defeat the might of two such great nations."

"You're lying. You're a frightened child making up wild stories. Kill them, Almodavar—just don't leave the corpses where I can smell them." He turned his back on the youths and pushed back the flap of the tent.

"I do not lie!" the boy yelled after him. "Our father is the Duke Laetho's Third Steward in Yarnarrow, and he was there when the King received the offer from King Hablet."

That had the ring of truth to it, Damin decided, although he did not stop or turn back. Once they were clear of the tent, he turned to his captain, his face reflecting concern and firelight in almost equal measure.

"You think he speaks the truth?"

"Aye, he's too scared to think up a convincing lie."

"This changes the rules of engagement somewhat," he said thoughtfully. "Perhaps our visitor from the Citadel can shed some light on the news. He's supposed to be in Intelligence, after all."

"And the boys? Did you really want me to kill them?"

"Of course not. They're children. Put them to work some place they can't cause any trouble. I believe the Kariens think hard work is good for the soul."

The captain smiled wickedly. "And deny them a chance to die as martyrs for the Overlord? You're a cruel man, my Lord."

chapter 9

drina's departure from Talabar was an occasion of some note, and Hablet was determined to see his daughter off in style. The hastily repaired wharf was lined with soldiers in their white dress uniforms, a band played merry tunes to keep the spectators entertained, and even Bhren, the God of Storms, was smiling on Fardohnya this day. The weather was perfect—a flawless sky, a calm sea. The sprawling city of Talabar glowed pink in the warm sunlight; the flat-roofed houses closest to the docks were lined with curious Fardohnyans come to see the last of their princess.

Hablet stepped down from his litter and looked around with satisfaction, waving to his people and accepting their cheers with a wave of his bear-like arms. He had just about everything he wanted from this treaty and was feeling unusually magnanimous. He had secured enough of the tall, straight Karien lumber to build the ships he wanted, enough gold to pay for their construction and, in a few months, with the Kariens and the Defenders embroiled in a war in the north, he would have a clear run across the southern plains of Medalon into Hythria. Best of all, he would finally destroy Lernen Wolfblade, the Hythrun High Prince—and his heirs—for an insult over thirty years old that very few people even remembered.

Hablet never forgot an insult.

He had conceded surprisingly little to the Kariens in return. True, he had agreed to allow Karien ships unhindered access to Solanndy Bay, where the Ironbrook River met the ocean, but they would pay dearly for the privilege. He had granted the Kariens sovereignty over the Isle of Slarn too, but that measly lump of rock perched in the Gulf was hardly a prime piece of real estate and it had no value to anyone but the Kariens. Of course, the casual observer would never have guessed how little the island meant to him. He had the Kariens believing it was as dear to him as one of his limbs, and had made them pay accordingly.

As for the secret of gunpowder, he had promised that, too, but had wisely proposed sending an expert in the science to Karien to suggest an appropriate location for a mill, before divulging the formula. When Hablet finally got around to sending someone, it was a foregone conclusion that the search for such a location would take years. A lot could happen in that time.

But the unexpected bonus was that he had finally found a way to get rid of Adrina.

He loved his eldest child, it was true. In fact he had often lamented the twist of fate that had seen her born a girl. She would have made a fine son. Unfortunately, that fiery spirit, that biting wit, that piercing intelligence, was positively dangerous in a woman. Adrina was, to put it bluntly, a troublesome, spoilt little bitch. Hablet was quite certain he would find it much easier to dote on his daughter from a distance.

His previous efforts to find Adrina a husband had all failed miserably. The last potential suitor, Lord Dundrake, had even suggested that he would rather face a century of Hythrun Raiders, alone and unarmed, than spend one night with Her Most Serene Highness. He claimed he would have a better chance of survival. Adrina had despised the man on sight, declaring she would never marry a man who couldn't tell the difference between a dinner fork and his fingers. Dundrake was a little rough around the edges, certainly. Hablet had hoped his provincial charm would entice her. It had proved an idle hope. Adrina was attracted to power, and there was no way that Hablet would allow her to wed a powerful man. She needed a husband who would hold her back. There were other men who would have married her gladly, and she them—not for love, but the power they brought each other. Hablet had refused all such offers out of hand.

The Karien Prince had turned out to be the perfect solution. He was a meek boy, so constrained by the edicts of his religion that Adrina would never be able to cajole him into anything. He was so inhibited by his religious distaste of all matters sexual, that even her legendary powers of seduction would be wasted. He believed in his God and little else. Poor Adrina. She would be the Karien Queen one day; she had agreed to go north for no other reason than the power it might eventually bring her. She was going to be very disappointed.

The band finished their tune and struck up a dour Karien number, heralding the arrival of Prince Cratyn and his party. The brightly painted Karien brigantine was tied up at the end of the wharf, awaiting her prince. Hablet frowned at the ship and decided he probably had no one but himself to blame for its hideous design. Fardohnyan ship builders were the best in the world, but their secrets were guarded more closely than his treasury. The Kariens built poor copies that were vastly inferior to their Fardohnyan originals. The irony was, Fardohnya had little in the way of timber for shipbuilding. It all had to be imported from Karien. What the Kariens did not have, besides generations of skilled craftsman, was the Fardohnyan secret of hardening and waterproofing the timber.

The King turned his attention back to the ceremony, smiling expansively at the young prince. For a moment, as Hablet studied his solemn face, he felt sorry for the boy. He was stuck with Adrina for life. The sorry fool was not even able to take a lover to console him. Ah well, that was the price one paid for being a Karien Prince. Cratyn bowed politely to the King and began a rather long-winded speech, thanking the King for his generosity, his kindness, his hospitality, and so on—in the Karien language, as the prince did not speak Fardohnyan. Hablet only half listened to the young man, thinking that he looked a little inbred. They were always marrying their cousins up north. The Karien Royal Family would benefit from a bit of fresh blood.

"Her Most Serene Highness, Princess Adrina!"

The fanfare that accompanied Adrina's arrival was not on the program that Hablet had approved. He smiled at her audacity, and she was handed down from her open litter by a handsome young slave wearing nothing but a white loin cloth and a great deal of oil on his well-formed muscles. She was planning to make her departure memorable, it seemed.

A number of white-robed young girls hurried to assemble in front of the princess and proceeded to scatter petals on the ground before her, so that her feet would not have to touch the grubby docks. Hablet considered that the ultimate irony, considering a week ago she thought she could sail a damned warship. He glanced at Cratyn's disapproving frown and forcibly swallowed his laughter. The boy was only just beginning to discover what he was marrying.

Adrina trod the flower-strewn path regally until she reached her father and curtsied gracefully. She was a beautiful woman, and in her prime. Although she was not particularly tall, and lacked Cassandra's delicate perfection, she had outgrown her sister's awkwardness of youth and had blossomed into a stunning creature. Her eyes were her best feature: emerald green and wide set. Her body was voluptuous and well-toned, rather than the slender gawkiness of a teenager. Cratyn would be a lucky young man if he had the sense to appreciate what he was getting. Provided Adrina kept her mouth shut.

Lecter Turon waddled forward and presented Hablet with a slender blade wrapped in a jeweled sheath. He took the dagger and held it out to Adrina.

"This is the Bride's Blade your mother carried."

"I hope it brings me better luck," Adrina replied, accepting the gift. Adrina's mother was not a topic discussed at court.

"It breaks my heart to lose you, my petal," he declared, almost, but not quite believing it.

Adrina's eyes glittered dangerously. "It's not too late to change your mind, Father."

He knew that look. She had learnt it at his knee.

"Oh yes it is, my petal."

"Then you will just have to live with the consequences, won't you?"

Hablet smiled. Only Adrina would dare threaten him. He swept her up into a bear hug and the crowd cheered at this obvious display of affection between the King and the princess.

"If you cross me, I'll personally see to it that you spend the rest of your life suffering in the coldest, most miserable place I can imagine," he whispered affectionately as he held her.

"Think up a better threat, Daddy," she whispered back. "You've already done that."

He let her go and held her at arm's length for a moment. She met his gaze evenly. Her mother had been like that. Fearless and ambitious. It was such a pity her ambition had run away with her. Had she learnt to

control it, she might not have lost her head . . . But Adrina was everything her mother was and more. He felt overcome with love for his child.
Hopefully, the feeling would soon pass.

He took her hand and ceremoniously placed it in Cratyn's hand. The
crowd went wild. Hablet suspected it had more to do with the idea of
Adrina finally getting married than any affection for the Karien groom.

"May the gods bless this great union!" Hablet boomed. "May Fardohnya and Karien, from this day forward, live in peace!"

The crowd cheered, although most of them knew Hablet's declaration had little to do with his own feelings. By law, no Fardohnyan could
declare war on the house of a family united by marriage. That law
included the King. The Kariens knew about it too, which was no doubt
why they had put aside their prejudice and accepted a foreign bride. A
Fardohnyan queen was a small price to pay for the guarantee that Hablet
was unable to make war on them.

Cratyn squirmed a little as he stood there holding Adrina's hand. His
daughter smiled and waved to the people. They liked the princess. She
was an astute politician and had made a point of being generous to those
lesser creatures outside the palace. She was a tyrant around anyone else,
but the people remembered her small kindnesses and were probably
genuinely sorry to see her go.

The guard snapped to attention as the Karien Prince and Adrina
walked down the dock toward the ship. Hablet watched them leaving
with some relief. As they boarded the gangway, he waved his hand to the
Captain of the Guard. Tristan dismissed his men and came to stand
before his father.

"You can come back next winter," he told the young man brusquely.
"I should have forgiven you by then."

Tristan grinned. "You are too kind, Sire."

"Don't take that tone with me, boy. You're lucky I didn't send you to
the eastern passes."

"To be honest, Father, I would have preferred that you did. I'd
rather fight Hythrun bandits than play toy soldiers in Karien."

"I need you to look after Adrina."

"Adrina doesn't need looking after."

"Well, keep an eye on her, then. And don't get mixed up in her
schemes. I want you back in a year, boy. I expect you to stay out of trou-

ble." He hugged his eldest bastard with genuine affection. "I'll have a legitimate son by then."

Tristan shook his head wryly. "Father, don't you worry sometimes that one of us might want the throne for himself?"

"There's none of you strong enough to challenge me, Tristan."

"But if you were to die before you name your heir . . ."

Hablet laughed. "Then you'll have Adrina to contend with, my boy, and I'm damned certain none of you is strong enough to challenge her."

chapter 10

nights. About five hundred of them."

Damin handed Tarja the small hollow tube he was using to examine the golden plain below. It had taken them most of the morning to climb up to this vantage on the side of the mountain that overlooked the border. Although rocky, the ledge was comfortably wide and he, Garet and Damin were stretched out on their bellies as they watched the tents of the enemy below, occasionally brushing away curious insects come to investigate the intruders.

Tarja put the tube to his eye and was enthralled to see the distant figures of the knights, their white circular tents and impressive entourage, grow larger through the lens. Damin called it a looking glass.

The knights camped on the Karien side of the border did not bother Tarja nearly so much as the infantry Jasnoff could throw against them. The knights were impressive, but they would be a minority in the final battle. More worrisome were the countless foot soldiers that the Kariens could muster. They had yet to arrive at the front. The knights below were as much an intimidating show of force as a serious vanguard of any incursion over the border. With a sigh, he moved the looking glass around to examine the fortifications on their side of the border.

The Defenders only hope to keep the conflict manageable was to force the Kariens to attack down a path chosen by the Medalonians. Trenches filled with sharpened stakes scored the plain like sword cuts in the red earth. The ground was pockmarked with holes dug to hamper the movement of the heavy Karien destriers. Mangonels, protected by earth mounds, stood silently out of Karien bow range, waiting for the coming battle like giant insects. But they had a vast front to cover and their defences looked woefully inadequate from this height.

"I thought there'd be more of them," Garet remarked as he took the looking glass from Tarja to study the Kariens.

"Ah, now that's the problem with a feudal government," Damin remarked sagely. "You have to waste an awful lot of time getting your army together. You have to call in favors, bribe people, marry off your children, and convince your Dukes that there's a profit in your war. Monumental waste of time and money, if you ask me. Standing armies are much more efficient." The fair-haired Hythrun frowned at Garet's surprised expression. It was obvious that Damin neither liked nor trusted Garet Warner. "I'm not a complete barbarian, you know, Commandant. Even Warlords need an education. What were you expecting my tactical assessment to be? Me Warlord. Me kill Kariens."

Garet smiled thinly. "Not exactly."

Damin grinned suddenly and pushed himself backward along the ledge. He sat against the cliff, leaning comfortably in the shade, with his long legs stretched out in front. He crossed his booted feet at the ankles as he took a long swig from his waterskin.

"You underestimate me again, Commandant," he said, offering Tarja the waterskin as Garet turned to face him. "But, for your information, I was educated by the finest tutors in Hythria. And I'm right. The Kariens don't keep a standing army, for all that they can field a huge one, once they finally get organized. It's a fatal flaw. Jasnoff's vassals owe him sixty days each a year, which means that by the time they get here, it will almost be time to go home again, but they're stuck here while the Church supports the war. Even fighting for the glory of the Overlord starts to pale when it's costing you money and there's no plunder in sight." He swatted idly at an annoying insect. "You Medalonians have the right idea. Toss the nobility, promote on merit and keep a standing army."

"Toss the nobility? If Hythria adopted that policy, you'd be out of a job."

Tarja wondered if he should warn Garet about the inadvisability of getting into a discussion about the merits of various systems of government with this man.

"Worse, Commandant, I'd be the first in line to be beheaded. My uncle is the High Prince of Hythria. I'm his heir, unfortunately."

"Unfortunately?" Tarja asked.

"Taking the Hythrun throne isn't going to be easy, and keeping it will be even harder. The other Warlords think I'm a bit . . . precocious. There may come a time when I call on Medalon for assistance. Assuming the Kariens and their Fardohnyan allies don't come pouring over your border to wipe us all out."

Tarja had wondered what the price of Damin's assistance would be. "I'm sure Medalon will remember your aid when the time comes."

"You're very free with your promises, Tarja," Garet remarked. "You're not the Lord Defender yet."

Tarja glanced at the commandant, but did not answer him.

"Well, for the time being, I think we're safe enough," Damin said. "Jasnoff can order his knights to the border with little ceremony, but we've time yet before the bulk of his army arrives. Although if they don't get here soon, winter will be on us."

"That would be too much to hope for," Tarja remarked. "The Kariens must know how hard a winter campaign will be."

"Lord Setenton is Jasnoff's Commander-in-Chief," Damin agreed. "He's too experienced to try campaigning in the snow."

"You need to train your men to deal with armored knights, too," Garet added. "A man encased in armor can be hard to kill, and neither the Defenders nor the Hythrun have much experience fighting them."

"But he's easy enough to disable. Just knock him off his horse and jump up and down on him for a while. That'll knock the fight out him."

Tarja smiled. "I'll let you inform the troops of that sage piece of tactical advice."

Damin shrugged. "It sounds silly, but it works. Have you any idea how hard it is to get up wearing a suit of armor? Hell, they can't even mount their horses without a block and tackle rig. Knock them on their backs and thrust your sword through the eye slit. Works like a treat. But the knights aren't our problem. The true problem lies with Hablet and the Fardohnyans if he puts his artillery at Jasnoff's disposal."

"Cannon, you mean?"

Damin nodded. "I've never seen one myself, but I've spoken to a few who have. The only thing in our favor is that Hablet guards the secret of what makes them work as if it's more precious to him than all his children put together. I suspect he'll find it a lot easier to give away his daughter than his precious cannon."

"I'd heard rumors of an alliance," Garet added, taking the waterskin from Tarja. "But nothing substantial. I've also heard rumors that the reason Hablet guards the secret so closely is because his cannon are notoriously unreliable, inaccurate, and just as likely to kill the cannoneers as they are the enemy. Hablet's weapon is his enemies' fear of the cannon, not the cannon themselves."

"Even if that's true, I don't want to face cannon fire with swords and arrows."

"Even without cannon, if there is an alliance, Fardohnya could attack from the south," Garet pointed out. "We can't afford to split our forces."

He said *our forces*, not *your forces*. Tarja wondered if the slip was accidental, or if it meant Garet had finally chosen which side he was on.

"We'll need time," Tarja agreed with a frown. "Until we gain control of the Citadel, the Defenders we can put in the field are barely half the number we need."

Damin nodded in agreement. "I can spare another three centuries of Raiders, but any more than that and Krakandar Province will begin to look a little bit too inviting to my neighbors. I can always send to Elasapine, if worst comes to worst. Narvell would send me five centuries of his Raiders if I asked him nicely. I imagine that many Hythrun troops garrisoned in Bordertown would make Hablet think twice about sailing up the Glass River."

"Narvell?" Tarja asked.

"Narvell Hawksword, the Warlord of Elasapine," Damin explained. "He's my half-brother. My mother's second husband was his father."

"How many husbands has your mother had?" Tarja asked.

"Five, the last time I counted," Garet remarked, obviously surprising Damin with his knowledge. He looked at the Warlord and shrugged. "I run the Defender Intelligence Corps, my Lord. I'm supposed to know these things."

"Then you should know she might have married again, by now. She had her eye on a very rich Greenharbour gem merchant when I saw her last."

Tarja shook his head in amazement. It was rare for Sisters of the

Blade to marry or have more than one or two children. Only the farmers of Medalon, for whom children were a convenient source of cheap labor, tended toward large families.

"But even with a thousand Hythrun raiders, we still need the Defenders in full force," Tarja pointed out with a frown, getting back to the problem at hand. "At the moment, we've got your seven hundred Raiders and about six thousand Defenders here, and that's less than half."

"How many longbowmen do you have?"

"Five hundred. The rest are still at the Citadel. Why?"

"I've been watching them train. I doubt if I could draw one of those damned bows."

"We train them from boyhood," Tarja told him. "They're selected from the cadets and they grow up with their bows. As they get stronger, the bows get longer, until they can draw a full-sized weapon. They're very good, I'll grant you, but they're irreplaceable. You can't just hand the bow along to the next man in line when a longbowman falls. And even with the others still at the Citadel, they number less than fifteen hundred."

"We can use them to our advantage. Assuming Hablet doesn't arm the Kariens with cannon, your longbows out-range any weapon they can bring to bear against you. Kariens consider the bow and arrow a peasant weapon. They have archers, but nothing of the calibre of your longbows. If we concentrate on protecting *them*, you could cut down any advance like a farmer mowing hay with a scythe."

"And your mounted archers?" Garet asked.

"We're hit-and-run specialists," Damin shrugged. "Any man of mine can fire three arrows into a target the size of an apple at a gallop in under a minute, but our bows are short-range weapons. There are too many Kariens for that sort of tactic."

"What about the rebels?"

Tarja shrugged. "Another thousand at the most. Most of them have never held a weapon. Jasnoff can field an army of over a hundred thousand with the Church supporting him. With the Fardohnyans as allies . . . I'm not sure I can count that high. I suppose they could pray for us."

"Never underestimate the power of prayer," Damin warned. "If Zegarnald, the God of War, takes our side, we should do well. And we've yet to hear from the Harshini."

Tarja did not argue the point. He had no faith in Damin's gods.

"I thought the Harshini were incapable of killing?" Garet asked.

"There's plenty of ways to frustrate the enemy without killing him."

"I suppose," Tarja agreed, a little doubtfully. "Maybe they could bring their demons and scare the Kariens to death."

"If the Kariens bring their priests with them, we will need the protection of the Harshini and their magic," Damin warned. "When Lord Brakandaran returns, we will know more."

Tarja frowned at the mention of Brak. "He's been gone more than five months. What makes you think he's planning to return at all?"

"He'll be back," Damin assured him.

"I wish I shared your confidence."

The fact was he wanted to see the Harshini rebel very badly—and not simply because he needed to know what help the Harshini could offer in the coming battle. Brak would know if R'shiel lived. Months had passed since she had vanished, quite literally, but he had seen enough wounds in his time to know that hers was fatal. Yet the Harshini were magical creatures and R'shiel was half-Harshini. A small spark of hope still burned in him that she had somehow survived Joyhinia's sword thrust, but as the days, weeks and then months passed with no word from her, his hope was fading.

"Is something wrong?"

Tarja shook his head. "I was just thinking of someone, that's all."

"The demon child."

"I wasn't thinking of her in those terms," Tarja said wryly. "But I was thinking of R'shiel, yes."

"Her fate is in the hands of the gods, my friend," Damin reminded him. "There is nothing you can do about her. On the other hand, there is something we can do about those damned knights."

"What did you have in mind?" Garet asked, a little suspiciously.

"They're looking a bit too comfortable for my liking. I think we should wake them up."

"What does that mean exactly?"

Damin laughed. "It means putting aside your damnable Defender's honor for a time and learning to be sneaky." He climbed to his feet and dusted off his trousers. "We need to do something about their supply lines, for one thing. What about it, Commandant? Are you with us?"

Tarja glanced at Garet curiously, knowing there was much more to Damin's simple question than whether or not he wanted to attack the Karien camp. The older man studied them both in silence for a moment.

"I'll not be a party to anything that reeks of stupidity," he warned, climbing to his feet and handing the looking glass back to Damin. "That also includes your ludicrous scheme for replacing Joyhinia, Tarja. Come up with something workable, and I'll back you to the hilt. But what you are planning is insane. And I plan to die in my bed a very old man."

"That's the most uncommitted excuse for an agreement I've ever heard."

"Be satisfied with it. It's the best you're likely to get until you show me something devised by brains, not wishful thinking."

Damin glanced at the two of them and shook his head. "Let's just push him off the cliff and be done with it, Tarja," he suggested.

"I hear you have a reputation as a cunning warrior, Lord Wolfblade. I can't for the life of me imagine how you came about it." He pushed past Damin on the ledge and began to climb down to the narrow trail where their horses were tethered below.

"If this man was not your friend, Tarja . . ." Damin began.

"He's just testing you. We need him."

"No, *you* need him. I'd just as soon see him dead. And I warn you, every moment I spend in his company, the idea becomes more attractive."

Damin slammed the delicate-looking glass back into its leather case and began to follow the path that Garet had taken.

Tarja shook his head. The last thing they needed was Damin Wolfblade threatening to kill Garet Warner. With Garet's assistance, it would be far easier to fool the Quorum into believing all was well with the First Sister and his help was essential if they were to eventually replace her. And if the Kariens really *had* allied with Fardohnya, their only hope of preventing a southern incursion was Damin's Hythrun Raiders.

Not for the first time since Joyhinia had won the First Sister's mantle, Tarja wished he had let her hang him. He would never have become involved in the rebellion. He would never have led the raid to rescue R'shiel that resulted in the death of the Karien Envoy, and they would not be facing an invasion. But what hurt most, when he let himself think on it, was R'shiel. If not for him, she would be alive and probably in blissful ignorance of what she really was.

But then again, maybe nothing would be different, even if he had
died. The Harshini had known all along what R'shiel was and had sent
Brak to find her. Garet and he had identified the Karien threat long
before any of these other events took shape. Whichever way he looked
at it, he was caught in circumstances that seemed to be constantly spi-
ralling out of control. He remembered thinking, more than a year ago,
when he was riding toward capture in Testra at the hands of Lord Draco,
the man who turned out to be his father, that life was no longer certain.

He was starting to wryly think of those times as the good old days.

The ride back to the Defender's camp was tense. Damin was angry and
Garet silent. Tarja wished he could think of something to say that would
bring some sanity to the situation. He had always liked and respected
Garet Warner, yet he had found a rare friendship with Damin Wolfblade—
ironically, a man he had spent four years on the southern border trying
to kill.

It was late afternoon when Treason Keep appeared on the horizon.
Although the engineers had done their best, it was unlikely the Keep
would ever be useful as anything but a temporary headquarters. Tarja
wondered what had happened to Bereth and her orphans. There was no
sign of them at the Keep. Had they survived? Or had Bereth found a
safer place for her brood? Tarja wished he had the time to discover their
fate.

The tents of their army covered a vast area surrounding the old ruin.
The Hythrun were camped on the western side of the plain, and as they
neared the sea of tents, Damin reined in his mount and studied the
camp thoughtfully. Tarja stopped beside him. Garet rode on, not interested in the view.

The Defenders' tents were laid out in precise lines, each housing
four men, with spears and pikes stacked in neat piles between them.
Their camp was as neat and orderly as Defender discipline demanded.
The much smaller Hythrun camp looked like a motley collection of
warriors out on a hunting expedition. No two tents were alike, and they
had been erected anywhere the Raiders felt like making camp. A pall
of smoke hung over the camp from the cook fires and the huge open-
air forge built against the southern wall of the Keep. Even from this

distance, Tarja could faintly hear the rhythmic ringing of the smiths' hammers as they pounded the metal into shape. The need for additional swords, pikes and arrowheads was urgent. Jenga had decided that making them on site was preferable to shipping them from the Citadel, although the lack of fuel for the hungry fires almost outweighed the advantages of being able to make and repair their weapons at the front.

North of the camp lay the training grounds, marked by a vast expanse of scuffed ground and lines of tall hay bales, to which rough outlines of man-shapes had been secured to give the trainees something to aim at. Mounted, red-coated sentries patrolled the camp perimeter in pairs. The Hythrun sentries were out of sight, hidden by the long grass.

To the south was the sprawling tent city that housed the rebels, the camp followers and anyone else in Medalon who thought there was a quick fortune to be made in a war. Jenga had given up trying to make them leave.

"The Fardohnyans have me worried," Damin admitted eventually, once Garet was out of their hearing. "Karien knights are fools. They expect everyone to play by the same rules as they do, and are therefore predictable."

"And the Fardohnyans?" Tarja had never fought them. In his experience they preferred trade to conflict. But an enemy that caused the Hythrun Warlord concern was an enemy to fear.

"Hablet keeps a huge standing army. His troops are well trained and they think on the run," Damin warned. "They won't play by the same rules as the Kariens. It's one of the reasons Hythria has avoided an open conflict with Fardohnya. And then there's Hablet's cannon . . ."

"What do you suggest?"

Damin shrugged. "I think we need help."

"Point me at it," Tarja said wearily.

Damin glanced at him and then laughed. "I think it's time I spoke to my god. I am, after all, His most worthy subject. Zegarnald owes me a favor or two."

"I thought you said you didn't know how to contact the gods?"

"I believe I said I didn't know how to contact the God of Thieves. The God of War is a different matter entirely. He speaks to me often."

"What does he say?" Tarja asked curiously.

"Ah, now that is between me and my god. You return to the Keep and try to keep things under control. I will see what I can do about some divine assistance."

"Damin!" Tarja called uselessly, as the Warlord spurred his magnificent stallion forward. Damin ignored him and galloped toward the camp.

Tarja watched him go, wondering about the wisdom of allying himself with someone who thought the fickle Primal gods could help them against the might of the Karien army, allied with the almost uncountable Fardohnyans.

Garet was right, he thought heavily as he spurred Shadow on toward the camp. He was trying to win a war with wishful thinking.

chapter 11

The Isle of Slarn was a miserable, bitter place; shrouded in mist and surrounded by a treacherous reef that made even the most seasoned sailor nervous. Adrina watched the island growing larger through the mist, as she shivered in the chilly spray that splashed over the bow in the gray, overcast morning.

"It's a great honor," Cratyn told her solemnly, "to be allowed to visit Slarn."

"You think so?" she asked, gripping the rail tightly. "I'll try to remember that as I'm being dashed against the reef, just before I drown."

Cratyn looked at her unsmilingly. He had solemn eyes in a not-unpleasant face, but he had no sense of humour that Adrina had been able to detect thus far.

"The Overlord will protect us and see us safe into the harbour."

"That makes me feel so much better."

"I am pleased to see that you are beginning to appreciate the power of the Overlord," he noted, as if her comment had been a profession of faith rather than a snide dig at his boring old god. "When we reach Slarn, the priests will appoint a Confessor to aid your conversion to the true faith."

"You're assuming I plan to convert, then?" she asked, bracing herself against the violent lurching of the hideously painted ship. The captain was screaming orders to his crew, fighting to be heard over the crashing waves and the creaking boat.

Cratyn looked astonished. "As the wife of the Crown Prince, you must set an example of faith and virtue for all the women of Karien."

"*Me?* An example of virtue? I fear I am not worthy of that honor, your Highness."

Completely oblivious to her meaning, Cratyn nodded. "Your humility does you credit, Princess. I am sure the Overlord will look most kindly on your character."

Just so long as he doesn't look too closely, she told herself. Still, the trip from Fardohnya so far had been bearable. She had only had to socialise with her Karien fiancé and his priests during meals. The rest of the journey she had been left to her own devices in her small but sumptuous cabin, which was quite appallingly decorated by someone who had either been very devout or blind drunk when he chose the colors. Every flat surface was emblazoned with the five-pointed star and lightning bolt of Xaphista.

Tristan and the rest of his regiment were not invited to Slarn. Their small fleet of Fardohnyan ships was sailing straight onto Karien.

"Your ladies-in-waiting will also join us when we reach Slarn," Cratyn added carefully. "I will then make arrangements to return your slaves to Fardohnya."

Adrina turned to face Cratyn determinedly. "My slaves aren't going anywhere, your Highness. They will stay with me."

Cratyn took a deep breath before he replied, as if he had known what her reaction to such a suggestion would be. It explained his sudden desire for her company this morning. She wondered how long it had taken to work himself up to delivering the news.

"The Overlord says that man can have only one master, and that is God. We do not condone or tolerate slavery in Karien, your Highness. Your slaves must be sent home."

"I don't give a damn what the Overlord says. My slaves are staying with me." She tossed her head imperiously. *Pretentious little upstart!* "Did my father know you were planning to deprive me of my slaves the moment we left Fardohnya?"

"He suggested that it would be wise not to broach the subject until we reached Slarn." Cratyn agreed. "But he assured us you would understand the necessity—"

"Well, he was wrong!" she declared. "I do *not* understand."

"I realize you are quite attached to them, your Highness, but as the Crown Princess of Karien, you cannot be seen to be supporting such a barbarous custom."

"Barbarous!" she cried. "My slaves live in more luxury than most of your damned knights. They are cared for, looked after, and secure. How dare you call my treatment of them barbarous!"

Cratyn looked rather taken aback by her outburst. "Your Highness, I did not mean to insult you. I'm sure you take great care of your slaves, but they are not *free*."

"Free to do what, exactly? Free to work like drudges for a pittance? For lordlings who think tossing their underlings a coin liberates them from any further responsibility for those less fortunate than themselves? It is harder to be a master than a slave, your Highness. A master must see to the welfare of his slaves. A master must ensure that everyone in his charge is taken care of. How many of your noble lords own the same level of responsibility?"

Cratyn sighed, unaccustomed to defending his position, particularly to a woman. In truth, Adrina was not surprised by the order to send her slaves home. She was far better versed in Karien customs than Cratyn knew, and had been expecting something like this for days. But she was enjoying watching him squirm.

"Your Highness, you must see that keeping your slaves is impossible . . ."

"I see no such thing," she announced petulantly. "Isn't it enough that I will never see my home again? Now you want to take away the only familiar faces I know. How can you be so cruel? Does your Overlord preach thoughtlessness along with virtue and piety?"

That left him speechless for a moment. Cratyn had not expected her to use his God to support her argument. "I . . . of course not . . . perhaps a compromise might be reached?"

Adrina smiled sweetly as he gave her the opening she was fishing for. "You mean I can keep some of them? Maybe just one or two?"

"You would have to emancipate them," Cratyn warned her. "But as free servants, I'm certain the priests would not object to their presence."

"Oh, thank you, your Highness," she gushed, with vast insincerity. Taking his bare hand in hers, she turned it over and kissed it, in the Fardohnyan tradition, letting her tongue trail lightly along the sword-callused palm. Cratyn snatched his hand away at the intimacy. He actually blushed.

"Perhaps we should go below now, your Highness," he suggested.

Adrina had to bite her lip to prevent herself laughing aloud. She realized, with mild surprise, that this young man was probably a virgin. The Overlord preached abstinence from sex except in marriage—and then only for the purposes of procreation. Cratyn was so annoyingly devout, he probably felt the need for penance if he had an impure thought. Adrina decided the wedding night was going to be quite an event, with Cratyn trying to pretend he knew what he was doing, and her trying to pretend she didn't.

"Perhaps we should," she agreed, with a smile that had nothing to do with the conversation and a great deal to do with her vision of her upcoming nuptials.

The Monastery of Slarn was as depressing and dark as the rest of the island. What little Adrina saw of the place in the carriage ride from the wharf was bare and rocky and windswept. The island sat in the middle of the Fardohnyan Gulf, but its fame stemmed more from its occupants than its strategic value. Slarn was home to the priests of Xaphista and a colony of Malik's Curse sufferers. For some reason, the priests were immune to the wasting disease, and anyone diagnosed, regardless of nationality, was packed off to Slarn as soon as their condition was identified. Cratyn had assured her that the sufferers were kept well away from the monastery, but she wondered just how safe this place was. Her half-brother Gaffen's mother had contracted the disease when he was a small boy, and Adrina still remembered standing outside the palace watching everything burn as the mother was taken away, screaming and crying to be allowed to say goodbye to her son. Everything Emalia had touched was destroyed with fire, lest it infect anyone else in the palace. Was Emalia still here, Adrina wondered, or had the disease taken her by now?

She glanced at Cratyn and frowned. He was seated across from her in the unadorned, but serviceable, carriage that had met them at the wharf. His head was bowed and he seemed to be muttering something. *Praying, no doubt*, she thought impatiently. Slarn was holy ground, after all.

"I hope they have a fire going when we get there," she remarked, as much to disturb his concentration as to make conversation. "Is it much colder than this in Yarnarrow?"

Cratyn looked up, and silently finished his prayer before answering. "Much colder, your Highness. We are snowbound for part of the year."

Adrina clapped her hands in delight. "I've never seen snow."

"You'll see plenty in Yarnarrow."

"Then I'll have to rely on you to keep me warm, won't I?" Baiting Cratyn was proving to be a most distracting pastime.

To her delight, he blushed again. "I'll . . . do my best to see you are . . . comfortable, your Highness."

The carriage finally clattered to a halt before the forbidding façade of the monastery. The door opened and a hand reached in to help her down. There was a gaggle of tonsured priests waiting for them, in addition to a dozen or more Church knights and five women, all but one of them younger than Adrina. She looked about with interest as Cratyn disembarked beside her.

The older woman in the group stepped forward and smiled with the ease of a professional diplomat.

"Welcome to Karien, your Highness," she said with a deep curtsy.

"Princess, may I present the Lady Madren," Cratyn announced, sounding surer now that he was on familiar ground among his own people. "Lady Madren, this is Her Serene Highness, Adrina of Fardohnya."

The woman glanced at Cratyn questioningly. "Adrina? We were expecting the Princess Cassandra."

"Princess Cassandra proved unsuitable," Cratyn informed the woman uncomfortably, although he managed not to blush this time. "Adrina is the eldest daughter of King Hablet, and as such, is an eminently qualified consort."

"Of course, your Highness." Adrina could tell she was burning with curiosity over the sudden change in brides. She wondered if Cratyn would admit to the real reason, or if it would prove too embarrassing for him. "You are most welcome, Princess."

"Thank you, my Lady."

"Please allow me to introduce your ladies-in-waiting."

Adrina was tempted to ask if it could wait until they were inside. The wind was bitingly cold, and the idea of standing out here on the bleak steps of the monastery while she was introduced to everybody was distinctly unappealing.

"This is Lady Grace, Lady Pacifica, Lady Hope and Lady Chastity,"

Madren announced as the young women in question stepped forward. Adrina glanced at the pale young women for a moment in astonishment.

"Are those really their names?"

Madren stiffened at the insult. "In Karien, it is the custom to name one's daughters after the virtue they hope the child will emulate, your Highness."

"Poor Chastity," Adrina murmured, then she smiled apologetically at the older woman. "I'm sorry, I should not have been surprised. We have a similar custom in Fardohnya. My own name means 'she whose beauty will tempt men to insane acts of bravery for the chance to spend the night with her'."

Adrina's name meant no such thing, but it was too tempting an opportunity to pass up. The looks on the Kariens' faces alone made the lie worthwhile. Cratyn looked as if he wished the ground would open and swallow him whole, and the ladies Grace, Pacifica, Hope and Chastity were on the verge of swooning.

"What virtue does 'Madren' represent?"

"I was named for my mother's home province, your Highness," Madren replied haughtily. "The naming after virtues is a relatively new custom."

"Well, with luck, it will prove a passing fad," Adrina announced airily. "Shall we continue the introductions inside? I've no wish to keep you all out here in this wind on my account."

She smiled sweetly at Cratyn and Madren as she swept up her cloak. There was little they could do but follow her inside.

Everything on Slarn was damp and the monastery was no exception. The black stone walls wept moisture and the rushes scattered on the stone floor of the main hall squelched faintly underfoot. There was no noticeable difference between the temperature inside or out. Two huge pits, evenly spaced in the floor of the lofty hall, hosted blazing fires that did little to warm the cavernous room. Adrina looked about with a frown. *Xaphista must be one of those gods who thinks suffering and misery is good for you*, she thought, rather depressed at the prospect of spending the rest of her life among his worshippers. She hoped the castle at Yarnarrow was better appointed than this miserable place.

An acolyte stepped forward to take her wrap, but she waved him away. It was too cold to shed the warmth of her cloak, and underneath she wore a Fardohnyan costume ill-suited to the bitter cold. She had been planning to make an issue of that too, knowing her mode of dress would appall the straight-laced Kariens. Now she was not so certain. The concealing, drab woolen dresses of her ladies-in-waiting looked decidedly warmer than her gloriously provocative gown.

The introductions continued once they were inside. Adrina smiled and nodded as Madren introduced her to an endless stream of priests and knights. Without exception, they greeted her solemnly; their eyes wide as they studied the exotic Fardohnyan bride Cratyn had brought home. Each priest ceremoniously laid his elaborate star-and-lightning-bolt-tipped staff on her shoulder, to satisfy himself that she was not an evil spirit—or worse, a Harshini, in the guise of a mortal. As for her future husband, he was nowhere to be found. He had vanished in the company of a young sandy-haired knight almost as soon as they crossed the threshold of the monastery.

"And this, your Highness, is Vonulus," Madren announced, as the last of the supplicants stepped forward. "He will be your Confessor and will instruct you in the doctrine of the Overlord, as well as advising you on pastoral matters."

Vonulus laid his staff on her shoulder gently, then bowed, his tonsured head shining in the damp morning light. Adrina studied him with interest. He was a little older than she, with intelligent brown eyes, and a serene expression that came from an inner peace Adrina doubted she would be able to disrupt easily.

"Your Serene Highness," Vonulus said in fluent Fardohnyan. "I am honoured to serve you."

First mistake, Adrina thought. *He should not have let me know he spoke Fardohnyan.* "Vonulus. I look forward to receiving your wisdom."

"I claim no wisdom, your Highness. I am a simple man, but moderately well read."

"Finding anyone who can read at all in Karien is a surprise," she remarked, watching for his reaction. The Kariens she had met so far were a universally dour and humorless lot. And they were insulted by the slightest hint of criticism. But not Vonulus. He met her eye unblinkingly, accepting her unspoken challenge.

"Your Highness, I hope you receive many surprises in your new home."

"I'm sure I will, sir."

"My first official duty will be to prepare you to accept the Karien wedding vows," he told her. "The ceremony will take place in Xaphista's Temple, as soon as we reach Yarnarrow. Lady Madren will advise you on matters of dress and protocol. I will, if the Overlord wills it, assist you to steer an easy course through the many intricacies of our religion."

"Tell me, Vonulus," she asked. "Hypothetically speaking, what would happen if I chose not to embrace your god?"

Madren hissed, shocked at the mere suggestion. Vonulus was less easily roused. "You will be the Crown Princess of Karien, your Highness. To worship another god would be considered treason. I imagine Fardohnya treats traitors much the same as we do."

She patted Madren's hand comfortingly. "I was simply asking out of curiosity, my Lady. Never fear."

"Of course, your Highness," Madren agreed. "I knew that."

"And will you be joining us for lunch, Vonulus? It is a pleasure to hear my native tongue spoken so fluently."

"I would be honoured, your Highness."

"Perhaps you would be more comfortable dressed in something more . . . appropriate?" Madren suggested, waving the silent ladies-in-waiting to her. "I shall have your ladies escort you to the chamber put aside for you."

Hoping that the chamber would be warmer than the draughty, cavernous hall, Adrina acquiesced graciously to the suggestion. Surrounded by the Ladies Grace, Hope, Pacifica and Chastity, she walked the length of the hall to the entrance where, not surprisingly, the five-pointed star and lightning bolt was carved into the large wooden doors. They opened as she approached to reveal Cratyn and a young knight entering the hall. The men stopped as they neared them. Cratyn's eyes flickered over Adrina then fixed on the Lady Chastity, who walked on her right. The look he gave the young woman was filled with remorse. Adrina glanced at Chastity, startled to see her soft brown eyes misted with unshed tears and unmistakable longing.

"Prince Cretin, I thought you were lost," she said brightly. Was the pale and insipid Chastity the reason Cratyn was so unhappy about being forced to take a Fardohnyan bride?

"It's *Cratyn*, your Highness," Lady Pacifica corrected her, rather crossly.

"That's what I said, isn't it?" Adrina asked innocently. "Cretin." It was an unfortunate, if rather delightful, result of her accent, that she mispronounced his name. It was also quite deliberate. Adrina spoke Karien fluently. Much more fluently than her somewhat contrived accent led her hosts to believe. Her first *court'esa* had been a linguist of some note and he had taught Adrina to speak a number of languages fluently. Another thing better kept from the Kariens. She had not thought of the *court'esa* in years—a slender, gentle young man with dark eyes and long, graceful limbs.

"It's nothing to worry about, my Lady," Cratyn assured Pacifica, not wishing to make an issue of it.

"Your Highness, this is my cousin, Drendyn, Earl of Tiler's Pass. Drendyn, this is Her Serene Highness, Princess Adrina of Fardohnya."

The young Earl bowed inelegantly, smiling like a child confronted with a new and exotic toy. Adrina took an instant liking to him. He was the first Karien she had met who did not feel the need to mope about as if they were perpetually in mourning.

"Welcome to Karien!" he gushed. "I do hope you'll be happy here. After the wedding, you should come to Tiler's Pass. We have the best wines in Karien and the hunting is just marvellous. You do hunt, don't you?"

"Every chance I can get. I shall look forward to your hospitality, my Lord."

"This way, your Highness," Pacifica interrupted stiffly, with a frown at the Earl. She did not seem to like the idea of Adrina getting too friendly with him.

"If you will excuse me, my Lord, Prince Cretin." She curtsied gracefully and followed her ladies-in waiting into the hall.

As the door closed behind them she stopped and called the women to her. They all turned to face her expectantly. Pacifica was tall and plain, with protruding pale eyes and pockmarked skin. Hope was a pleasant looking girl with rich brown hair and a vacant expression. Grace was a plump brunette with a button nose and a receding chin. Chastity was pale and fair and by far the beauty of the group. "Ladies, I'd like to make sure we understand each other."

"Your Highness?" Pacifica asked, still a little put out, she thought, by Drendyn's enthusiastic welcome.

"As my ladies-in-waiting, your actions reflect on me. If I ever see *you*, Pacifica, acting like a jealous fishwife again, or *you* Chastity, lusting after my fiancé, I shall have you both whipped. Is that clear?"

Pacifica turned a brilliant shade of red. Chastity burst into tears. Grace and Hope simply stood there, dumbstruck. Adrina marched on ahead, not waiting for them to catch up. That way, they couldn't see her laughing.

chapter 12

The Harshini were the strangest creatures R'shiel had ever encountered. All she had been taught to believe about them, since her earliest childhood, was proving to be wrong. They were not evil or wicked or even particularly threatening. They were a gentle, happy people who seemed to want nothing more than the same happiness for all living things.

For R'shiel, raised in an atmosphere of political intrigue and ambition, she found it hard to believe that the Harshini could be so innocent. She questioned them constantly, looking for the crack in their serene complacency, but found none. In fact, she suspected there were even some of the Harshini who deliberately avoided her, for fear of being asked questions they simply didn't understand. They had no ambition beyond that which the gods had created them for. They were the guardians of the gods' power. That was all they needed to know.

The demons were a different matter, however, and R'shiel found herself enjoying their company much more than the placid Harshini. Lord Dranymire was a bit of a bore, but she supposed that came from being older than time itself. The other demons, the younger ones, were much more interesting.

Korandellan had tried to explain the bond between the Harshini and the demons in some depth, but R'shiel understood so little about the gods that she had trouble grasping the concept. She could feel the bond, though, like an invisible cord that tied her to the demons. She only needed to think of them, and they were there, eager to show her Sanctuary, or have her tell them something of the outside world. Their hunger for new things was insatiable, particularly in the younger demons, although "young" was a relative term among the demonkind. "Young," when compared to Lord Dranymire, the prime demon in the brethren bonded to the té Ortyn family, might be anything less than a thousand years.

"We are all one," Korandellan explained patiently. "The gods, the Harshini and the demons. We are all made of the same stuff."

"Then why aren't the Harshini gods?" she asked.

"We are a part of the gods."

"And the demons?"

"They are also a part of the gods."

"So gods created the Harshini and the demons, right?"

"That is correct."

"Why?"

"Because they feared that without some way of limiting their power, they would destroy each other."

"So the gods gave you their power? That's a pretty dumb thing to do. What happens if they want to use it?"

Korandellan sighed. "They did not give us their power, R'shiel, they share it. The power you feel is the same source of power that the gods draw on."

"Then that makes you gods, too, doesn't it?"

"Think of it as a rope made up of many strands," the King said, trying to put his explanation into words she could grasp. "Each of the Primal gods has divinity over a different aspect of life. Each god draws on their own strand. Depending on what is happening in the world, the strands grow thicker and stronger, or weaker and thinner."

R'shiel thought on that for a moment. "You mean if everyone started stealing, then Dacendaran's strand would grow and the others would diminish, because he's the God of Thieves?"

Korandellan nodded happily. "Yes! Now you are beginning to understand!"

"Don't count on it," she warned.

"The Harshini use the gods' power, R'shiel; they use it constantly."

"So they drain off the excess?"

"In a manner of speaking."

"But how can that work? You can't abide violence, so you would only draw on the power of some of the gods, wouldn't you?"

"That is what the demons are for," he replied. "To maintain the balance."

She nodded as it finally began to make sense. The demons were childlike and innocent and took thousands of years to reach maturity. They embodied all the violence, mischief and destructive capabilities of the power the Harshini could not draw on, but their childlike innocence and their blood bond to the gentle Harshini prevented them from causing harm.

"And only the té Ortyn family can draw on all the power at once, can't they? That's what makes me so dangerous?"

The King smiled, as he usually did when she asked such blunt questions. Then again, he would probably smile if someone chopped his leg off. No wonder Brak spent so much time out in the human world. Eternal happiness could be rather wearing at times.

"Your human blood allows you to circumvent our instincts against violence, yes," he agreed.

"Is that why they call me the demon child? Because I'm human, with the same ability for causing violence as a demon?"

This time the King laughed out loud. "I never really thought of it like that, R'shiel. The name 'demon child' is a human one, but now that you mention it, yes, I suppose that's exactly what you are."

It made sense now. She wasn't sure she actually believed it, but it did make sense.

"So tell me about Xaphista? How did he get to be a god?"

For the first time since she met him, Korandellan's smile faded. "Xaphista learnt too much, too quickly, I fear. The family he was bonded to were travelers. They roamed the world seeking knowledge, and in time too much human blood became mingled with the Harshini line. The restraint on violence broke down and Xaphista learnt that if he could gather followers to believe in *him*, his power would grow to rival the Primal gods."

"And how am I supposed to destroy him?"

"I have no idea, child. I cannot contemplate destruction. That is a human quality. You must find the answer within yourself."

· · ·

Find the answer within yourself.

R'shiel didn't even try. She liked the Harshini—it was impossible to dislike them—but she had no desire to become embroiled in some divine conflict. She accepted that there were gods. She had even met a few of them since coming here, but they did not impress her, and she certainly felt no desire to worship them. If the gods didn't like one of their underlings getting above his station, then they should have thought about that before creating the problem in the first place.

She did not share her opinion with Korandellan. He was willing to answer any question she asked and teach her anything she wanted to know, but his aversion to violence made the subject of Xaphista an awkward one. That suited R'shiel just fine—she had no desire to discuss the matter anyway.

Time was a fluid quantity in Sanctuary, so R'shiel had no way of gauging how long she had been here. It seemed as if every day she learnt something new, but if each day was a new one, or simply the same day repeated over and over, she could not tell. She regained her strength and then grew even stronger, exploring the vast network of halls that made up the Harshini settlement.

There were rooms here that were so like the Citadel she sometimes had to remind herself where she was. The artwork that was so determinedly concealed in the Citadel was exposed here, in all its glory. Although the walls were generally white, there wasn't a flat surface in the place that was not adorned with some type of artwork, large or small. It seemed every Harshini was an artist of some description. There were delicately painted friezes lining the halls and crystal statues in every corner. There were galleries full of paintings depicting everything from broad sweeping landscapes to tiny, exquisitely detailed paintings of insects and birds. The Harshini studied life and then captured its essence in their art.

Curiously, the one thing she expected did not happen here. The walls did not glow with the coming of each new day and fade with the onset of night. The Brightening and Dimming that characterised the Citadel was missing. The Harshini used candles and lanterns like any normal human, although admittedly they could light them with a thought and extinguish them just as easily.

The valley floor, which looked so wild and untended from the balconies, proved to be a complex series of connecting gardens and the source for much of the Harshini food in the settlement. At least it should have been, Korandellan had explained, with a slight frown. The abundant gardens were trapped in time, as was the whole settlement. The vines never wilted, the flowers never faded. Bees buzzed between the bushes, crickets chirruped happily, worms wiggled their way through the fertile soil—but a picked berry was gone forever. Like the Harshini, and every animal in Sanctuary, they could not reproduce. The issue of food was becoming critical, so much so, that Korandellan had allowed a number of Harshini to leave the settlement. Some of them went openly, like Glenanaran, who had returned to Hythria to teach at the Sorcerers' Collective. Others went out into the human world, disguised and cautious, to barter or trade for some badly needed supplies. Although he never said it aloud, R'shiel guessed it was fear of Xaphista and the Karien priests that kept them hidden.

They were performers, too, R'shiel discovered soon after she was allowed the freedom of Sanctuary. In the amphitheater in the hollow center of the gardens, against the permanent rainbow that hovered over the tinkling cascade, they held concerts in the twilight as the sun settled behind the mountains. The first time R'shiel heard the Harshini sing she had cried. Nothing had prepared her for the beauty of their voices or their skill with instruments she had never seen in the human world.

Sometimes the concerts were impromptu affairs, where members of the audience would step forward, either alone or in groups, to perform for their friends. Other times the concerts were as well organized as any Founder's Day Parade, and then the massed choir of the Harshini would transport R'shiel to a place she had never even glimpsed before. "The Song of Gimlorie," the Harshini called it. The gift of the God of Music. A prayer in its own right, it had the power to devour one's soul. The cadence of the song, the subtle harmonies, and the pure, crystalline voices of the Harshini, combined to create images in the mind that could be as euphoric as they were dangerous. The demons would appear in the amphitheater whenever they sang for Gimlorie, their eyes wide, their bodies uncharacteristically still as they listened to the music with rapt expressions. R'shiel understood their fascination with the music and lamented its loss to the human world.

It was following the last concert she attended that R'shiel came to an important decision. Tarja was a pleasant, fading memory. Joyhinia and Loclon were so far buried in the back of her mind that she barely even acknowledged their existence. Xaphista was the gods' problem, not hers. There was supposed to be a war going on, but it did not intrude on the serenity of this otherworldly realm. Sanctuary was peaceful, and the troubles of the outside world could not touch her in this magical place. She was half-Harshini after all, and welcome here.

R'shiel decided that she didn't really care if she never returned to the outside world at all.

chapter 13

arien was a vast country, full of tall evergreens, rugged val-
leys and steep, but distant, snow-capped mountains to the
east. With autumn approaching the weather grew colder as
they sailed north. Adrina found herself shivering each
morning when she took her daily exercise on deck.

The Ironbrook was a heavily populated waterway. They sailed past
numerous villages, some large and prosperous, some mean and depressing, some barely deserving of the name at all. They seemed dirty and
crowded to a princess raised in the spacious, pink-walled cities of Fardohnya. In fact, Karien seemed a nation lacking in color. The villages
were drab, the people even more so, and the frequently overcast weather
leached the remaining pigment from the world. She was not looking forward to spending her life among these people, not even as their queen.

Adrina was easily bored and the seemingly endless journey up the
Ironbrook River toward Yarnarrow offered little in the way of entertainment. She had exhausted most of the opportunities for distraction available to her. She had admired all the scenery she could bear and waved at
so many ragged peasants lining the riverbank that her arm felt ready to
drop off. When she wasn't being hounded by Madren regarding the
proper way to behave in a Karien court, Vonulus dogged her heels with
his instruction in the unbelievably demanding laws of the Karien
Church. Adrina was beginning to think the reason so many people
sinned was because it wasn't humanly possible to remember everything
that would lead one into temptation.

The only other activity Adrina had to while away the long days on the river was socializing with her ladies-in-waiting. She was not certain what a lady-in-waiting was supposed to do. They hovered around her like flies around a corpse, and seemed anxious to perform small, meaningless tasks for her, but they were offended if she treated them as servants and too sheltered to serve as entertaining companions.

Adrina was unusually cautious in dealing with them. It would not do for these young women (virgins one and all) to learn that for her sixteenth birthday her father had given her a handsome young *court'esa*. Nor would it do to disillusion the Ladies Hope, Pacifica, Grace and Chastity regarding her virtue. As far as Adrina could tell, every one of them had been raised in finest Karien tradition, which meant they could read (barely), sing (acceptably), play a musical instrument (tolerably well) and discuss such riveting topics as needlework, banquet menus and the convoluted family bloodlines of the Karien nobility. All of these topics left Adrina cold, so she listened and smiled and pretended she didn't understand them when the conversation became unbearable.

Today was proving particularly trying. Tall, dour, Pacifica had taken it upon herself to enlighten Adrina regarding the long and incredibly dull history of her family, the Gullwings of Mount Pike. She had only got as far as Lord Gullwing the Pious, who lived three centuries past, when Vonulus disturbed them. Adrina welcomed him into the crowded cabin. Even a lesson in the complex duties of a woman according to the Church of Xaphista was preferable to another three hundred years of *Dullwings*.

"Vonulus! Have you come to instruct me?" she asked. "Or perhaps another discussion about the definition of sin?"

"You would do well to heed both, your Highness," Pacifica advised, a little put out at Adrina's shift in attention.

"We may discuss whatever you wish, your Highness."

Adrina glanced at Pacifica and her companions thoughtfully. "Sin shall be the topic today, I think. I am interested in your definition of adultery."

Predictably, the Ladies Hope, Pacifica, Grace and Chastity gasped at the suggestion. Vonulus, however, was not so easily rattled.

"Certainly, your Highness. What were you planning?"

Adrina's eyes widened innocently. "Planning? Why nothing, sir. I simply seek to avoid pitfalls. I have no wish to do or say something that in my country would be considered perfectly normal, but in yours would see me stoned."

"A reasonable precaution," he noted with a look that said he didn't believe her for a minute. "What exactly did you want to know?"

"Define adultery. The Karien definition."

"It is not the Karien definition, your Highness. It is the Overlord's definition, and therefore, the only acceptable definition."

Adrina chose not to pursue that particular argument. "As you wish, define it for me."

"Adultery, according to the Overlord, is any thought or deed that causes a man to lust after another man's wife, or a woman to lust after another woman's husband."

Adrina's brow furrowed. "So, let me see if I understand you. If I lust after an unmarried man, then I have not committed adultery, but if I lust after a married man, I have? Is that right?"

"I think you take my meaning too literally, your Highness," Vonulus began with a shake of his head, but Adrina did not allow him time to continue.

"So that would work the other way, too, I suppose?" she asked. "If my husband . . . well, for argument's sake, let's pretend Cretin falls madly in love with one of my ladies . . ." she glanced around at the four rather appalled young women, before fixing her eyes on Chastity. "Say . . . the Lady Chastity here . . ."

"Your Highness!" Chastity cried in horror.

Adrina smiled sweetly. "Oh never mind, Chastity, I only use you to demonstrate my point. With a name like yours, how could you be anything *but* pure? Anyway, let's pretend that Cretin and Chastity . . . indulge in a bit of . . . sin . . . then by your definition, Cretin would get off free as a bird, because Chastity is unmarried, yet my poor Lady would be stoned, because Cretin is married to me. Is that right?"

Vonulus did not look pleased. "That could be regarded as the strictest definition, I suppose, however—"

"I see," Adrina cut in. "And I can sin merely by *thinking* something lustful?" *Gods! Am I in trouble!* "How would you know what I'm thinking?"

"I don't need to know, your Highness. Xaphista sees all. The Overlord would know."

"He must be a very busy god, then," she remarked irreverently.

"It is by resisting such thoughts, that we spare our god the need to constantly watch over us," Vonulus replied.

"And do you ladies resist temptation?"

The young women nodded quickly in agreement. *Too quickly*, she thought, with a private little smirk.

"The Overlord teaches us that to resist temptation is to ensure a place at His table in the next life," Pacifica said.

"You mean if you're a good little girl in this life, you won't come back as a cockroach in the next?"

Vonulus sighed heavily. "Your Highness, I believe we discussed the matter of reincarnation several days ago. There is no such thing. We are given one life. When we die, our spirit ascends to the Overlord's table if we have lived according to his rules."

"And you drown in the Sea of Despair for eternity, if you don't," Adrina replied with a nod. "I remember our discussion. That would mean, that by your definition, every soul who ever lived, who didn't worship Xaphista, is splashing about in the Sea of Despair, wondering where they went wrong. It must be pretty crowded down there."

"Your irreverence will lead you into trouble, your Highness," Vonulus warned. "Have a care when you reach Yarnarrow. Such comments will not sit well at court."

Adrina met the priest's gaze evenly. "Can't your religion stand a bit of scrutiny, Vonulus? You wish me to believe in your god, yet you resent me questioning anything I do not understand. My gods may be numerous, but at least they have a sense of humour."

"Your Highness, a sense of humour will be of little help to you, should you be out of grace when you die. The Primal gods you worship are nothing more than natural events to which the unenlightened have attached divinity. You should be thankful that by marrying Prince Cratyn, you have an opportunity to embrace the one true god."

Adrina smiled apologetically, realizing that she had pushed the priest far enough for one day. It did not particularly matter to her that they expected her to worship their god. She wasn't a fool and had every intention of acting as if she had converted. But her own beliefs ran too deep to be overturned by a priest, no matter how clever or articulate.

"I appreciate your advice, sir," she demurred. "I hope the Overlord will forgive my pagan ignorance."

Vonulus looked a little suspicious, but he nodded. "The Overlord can see into your heart, your Highness. He will judge you accordingly."

"Well, I don't have anything to worry about then, do I?" she asked brightly.

"I'm sure you don't," Vonulus agreed warily.

Two days later, they docked at Setenton, the first real city Adrina had seen since coming to Karien. The city boasted a sizeable wharf district and an impressive market, but it was as dirty and crowded as every other town she had sailed past these last few weeks. A bleak, thick-walled castle, built on a rise that gave it a commanding view of the river and the surrounding countryside, dominated the walled city. This was the home of Lord Terbolt, the Duke of Setenton, and coincidentally, Chastity's father—so Lady Hope informed her. As they waited for the ship to dock, Adrina glanced at the young woman, but she showed no obvious pleasure to be home. Rather, she kept surreptitiously glancing at Cratyn, as if trying to catch his eye. To his credit, the young prince studiously ignored her.

The sight that greeted them as they docked brought a smile to Adrina's lips. A full guard of honor awaited them—her own Guard, Fardohnyan one and all, in full ceremonial uniform.

Her father held to the notion that vast wealth was only fun when you got to flaunt it, and he had spared no expense equipping her Guard. Five hundred strong, every man was mounted on a sleek black steed stamped with the unmistakable breeding of the Jalanar Plains. The soldiers were dressed in silver and white, from their ornate silver helms and short white capes, trimmed with rare Medalonian snowfox fur, to their white, silver-trimmed, knee-high boots.

According to Fardohnyan legend, the custom of the royal guard wearing white had come about almost a thousand years ago, when King Waldon the Peaceful seized the throne from his cousin Blagdon the Butcher. His Guard wore white so that the people would know there was no innocent blood on the hands of his soldiers. Whatever the reason, the ceremonial uniforms were gorgeous, and Tristan wore his with the confidence of one born to show off. He really was much too good-looking for his own good, Adrina decided. She had worried that Cassandra might cause trouble in Karien. It occurred to her that Tristan was just as likely to get into mischief. All that repressed emotion at court, mixed with her brother, was a recipe for disaster.

Impressed by the sight of her Guard, Cratyn offered her his hand as they walked down the treacherous gangplank, followed by their retinue. Tristan met them at the bottom and bowed ostentatiously.

"Your Serene Highness, your Royal Highness, the Fardohnyan Princess's Guard awaits the honor of escorting you to Setenton Castle," he announced, rather dramatically, in Fardohnyan. "Which, I might add, is as draughty and flea ridden as every other building in this godforsaken country and I would very much like to go home," he added, without changing his smile or tone.

Adrina turned to Cratyn. "My brother welcomes us, and pledges his life to see us safely to the castle," she translated calmly, grateful that Vonulus was still back on the ship. Tristan really should learn to be more careful.

Cratyn frowned. "Your brother?"

"Half-brother," she amended. "Tristan is one of my father's bastards."

A shocked gasp escaped Pacifica's lips at Adrina's casual remark, a fact that was not lost on Tristan, who was not supposed to understand Karien. He bit back a grin as Cratyn, predictably, blushed crimson.

"Ah, please tell your . . . captain . . . that we are honoured," Cratyn stammered. "Although I hardly think the ride from here to the castle will be life threatening."

"His Highness appears to be having some difficulty coping with your baseborn status," she translated.

"His Highness looks like he's about to burst something. I'll bet you can't wait for the wedding. Shall we?" He offered Adrina his arm, which she accepted gracefully, with a smile over her shoulder for her fiancé.

They rode in an open carriage up the steep, cobbled streets of Setenton toward the castle. Crowds lined the route to catch a glimpse of the foreigner who would one day be their queen. Adrina smiled and waved. She was born to this, and the Kariens seemed to appreciate her acknowledgment of them. At least the townsfolk did.

After a while, Lady Madren leaned over with a frown. "You must not encourage them, your Highness."

"Encourage them, my Lady? These are to be my people, are they not? I want them to like me."

"It doesn't matter that they like you, your Highness," Madren said. "Only that they respect and obey you."

"In Fardohnya we have a saying, my Lady: 'A king who has the love of his people is harder to kill than one who has their enmity.' Being pleasant costs nothing."

"It is unseemly, your Highness," Madren insisted.

"And what of you, Prince Cretin? Don't you care that the people love you?"

"The people love the Overlord, your Highness. It is His blessing that gives my family the right to rule. What they feel for me is irrelevant."

"Well, you trust in the Overlord," she told him. "I'll just keep smiling and waving. I'm not actually a member of your divinely sanctioned family yet."

Adrina turned back to the peasants, ignoring Madren's frown and Cratyn's despairing look. Tristan glanced back over his shoulder from his position at the head of the Guard and she rolled her eyes at him. He laughed and spurred his horse forward. Adrina had a feeling it was going to be a very long day.

Fardohnya was a nation ruled by a single line of monarchs for a millennium. A thousand years of Fardohnyan kings governed on the principal that a nation that prospered was a nation relatively free of internal unrest. It had proved a sound theory and consequently, little Fardohnyan architecture was designed with defense in mind. Aesthetics was the overriding concern. Besides, if one was wealthy enough, one could hire the best architects to construct fortifications that didn't constantly remind one of their true purpose.

The Kariens did not subscribe to the Fardohnyan notion of beauty first, usefulness second. Setenton Castle was a fortress and pretended to be nothing else. The walls were thirty paces high and thicker than two men lying end to end, and the courtyard bustled with the panoply of war. Looking around her as she alighted from the carriage in a courtyard crowded with men, horses and the ringing of smiths' hammers, Adrina wondered if the Medalonian Defenders were as good as their reputation held them to be. She privately hoped they were. Karien was much larger than Medalon, and could overrun the smaller country through sheer weight of numbers, if nothing else.

Hablet needed a drawn-out conflict on the northern border of

Medalon. He could not go over the Sunrise Mountains into Hythria with an invasion force, but once on the open plains of Medalon, he could turn south with ease. Of course, the Kariens thought he was planning to attack Medalon to aid their cause. It would not be until they discovered his true destination that his treachery would be revealed. Adrina was not in favor of the plan, mostly because she would be the focus for the Kariens' fury when they realized they had been duped. Her father had advised her to plan an escape route when the news came. He had seemed singularly unconcerned that his plan might cost Adrina her head.

Lord Terbolt greeted them from the steps of his great hall. He was a tall man with hooded brown eyes and a weary expression. But he greeted Cratyn warmly before he turned to Adrina.

"Your Serene Highness," he said with a small bow. "Welcome to Setenton Castle."

"Thank you, Lord Terbolt," she replied graciously. "I hope our presence will not tax your resources unduly. And you have been playing host to my Guard. I trust they have not been a burden to you."

Terbolt shook his head. "A few language difficulties, your Highness, nothing more. Please, let me have you shown to your rooms. You must be tired, I'm sure, and we men have things to discuss that will not interest you."

On the contrary, Adrina was vitally interested, but it would be difficult to convince these barbarians that as a woman she might have any idea of politics or war. "Of course, my Lord. Perhaps Tristan might be of help, though? I am sure he could learn something from your discussions and he might be able to offer a new perspective, don't you think?"

"But he doesn't speak Karien, your Highness," Cratyn pointed out, with a rather horrified expression.

"Oh that's all right, I'll translate," she offered brightly. "I'm really not tired, my Lords, and although as Lord Terbolt pointed out, I will no doubt be bored witless by the discussion—we are allies now, are we not? All that I ask is that you not speak too quickly so that I may follow the discussion. Tristan!"

Neither Terbolt nor Cratyn looked pleased by her suggestion, and poor Madren looked ready to faint, but she had left them little choice.

"As you wish, your Highness," Terbolt conceded with ill grace.

She picked up her skirts and, with Tristan at her side, marched indoors.

"Adrina, does something bother you about these people?" Tristan asked her quietly as they entered the gloom followed by the rest of the entourage. A quick glance over her shoulder revealed Terbolt greeting Chastity with all the warmth of a man renewing his acquaintance with a distant relative.

"What do you mean?" she asked as she looked back at him. "They are fools."

"Maybe. I just wonder if we are the ones being played for fools."

"You pick a fine time to have second thoughts, Tristan," she muttered as they walked the length of the rush-strewn stone floor. Tall banners, depicting both the sign of the Overlord and the Lord Terbolt's silver pike on a field of red hung limply from the walls. Presumably the red background was a romantic representation of the muddy Ironbrook. "You were the one who encouraged me to accept this arranged marriage."

"I know," he sighed. "I just have this feeling. I can't define it, but it worries me. Be careful."

"You're the one who should be careful. Although, I have it on good authority that provided you confine your attentions to unmarried women, you shouldn't need to worry about being stoned."

"It's going to be a long, cold winter, I fear, Rina."

He had not called her Rina since they were small children. "You at least have the option of going home someday. I have to spend my life with these people. Not to mention Prince Cretin the Cringing."

He leaned closer to her and, although speaking Fardohnyan, even if he was overheard, nobody here would understand him. "Look on the bright side. He'll be off to war in a month or two. With luck the Medalonians will keep him there for years."

"With luck, they'll put an arrow through him," she corrected with a whisper, then turned to her fiancé and smiled serenely, every inch the princess.

Cratyn was looking at her with an odd expression. Not dislike, exactly. It was stronger than that. She had a bad feeling it was distaste.

chapter 14

Tarja returned to the camp late in the day, letting Shadow set her own pace, still brooding over his last argument with Jenga. The Lord Defender was trying to hold together a disparate force, Tarja knew that, and the knowledge that he was doing it through deception weighed heavily on him. But it didn't excuse his intransigence over the matter of attacking the Kariens. The Lord Defender was willing to defend his border, but he refused to make the first move. He wanted to wait until the Kariens invaded. Tarja disagreed. The Karien camp had grown considerably from the five hundred knights that had been camped there all through summer. They should be taking the fight to the enemy and they should do it now, before the Karien force grew so large that they would simply be overrun.

Jenga was furious when he heard that Tarja had crossed the border. Using the same Hythrun tactics that were so effective in the south, on their numerous cattle raids into Medalon, he had taken a handful of men into Karien under cover of darkness and stampeded the enemy's horses through their camp. The ensuing destruction had been extremely gratifying—it had probably set back their war effort by weeks. He'd only lost three men to injury, and had considered the entire affair a small, if significant, victory.

Jenga did not see it that way. He had exploded with fury when he learnt of the attack, accusing Damin of being a reckless barbarian for suggesting the idea, and Tarja of being an undisciplined fool for listening to him.

Following his desertion two years ago, Tarja had often longed for the chance to return to the security and brotherhood of the Corps. But now that he was back, he discovered it was not the easy ride he had hoped. He had *liked* being in command of the rebels, he realized now. He had been raised to command, and knew, without vanity, that he was good at it. Tarja respected Jenga, but had grown accustomed to making his own decisions. Jenga was a good soldier but he'd been Lord Defender for more than twenty years, and that meant he had more practice with politics than war. Tarja had spent the best part of his adult life at war with the Hythrun, the Defenders and now the Kariens. Jenga had not raised his sword in anger in decades.

They still had only six thousand of the twelve thousand Defenders they could count on, and a thousand Hythrun Raiders from Krakandar. As he thought of the Hythrun, he wondered, as he had already done countless times, where Damin Wolfblade was.

Nobody had seen the Warlord for nearly a month—not since the argument with Jenga after the raid, when he announced that he was going to speak with his god. If Almodavar knew where he was, he wasn't saying. The grizzled Hythrun captain seemed unconcerned by his Lord's absence. If Damin wished to speak with the God of War, to seek his blessing, then his troops were not about to object. They fervently believed Zegarnald would help them. They were counting on it, in fact.

When he reached the camp, on impulse Tarja turned toward the scattered Hythrun tents. Perhaps Almodavar had heard something. It was becoming increasingly difficult to reassure Jenga that Damin had not simply deserted them.

He rode through the camp, acknowledging the occasional wave from the Hythrun troops. The Raiders were much less respectful of rank than the Defenders. Among the Raiders, one earned respect through battle, not promotion or pretty insignia. But some of these men had faced Tarja on the southern border. They knew him for a warrior and found nothing strange in their Warlord's alliance with his former enemy.

The Defenders had been far less accommodating. They resented the presence of the Hythrun and made no secret of it. Tarja thought that much of the impressive discipline the Defenders displayed was designed to show the Hythrun how things were done in a "proper" army. The Defenders despised mercenaries, and most of Damin's Raiders were just that. Tarja was a little more tolerant. Had the rebellion not intervened, he would likely be a mercenary himself, by now. But feelings ran strong between the two camps and fights broke out frequently. In the beginning, Tarja and Damin had organized training bouts between the two armies, ostensibly to foster some sort of cohesion between the two forces. Three fatalities put paid to that laudable sentiment, and Jenga had ordered them stopped. Now the training was strictly segregated.

He reached the center of the Hythrun camp and discovered a large number of the Raiders in a cheering circle, obviously wagering on some sort of contest. As he neared the group a cheer went up, almost drowning out an unmistakable cry of pain. Tarja dismounted curiously, threw the reins over Shadow's neck and pushed his way through the crowd.

The source of the Hythrun entertainment proved to be two boys, both bloodied and wounded. The brawl must have been going on for quite some time, by the look of the two combatants. The older of the two was a well-muscled, fair-haired Hythrun lad of about sixteen, an apprentice blacksmith that Tarja had seen once or twice around the forge. The younger boy could not have been more than ten or eleven and was unmistakably Karien, but despite the difference in their sizes, he appeared to be giving a good account of himself, although he was clearly on the brink of collapse. His freckled face was almost totally obscured by blood, his clothes torn, his eyes burning with hatred. He was staggering to his feet as Tarja pushed through to the front of the crowd.

Tarja winced sympathetically as the older boy ran at the disoriented Karien lad and delivered a kick to the boy's chin that snapped his neck back almost hard enough to break it. With a pain-filled grunt, the Karien boy dropped to the ground. Breathing heavily, the apprentice laughed, triumphantly standing over his vanquished foe. He reached down and snatched the pendant from around the boy's neck and held it up high to the cheers of the spectators. The five-pointed star and lightning bolt of the Overlord glittered dully in the afternoon light. Someone started up a cry of "Finish him!" which was quickly taken up by the rest of the spectators. The apprentice grinned at the chant and pulled his dagger from his belt. Tarja glanced around the Hythrun and realized, with horror, that they were serious.

"Enough!" he shouted, stepping into the clearing, his red jacket stark against the motley browns and black chain mail of the Hythrun.

Silence descended on the circle of Raiders. Only then did Tarja wonder about the advisability of walking into the center of thirty-odd Hythrun Raiders crying for blood. The Raiders stared at him, their stillness more threatening than their chanting. He covered the distance to the startled apprentice and snatched the dagger from his hand.

"Get back to work, boy," he ordered in a tone that brooked no argument.

The Hythrun boy glared at him, but stepped away from the fallen Karien. A discontented mutter rippled through the men, until one of them, a slender man, with a puckered scar across his throat that looked as if he had survived having it cut, stepped forward.

"You've no authority here, Defender," he said. "Go back to your pretty-boys and leave us to deal with the Karien scum as we wish."

Tarja could feel the animosity from the Hythrun mercenaries surrounding him. He was far from his own troops, and Damin's restraining influence had weakened in his absence. With a jolt, Tarja realized he might not get out of this alive. The mercenary stepped closer and Tarja did the only thing he could think of, under the circumstances. He brought his elbow up sharply into the Hythrun's face and then kicked the stunned mercenary's legs from under him. The Hythrun hit the ground before the others could react. Tarja slammed his boot down across the man's scarred throat and then looked up at the startled Raiders.

"Anyone else?" he asked with an equanimity he did not feel. The man beneath his boot squirmed desperately, gasping for air, lack of oxygen draining his strength to escape the pressure of Tarja's boot.

"I think you've made your point, Captain."

Tarja had to consciously stop himself from sagging with relief as Almodavar appeared in the circle. The Hythrun captain barked a harsh order at his men in their own language and the circle dissolved. Tarja took his boot off the throat of his challenger and the man scrambled to his feet and ran off without looking back, clutching at his neck. Almodavar smiled grimly.

"I never thought you had a death wish, Captain," the Hythrun remarked with a shake of his head. "You should know better than to interfere with Raiders when their blood is up."

"Your Raiders should know better than to encourage cold-blooded murder," Tarja retorted, turning to the prone form of the Karien boy. He knelt down beside the lad and was relieved to see his eyes fluttering open blankly.

The Hythrun captain looked down at the boy and shrugged. "Don't blame my Raiders too quickly, Captain. That one asks for it daily. He wants to die for his Overlord."

Tarja pulled the boy to his feet. Far from being grateful, the boy seemed disappointed that Tarja had saved him. He shook himself free and staggered a little before drawing himself up to his full height.

"I need no help from an atheist!" he spat defiantly in broken Hythrun. He had obviously been in the camp long enough to pick up some of the language. He would never have learnt a heathen language in Karien.

Tarja glanced at Almodavar and then back at the boy. "Ungrateful little whelp, isn't he?" he said in Karien, so the boy would understand him.

Almodavar, for all that he looked like an illiterate pirate, spoke Karien almost as well as he spoke Medalonian and Fardohnyan. Damin held that understanding an enemy's language was the first step to understanding an enemy. He had been surprised to learn that most of Damin's Raiders spoke several languages. His Defenders, the officers at least, could speak Medalonian and Karien. It had been considered polite to converse with one's allies in their own language, but few bothered to learn the languages of the south. It was a lesson Tarja had taken to heart, although trying to convince Jenga that the Defenders should learn to speak Hythrun was proving something of a chore.

"Aye," Almodavar agreed, easily falling into the language of their enemy. "This isn't the first time, and I'll wager it won't be the last, that he's caused trouble. He and his brother were the ones who brought the news of the alliance. His brother isn't much trouble, but you'd think this one planned to defeat us single handed."

Tarja studied the boy curiously for a moment. "*This* is the Karien spy?"

The boy bristled at Tarja's amusement. "Atheist pig! The Overlord will see you drown in the Sea of Despair!"

"I'm starting to regret saving your neck, boy," Tarja warned. "Have a care with that mouth of yours."

"The Overlord will protect me!"

"I didn't see him around just now," Almodavar chuckled, and then he changed back to speaking Medalonian without missing a beat. "You wouldn't consider taking him back with you, I suppose?" he asked. "I doubt he'll last much longer around here with that attitude."

Tarja frowned. The last thing he needed was an uncontrollable ten-year-old reeking havoc in their camp in the name of the Overlord. But Almodavar was correct in his assertion that he would not last long among the Hythrun. He pondered the problem for a moment, then turned to the captain.

"Very well, I'll take him back with me," he agreed, speaking Karien so the boy could follow the conversation. "You keep his brother here. If the boy gives me any trouble, I'll send word. You can send back a finger from his brother's hand each time you hear from me. When we run out of fingers, start on his toes. Perhaps the prospect of seeing his brother dismembered bit by bit will teach him a little self-control. It's obviously not a virtue the Overlord encourages."

The boy's blood-streaked face paled, tears of fear and horror welling up in his eyes. "You are a vicious, evil, barbarian bastard!" he cried.

"A fact you would do well to remember, boy," Tarja warned. He dared not look at Almodavar. The Hythrun captain made a noise that sounded like a cough, but which Tarja suspected was a futile attempt to stifle a laugh. "Go and fetch your belongings. If you're not back here in five minutes, you'll find out what your brother looks like without his left ear."

The boy fled as Almodavar burst out laughing. "Captain, I swear you're turning into a Hythrun."

"What did you expect from a vicious, evil, barbarian bastard?"

"Truly," Almodavar agreed. "You've had a busy day. First you take on my Raiders, and then you subdue a Karien fanatic with a few words. What's next?"

"I was hoping you could tell me," Tarja said. "You've no word from Lord Wolfblade?"

"None. Don't let it concern you, Captain. He'll be back."

Tarja sighed, not really expecting any other answer. *He'll be back. But before or after the war is over?* he wondered.

chapter 15

arnarrow was a huge city, rivalling Talabar in size, although it lacked the southern capital's grace and aesthetic beauty. Steep pitched roofs of gray slate covered the more substantial buildings; while the poorer districts were simply hovels thrown together with whatever material their pitiful inhabitants could scrounge. The vast Yarnarrow Castle loomed over the city like a shadowed hand, and was even more forbidding than the city, which had grown up around its slanted walls. Adrina longed for the flat-roofed pink stone villas of Talabar, the broad balconies, the flowerladen trellises and the heavy scent of their perfume on the still air. She missed the wide, tree-lined streets and the gaily-dressed citizens. Everything was gray here—the city, the sky, even the people. Yarnarrow was depressing and dirty, and the most pervasive odor was stale wood-smoke that hung like a pall over the city as if it were constantly wrapped in fog.

She despaired at the thought of spending her life here.

The wedding took place with almost indecent haste, the day after Adrina arrived. Vonulus had instructed her in the Karien wedding vows, and Madren had ensured that she knew exactly what was expected of her. They had barely landed in Yarnarrow when she was whisked away to her large and rather draughty apartments to prepare herself for the ceremony the following day. She was not even accorded the honor of an introduction to King Jasnoff or Queen Aringard, a slight against her that had her fuming.

Tamylan, the only slave she had been allowed to keep, helped her dress on the morning of the wedding. Her ladies-in-waiting had other duties to attend to, it seemed, which did not bother Adrina at all. She defiantly ignored the stiff, gray silk dress that Madren had informed her was her wedding gown, and dressed instead in the traditional Fardohnyan bridal outfit she had brought with her. It had been made for Cassandra originally, but they were about the same size, so Adrina had appropriated the gown from her younger sister, rather than explain why Japinel had not designed a new one. It was a little tight, and she knew it would cause a commotion, but she was still smarting over Cratyn's obvious distaste for his Fardohnyan bride.

Among the more interesting things she had learnt during her short stay at Setenton Castle was that prior to the treaty with her father, Cratyn had previously been betrothed to Chastity, and that he had broken the engagement to marry Adrina. It accounted for Cratyn's reluctance, and Chastity's pitiful demeanor whenever the prince was in the room. The girl was obviously hopelessly in love with him and Adrina suspected he reciprocated the young woman's feelings. She had every intention of making him forget the silly cow ever lived, and if anything was going to advertise her matchless beauty, it was the traditional gown of a Fardohnyan bride.

The gown was in two pieces. The bodice was made of deep blue lace, threaded with diamonds, with long narrow sleeves and a low neckline that offered a tantalising view of her ample bosom and left her midriff bare. The skirt sat snugly on her hips, the same glorious blue as the bodice, made up of layer upon layer of transparent silk that flowed like a waterfall against her legs. The skirt was belted with a layer of silver mesh. In the mesh was sheathed the small jeweled dagger that had once belonged to her mother. Centuries ago, Fardohnyan brides had carried a sword, but it was tradition, rather than necessity, that required the Bride's Blade these days, and the blade was more ornamental than practical. It was sharp, though. She had cut her finger testing its edge after Hablet had presented it to her the day she left Talabar.

The Fardohnyan bridal jewels completed her outfit. In her navel nested a blue diamond of immeasurable value, matched by the sapphire and diamond choker that encased her long neck. She wore her hair down, and it hung past her waist in an ebony fall of silken waves, as was the tradition for all Fardohnyan brides. Over it all, she wore a shimmering blue veil that covered her head and the lower half of her face. The veil trailed ten paces behind her, floating on the slight current of air created by her passage as she took the long walk down the aisle of the vast Temple of Xaphista to the shocked gasps of the gathered Karien nobility.

As she traversed the length of the vast temple, Adrina was quite overwhelmed by the opulence of the building. Having seen the bleak, austere monastery on the Isle of Slarn, the Temple of Xaphista seemed almost garish by comparison. Tall, fluted columns of gold-flecked marble were spaced evenly down the center of the cathedral, supporting a vaulted ceiling that led to a dome over the altar. The dome was lined with thousands of tiny mother-of-pearl tiles, which reflected the sun onto the worshippers in a spray of rainbow light.

The temple was filled to capacity with every nobleman and noble-woman in Karien who had managed to get themselves invited to the royal wedding. Adrina heard their shocked whispers. There was no sign of warmth among the gathering. No familiar faces or encouraging smiles. Tristan had not been allowed to attend, nor had any of her Guard. They waited outside, not permitted to sully the sacred temple with their pagan presence. The only familiar face she saw during her interminable walk down the aisle was Vonulus, standing with the other priests at the front of the temple, dressed in his elaborate ceremonial robes and clutching his precious staff. The priest shook his head faintly as she caught his eye, as if scolding her for her defiance.

She turned her attention back to the altar and the somewhat aghast figure of Prince Cratyn. He wore black, from head to toe, the severity of his outfit relieved only by a thin golden coronet on his head and a gold and silver pendant in the shape of the star and lightning bolt of the Over-lord. His expression was as close to anger as she had ever seen it, in her limited acquaintance with him. *To the Seven Hells with him*, she decided. *To the Seven Hells with all of them.*

The ceremony was blessedly short, requiring little more from her than her agreement to obey Cratyn in all things and be a good and upstanding Defender of the Faith. Almost before she knew it, she was married. The High Priest, who had spent the entire ceremony trying not to see the considerable amount of bare flesh she was displaying, declared them man and wife and then prostrated himself on the floor of the altar. Carefully instructed by Vonulus, Adrina knew this was coming, and with Cratyn at her side, followed suit. Biting back a gasp as her bare skin touched the icy marble floor of the temple, Adrina momentarily regretted her impulse to wear her own gown. She had forgotten about this part of the ceremony. Every person present was required to prostrate themselves before their god and by the sound of the muffled grunts and groans behind them, some were finding the task easier than others.

They lay prone on the floor of the temple for a full ten minutes, the entire temple hushed, as each member of the congregation examined their conscience and contemplated their service to the Overlord. Adrina spent the time wishing she could get up. That floor was *freezing*.

Finally, the High Priest climbed awkwardly to his feet, and the congregation followed. Adrina turned to Cratyn and smiled, deciding to be gracious, at least in public. He took her hand uncertainly and led her through the temple to the muted, and rather unenthusiastic applause of the wedding guests.

When they reached the entrance, she was relieved to find Tristan and her Guard, once again in their glorious dress whites, waiting to escort them back to the castle. He smiled at her encouragingly, his men holding back the crowd, as Cratyn handed her up into the open carriage for the ride through the streets.

She sat down and smoothed her skirts before glancing at her new husband. He was not looking at her, but back at the temple where a sobbing Chastity had just emerged into the rare sunlight. Adrina frowned. How did one compete with such an insipid rival?

"You *could* smile, you know, husband. Getting married is supposed to be a joyous occasion. At least in Fardohnya, it is."

"We are not in Fardohnya now," Cratyn pointed out, as they moved off with a jerk. "You would do well to remember that."

Startled by his icy tone, Adrina retorted without thinking. "You would do well to remember *who* you married. Chastity will just have to stay that way, I'm afraid."

Cratyn glared at her, but did not reply. Despite the unusually warm day and the waving crowds, the ride back to Yarnarrow Castle was thoroughly unpleasant.

Had she been married in Fardohnya, the rest of the week would have been spent feasting and dancing to celebrate the occasion of her marriage. In Karien such revelry was considered wasteful and unseemly. On reaching Yarnarrow Castle, Adrina was escorted to the royal apartments to meet the Karien King—not to celebrate her marriage, but to formalize the treaty between Fardohnya and Karien.

Jasnoff proved to be a more rotund version of his son, with the same brown eyes and hair, although his was flecked with gray. He also wore the same shocked expression when he saw what she was wearing. He made no comment about it, however, and simply rose from his small throne and accepted her curtsy as was his due.

"You will sign here," Jasnoff ordered, as soon as the pleasantries were taken care of. He pointed to a parchment scroll waiting on the small, slanted desk, a tonsured scribe holding out an inked quill expectantly.

"Certainly, your Majesty. What exactly is it that I'm signing?"

"It is a letter to your father," Cratyn explained behind her. "It informs him that you are married in accordance with Karien law, and that we have kept our side of the bargain. On receipt of this letter, he will send your dowry and begin preparations for the invasion of Medalon."

"My dowry? Ah, you mean he will sign over sovereignty of the Isle of Slarn, don't you?"

Adrina took the quill from the scribe. There was something vaguely degrading about being traded for a lump of rock. She signed the letter with a flourish and handed the quill back to the scribe.

Jasnoff nodded with satisfaction and turned to his son. "Your mother and I will look forward to seeing you at dinner. And your wife, of course," he added as an afterthought.

Cratyn bowed to his father and Adrina dropped into another low curtsy as the King and his scribe strode from the room, leaving them alone. Adrina turned to Cratyn questioningly. Vonulus and Madren had spent a great deal of time instructing her on the Karien wedding ceremony, but had barely mentioned what was supposed to happen afterward.

"So what now, Cretin?" she asked. She waited for him to blush. This was the first time they had ever been alone, and she had no doubt the poor boy was probably dreading his marital duty. That, or he'd rather be doing it with Chastity.

The slap, when it came, took her completely by surprise. Her head snapped back and his signet cut her cheek, leaving a thin smear of blood on the back of his hand.

Cratyn was not blushing, he was furious.

"Fardohnyan whore!" He slapped her again, this time even harder, and she staggered under the blow. "You will *never* disgrace me or the Royal House again by such a wanton public display!"

Adrina quickly decided to forgo trading blows with him. Cratyn might be a fool, but he was stronger than she was. Such rare common sense was the last rational thought she had as her own anger exploded.

"*You* will *never* lay a hand on me again, you gutless little turd! How dare you hit me!"

"I dare what I please, your Highness," he told her, his voice a quiet rage. "I am your husband!"

"That remains to be seen! I seriously doubt your manhood is going to be up to the task. Perhaps if I simper and pout and let you call me Chastity, it will be easier for you?"

Cratyn raised his hand to strike her again, but this time she was ready for him. She had her delicate and wickedly sharp Bride's Blade at his throat, faster than he could credit. With eyes wide, he slowly lowered his arm.

"That's better," she said, holding the thin blade to his neck with her outstretched hand. "Husband you may be, Cretin, but if you *ever* lay a hand on me again, I will slit your miserable throat. Do we understand each other?"

Cratyn nodded slowly and she lowered the knife. He rubbed his neck where she had jabbed him, fingering the small bead of blood that came away on his finger. He stared at her, but his expression was far from apologetic.

"I should not have hit you," he conceded. "It was unworthy of me. But don't play me for a fool, Adrina, or think your threats and a table dagger have me cowed." He moved to the side table and poured himself a generous cup of wine before he turned back to her, his anger replaced with quiet certitude. "Did you really believe that we knew nothing of your reputation? Of your lovers? I have known since we first met what you are. Your sister's wanton behavior in Talabar merely played into our hands."

The admission stunned her. "What are you saying? You actually *wanted* to marry me?"

"I married Hablet's eldest legitimate child," Cratyn corrected coldly. "Any issue of yours will be heir to the Fardohnyan throne."

"Not if my father has a legitimate son. And I have fifteen bastard half-brothers. Father could legitimize one of them any time he wanted to."

"If he does, they will die. The Overlord has willed it. Fardohnya will become the Overlord's through the ascension of a Karien king to the throne."

"You are out of your mind if you think I will aid you in this!"

"You are my wife, Adrina," he insisted stubbornly, as if there was nothing further to be discussed on the matter. Then he added, almost as an afterthought, "Another thing, I will require you to order your Guard to place themselves under my command. I will be taking them to the front with me."

"Oh no you won't! My father never gave you leave to use my Guard in battle. They are under *my* command."

"Then you will command them according to my wishes."

"*The Seven Hells I will!* My Guard isn't going anywhere without me, least of all to some soggy battlefield to fight your wars for you."

"As you wish, Adrina," Cratyn shrugged. "If you insist, you will accompany your Guard, but they *will* fight."

"How in the name of the gods do you plan to make me order them into battle? I'll die before I give such an order."

Cratyn placed the cup down carefully and crossed his arms as he studied her. "You swear by the Primal gods. That is an offense punishable by death. You are my wife and have sworn to obey me in the eyes of my God and every nobleman in Yarnarrow. To defy me is punishable by death. If that does not convince you, I am sure it will only take your bastard half-brother and his pagans a few days to break some church law punishable by death."

"You hypocritical son-of-a-bitch! You have the gall to preach piety to me yet you would calmly murder my brother in the name of your pitiful god!"

"Be careful, Adrina," Cratyn warned. "Insulting the Overlord is punishable—"

"By death," she finished impatiently. "I get the idea, your Highness."

"Then you will do as I command?"

Adrina could barely credit the change in him. He seemed so sure of himself, here in Yarnarrow. The blushing princeling who had almost fainted at the sight of the barely dressed Fardohnyan women was still there, underneath the confident exterior, but this was his God speaking. His faith ran so deep it was impossible to shake his belief that everything would turn out as Xaphista willed it. As the realization came to her, Adrina forced her anger down. She could not fight this by having a tantrum. She needed to have her wits about her to find a way out of this terrible bargain.

"I have conditions," she said.

"I have no need to grant you anything, Adrina."

"No, you don't," she agreed. "But you want my cooperation, and believe me, I am much more tractable when I have my own way."

He nodded slightly. "As you wish, what are your conditions?"

Adrina's mind was racing ahead, trying to think what she could ask for that would not raise suspicion. "If I am to accompany you to the Medalon border, I wish to do so in a manner befitting my station as your wife. I want my full retinue, including my ladies-in-waiting." *There! Let's see how your precious Chastity likes roughing it on the front with a few thousand smelly soldiers*, she thought.

"I believe that can be arranged," he conceded. "Was that all?"

"No. I want to be included in your war council. I will not allow you to waste Fardohnyan lives without being fully informed as to your plans."

"Absolutely not! A council of war is no place for a woman."

"Suit yourself," she shrugged. "If you refuse me, then I will stand up at dinner tonight and scream at the top of my voice that Xaphista is a lying, hypocritical bastard. Somewhat like you, I imagine. Such an act would be punishable by death, would it not? If I die, you'll have no heir to the Fardohnyan throne and no troops to throw at the Medalonians. If you think I'm bluffing, then by all means, refuse me."

He thought for a moment, weighing up, no doubt, the advisability of calling her bluff, against the reaction of his Dukes to a woman in their war council.

Finally he nodded, albeit reluctantly. "Very well."

"And one other thing," she added as an afterthought. "I want every Fardohnyan under my command given special exemption by the Church. As you pointed out, they are bound to break some unknown Church law, sooner or later. It will be a lot easier for both of us if you don't whittle away at their numbers by hanging every transgressor for some slight, real or imagined, against your precious god."

Although he bristled at her tone, he was not so foolish as to deny the logic of her request. He nodded.

"That's it then," she said. "I will do as you ask." *For now*, she amended silently.

"I have some conditions of my own," Cratyn told her as she turned away.

"Such as?"

"You will never dress in such a provocative manner again. You will behave in a manner befitting a Karien Princess, or, Fardohnyan heir or not, I will see you stoned."

"Of course, your Highness," she agreed, her voiced laced with sarcasm. "Perhaps a hair shirt would be more suitable?"

He ignored the jibe. "And you will not speak to your half-brother, or any of your Guard unless Vonulus is present. I will not have you making your own plans behind my back."

Now that could prove awkward, she thought in annoyance, but she did not see a way around it. "You show a disturbing lack of trust in me, your Highness."

"A warranted lack of trust," he retorted. "Do you agree?"

She nodded slowly. "I agree."

"Good. In that case, you may return to your rooms and dress in something more . . . appropriate . . . for dinner. Tomorrow, I will have the nuns sent to you, to discuss the most opportune time in your cycle to consummate our marriage. I do not intend to spend one moment longer in your bed than I have to."

Of all that had been said in the past hour, that shocked her the most. It even hurt! How dare he!

"Just be sure that when you do deign to come to my bed, you have some idea of what you're supposed to do," she retorted coldly. "As you apparently know, I have been taught the art of lovemaking by professionals. It would be most unfortunate if your much-needed heir to the

Fardohnyan and Karien thrones fails to be consummated because I couldn't stop laughing."

The insult hit the mark as she intended, but she swept up her skirts and strode from the room before he had a chance to answer her.

chapter 16

For longer than human memory, Sanctuary had remained hidden in the mountains named for it. It had weathered nature's inevitable passage of time, untouched by anything but the magical peace and serenity that seeped through its very walls. The vast white-spired complex had watched ages come and go, kingdoms rise and fall, mortals live and die. The gods roamed its halls at will and the Harshini who lived there sought nothing more than wisdom and knowledge and safety from the foibles of humanity.

Nothing had ever disturbed it.

Until now.

Until the demon child.

Brakandaran heard the laughter as he approached Korandellan's chambers and winced. It wasn't that nobody laughed in Sanctuary, on the contrary, the Harshini were happy by nature. But this was not the polite, considerate laugh of an amused Harshini. This laugh was loud and heartfelt and unmistakably female. The laughter echoed through the halls with startling clarity, turning the heads of the white robed Harshini who glided silently past him in the hall. Their black eyes were either curious or indulgent, depending on whether or not they had any knowledge of its source.

Brak hurried on, almost afraid to discover the reason for the demon child's mirth. Korandellan was a tolerant king—he had ruled the Harshini through some of its most turbulent history—but he was ill-equipped to handle R'shiel. She had a knack for saying the wrong thing at the wrong time, asking awkward and frequently unanswerable questions, and she was totally unimpressed by the pivotal role she was expected to play in the conflict of the gods. Nor was the Harshini King easily able to deal with the fact that she was an instrument of destruction. It was hard for him to accept that the demon child's purpose was to destroy. Harder yet for him to teach her what she needed to know to enable her to complete the task. Lorandranek, R'shiel's father, had been driven insane by the knowledge.

Brak opened the door to Korandellan's chambers with a thought. The King leapt to his feet with a relieved smile at the sight of him. He and R'shiel were on the balcony, overlooking the hollow valley that Sanctuary encompassed, a crystal pitcher of chilled wine between them. Both the King and the demon child were dressed in the light linen robes that were all the protection one needed in the atmosphere-controlled vicinity of the Citadel. His black leathers seemed out of place. Brak crossed the white tiled floor and bowed to his king, who seemed inordinately glad to see him.

"Brakandaran!" Korandellan cried. "You're back!"

"So it would seem."

"R'shiel and I were just discussing her childhood at the Citadel," the King explained. "She has had a most interesting life."

Interesting is something of an understatement, Brak thought, but it did not explain R'shiel's laughter.

"The King asked me if I missed my mother," she explained, as if she understood his confusion. "It struck me as rather funny."

"Our worthy monarch has no concept of a personality like the First Sister's," Brak agreed wryly. "But it's good to hear you laughing. You're looking much better."

Another understatement. He had never seen her look better. Cheltaran, the God of Healing, had done more than heal the near-fatal wound she received in Testra. It was as if he had healed her soul as well. Or maybe it was because Death had forsaken any claim on her until the life Brak had offered in return for hers was forfeited. Her violet eyes were shining, and her skin was golden rather than sallow. She had put on weight, too, now that she was eating a diet more suited to her Harshini metabolism. He realized they would not be able to keep her here much longer, and wondered if Korandellan realized it too. They would have taught her much about her Harshini heritage and the power she had at her command, but this girl was destined to destroy a god. She would not, *could* not, learn all she needed within Sanctuary's peace-filled walls.

"What news have you, Brakandaran?" the King asked. He waved his arm and a chair appeared at the table for him. Korandellan took his own seat and poured him a cup of wine with his own hand. Brak wanted to tell him it wasn't necessary, but it would have been useless. For more than twenty years, Korandellan had been trying to prove to him that he did not hold him responsible for Lorandranek's death. Every small gesture meant something to the King. Brak took the offered seat and accepted the wine.

"Not good news, I fear," he said, glancing at R'shiel. He wondered what her reaction would be to the news he carried. Much of her current serenity was a direct result of Sanctuary's magical atmosphere. And, he privately suspected, a deliberate glamor laid on her, to take the edge off her more extreme human emotions while her body and mind recovered. That glamor would not hold if she ever realized it was there. She was easily powerful enough to break through it. Ignorance of the spell was the only thing protecting the gentle Harshini from her violent human side.

"Are the Kariens still planning to invade Medalon?" Korandellan asked with concern. The mere thought of a war made him pale. It wasn't cowardice; it was simply part of being a Harshini. A part that neither Brak nor R'shiel, being half-human, were susceptible to.

"It's worse than that," Brak told him. "They have allied with the Fardohnyans."

Korandellan shook his head, tears glistening in his totally black eyes. "Foolish humans. Don't they realize what such a war will cost?"

"They realize," Brak said. "They just don't care."

R'shiel frowned. "Even if the Fardohnyans don't join in the conflict in the north, they could still send troops up the Glass River in the south. The Defenders can't fight a war on two fronts. They barely have the numbers to fight on one, even with Hythrun allies."

Brak wondered who had told her about the Hythrun. Probably the demons. They could gossip like old women when something caught their fancy. Korandellan said nothing, just shook his head. He was no more able to discuss tactics than he was able to contemplate murder.

"It's liable to escalate beyond Medalon," Brak agreed. "If the Fardohnyans enter Medalon from the south then they can cross into Hythria without having to go over the Sunrise Mountains. Hablet has no interest in Medalon, but he'd love to get his grubby little hands on Hythria."

"We must do something!" Korandellan exclaimed. "We cannot allow the entire world to be plunged into war. Perhaps if I ask the gods . . ."

"Well, I don't suggest you mention it to Zegarnald," Brak suggested. "A global conflict would rather please the God of War. In fact, I wouldn't mind betting that he's been giving it a bit of a nudge. It must get pretty boring looking down on all those measly little border skirmishes. We haven't had a decent war in years."

"Your disrespect will prove fatal one day, Brakandaran."

Brak started at the voice as the overwhelming presence of the God of War suddenly filled the chamber. Brak should have known better than to even mention his name. Here in Sanctuary, more than any other place, to name a god was to call him. He turned in his chair but did not rise, although R'shiel and Korandellan did. Zegarnald took shape before them, so tall his golden helmet brushed the ceiling, dressed in a simple dark robe that covered him from head to toe, out of respect for Korandellan, no doubt. The Harshini were uncomfortable with weapons and Zegarnald carried at least one of every weapon his worshippers had devised, from a dagger to a longbow. Brak would have bet money he had the odd catapult stashed about his person somewhere.

"Divine One, you honor us with your presence," Korandellan greeted him somberly.

The War God smiled, if such a grimace could be called a smile. "Well, some seem more honoured than others. I would think, Brakandaran, that you of all the Harshini would be pleased to see me. I do not offend your sensibilities, as I do your king's, yet he can find it in himself to be gracious."

"I'm half-human," Brak shrugged. "What can I say?"

"You could start by not saying anything," Zegarnald retorted. "Particularly about matters you know nothing of."

Korandellan laid a restraining hand on Brak's shoulder—a silent plea not to argue with the god. "Brakandaran means no disrespect, Divine One."

"On the contrary, Korandellan, that's exactly what he intends. However, in this case, he is correct. I have been giving this war a *nudge*, as he so elegantly puts it."

"Why?" R'shiel asked curiously. She had come to accept the sudden appearance of the gods, along with a lot of other things that Brak suspected she would not be nearly so accepting of, were she outside Sanctuary's magical walls.

Zegarnald turned his gaze on the demon child, as if noticing her for the first time. "When you understand that, demon child, you will be ready to face Xaphista."

"I really think your faith in me is misplaced. I wouldn't know the first thing about killing a god."

Surprisingly, Zegarnald nodded in agreement. "Unfortunately, you speak the truth. Korandellan would have more chance of defeating him than you at present, a situation I have decided to remedy."

Brak looked at Zegarnald suspiciously. "How?"

"The demon child must leave Sanctuary and return to the humans," the god decreed. "You have helped her, Korandellan, but your peaceful ministrations and Sanctuary's magic are destroying the instincts she will need to survive Xaphista."

Korandellan did not appear pleased by the order. "No Harshini will be turned out of Sanctuary, Divine One, not even when decreed by a god. The demon child may leave if she wishes, but I will not send her away."

"As you wish," Zegarnald agreed, then he turned to R'shiel. "What say you, child? Do you wish to return to your human friends?"

R'shiel barely hesitated. "No. I want to stay here."

Zegarnald seemed almost as surprised as Brak by her words. The god studied her closely for a moment then nodded. "I see. You are more devious than I suspected, Korandellan, but the glamor that holds back her emotions cannot last forever. Brakandaran, I suggest you take the demon child into the mountains for a day. Let her breathe the air outside of Sanctuary for a time and then ask her the same question. Her answer will differ a great deal, I suspect."

"What do you mean? I feel fine."

"And happy, and calm, and contented," Zegarnald agreed. "But can you feel pain? Or anger? Or grief? I think you will discover such emotions beyond you while you live within these walls."

R'shiel looked puzzled, uncertain. Korandellan looked decidedly unhappy.

"Is this true?" she asked the Harshini king. "Have you done some-thing to me that stops me feeling those things?"

"It was necessary, child," Korandellan told her, as incapable of lying as he was of causing pain.

"But it can't be," she insisted. "I have no holes in my memory. I remember everything. And everyone."

"And yet you feel nothing?" the god asked. "You feel no loss for your friends, no anger at being betrayed, no fear for their safety? Take my advice, leave these walls for a time and see if you feel the same. When you wish to return to your friends, call me. I will see you delivered safely to them."

The god was gone an instant later, leaving a very confused young woman behind. Brak glanced at the King and shook his head. "You can-not fight the inevitable, Korandellan."

The King sighed. "I'm Harshini, Brakandaran. I cannot fight any-thing."

chapter 17

Adrina intended to make Cratyn pay for striking her, and pay dearly. Such an act was beyond unforgivable. In the finest traditions of *mort'eda*—the ancient Fardohnyan art of revenge—she quite coldly and deliberately planned to make him rue the day he ever laid eyes on her.

Her first step was acquiescing to his demands. Overnight, Adrina became the perfect Karien Princess—so perfect that it brought stares from Madren and Vonulus, both of whom viewed her transformation with suspicion. Lacking proof to the contrary, however, there was little they could do, given Adrina's exemplary behavior. Cratyn did not seem surprised. He no doubt considered it a direct result of his ultimatum, and Adrina was happy to let him think that way until she was ready to teach him otherwise.

Adrina dressed according to Karien custom, wore her hair in a snood, as was proper for married Karien Ladies, and followed Cratyn the required three paces behind him whenever they appeared in public together. She converted to the Overlord with remarkable conviction and even attended morning prayers in the chilly Temple with Queen Aringard each morning at dawn. She embroidered with her ladies and planned menus with commendable frugality. She gave alms to the poor on Fifthdays and met with the nobles of her husband's court with eyes lowered demurely. She wore no cosmetics and trimmed her long nails to the short blunt shape the Kariens preferred. In short, she gave nobody a single excuse to fault her behavior.

Of course, there were any number of ways to get at Cratyn, the easiest target being the hapless Lady Chastity.

Adrina suddenly decided that she preferred the Lady Chastity's company to all others'. She began to foster a friendship with the girl that culminated some three weeks after her wedding in a long session of "girl-talk," which centerd mostly on Cratyn. A single afternoon was all it took to reduce the poor girl to tears as Adrina waxed lyrical about the prince, about how many children they would have, about how handsome he was and how lucky she was that some other woman hadn't snatched him up before now. When Chastity had all she could stomach she excused herself hastily. Adrina could hear her sobbing from down the hall.

Teasing Chastity was poor sport, though, and it put Cratyn in a foul mood. He burst into her rooms as she bent over her needlework and ordered Tamylan out, his pale face flushed with rage.

"What did you do?"

"I wasn't aware that I had done anything, your Highness. Could you be a little more specific?"

"The Lady Chastity is distraught! What did you say to her?"

"We were merely discussing married life. I was endeavouring to enlighten her about the joys of conjugal bliss." She smiled at him sweetly and added, "Such that it is."

"You are not to discuss such things with her!"

"Why ever not?" There was nothing she had said or done that he could fault her for without crossing into dangerous moral territory, and they both knew it. "Could it be that the Lady Chastity still harbours some affection for you, my dear? Now that would be awkward, wouldn't it, you being married to me . . ."

She let the rest of the sentence hang. The young prince stormed out of the room, muttering to himself about foreign whores.

Adrina was getting very tired of being referred to as a foreign whore.

But there were other ways to punish him. Her first real chance came when they began their preparations for their trip to the border. Adrina held Cratyn strictly to his promise to see her accommodated in a manner befitting her station, and by the time they left Yarnarrow, her entourage was almost as large as the force of knights and foot soldiers accompanying them. She would happily have beggared him, given half a chance, and it was only Jasnoff's intervention that prevented her from doing just that. As soon as the King complained, Adrina ceased her outrageous demands, but by then the damage had been done. Adrina and her ladies were going off to war in style.

Adrina's most subtle, and by far her most effective revenge she aimed at Cratyn's manhood. The nuns had dutifully visited Adrina the day after her wedding to discuss her cycle in rather unpleasant detail, and they determined the most opportune time to conceive was eight days after the wedding. Adrina's bed remained empty until that time. When the designated night finally arrived, Adrina excused herself early and spent a considerable amount of time preparing for Cratyn's visit, including preparing a small quantity of the mixture that would ensure that in the unlikely event that Cratyn actually desired her, his body would not respond.

Getting Cratyn to accept the laced wine had been easy. She had a feeling he could only bring himself to touch her if he wasn't entirely sober. She then waited, with an expectant look, for Cratyn to make the first move. His fumbling and ultimately futile attempts to consummate their union left her weak with ridiculing laughter. Cratyn fled the chamber in embarrassment and she did not lay eyes on him for two whole days afterward. Altogether an entirely satisfactory outcome, she decided.

But Adrina was determined that no child would ever come from this union, so she set about making certain it never did. She knew enough herb lore to ensure she would not suffer an unwanted pregnancy—it was a necessity for any woman in a society where *court'esa* were the norm. But the easiest way to prevent a pregnancy was simply not to let Cratyn into her bed on the days designated by the nuns as suitable. There was also the added bonus that if the marriage remained unconsummated for a year and a day, under Karien law she would be free of Cratyn entirely.

One of the lesser-known advantages of being instructed in the arts of love by a *court'esa* was learning how to cool a man's ardour as easily as arousing it. It was a skill every *court'esa* owned—even professional lovers needed a night off occasionally—but it was a skill rarely passed on to their masters or mistresses. If one's paramour knew what one was up to, it was impossible to guarantee success. It only worked on an inexperienced lover, and that description fitted Cratyn better than his custom-made armor. There were drugs too, one could use, although they were a closely guarded secret among the *court'esa*. Adrina had extracted those secrets from Lynel, a dark-eyed *court'esa* from Mission Rock in southern Fardohnya, for the promise of a minor title. So grateful had she been to learn the arts and acquire the drugs, that she even kept her promise, and as far as she knew, Lynel was still happily ensconced in his own small manor near Kalinpoor on the Jalanar plains. In the days and weeks that followed her marriage to Cratyn, she often had cause to silently thank the man.

But her revenge did not stop there. While it was intensely satisfying to her to watch Cratyn crumble with mortification every time she glanced at him, the real fun came from making it known that the Crown Prince of Karien was impotent.

Her first step was to cry, quite convincingly, on Madren's shoulder about her inability to arouse her husband. Madren, of all her retinue, was the most suspicious and the most watchful. Adrina blamed herself, of course, and almost choked when Madren delivered her stiff and rather unimaginative suggestions on how to deal with the situation. As she had made certain that the servants would overhear her heartbroken confession, within a day the news was all through the castle. Tamylan reported that the kitchens were abuzz with rumors and that even the stableboys had heard. By the time their vast caravan left Yarnarrow there was not a man or woman in the castle, serf or noble, who had not heard the rumor that Cratyn's manhood was in doubt.

The effect such rumors had on Chastity was predictable. The girl was torn between horror that her love might be impotent and delight that he had not slept with Adrina. That the pale skinned blonde lusted after Cratyn was so obvious, Adrina wondered that she hadn't been hauled off and stoned for her adulterous thoughts. On the other hand, there was many a duke who would have preferred a Karien queen, and Adrina wondered if she would survive the birth of a son, should she be so foolish as to conceive. A claimant to the Fardohnyan throne did not need a Fardohnyan mother to raise him, and everybody knew how perilous childbirth could be.

Adrina refused to give any of these fanatics an opportunity to rearrange the world to their liking. She would suffer the humiliation of Cratyn only coming to her rooms when she was likely to conceive; she would tolerate Madren's hawk-like scrutiny and Vonulus' pious instruction. She would bear King Jasnoff's obvious distaste and Queen Aringard's sour disapproval. She would even put up with the miserable Karien weather.

Until she found a way out of this mess, Adrina didn't really have much choice.

Tristan was predictably unhappy about being ordered to the border, but as she had promised Cratyn she would not speak to him alone, she had not had the chance to explain it to him before they left Yarnarrow. In fact, getting a message to Tristan became more and more important as they drew closer to the border. She was afraid he would do something reckless. He knew the terms of the agreement under which he and his soldiers were in Karien, and knew that she was flying in the face of Hablet's express wishes by ordering her Guard to the front.

Hablet wanted the Hythrun so involved in the Medalon conflict that they would not notice the direction his army was heading when they crossed the southern border of Medalon. Loaning her Guard to Cratyn to ensure a quick victory in the north was not liable to help her father's cause, and she was far more concerned about his reaction than anything Cratyn might threaten her with. Hablet was not a man who took disruption of his plans well. The problem kept her awake night after night, until one morning, as she sat on a small stool in her sumptuous traveling tent, while Tamylan brushed out her long hair before she dressed for the day's travel. She studied the former slave in the mirror thoughtfully. She really was quite a pretty young woman.

"Tam, do you like Tristan?"

The question startled her. "Tristan?"

"Yes. You know, Tristan. Tall. Fair. Golden eyes. Good looking and entirely too aware of the fact?"

Tamylan smiled. "Do I like him? I suppose."

"Good," Adrina announced with satisfaction. "I want you to become his lover."

The brush halted mid-stroke as Tam stared at her in the mirror. "You want me to be Tristan's lover?"

"Don't act so thick, Tam. You heard me. You're both Fardohnyan, far from home. Nobody would look twice."

"Your Highness, I appreciate your . . . thoughtfulness . . . but somehow, I don't think your brother is interested in the likes of me."

"Don't be so hard on yourself, Tam," Adrina told her cheerily. "You're very pretty and there isn't a *court'esa* for a thousand leagues, so Tristan can hardly afford to be choosy now, can he?" She laughed at the young woman's expression. "Oh Tam, don't look so horrified. Don't you see? I can't speak to Tristan without that vulture Vonulus around. If everyone thinks you and Tristan are lovers, they won't question you visiting him."

"If they think Tristan and I are lovers, I'm likely to get stoned."

"No you won't. The Fardohnyans have been given a special exemption by the Church. You'll be safe enough. Far safer than me, in fact."

Tamylan scowled unhappily. "I don't like this place, your Highness. I'd rather you figured out a way to get us home."

"I'm working on it, Tam," Adrina assured her. "Believe me, I'm working on it."

There was one bright spot in her miserable existence, and it came from the most unexpected source. The day after her wedding, Drendyn, Cratyn's cheerful cousin, had paid her a visit carrying a large wicker basket, which he placed gently on the rug in front of the hearth before turning to her with a beaming smile.

"I have brought you a wedding gift," he announced.

"And it's a beautiful basket, too," she agreed graciously.

"Basket? Oh! No! It's what's inside!"

Adrina lifted the lid and peered inside with curiosity. A wet nose thrust itself at her and a long sloppy tongue slapped her face. Laughing delightedly, she threw back the lid and lifted the puppy out. He was tan in color, his shaggy coat thick and soft. The pup was enormous, even at such a young age, and she struggled to lift him.

"He's beautiful!" she cried. "What is he?"

"He's a dog," Drendyn explained, a little confused.

"I *know* he's a dog, silly, but what sort of dog? We have nothing this big in Fardohnya. If he gets much bigger I'll be able to saddle him!"

"He's a Karien hunting dog," the young Earl told her. "You said you liked hunting, so I thought you could train him now. We breed the best hounds in Karien in Tiler's Pass. Do you like him?"

She pushed away the sloppy kisses of her new friend and laughed. "Oh Drendyn, I love him. Thank you so much."

The Earl looked very pleased with himself. "Nothing is too good for our future queen. You will have to think of a name for him."

"I shall call him . . . Tiler! In honor of your home."

Tiler had not left her side since. The dog grew at an alarming rate, and consumed enough to keep a peasant family well fed. He was, besides Tamylan and Tristan, the only soul in Karien who seemed to love her unreservedly. Adrina found it strange that she, having been raised in excessive luxury with anything she wanted there for the asking, should find such joy in such a shaggy, clumsy beast.

chapter 18

rak could have followed R'shiel's path through the mountains with little difficulty, even had a demon not appeared to show him the way. The little gray creature was young and it could barely speak, but it tittered with concern and kept looking over its small gray shoulder to ensure Brak was still following, as it led the way through a forest carpeted in the fiery shades of autumn.

When he finally reached her he hesitated. She was sitting on the edge of a precipice, dressed in dark riding leathers, her feet dangling over a long sheer drop that disappeared into mist.

"I'm not suicidal, if that's what you're worried about," she said without looking at him. The little demon scrambled up the rest of the path and climbed into her lap.

"Did you bring him here? Traitor."

She turned to face Brak. Her eyes were red and swollen, her cheeks tearstained. "Did they send you to find me?"

"It's a curse. All I seem to do these days is chase after you." When he reached the ledge he sat down beside her and admired the view silently for a moment. The steep mountains were still snowcapped, even at this time of year, and the air was pleasantly cool. He could see Sanctuary's tall spires in the distance, but only because he knew they were there. To mere human eyes, the spires looked like any other steep peaks in this vast range full of them. "Korandellan was worried about you."

"He did this to me. It serves him right."

"Nobody meant to hurt you, R'shiel. They did it to protect you."

"Did they know how much it would hurt when it wore off?"

"Probably not. Harshini don't really understand human emotions. But when you came here, you were dying. They did what they had to."

She wiped her eyes impatiently. "I know that. That's what makes it so infuriating. You have no idea how hard it is to stay angry at these people."

"I do know," he assured her. "Better than you, girl. I've lived between two worlds for centuries."

She glanced at him curiously. "Will I live as long as you?"

Brak shrugged. "I don't know. I suppose you will. Most half-humans seem to inherit Harshini longevity. You might fall off this precipice at any moment too, so don't tie yourself into knots trying to predict the future."

"Is that how you get by?"

"That and large quantities of mead," he replied with a thin smile.

She looked at him sharply, then smiled when she realized he was joking. "You don't really fit in here, do you Brak?"

"No more than I fit in a human world. But don't let my inability to find my niche in the world deter you from trying to find yours."

"I was under the impression my niche was already carved in stone," she pointed out sourly. "I am the demon child, am I not?"

"R'shiel, nobody is going to make you face Xaphista until you're ready. Stop worrying about it. If you really are meant to tackle Xaphista, there will come a time when you won't need to be asked. You'll want to do it."

"I can't see that happening anytime soon."

"As I said, don't tie yourself into knots trying to predict the future."

R'shiel did not answer him for a while. She stared out over the mountains, idly scratching the young demon behind its large wrinkled ear. Finally she turned to him, the tears under control for the time being.

"Does Tarja think I'm dead?"

The question surprised him a little. He had not expected her to be able to think things through so rationally yet. The first time he had broken through a glamor designed to suppress his emotions, he'd been incoherent for days.

"I suppose so. Nobody has told him otherwise that I'm aware of."

"He's done his grieving then," she sighed. "And I will live to see him whither and die an old man. I'm not sure I can deal with that."

"The way Tarja finds trouble, it'll be a bloody *miracle* if he lives to be an old man, so I wouldn't let that stand in your way."

She frowned at his poor attempt at humour. "You're pretty tactless, for a Harshini, aren't you?"

"I'm the bane of their existence," he agreed. "At least I was until you came along and relieved me of the title. However, it seems I am doomed to serve your cause, whether I like it or not."

"There's no need to be so gallant about it." She turned back to the glorious view and was silent for a time before she spoke. "I wish I knew what to do, Brak."

"What do you *want* to do?"

"I want to go home. But there's a small problem. I don't seem to *have* a home any longer. Sanctuary isn't where I belong, I know that now, and I can hardly go back to the Citadel."

"No, that's probably not a good idea," he agreed with a faint smile.

"What happened to Joyhinia?" she asked abruptly. "Did Tarja kill her?"

"Dacendaran stole her intellect. Then Tarja destroyed it. She lives, but she's as innocent and harmless as a child, now. I suppose she's on the border with the Defenders. We'd have heard if she returned to the Citadel in that condition."

"And this Hythrun who is helping Tarja, what's he like?"

"Damin Wolfblade? You'd like him. He's almost as good at finding trouble as Tarja. I sometimes think it was a mistake bringing those two together. I'm not sure the world is ready for either of them."

"And Lord Draco?"

Brak sighed heavily. "R'shiel, if you're so anxious to see how they are, go to them. Zegarnald has already offered to take you. You can't stay here forever and you don't want to, anyway. Follow your instincts. Destiny has a habit of catching up with you, no matter how hard you try to outrun it. Believe me, I speak from experience."

"were you destined to kill my father?"

Brak stared at her, aghast at the question. It took him a moment to recover himself enough to answer her. "I don't know, R'shiel. Perhaps I was. One of the advantages of being *destined* to do things, is that it can take the place of a conscience for a while."

"Korandellan says you've been trying to outrun your destiny your whole life."

"Does Korandellan often discuss my failings with you?"

"He uses you to illustrate the pitfalls of being half-human."

Brak scowled at her but offered no comment.

"You think I should go back, don't you?" she sighed.

"It doesn't matter what I think. It's what you think that counts."

"I'm afraid," she admitted.

"Of what?" he asked curiously. "Tarja?"

She nodded. "I'm afraid he's accepted that I'm dead. Suppose he's moved on? Suppose he's found someone else?"

Brak snorted impatiently. "Suppose you stop being such an idiot! Gods, R'shiel! Zegarnald was right. You're turning into a mouse. Have a bit of faith, girl! The man loves you. Six months wondering if you're dead isn't going to change that. If it has, then he never loved you in the first place, so you might as well be rid of him. Either way, put us all out of our misery and go find out for yourself instead of sitting here on the top of a mountain bemoaning your lot in life." He did not add that Kalianah had made certain Tarja would never love another. She did not need to know that.

R'shiel glared at him, startled at his outburst. Months of the eternally accommodating Harshini had left her unprepared for a little human aggravation.

"Don't tell me what to do!"

"Why not? That's what you've been asking me. You want me to tell you what you should do, so that if it doesn't work out you won't have to blame yourself. Well, thanks, R'shiel, but I have enough of my own burdens to lug around without taking on yours as well."

He watched the anger flare in her violet eyes with relief. Her spirit was still there, underneath the shock from the glamor and the effects of her time spent in the smothering peace of Sanctuary. It was rare that he agreed with the War God, but in this case, Zegarnald was right. R'shiel would wither if she stayed here much longer. This girl had faced down three hundred angry rebels, she had been raped, imprisoned, and mortally wounded by the woman she grew up thinking was her mother. None of it had been able to break her. But much longer within Sanctuary's calming walls and the human shell that had protected her inner strength would be dissolved.

Pushing the demon from her lap, she scrambled to her feet and brushed down the leathers before turning on him. "I don't need you to tell me what I want to do. I'll go where I want, when I want, and you can go to the lowest of the Seven Hells, for all I care!"

She stormed off down the path, the little demon tumbling in her wake. Brak watched her go with a faint smile.

"Deftly handled, Lord Brakandaran."

Brak turned toward the deep voice, unsurprised to find the old demon Dranymire behind him. "I thought you'd be around somewhere. You could have helped, you know."

The little demon sat down beside Brak with a smug expression. "If she had fallen off this cliff, I would have been there in an instant. But some things are best left to one's own kind."

"It's not my responsibility to protect her. That's supposed to be your job."

Dranymire nodded sagely. "And protect her I will, Brakandaran," he said. "But I can only save her from outside danger. I cannot save her from herself."

chapter 19

ikel of Kirkland found it hard to be brave in the Defender Camp. Among the Hythrun it had been easy. There he had Jaymes to support him. Jaymes was always brave. Jaymes hadn't blabbed about the Fardohnyan alliance trying to make himself sound important. Jaymes had been quiet and sullen and strong.

The Hythrun were quick to anger and easy to provoke, and Mikel felt it was his solemn duty to do what he could to sabotage their war effort. He had honored the Overlord countless times in the weeks he spent among them, cursing the soldiers, spitting in their stew whenever he got the chance, and making a general nuisance of himself. It had been easier once the Warlord left. The big blonde Hythrun had frightened the boy more than he was willing to admit, but once he was gone, Mikel found his courage increased. The fight with the blacksmith's apprentice had been the last in a long line of skirmishes with his captors.

The Defenders were different, however. They did not listen to his insults or his curses, or if they heard them, they simply laughed indulgently at him. Even more humiliating was the fact that the captain who had saved him from the apprentice and taken him to the other camp had placed him in the care of a woman! Her name was Mahina and he was supposed to call her Sister, even though she wasn't a nun and didn't deserve the title. Worse, when the little old lady, who reminded him of his own Nana, had gotten hold of him, she took one whiff of his ragged tunic and ordered him to bathe. She then stood over him while the deed was done, to ensure he was properly clean. Everybody knew that taking off all your clothes was a sin against the Overlord and it was a well-known fact that total immersion in water was bad for you and gave rise to unhealthy vapors. But she had stood there like a slave-master on a Far-dohnyan galley and made him wash every part of his body. She then added insult to injury by trimming his hair and making him wear a pair of cast-off Defender's trousers and a pleated linen shirt several sizes too big for him. His tunic and hose she rather ceremoniously burned on the hearth, holding her nose as she did so.

As praying to the Overlord had always evoked a reaction from the Hythrun, he was startled when his prayers drew nothing from Mahina and the Defenders but bored looks and, in some cases, stifled yawns. The Defenders did not seem offended by his prayers. They just didn't *care*! His devotions meant nothing to them. They were atheists who considered worshipping the gods a quaint and rather laughable custom. That hurt almost as much as the thought that his misbehavior might cost Jaymes a finger.

The Defenders were frighteningly well disciplined, a fact which surprised the boy. They were under the command of a tall, hard-looking man called Lord Jenga, but it was the captain who had brought him here who scared him most. His name was Tarja Tenragan, and every night, when Mikel said his prayers to the Overlord, he prayed his god would strike the man down.

Mikel burned with hatred for the tall Medalonian who had so calmly ordered Jaymes dismembered if Mikel misbehaved. Although he was only a captain, everybody seemed to listen to him, even Lord Jenga, and he had faced down the Hythrun Raiders without blinking. Mikel was sure there was nothing on this world that could scare him—and that scared Mikel, because he knew that in battle, the Medalonians would not run in the face of the first concerted charge, as he had often heard Duke Laetho boast.

In fact, much of what Mikel had heard in the Karien camp was proving to be incorrect. The Hythrun did not eat human babies for breakfast and the red-coated Defenders weren't weaklings dressed up in fancy uniforms and playing at being soldiers. They were hard men and well trained. Much better trained than the Kariens, Mikel suspected. Where the Karien camp spent time boasting of past victories on the jousting field or anticipating future glories, these soldiers were on the training field in Medalon.

They were much better supplied too, Mikel discovered. Unlike the

Kariens, the Medalonians and their Hythrun allies had a constant supply line from the Glass River, and they lived like kings compared to his own people. He had eaten more since being a captive than he had since arriving on the front as Lord Laetho's page some four months ago. He began to wonder if it was a sin to eat so well, but when he refused to eat, Mahina had threatened to have him force fed. When that threat had not worked, Mahina called Tarja in. The captain had looked at him coldly and simply asked one question.

"Left hand or right hand?"

Mikel had not missed a meal since and never again brought up the topic of sinning by eating too well.

Mahina had set him to performing chores around the camp, which in truth did not vary much from what had been asked of him as Lord Laetho's page. He waited tables and filled wine jugs and ran errands for the old woman, all the while keeping his eyes and ears open. Mikel was certain he would eventually be rescued. If not, there was always a chance he could escape—except that if he did, Tarja was likely to kill Jaymes, so he tried not to think about it too much. But if the chance ever arose, he wanted to take back as much intelligence as possible to Lord Laetho. Perhaps even Prince Cratyn or King Jasnoff would want to hear his information. Mikel managed to spend a good deal of time in idle dreams of his triumphant return to the Karien camp, bearing the one vital piece of information that would ensure a Karien victory.

In the meantime, he performed his chores doggedly, determined to give Tarja no reason to harm his older brother. Mahina was often distracted, but she was not unkind and it was hard to hate her. In fact, it was hard to hate many of the Medalonians, although his loathing of Tarja Tenragan never wavered. Most of them treated him well, if not out of kindness, exactly. Mikel suspected it was because they did not consider him a threat. He had grandiose, if rather vague plans to disabuse them of that notion some day and he prayed to the Overlord every night before he slept that his god would show him the way.

The Defenders' camp spread out across the plain in neat lines of identical tents, radiating from the old keep in the center, which served as the temporary command post for the Medalonian forces. The Defenders called it Treason Keep, which Mikel thought the strangest name. It was here that Mikel did his chores for Mahina. It was here that Lord Jenga,

Tarja Tenragan and another dangerous looking man called Garet Warner met with the savage Captain Almodavar and a passionate young man called Ghari, to make their plans. Mikel had not worked out exactly what Ghari's position was in the Medalon forces, but he was often called in to discuss matters of import, although he had little to offer in the way of tactical advice. He seemed to be in charge of all sorts of other things—tasks that were vital to the war effort but not directly involved in the fighting.

Mikel was amazed at how little time the Medalonians spent discussing actual battle plans. They spent a lot more time worrying about supplies and ammunition and feed for the horses and securing enough fuel to see them through the winter. He supposed it was because they did not have the Overlord to protect them. Such mundane matters were rarely discussed in the Karien camp. The Overlord would provide.

Mikel had a natural ear for languages, and it was not long before he could make sense of what they were saying. Astonishingly, once Mahina realized he could understand what was being said, far from discouraging him, she took time out to give him lessons and even boasted to Tarja about how quickly he was picking up the language. Tarja had actually smiled!

Of all things in the Defenders' camp that confused or surprised Mikel, the strangest by far was the Crazy Lady. She had rooms in the restored upper level of Treason Keep, heavily guarded by Defenders and a sad looking man called Lord Draco who said little and kept to himself in the chambers above the great hall. Lord Draco frightened Mikel, and not simply because of his physical resemblance to Tarja. The man had an air about him that spoke of emotions Mikel was too young to define. The only redeeming features that Mikel could see were his devotion to the Crazy Lady and the fact that any time Lord Draco and Tarja were in the same room you could almost see the hatred between them like streaks of jagged lightning. He did not know why Tarja hated Lord Draco and was too afraid to ask anyone the reason, but it made him feel a little better to know that all was not as perfect as it seemed in the Medalonian camp.

The Crazy Lady never left her room. Mikel had seen her once, when Mahina had sent him to her chamber with a document she had to sign. The guards had opened the door for him and Affiana, the tall, no-nonsense woman who seemed to be the Crazy Lady's nurse, had met him inside. Affiana had relieved him of the scroll and bustled him out the door, but not before he caught a glimpse of the Crazy Lady sitting on the floor in the center of the chamber, clutching a ragged doll and humming tunelessly. The guards outside had shooed him away, leaving him burning with curiosity regarding the Crazy Lady's identity.

The third week into Mikel's internment in the Defender camp, Mahina sent him to find Tarja. A messenger had arrived from the front with news, and she wanted to see him. It must be something important, he knew, but he was sent away before he could learn what it was.

While Mikel dreaded the thought of seeking Tarja out, he was looking forward to the opportunity to visit the training ground legitimately. He hurried through the camp, ignored by Defenders who considered him not worth noticing. The day was quite cold and still. Swirls of dust floated through the camp like smoke eddies. Mikel all but ran, knowing the quicker he got there, the more time he could spend watching the Defenders before he had to approach Tarja.

The training ground covered a vast area north of Treason Keep. It was dusty and noisy, the long grass scuffed bare by the boots of thousands of men training for war. He slowed as he reached the field, weaving his way cautiously between groups of men charging with pikes at targets nailed to posts buried deep in the ground. A little further on another troop bearing red-painted shields was practising a set of striking sword blows. The sergeant in charge bellowed impatient instructions about turning hands, and standing side-on, and told one hapless young man that if he continued to use his shield as a counter-balance instead of protection he would undoubtedly have the honor of being the first trooper to die in defense of Medalon.

A little further on Mikel watched in awe as a troop of Hythrun Raiders practised, mounted on their beautiful golden steeds. They were shooting into melons mounted on short poles, which exploded in a ruddy mess as wave after wave of them galloped toward the targets; they loosed their arrows side-on, reloaded and fired at the next target without missing a beat. The Raiders steered their horses with their knees and rode as if nothing could unseat them. Karien knights picked their horses for their ability to carry the weight of an armored man. Agility and speed were secondary concerns. Mikel thought of Lord Laetho's huge and very expensive warhorse, which looked clumsy and cumbersome compared to the sleek Hythrun mounts, and wondered how he would fare in a battle.

He moved on in the direction Mahina had told him Tarja would be, watching the Hythrun horsemen over his shoulder as he hurried forward. He stopped again for a moment to watch another group attacking a number of armored targets, practising slowly and deliberately as they aimed for the vulnerable places in the armor with deadly precision. Mikel frowned as he watched them. Although every man here was training for war, these men were specifically training to kill or disable the knights who would lead the charge. He shuddered at the thought. The Medalonians seemed to be taking this war a lot more seriously that his own people. *But then they had to,* he reminded himself. *They were outnumbered and they did not have the Overlord on their side.*

"Here, lad, what are you doing hanging about the field?"

Mikel jumped guiltily and turned to the man who had challenged him. It was Ghari, he discovered with relief. Ghari did not frighten him nearly as much as the Defenders.

"Sister Mahina sent me to find Captain Tenragan."

Ghari placed his hand on Mikel's shoulder with a friendly smile. "Let's go find him then, shall we? I'm looking for him too."

Mikel nodded a little uncertainly and let Ghari lead the way. He watched the man out of the corner of his eye, expecting to see some sign that Ghari's friendliness was feigned, but the young man simply glanced down at him and smiled again. Mikel could not understand these people at all.

Tarja was on the far side of the training ground, stripped down to trousers and boots and sweating in the cold sunlight. He was training with another man, a little older than he, and both men were breathing hard, dust clinging to their sweaty skin as they traded blows. Both had the musculature of men who spent hours with a sword, but Mikel was astounded to see Tarja's back scarred with the unmistakable mark of the lash. He was savagely pleased to think that someone had lashed Tarja. He would like to meet the man and thank him.

The sound of metal against metal rang loudly as Tarja and his opponent moved back and forth, neither man trying to gain the advantage, simply working muscles to the point of fatigue and beyond to strengthen them. Mikel had heard one of the Medalonians say that it was the training you did after you reached the point of exhaustion that really counted. Everything you did up to that point was just warming up.

Tarja saw them approaching and held up his hand to halt the fight. His opponent lowered his sword and glanced at Mikel and Ghari. Realizing that their appearance heralded the end of their bout, he raised his blade in salute to Tarja with a weary smile.

"You're getting slow, Tarja. I can still stand up."

"*I'm* getting slow," Tarja laughed as he returned the salute. "More likely some Karien knight is going to make a trophy of your hide."

The older man chuckled. "Perhaps, but he'll have trampled you getting to me." Captain Alcarnen picked up his shirt off the ground and wiped his forehead with it, then threw it over his shoulder. "Ghari," he said with a nod as he walked past the young man.

"Captain," Ghari replied, with a surprising amount of angst. Mikel looked at him curiously. He didn't like Alcarnen at all, that much was obvious.

"You didn't come looking for me for the pleasure of my company, I suppose?" Tarja asked. He slipped his shirt over his head but did not bother to tuck it in to his trousers.

"No," Ghari agreed. "There's a bit of trouble brewing in the followers' camp. I thought maybe you could do something."

The captain did not seem pleased. "What is it this time?"

"Some of our people tried to set up a temple to Zegarnald. The Defenders tore it down."

"Heathen worship is against the law, Ghari. You know that and so do they."

Ghari placed his hands on his hips and glared at Tarja. "Damn it, Tarja, we followed you here to save Medalon from the Kariens. You told us things would change, that we'd be free to worship our gods—"

"All right, I'll speak to Jenga," Tarja promised, obviously not pleased by the prospect, then he turned his gaze on Mikel, who shivered with apprehension.

"And what of you, boy?" he asked abruptly. "What are you doing here?"

"Sister Mahina . . . she sent me to . . . a messenger came . . . from the front . . . she said . . ." Mikel could have cried as he stuttered under the scrutiny of the captain.

"I gather that means Sister Mahina has received a messenger from the front and she wants to see me?" he translated condescendingly. Mikel's hatred surged through his veins like lava. *I will kill this man one day*, he swore silently. Tarja seemed oblivious to his animosity. "This could mean things are about to get interesting."

"You think the rest of the Kariens have arrived?" Ghari asked.

"Either that, or they've packed up and gone home, which would be too much to hope for," he said, sheathing his blade. "Has anyone told—" Tarja's words were cut off by an ear-shattering whoop as the Hythrun Raiders suddenly thundered past them at a gallop, leaving them coated in a cloud of fine dust. Tarja glared at the troop angrily, spitting grit as he watched them vanish into the dust. "What in the name of the Founders are they up to?"

Ghari wiped his eyes. "Something's caught their attention."

Tarja shook his head in annoyance and followed the path of the Raiders. He strode ahead of Ghari and Mikel, who had to run to catch up. The Raiders had not gone far. They were milling about, shouting incomprehensibly a mere fifty paces from the edge of the camp, kicking up a cloud of dust as thick as a winter fog in Yarnarrow. Mikel watched the Raiders curiously, coughing as the dust tickled the back of his throat. He glanced over his shoulder and discovered most of the men on the training ground had stopped what they were doing and had turned to see what the commotion was about.

Tarja strode on, then suddenly stopped, frozen to the spot, as three figures began to materialise out of the dust. All three were on foot, and Mikel immediately recognized the figure in the center, leading his lathered golden stallion, as the Hythrun Warlord who had been missing these past weeks. The man on his left Mikel had never seen before, but he was tall and lean with dark hair and walked with long, easy strides. Damin Wolfblade was grinning like a fool, obviously enormously pleased with himself. The tall man beside him simply looked satisfied. The figure to the right of the Warlord made Mikel gasp. It was a woman, he realized, wearing close-fitting dark leathers that showed every line of her statuesque body in startling detail, an outfit that would have seen her stoned had she dared wear it in Karien. As she neared them, the Warlord and the other man stopped and waited, letting her walk on alone. She was very tall and had long, dark red hair that fell in a thick braid to her waist. She was the most beautiful woman Mikel had ever seen, even when he was at court; prettier even than the Lady Chastity, who was supposed to be the most beautiful woman in all of Karien.

He glanced up at Tarja, whose expression had changed from anger to awe. As the woman walked toward him, Mikel thought he could have killed Tarja, had he a knife, and the captain would not have noticed, so enthralled did he seem at the sight of the pretty lady.

"By the gods!" Ghari breathed softly behind him. "She's alive!"

Ghari apparently knew who the pretty lady was, but his words seemed to break the spell that held Tarja motionless. The captain walked out to meet her, and as soon as she saw him, the pretty lady broke into a run. She collided with Tarja, who swept her off the ground and spun her around in a full circle with an inarticulate cry. He was kissing her before her feet touched the ground, a deed that had the gathered army cheering and Mikel blushing with embarrassment at such a wanton public display.

"Who is she?" Mikel asked Ghari. He looked up at the young man and was startled to see his eyes misted with tears.

"R'shiel," Ghari explained, although the name meant nothing to him. Ghari glanced down at him and ruffled his cropped hair with a grin. "She's the demon child. She's come back to us!"

That description meant as little to Mikel as the lady's name, but it seemed fitting that a man as evil as Tarja would be attracted to a demon. The crowd flowed past him as the soldiers all converged on the returning Warlord and his companions. He quickly lost sight of Tarja and R'shiel as the crowd swallowed them.

Mikel turned away, his heart heavy. It was bad enough that these Medalonians seemed so organized and battle ready, but it was patently unfair that Tarja Tenragan was allowed to be happy, or that they had demons on their side. He impatiently brushed away tears of anger and said a silent prayer to Xaphista.

Help me, he prayed. *The demon child has returned to help our enemies.*

Mikel had no way of knowing if Xaphista had heard him or not.

He would have been astonished and delighted to know that he had.

chapter 20

The Karien war camp proved to be as uncomfortable as Adrina had feared. Cratyn's army was slow in gathering and many of his knights had been here far longer than they ever intended. The sixty days they owed their king was long past. What kept them at the border now was the hope of recovering some of the cost of their expedition once they reached Medalon, and the exhortations of the priesthood that this was a holy war. When one feared eternal damnation, it was easier to stay and fight. Food was scarce and so was fuel; winter was fast approaching. Nobody had expected the Defenders to be waiting on the border when the knights arrived.

The original force of five hundred had been deemed sufficient to cow the unprepared Medalonians and punish them for their temerity. Instead they were met by a large force of Defenders with Hythrun allies and defenses that left the knights gasping. There was nothing hurried or hastily thought-out about their earthworks. Even to the inexperienced eye it was obvious that the Defenders planned to force the battle along a path of their choosing. Although Adrina heard some of the knights boast that the first sight of an armored charge would send the Defenders scurrying, she knew better. Whoever had planned the defense of the Medalon border had planned this long ago—and planned it well. Taking Medalon was not going to be easy, despite the Kariens' numerical superiority and the much-talked-about blessing of the Overlord.

Not surprisingly, Adrina's first appearance at the war council caused a stir, even more than Tristan's inclusion. Tristan was a man, after all, and a warrior, for all that he was foreign. It was not considered seemly for a woman to involve herself in such manly pursuits as war, even in the unlikely event that she would have anything constructive to offer. Adrina bore the insults stoically, letting Cratyn defend his decision to his vassals. If he was going to lead these men, he needed the practice, anyway.

The war council was made up of the eight Dukes of Karien. The loudest was a heavy-set man with a thick neck and an even thicker intellect—Laetho, the Duke of Kirkland. Adrina marked him as a dangerous fool. He had apparently lost two of his servants a few months back, having sent the children over the border to spy on the Medalonians. It was safely assumed they were both dead. Only an idiot would, quite literally, send boys out to do a man's job.

The man next to Laetho was as tall, but only half his girth. Lord Roache, the Duke of Morrus. He said little and gave the impression that he wasn't listening, more often than not, but when he did comment, it was obvious he had not missed a word of the discussion. Adrina regarded him with caution.

Next to Roache, she was delighted to discover Cratyn's cousin Drendyn, the Earl of Tiler's Pass. His father was too infirm to make the journey to the border and had sent his son in his place. Drendyn was young and enthusiastic, but dangerously inexperienced. He had never faced a man in battle, never had his life seriously threatened. Adrina thought it likely he would die, sooner rather than later, no doubt doing something exceptionally foolish, which he considered exceptionally brave. It was a pity really, because she quite liked the young Earl.

The fourth member of the council was even younger and more inexperienced than Drendyn. Jannis, the Earl of Menthall, was also here in the place of his father, although Tam had heard it rumoured that the reason the old Duke was absent had something to do with the "wages of sin." Adrina wondered if it meant he'd caught the pox, but it was hardly a question she could put to any of her Karien companions, and the reason hardly mattered anyway. Dark and slender, Jannis was barely more than a child and agreed with everyone, even when they disagreed with each other.

On the other side of the long trestle table set up in the large command tent was Palen, the Duke of Lake Isony. He was a lot smarter than he looked. He had the ruddy face of a peasant and the mind of a general,

Adrina decided. If Cratyn listened to his advice, he might even win this war. On Palen's right sat Ervin, the Duke of Windhaven. His purpose seemed entirely decorative. He was dressed in blue velvet with snowy lace collar and cuffs, and spent more time fiddling with his moustaches than he did taking part in the conversation. When he did speak up it was usually on a point that had been passed over ten minutes before.

Next to Ervin was a stout, middle-aged man with a patch over one eye. The Duke of Nerlin, Wherland had the unfortunate nickname of Whirlin' Nerlin, but he was an experienced fighter, having spent time in the gulf fighting Fardohnyan pirates. His advice was always preceded with the comment, "When I was in the navy . . .". But he wasn't a fool, and when he finally figured out how to fight on dry land, he would be a dangerous opponent.

The last of the Dukes should have been Chastity's father Terbolt, the Duke of Setenton; however, he had sent his brother, Lord Ciril, in his place. A heavier version of his older brother, Ciril did not look surprised at her inclusion. He had already suffered through her unwelcome presence when she visited his brother's castle on the way to Yarnarrow. Adrina wondered why Terbolt had stayed at home, hoping there was nothing sinister in his unexplained absence. As for Ciril, she marked him as a stolid, if unimaginative knight, who would advise caution, but would see any battle plan through to the bitter end.

She said nothing during the first meeting of the council and had, via Tamylan, advised Tristan to do the same. If they asked him a direct question, she translated it for him and then dutifully repeated his answers to the Dukes. To his credit, Tristan gave no sign that he understood a word of the discussion going on around him, even when the Kariens suggested things that, under normal circumstances, would have made him laugh out loud. By the time the meeting broke up, nothing had been decided, and there were eight dukes with eight different ideas as to how the battle should be engaged, well, seven in reality—Jannis agreed with everyone—and one very confused young prince.

When the tent finally emptied, leaving Cratyn and Adrina alone, she turned to him with a hopeful smile.

"It is the right time in my cycle, your Highness. Can I expect you tonight?"

"I'll see. I have a lot to do."

"Of course, however, it's been several months now and we still haven't consummated our union. Perhaps here, on the battlefield, you might find the . . . fortitude . . . to get the job done."

Cratyn glared at her, his expression a mixture of hatred and despair. "Don't push me, Adrina."

"Push you, husband? I doubt pushing you would achieve any more than pulling your limp sword has so far."

"You taunt me at your peril, Adrina."

She laughed. "Peril? What peril? What are you going to do, Cretin? Hit me again?"

"I'm warning you . . ."

"Does your sword get hard when you think of Chastity, my dear?"

Cratyn flew out his chair and turned to face her. He was red faced with shame and shaking with fury. "Don't you even *mention* her name, you pagan whore! I'm not fooled by this act you are putting on! If I cannot lie with you, it is because the Overlord does not wish me to sully myself in your filth!"

Adrina took a step backwards, her hand on Tiler's collar. The dog took exception to Cratyn's tone and he was growling softly, warningly.

"Perhaps you're right, Cretin. Perhaps you *are* cast in the image of your god. He's undoubtedly an emasculated idiot, too."

Cratyn snatched up a map from the table and made a show of studying it. His hands were shaking with suppressed rage. "Return to your tent, Adrina, and take that damned beast with you. I will come to you when the Overlord assures me the time is right, not to satisfy your crude heathen lust."

"*Lust*? Now there's a word I never thought to associate with you. Are you sure you know what it means?"

"Get out."

"Get out, *your Highness*," she corrected.

He slammed the map onto the table. "Get out! Go back to your tent and stay there! I will not tolerate your pagan disrespect a moment longer!"

His shout had Tiler lunging against her hold. He bared his teeth at the prince defiantly.

"Don't you dare take that tone with me, you impotent fool! I am a Princess of Fardohnya!"

"You are a heathen slut," he cried angrily.

She could not hold Tiler any longer. He slipped her hold and lunged for the prince. Cratyn threw his hand up to protect his face as the dog flew at him. His cry brought the guards running from outside the tent.

It almost happened too quickly for Adrina to see. Tiler had Cratyn pinned against the table. The guards saw nothing but their prince under attack. Adrina saw the blade in the hand of the guard and screamed as she realized what they intended. She threw herself at the dog, but the guards were quicker. Tiler squealed with agony as the guard ran him through.

"No!" she sobbed as the dog slid to the ground.

"Sire? Are you all right?" the guard asked with concern as he helped Cratyn up. Tiler had savaged his arm, but he had managed to fend off the worst of the attack.

"You killed my dog!" Adrina accused, unaware of the tears coursing down her face. "I want him punished, Cretin! He killed my dog!"

"Your damned dog was trying to kill me!" Cratyn gasped, still shaking from fear and shock. "I'm more inclined to knight him."

Adrina brushed away her tears and gently kissed Tiler's limp head before climbing to her feet.

"You'll pay for this," she warned, then she turned and walked out of the tent with all the regal bearing her breeding and ancestry allowed.

When she reached her own tent she dismissed her ladies-in-waiting impatiently and called for Tam. When her maid found her, she was tearing at the laces of her bodice impatiently, sobbing inconsolably.

"Here, let me do that," Tam offered, as she saw Adrina struggling. The princess knocked the offered hand away.

"No! I can do it myself! I want you to go and see Tristan. We're getting out of here."

The young woman studied her closely. "Out of here? How?"

"I haven't the faintest idea. But we're leaving and I don't care what it does to the alliance, to the war, or to my father. I've had enough!"

"We're a thousand leagues from home in the middle of a battlefield on the border of an enemy nation," Tamylan pointed out. "Where are you planning to go, your Highness?"

Adrina glared at her in annoyance, then sagged onto her bed. It was a large four-poster that had taken a full team of oxen to bring it to the front. One of the trappings of her station designed to inconvenience Cratyn.

"I don't know," she sniffed, wiping her eyes. "Oh, Tam, they killed Tiler!"

The slave opened her arms and she sobbed against Tamylan's shoulder hopelessly. Grief was a new emotion for Adrina. She had never before lost a living soul she had loved.

"There, there, I know it hurts, but it will pass in time," Tam advised.

Adrina wiped her eyes and sat up determinedly. "I can't do this any more, Tamylan. I don't care if there's a crown at the end of it. I cannot bear these people. It's like a prison."

"I understand, your Highness, but think it through before you act too hastily. This might be a prison, but it's a sight more comfortable than the one awaiting you on the other side of the border, or worse, if you were caught by the Kariens trying to run away."

Adrina looked up at the slave who had been by her side for as long as she could remember. "You always did say more than was proper for a slave."

"That's because I've always been your friend first, Adrina."

Adrina smiled wanly. "Even though you were my slave?"

"Slavery is a state of mind, your Highness," she shrugged. "You're a princess, yet you've less freedom than I have. I never minded being a slave. It just meant that I knew where I stood."

After Tamylan left, Adrina lay on the bed and thought on what the slave had said. She was right. Even being a princess didn't stop you from being used by other people for their own ends, or save you from being hurt. If anything, it made you more vulnerable. Well, enough was enough. She would find a way out of this and she would never, as long as she lived, ever allow a man to hurt her again.

And by the gods, she vowed, she would make Cratyn pay.

part two

BATTLE LINES

chapter 21

Loclon may have been responsible for letting Medalon's most notorious criminal escape, but his expertise with a blade was widely acknowledged. Commandant Arkin assigned him to the cadets. His days were spent in the Arena teaching future Defenders the finer points of swordplay.

Following his initial annoyance at not being assigned to active duty, he found he enjoyed the job. He had regained his fitness quickly. The cadets were in awe of both his skill and his fearsome scars, and the rumor that he had killed a man in the Arena enhanced his reputation considerably.

The work gave Loclon a rare feeling of omnipotence. While they were in his charge, he had the power of life and death over these young men, and he wielded it liberally. Demerits were earned easily in his classes and, almost without exception, the cadets treated him with gratifying obsequiousness to avoid incurring his wrath. Of course, there was the odd dissenter. Occasionally, a cadet would fancy himself a cut above the rest of his classmates. There was one such foolhardy soul in the Infirmary now. His temerity had cost him his right eye. Commandant Geendel, the officer in charge of the cadets, had demanded an explanation, of course, but the word of an officer was always taken over the word of a mere cadet.

Loclon smiled to himself as he rode through the Citadel toward his lodgings, thinking of the expressions on the cadets' faces when he had appeared in the Arena this morning. No doubt they had all been hoping Geendel would relieve him of his duty. Well, they had learnt a valuable lesson today. In the Defenders, the officers would always close ranks around their own. Loclon had learnt that lesson the hard way, too.

On impulse, Loclon turned down Tavern Street, deciding he owed himself a drink to celebrate his victory over the cadets. He reined in outside the Blue Bull Tavern, handed his mount over to a waiting stableboy and walked inside, his boots echoing hollowly on the wooden verandah. Business was slow this early, but he spied a familiar figure hugging his ale near the fireplace. He ordered ale from the barkeep and crossed the room to join his friend.

"Gawn."

The captain looked up. "Loclon. Finished for the day?"

Loclon nodded and took the seat opposite. Although Gawn had been a year or two ahead of Loclon when they were cadets, their friendship was a recent one. They had discovered they shared a loathing of Tarja Tenragan that few in the Defenders understood. Gawn had spent time on the southern border with Tarja and blamed him for just about everything that happened to him while he was there, starting with an arrow he took during a Hythrun raid, to the tavern keeper's daughter he had impregnated and been forced to marry.

Loclon had met the girl once, a slovenly, lazy slut who spoke with a thick southern accent. To make matters worse, the child had been stillborn and Gawn was left with a wife he loathed, who would hold back his career just as surely as Tarja and R'shiel's escape from the Grimfield would hold back Loclon's.

"I heard there was some trouble with a cadet."

Loclon shrugged. "Nothing I can't handle. What are you doing here so early?"

"Parenor was called to a meeting with Commandant Arkin." Captain Parenor was the Citadel's Quartermaster. Gawn had been assigned as his adjutant on his return to the Citadel. It was an administrative position and a grave insult to a battle-experienced officer. "They are asking for even more supplies on the border."

Nobody in the Citadel was exactly sure what was really happening on the northern border. Near half the Defenders in the Citadel had been sent north, supposedly to push back an attack by the Kariens. The reason the Kariens were attacking varied, according to which rumors one believed. Loclon believed the one that fitted with his own view of the world—that the Kariens were invading to avenge the death of their Envoy at Tarja's hand. But it did not explain Tarja's reinstatement to the Defenders, or the sudden alliance with the Warlord of Krakandar, or the First Sister's change of heart. Even Gawn, who knew the southern border well, was at a loss to explain how near a thousand Hythrun Raiders could cross into Medalon without being noticed.

"I heard something else today that might interest you."

"What's that?"

"The Warlord of Elasapine crossed into Medalon with five hundred Raiders and placed himself at the disposal of Commandant Verkin in Bordertown, supposedly to help fight off an expected attack by the Fardohnyans."

"I though we were fighting the Kariens?"

"Apparently, the Fardohnyan king married one of his daughters to Prince Cratyn. Parenor is furious because now Verkin is sending in supply requisitions that he can't fill, and the local merchants have got wind of the fact. The price of grain has doubled in the past month."

Loclon could not have cared less about the price of grain, but it irked him that he was sitting here in the Citadel while there was a war going on.

"If we have to fight on two fronts, they'll need every officer they can get their hands on. You and I might finally get a chance to do what we were trained for, my friend."

"Instead of me pushing parchment around and you nursemaiding a bunch of homesick cadets? I'll drink to that!" Gawn swallowed his ale in a gulp. Loclon signalled the barkeep for another but the captain shook his head. "Better not, Loclon. If I don't get home soon she'll be after me with a carving knife. Founders, how I loathe that bitch!"

Loclon smiled sympathetically. "Why go home at all?"

"I've not the money for any other sort of entertainment. She takes every rivet I earn. Speaking of which, could you fix up the tavern keeper for me? I'm afraid I've overspent, somewhat."

"Very well," he agreed, thinking of what Gawn already owed him. The amount did not bother him. He had no problem with cash these days, but it was time Gawn did something to earn such generosity. "On one condition. You come with me to Mistress Heaner's tonight."

Gawn pulled a face. "If I can't afford to pay my tavern bill, how do you expect me to afford that sort of place?"

Loclon smiled. "The same way I do, my friend."

When Loclon had woken up in the Blue Room in Mistress Heaner's House of Pleasure, he had discovered, somewhat to his annoyance, that the redheaded whore was no longer breathing. Worse, he felt no relief. Killing her had done little to ease his torment. Peny had been too dull, too plain, too fat, and too damned ordinary to satisfy him. Even in his imagination, she had been a poor substitute for R'shiel. He lay there for a time, wondering what it was going to cost him to keep Mistress Heaner from having him kneecapped. She did not care about murder, but she did care about her assets and Loclon had just deprived her of one.

This was not the first time Loclon had killed one of Mistress Heaner's *court'esa*, but on the previous occasions he had been a champion in the Arena, and his winnings had provided him with the funds to pay whatever she asked in compensation. This time, however, he had spent everything he owned and was not due to be paid for another month. At the interest rate she charged, the debt would have doubled by that time. He was still pondering the problem when the door opened and Mistress Heaner entered the room, followed by Lork, her faithful bodyguard. Lork gave a reasonable impression of a living mountain, his dead eyes reflecting little intelligence and undying loyalty to the woman who employed him. Mistress Heaner held up the lamp and glanced at Peny with a shake of her head, before turning to Loclon.

"You've been careless, Captain."

"I'm sorry, Mistress. I shall see that you're compensated."

"With what, Captain? You've no career in the Arena any more. On a captain's pay, you can't afford a drink here, let alone indulge your rather exotic tastes."

Loclon swung his feet onto the floor and snatched his trousers up. "I said, I will see that you are paid, Madam, and I shall. Do you question the word of an Officer of the Defenders?"

"I question the word of any man who beats women to death for pleasure, Captain," she retorted coldly. "Perhaps I should just have Lork kill you now, and save myself any further trouble." Lork flexed his plate-sized hands in anticipation.

Loclon glanced at his sword that lay on the other side of the room, knowing there was no way he could reach it before the man was on him. "Perhaps we might come to . . . an arrangement?"

Mistress Heaner laughed. "What could you offer me, Captain, that I don't already have in abundance? Kill him, Lork."

Loclon jumped to his feet, but Lork moved with remarkable speed for one so huge. He had grabbed Loclon by the throat and slammed him against the wall with one hand. Loclon gasped from the pressure, his feet dangling as the big man squeezed the life out of him. He discovered he was sobbing, begging for mercy in a voice that was quickly losing strength. He was on the point of losing consciousness when Mistress Heaner stepped forward and signalled Lork to release him. The big man suddenly released him and Loclon dropped to his hands and knees, sobbing with fear.

"Perhaps there *is* something you can do for me, Captain."

"Anything!" he croaked, gulping for air. He wiped his streaming eyes and looked up at her.

"Anything? A careless promise, Captain."

"Anything you ask," he repeated desperately.

Mistress Heaner studied him for a moment, then nodded. "Bring him, Lork."

Lork grabbed hold of him again and half-dragged, half-carried Loclon down the hall to a narrow flight of stairs that led to the basement. Mistress Heaner led the way, holding the lamp, which threw fitful shadows onto the walls. Lork dropped him heavily and he spat dirt from his mouth as he looked around.

"Get rid of the body," the woman told her henchman. "And see that we are not disturbed."

Lork grunted in reply and returned upstairs. Mistress Heaner ignored Loclon and walked to the far end of the dark basement. She removed the glass from the lantern and lit a taper from the small flame, which she used to light a row of thick beeswax candles lining a long narrow table. He stared at the candles with growing horror as they illuminated a richly embroidered wall hanging that depicted the five-pointed star and lightning bolt of Xaphista, the Overlord.

"You're a heathen!"

"Heathens believe in the Primal gods," she corrected. "I serve Xaphista, the one true God. As will you."

Loclon climbed unsteadily to his feet. "No. I won't join your sick cult. I'll report you for this."

Mistress Heaner finished lighting the candles and turned to him. "*You'll* report *me*? Perhaps you should consider your situation more carefully, Captain. You might be able to walk away from murder in the Arena, sir, but I doubt your superiors will be quite so understanding about Peny's fate."

"I'm an Officer in the Defenders! I can't countenance this!"

"You are a monster who kills for pleasure, Captain," she reminded him. "I don't recall that being a virtue the Defenders hold dear."

"I don't believe in your god."

"A point that is quite irrelevant," she shrugged. "You *will* serve him, however, whether you believe in him or not."

"How?"

Mistress Heaner smiled, correctly interpreting his question as the beginning of his surrender. "The Overlord is a generous god. In return for your service, he will see that you are taken care of. All you have to do is keep me informed as to what is happening among the Defenders. Report any rumors you hear. Perhaps secure a document or two. I may even need you to kill, occasionally, something you have already proved is to your liking."

"That's treason!"

"You baulk at treason, yet you don't seem to mind murder. A curious moral stance, don't you think?"

"And if I refuse?"

"I believe we've already covered that."

Loclon stared at the symbol of the Overlord and thought over Mistress Heaner's offer. For all his faults, he believed in the Defenders and had been raised to think of anyone who practised heathen worship as a traitor to his nation. The decision was surprisingly hard to make.

"Perhaps I can offer you another incentive, Captain," she said softly. "You and the Overlord do share a common purpose, you know."

"What purpose?"

"You've heard of the demon child?"

Loclon turned to her, a little confused by the sudden change of subject. "Everybody has. It's just a stupid legend. The rebels claimed it was Tarja."

"The heathens were wrong, as they are about so many things. There is a demon child, however, and she was created to destroy Xaphista. Naturally, my god would like to see that she does not live long enough to fulfil her destiny."

"She?"

"The demon child is an old friend of yours, I believe. Her name is R'shiel."

Loclon started as a sudden image of black eyes and a cold blade slicing his throat filled his vision. He could hear Mistress Heaner laughing softly as the rage consumed him, blood pounding in his ears.

"Ah, you remember her, I see. Your service to the Overlord will provide you with an opportunity to redress the wrongs done you by R'shiel té Ortyn, Captain. A convenient arrangement on both sides, don't you think?"

In the months that had passed since then, Loclon never wanted for anything. His rent was paid on time by an anonymous donor. He often arrived home to find a small purse sitting on his side table, filled with gold rivets. He was welcomed at Mistress Heaner's and was never asked for payment, although he had been careful not to kill another *court'esa*. In fact, the urge had dissipated somewhat, now that the promise of a chance at R'shiel was in the offing. He no longer considered his actions treasonous. He had been offered a chance for revenge, a chance the Defenders had refused him. That justified everything.

But teaching cadets meant there was a limit to the information Loclon was privy to, and Mistress Heaner was growing impatient with him. Gawn, on the other hand, was far better placed to provide the intelligence she demanded. By bringing Gawn into the fold, his position would be secured and his chance at R'shiel would be certain.

Of course, he needed to find something to convince Gawn to join them, and as he settled his companion's account with the barkeep, it came to him. In return for his service to the Overlord, Loclon would relieve Gawn of his most onerous possession.

He would kill his wife for him.

chapter 22

Tarja lay awake for most of the night, simply watching R'shiel sleeping, thinking it was a pastime he would never tire of. In sleep her expression was peaceful, her breathing steady and even. The faint, familiar sounds of the camp slowly coming awake as dawn approached filtered through the canvas walls of his tent. Reality intruded rudely into his own, private, perfect world. He almost felt guilty for being so happy.

He also knew it would not last. They were on the brink of war and liable to be hanged for treason. The Gathering was almost on them and Garet Warner was already talking of returning to the Citadel to make his report. Damin kept fingering his sword threateningly every time Garet mentioned the subject, still of the opinion that the safest course of action was to slit the commandant's throat.

The rebels were growing restless, too. The shaky truce brought about in Testra was in danger of falling apart. Tarja felt responsible for the rebels, but his position here was ambiguous. He had been welcomed back into the Defenders, his desertion if not forgiven, then at least not mentioned, yet too much had happened for him to follow orders without question as he once had done. He was walking a fine line between loyalty to the Defenders and the responsibility he felt for the rebels who had put their lives in his hands because they believed he could help them.

And now R'shiel was back.

He loved R'shiel. He knew it as surely as he knew how to take his next breath, but he could not say why that night in the old vineyard in

Testra a year ago, he had suddenly realized it. He could remember wanting to strangle her. They were fighting, something that until that moment they had done a great deal. R'shiel was trying to get even with Joyhinia and did not particularly care how many rebels' lives she spent doing it. Tarja remembered wanting to slap some sense into her one moment, wanting to die in her arms the next. It bothered him a little. He felt no guilt that he had grown up thinking she was his sister. No thought that would in any way cloud his love for her seemed able to take root in his mind.

He reached across to gently lift an errant strand of long, dark red hair that had fallen over her face, then froze as he felt something move under the blanket. Certain he had not imagined it, he threw back the covers and yelped with astonishment. His cry woke R'shiel with a jerk.

"What in the name of the Founders is *that*!"

R'shiel glanced down sleepily. A small gray creature lay curled between them, seeking the warmth of their bodies, although Tarja's yell had obviously frightened it. With an incomprehensible chitter it scrambled up the pallet and wrapped its thin gray arms tightly around R'shiel's neck, staring accusingly at him with black eyes too large for its wrinkled gray head.

"It's only a demon," R'shiel laughed, peeling the creature off so that she could breathe.

"*Only* a demon?" Tarja asked, his heart still pounding.

She laughed again, a rich, throaty laugh that Tarja had not heard from her in a very long time. "It's bonded to the té Ortyn bloodline and I was the first té Ortyn it saw, I suppose."

"So . . . what . . . it thinks you're its mother?"

"Demons don't have mothers, silly. They . . . just . . . come into being. She won't be able to speak or do much at all until she's melded with the other demons a few times."

"She?" he wondered doubtfully, as he stared at the androgynous little creature. "How can you tell?"

"I can't," R'shiel shrugged, pulling the demon off her neck again as it tried to hide in her long hair. "Demons don't have genders, not really. They just sort of decide along the way somewhere. I just have a feeling this one wants to be a girl."

"You sound quite the expert." Nothing could have made the change in R'shiel more obvious, or pointed to what she was, than waking to find a demon in his bed.

"It's a necessary virtue, when you've got demons following you around everywhere you go. You're lucky there's only one in the bed. They were as thick as flies in Sanctuary."

He looked at her curiously, wondering if she would elaborate. She had said little in the days since her sudden return. Not, he thought wryly, that they'd spent a lot of time talking. But her time there had wrought a noticeable change in her. She was more certain of herself. Perhaps she had finally accepted what she was. Perhaps the Harshini had done something to her besides healing the wound that almost killed her, and they had certainly done that well. Not even a hint of a scar marred the golden skin below her breast where Joyhinia had thrust Jenga's discarded sword into her.

"I can feel it, you know," she added softly in the darkness, as if she knew what he was thinking. "It's like there's a tether linking me to Sanctuary that nothing can break. I think if I was lost in a snowstorm, I'd still be able to find it." She sighed wistfully. "I used to feel it when I was in the Citadel, but I never knew what it was. Which was probably a blessing," she added with a smile.

He wondered if this was how it would be. Would she tell him, bit by tantalising bit, or would he never hear the whole story of her stay in the magical halls of the Harshini? The little demon started chattering again, pulling on her hair. He knew he would learn nothing more for the time being.

"Is this," he asked, pointing at the little demon with a scowl, "an event that we can look forward to on a regular basis? Waking to find demons in our bed?"

"It could have been worse, Tarja. There could have been half a dozen of them melded into a cactus, or worse."

"Worse?"

"Well, they could have melded into a dragon," she laughed. "Or a snow cat, or a Karien knight in full armour or a beehive, or a—"

"What?" he cut in abruptly. Something she said sparked the germ of an idea in his mind, but it was elusive. It hovered on the edge of his awareness, just out of reach.

"I was kidding, Tarja," she said, looking at him oddly. "I'll speak to

Dranymire. He'll keep the demons out of our bed if it bothers you so much."

"No, I didn't mean that. You were talking about the demons melding."

"But I didn't really mean they'd do it—"

"But they can meld into anything, can't they?" he asked, afraid to give voice to the idea in case she thought him insane.

"I suppose," she agreed, a little doubtfully.

"Or anyone?"

"*Who* exactly?"

Tarja sat up and began pulling on his clothes hurriedly. "Get dressed. We have to talk to Brak."

"Tarja! What are you up to?"

"I'm not sure yet," he told her as he tugged on his boots. "I need to talk to Brak first. Hurry up!"

She threw her hands up in disgust, but did as he asked, although she was still lacing her vest as he hurried her out into the chill morning. The little demon had vanished, thankfully—at least Tarja hoped it had. The idea of one of his men waking to find an inquisitive demon poking around in his equipment did not bear thinking about.

"Tarja!" R'shiel demanded as she ran to catch up. "What's this about?"

"I've got an idea, but I need to find out if it's possible," he explained, as he strode through the waking camp toward the old Keep. Pink fingers scratched at the sky as dawn clawed its way over the Jagged Mountains.

"Maybe if you shared this brilliant idea, I could tell you."

He grinned at her as he strode past the guards in front of the Keep, but did not answer. He pushed open the door to the old great hall and strode toward the huge hearth at the far end, and a small figure curled up near the dying embers.

"Boy!" he snapped, jerking the Karien lad awake. "Find Lord Brakandaran and tell him I need to see him urgently!"

The child nodded hastily and scrambled off the hearth. He was running by the time he reached the door.

"You bully! That child is terrified of you!"

"I know," he agreed, taking the poker to stir some life back into the coals. "I threatened to chop his brother's fingers off."

"*Why?*"

He stopped stoking the fire and looked at her. "Because he's a fanatical believer in the Overlord and if I hadn't put an end to his antics, somebody would have killed him. Better to be terrified of me and live long enough to reach manhood, than find himself skewered by a Hythrun sword."

She smiled at him then and moved closer. She smelled of summer and leather and their lovemaking. It was a heady and very distracting combination.

"Don't you ever get tired of being so damned noble?" she teased.

He found himself unable to think of a suitably witty retort as she slid her arms around his neck and kissed him. He dropped the poker with a clatter as rational thought began to slip away, wondering what else the Harshini had taught her. Either that, or R'shiel had inherited that magical race's rather legendary libido.

"Can't you two make up for lost time somewhere else?"

He felt her smile as she broke off the kiss and turned to look at Brak. The Harshini rebel was shaking his head at them. The Karien boy looked mortified.

"Hello Brak," R'shiel said, making no attempt to leave the circle of his arms. "We weren't expecting you so soon."

"That's obvious. I was heading this way when the boy found me."

Tarja somewhat reluctantly let R'shiel go and glared at the boy. "Shoo! Go find us some breakfast!"

Mikel nodded wordlessly and fled. Brak watched him go with a frown. "I think you actually enjoy tormenting that child, Tarja."

"I'm an evil, barbarian bastard. I have a reputation to uphold."

Brak shook his head at the folly of humans. "The boy said you wanted to see me."

"I need to know about demon melds," he explained, throwing a small log on the fire as the exposed embers glowed red in the dim hall. The dawn striped the long chilly hall with slices of dull light and their breath formed small misty clouds as they spoke.

Brak glanced at R'shiel who shrugged, her expression confused.

"Would you care to be a bit more specific?" the Harshini asked. "If we had a week, I could tell you a tenth of what I know."

"Can they take on a human form?"

"I can't imagine why they'd want to, but they could do it."

"Can they imitate people? Take on a specific form?"

Brak's eyes narrowed suspiciously. "I've got a bad feeling I know where this is leading, Tarja, but yes, they can imitate people. Before you get too enamored of the idea, let me explain a few things. The more complex the shape, the more demons it takes, and the shorter length of time they can hold the meld. If you're thinking of doing what I suspect you're thinking of doing, it won't work. A human form is hard enough. To create one that walks and talks convincingly would take dozens of demons and you'd be lucky if they could maintain it for more than a few hours.

"That's assuming they would agree to such an idiotic idea. Then you have the problem of getting the meld to act the way you want. Your demon meld could say the wrong thing at the wrong time and blow the whole illusion."

"But it's theoretically possible, isn't it?" Tarja insisted.

Brak nodded reluctantly. "Theoretically."

R'shiel listened to the conversation, her eyes wide. "Founders! You're thinking of replacing Joyhinia with a *demon* meld?"

"Not permanently," he told them, trying hard to contain his enthusiasm. "Just long enough to get through the Gathering. If Joyhinia can stand up in front of the Gathering then she can appoint Mahina as the new First Sister."

R'shiel stared at him and then at Brak, her mind obviously racing. "It might work."

Brak threw his hands up in despair. "*R'shiel!* You're as bad as he is! *Think* about it. The only way it would work is if you went with the demons to the Citadel. And you'd need Joyhinia with you, too—they couldn't copy her convincingly with her so far away. You'd be putting everyone in danger, starting with yourself. Besides, Dranymire would never agree to anything so dangerous. The demons are bonded with the Harshini to protect them, R'shiel. Not aid them in committing suicide."

R'shiel seemed unfazed by Brak's tirade. "I didn't say it would be easy, Brak. I just said it might work."

The Harshini shook his head in disgust. "Korandellan must have suppressed your ability to think, along with your emotions, R'shiel."

Tarja glanced at R'shiel curiously, wondering what he meant. R'shiel simply shrugged. "Zegarnald said I needed toughening up, Brak. Just think of this as . . . training. Of course, if you don't want to help—"

Brak sighed heavily. "Gods! I don't believe this. This is rank stupidity. It is insane."

Tarja nodded in agreement, his enthusiasm for the idea waning a little at the thought of sending R'shiel to the Citadel. He had not considered that when the idea came to him. Perhaps it was a crazy idea. "Well, it was worth suggesting. But I won't do anything to endanger R'shiel."

"It's not your place to decide what might endanger me. Besides, it might well be the only chance we have." R'shiel's enthusiasm for the idea seemed to be increasing in direct proportion to his growing reluctance.

"Listen to Tarja," Brak told her. "You might be the demon child, but you're a long way from being invincible. It was worth considering, but it won't work. Forget it."

"You're right, it would never work," she agreed, capitulating with suspicious speed. "We'll have to think of something else."

Before he could question her willingness to drop the matter so easily, the Karien boy returned bearing a tray with steaming mugs of tea. Tarja took the tray from the lad before he dropped it and handed out the mugs. R'shiel smiled at him innocently over the rim as she sipped the steaming brew.

But something about that smile, full of ingenuous sweetness, sent a shiver of apprehension tingling down his spine.

chapter 23

ikel emptied the bucket of water from the well in the corner of the old Keep's yard into another bucket, grumbling as the icy water splashed his trousers. Today was not going well at all.

First, Tarja had so rudely awakened him to find Lord Brakandaran, and then Mahina had snapped at him for being late with her tea. And then the soldiers on the Keep gate had teasingly refused to let him pass when she sent him with a message for Lord Jenga. And then Lord Jenga had yelled at him when he almost got himself trampled by the horses milling about in one of the vast corrals south of the camp.

No, today was not going well at all.

To add to his misery, the atmosphere in the Defenders' camp had changed noticeably following the return of the Hythrun Warlord and his two unexpected companions. For one thing, Tarja was smiling a lot these days, which made him a little less fearsome but did not alter Mikel's loathing for him. If anything, it increased it. How *dare* he look so smug! As for the pair who had returned with Damin Wolfblade, Mikel had been horrified to hear someone say they were Harshini.

Mikel found that hard to swallow. Did they think him a child to believe such wild stories? Everybody knew that the Harshini were monsters with wart-covered skin, sharp pointed teeth and drooling mouths who ate wicked Karien children, particularly if they wavered in their devotion to the Overlord. Lord Brakandaran looked just like any other man and the pretty lady was more beautiful than Lady Chastity, so she couldn't possibly be a Harshini monster. Mahina had introduced her as

Lady R'shiel and warned him to treat her with respect, or suffer the consequences. The Lady had smiled at him pleasantly, but otherwise paid him little attention. Had it not been for her obvious attachment to Tarja, he could have almost allowed himself to like her.

Mikel hefted the bucket and turned toward the hall, muttering miserably to himself, but he had only taken a few steps when a scratching sound behind the well caught his attention. Glancing around to ensure he was unobserved, he put down the bucket and walked cautiously around the stone lip of the well. A heap of rubble from the crumbled outer wall was piled up on the other side. He heard the sound again and moved toward the source, wondering if it was a cat, or perhaps a fox who had inadvertently wandered into the Keep. He hoped it was a cat. He liked cats. Perhaps he could catch it and keep it for a pet . . .

The area near the well was one of the warmest in the Keep, with the forge on the other side of the wall. It would be a good place to hide. Mikel listened hard, trying to hear over the rhythmic clanging coming from the smiths on the other side. The scratching sound came again, louder this time, from a dark hole formed by the fallen masonry. With a careful hand, Mikel reached into the darkness.

Whatever it was, it bit him with a force that made him cry out in pain. He scrambled backwards around the well, tripped over the bucket and landed on his backside in a puddle of icy mud. His hand was bleeding profusely and throbbing, and tears of fright and pain and humiliation were streaming down his face. Laughter wafted down from the guards on the wall-walk who had looked down at the commotion. A gray streak emerged from the rubble with a screech and bolted past him toward the Keep. He watched it race past and into the arms of the Lady R'shiel.

She caught the creature with a smile and turned to Mikel. "Don't worry, I think you frightened her as much as she frightened you."

Mikel stared at the little monster with wide eyes. He didn't know what it was, but it was clinging to R'shiel, chattering unintelligibly in a screeching voice and pointing at him with huge black accusing eyes.

"Oh look, you're hurt."

She shooed the creature away and it literally vanished into thin air. Mikel traced the star of the Overlord on his forehead to ward off evil as the Lady walked over to him and squatted down, smiling reassuringly.

"Here, let me look at it," she said. He held out his throbbing hand wordlessly, too afraid to do anything else. She took his hand in her own and almost instantly the pain vanished. He snatched his hand back in astonishment. The bite was gone, the skin as smooth as if it had never been broken.

Mikel screamed.

R'shiel waved back a curious guard come to see what all the fuss was about. She sat back on her heels until he ran out of breath, then smiled.

"Feeling better?"

"Wha—what did you do to me?" he demanded. Had she used magic on him? Would he be condemned to drown in the Sea of Despair for eternity because she had infected him with evil spirits? Mikel was weak with fear at the prospect. "You used the power of the pagan gods on me!"

"Never fear, little one, it's the same power as that of the Overlord, so it shouldn't do you any lasting harm."

Mikel shrank away from her. She did not look like a monster, but she could use magic—and the little creature, who was obviously some sort of evil-spawned monster, had run to her for comfort. *Perhaps she was Harshini. Maybe under those close-fitting leathers was warty skin that peeled when you touched it and gave you diseases that had no cure and made you do nasty things to people and turned you into—*

"I said, your name is Mikel, isn't it?"

Mikel forced away the terrifying images that filled his head. He nodded, afraid that if he did not answer her, she would turn him into a beetle.

"And your brother? Where is he?"

Mikel's eyes narrowed at the question. *Why does she want to know that?*

"The Hythrun have him," he told her sullenly.

"It must be pretty scary for you, Mikel. You're a long way from home and surrounded by strangers. I know how that feels."

Try as he did to despise her, he knew she meant what she said. She really *did* understand how he felt. The thought frightened him. Had she used more magic on him? *There is only the Overlord*, he reminded himself. He was relieved when the prayer came so easily. Xaphista was still with him.

"Nothing scares me," he declared defiantly.

She laughed. "Maybe nothing does, at that. Are you all right now?"

He nodded and suffered her assistance as he climbed to his feet. As soon as she let him go, he snatched up his empty bucket and ran back to the hall as if all the demons of the Harshini were on his heels.

Several days later the Medalonians held their most important meeting since Mikel had been in the Defenders' camp. Everyone was in attendance. Tarja and Lord Jenga, Sister Mahina and Garet Warner, Ghari, Lord Wolfblade and the mean-looking Captain Almodavar, and Lord Brakandaran. The only one missing was the Lady R'shiel. Mikel did not know where she was. Perhaps even the Medalonians were afraid to share their battle plans with a Harshini magician. They obviously did not share the same feeling for the small Karien boy who served them. Mikel moved among the adults, filling wine cups and collecting empty platters left over from their meal. Nobody seemed to notice him. The hall was cold—it was not possible to seal all the cracks in the drafty old ruin—and torches sputtered fitfully, flaring occasionally as an errant draft fanned them into brightness. The fire did little to relieve the chill. If anything, it made the gathered people look more sinister, but if it was the cold or fear that made Mikel shiver, he could not say.

"This may sound like a stupid question," Lord Brakandaran was saying as Mikel silently filled his cup. "But has anyone thought to offer the Kariens a settlement?"

"*What*? You mean offer them *peace?*" the Hythrun Warlord gasped with mock horror. "Bite your tongue, man!"

"Perhaps not so stupid," Sister Mahina mused. "They must have realized by now that even if they win, it will be an expensive victory. Perhaps they would consider a peaceful settlement."

Tarja shook his head. "I doubt it, but I suppose it's worth a try."

"At the very least, it might delay them for a while," Jenga agreed. "That would take us well into winter before the first attack. Those big warhorses, weighted down with armor, will be a liability rather than an asset if it snows. Even a decent rainstorm will turn the battlefield into a quagmire."

"I'll be very disappointed if they agree," Damin said. "And surprised. They've too much at stake to withdraw at this point."

"You're right," Garet Warner said in his soft, dangerous voice, which seemed to startle the Warlord. Damin Wolfblade didn't seem to like the commandant much. "The banner flying over their command tent is Cratyn's, not Jasnoff's. He's young and he needs to prove himself. Agreeing to a settlement would imply weakness. He won't back down."

"And what of the Fardohnyans?" Mahina asked. "Perhaps they might persuade him?"

Garet shook his head. "Again, I doubt it. They were sent to Karien as the Princess's Guard, and the first thing Adrina did was bring them to the border to aid her husband. They obviously share a common purpose."

"Adrina?" Damin Wolfblade asked in surprise. "I thought he married Cassandra?"

"He married Adrina," Brak confirmed. "She left Talabar with Cratyn several months ago. Her progress up the Ironbrook was something of an event, I hear."

"Gods!" Damin muttered. He looked concerned.

"Is that a problem?" Lord Jenga asked.

"It could be," Brak answered. "Adrina is Hablet's eldest legitimate child. Adrina's son could claim the Fardohnyan throne."

"Who cares?" Mahina asked. "Our problem is here and now, not whether or not there is a Karien heir to Fardohnya."

"Our problem could be Adrina herself," Damin warned them. "If she's half as bad as her reputation suggests, then she's the one to look out for, not Cratyn." The Warlord glanced at his captain, who nodded in agreement.

"Do you know her?" Tarja asked Damin curiously.

"No, thank the gods! She was in Greenharbour a couple of years ago for my uncle's birthday." Suddenly he grinned. "Despite my uncle's wishes, and a number of dangerously close calls, I managed to avoid an encounter with Her Serene Highness."

"How bad can the woman be?"

"Bad," Damin assured him. "She's got the body of a goddess and the heart of a hyena. Hablet offered a dowry beyond the dreams of avarice—and he still couldn't marry her off. Adrina married to the Karien Crown Prince is not a happy prospect. I wonder how poor Cratyn is coping."

"He can't be doing too badly," Garet said. "She's followed him to the front with her troops. Maybe she's found her soul mate."

"If she has, then I'm packing up and going home now," the Warlord announced, although Mikel didn't think he was serious.

"I'd like to meet the woman that makes you turn tail and run, Damin," Tarja chuckled.

"Does it really matter?" Mahina asked, obviously annoyed by the banter between Tarja and the Warlord. "We were discussing the advisability of sending an emissary to the Kariens, I believe?"

"Assuming we do, who would we send?" Jenga asked. "I'm in no mood to give them a hostage, should they not honor our flag of truce." Mikel was quite offended at the idea that his prince would do any such thing. How dare they impugn Cratyn's honor!

"What about the boy?" Lord Brakandaran suggested. All eyes turned to Mikel curiously. He quivered under their unrelenting gaze.

"Are you crazy?" Tarja said.

"It's no crazier than some ideas I've heard lately."

He turned back to the others to explain. "His return could be considered a gesture of good faith. The child has been here for months and he will tell the Kariens everything he's seen. It might give them pause, even if your offer of peace falls on deaf ears."

"But he's a child," Jenga objected.

"All the more reason to send him home."

All eyes turned at the sound of the imperious voice and Mikel was suddenly forgotten. The Crazy Lady descended the stairs regally, dressed in a long, high-necked white gown. She had icy blue eyes and a haughty expression and surveyed the room as if everyone in it was beneath contempt.

"You will bow in the presence of the First Sister!" she snapped.

Instinctively, the stunned Medalonians almost did as she demanded. Lord Wolfblade's jaw was hanging slackly in astonishment and Tarja wore an expression of such hatred that it made Mikel take a step backwards. Only Lord Brakandaran did not seem startled by her appearance.

"Impressive, Lord Dranymire," he said.

Suddenly the Crazy Lady seemed to wobble and her expression changed from contempt to amusement.

"Spoilsport!" R'shiel accused, stepping out of the shadows on the staircase. She looked at the others who still sat frozen in various poses ranging from amazement to outright shock, and laughed. "You should see your faces!"

"Humans are far too easy to impress," the Crazy Lady remarked, in a male voice much deeper than the one she had spoken with a moment ago.

Mikel was certain he had been swallowed up whole and sucked into some sort of pagan hell. The Crazy Lady wobbled again and Mikel watched in horror as she literally fell apart. Then the room was swarming with little gray creatures like the one that had bitten him by the well. The creatures fell about laughing in high twittering voices, as if they were privy to some marvellous prank. It was more than Mikel could cope with. He screamed in terror as the creatures neared him.

His scream brought the others out of their torpor. They all began talking at once but Mikel could make no sense of what they were saying. He did not try. He could hear someone crying and it took a little while to realize it was he. R'shiel walked toward him, pushing the monsters out of her way impatiently. He shied away from her in fear.

"I'm sorry, Mikel. I didn't mean to frighten you. They're demons, that's all. They won't hurt you." She turned impatiently. "You're scaring the poor child to death. Be gone!"

The demons vanished almost instantly, shocking the grown-ups almost as much as Mikel. "*The Overlord will protect me. The Overlord will protect me. The Overlord will protect me,*" he chanted softly as the tears streamed down his face.

"Let the boy take the message to the Kariens, Lord Jenga," she pleaded. "Send him home. He doesn't belong here."

Jenga looked at Brak uncertainly. "You said he would tell his people what he's seen here. Do you really want him to report what he's seen here tonight?"

Brak shrugged. "The Karien priests will know we are here soon enough. It might even give them pause."

"Or they won't believe him," Garet pointed out. "I certainly don't believe what I just saw."

A meaningful glance passed between the adults before Jenga turned on him. "Boy! Go get your gear packed. You're leaving first thing in the morning. You will take our offer of peace back to Prince Cratyn, is that clear?"

Mikel nodded. Tears of joy, as opposed to fright, threatened to unman him. "And . . . my brother?" he ventured cautiously.

"He stays," the Hythrun Warlord announced, before anybody else could answer. "He will be a hostage to your good behavior. If your prince accepts our offer, we'll send him home."

It would have been too much to hope for any other answer, although he wondered if he'd waited and asked the Lady R'shiel when she was alone, the result might have been different. But it was too late now.

Mikel nodded and the Lady R'shiel smiled at him reassuringly. He was going home. The Overlord had finally answered his prayers—some of them, at least. By tomorrow evening, he would be standing before his prince and his priests and he could finally tell them of the evil that resided south of the border in the camp of the Defenders.

chapter 24

They sent him back to the Karien camp mounted on a nondescript dun gelding. Tarja Tenragan and Damin Wolfblade escorted Mikel as far as the earthworks that were constructed along the front. It was the first close look Mikel had got of the Medalonian defenses. He tried to remember every detail to tell Prince Cratyn, but it wasn't easy with Damin on one side of him on a huge golden stallion, and Tarja on the other on a sleek black mare. As if they knew the reason for his swivelling head and wide eyes, they began to point out various features of the defenses to each other over the top of his head, describing in rather graphic and gory detail the effect they would have on any attacking Karien force.

The earthworks gave cover for a vast number of bowmen, Tarja explained cheerfully to the Warlord, which would decimate the vanguard of any Karien attack. Even if the knights were armored, their horses would founder under the rain of arrows. Each archer carried around fifty arrows, and if they took their time, they could keep up the deadly hail for an hour or more. Being trapped under a dead warhorse while it rained arrows was not a happy prospect, Damin agreed with relish. And, he added, if they were so foolish as to send unarmored men to lead the attack, it would be a massacre. Mikel tried very hard not to listen to them. They were teasing him, he knew, and his courage was growing stronger the closer he came to the border. The Overlord was with him and he was on his way home. There was nothing they could do to him that would quell his growing excitement.

"This is as far as we go, boy," Damin said eventually, reining his horse in as they reached the edge of the field that the Medalonians ominously referred to as the "killing ground." He looked down at Mikel and grinned. "Just head north, boy. You'll reach Karien sooner or later."

"And carry this," Tarja added, thrusting a broken spear into his hand, to which had been tied a scrap of white linen.

"My people won't harm me!" Mikel said, quite offended by the flag of truce. "I am going home!"

"You're going home wearing a Defender's uniform," Tarja pointed out. "I'm sure they won't kill you if they know who you are, but you're not going to get close enough to tell them, dressed like that. Take it." He looked across at Damin and added with a grin, "Mind you, they'd never believe a Defender could be so short."

Reluctantly, Mikel accepted the flag.

"You have the message?" Damin asked.

He nodded glumly and patted the bulge under his jacket where the sealed letter from Lord Jenga was securely tucked, as the two men he hated most in this world talked to him like a small child. They would ask if he'd washed behind his ears next!

"Then scat!" the Warlord said, slapping the flank of the gelding. The horse surged forward and Mikel nearly lost his seat as he galloped headlong toward the border.

Not an experienced rider, Mikel clung grimly to the pommel until he remembered to use the reins. The slightest touch and the well-trained cavalry mount slowed his headlong rush to a more manageable pace. With a sigh of relief, Mikel remembered the flag, and propped it up against his thigh as he rode through the waist-high grass of the no-man's land between the two camps. Although he did not know the exact location of the border, he knew that he would soon be in bow range of the Kariens, and he would be hard pressed to deliver his intelligence about the Medalonians with an arrow through his chest.

It annoyed him intensely that it had been Tarja who pointed that out.

He was still half a league or more from the camp when the Karien sentries found him. The sight of Lord Laetho's purple pennant, with its three tall pines worked in red, brought tears of relief, which he hastily brushed away as the knights approached. The Overlord was truly with him, he knew now. Not only had he been released, but he had sent his own people to meet him. Mikel was giddy with relief as the tall knight in the lead lifted his faceplate. It was Sir Andony, Laetho's nephew, newly knighted last summer and enormously proud of the fact. Andony studied him for a moment, waving away the drawn swords of his three companions.

"Sir Andony!" he cried, urging his horse forward.

"Mikel?" he asked in astonishment. "We thought you long dead, lad!"

"They sent me back. I have a message for the prince."

Andony frowned. "You seem remarkably well fed for someone kept prisoner these past months, boy. And you wear the uniform of the enemy."

Mikel glanced down at his rolled up Defender's trousers and the too-big, warm red jacket they had given him in the Medalonian camp. "They took my clothes and burned them. You must take me to the prince! I've seen so much, Sir! I have to tell him!"

Andony nodded, not entirely convinced. "Well, we'll see if Lord Laetho wants you to speak with his Highness. Come!"

Andony wheeled his big horse around and fell in beside Mikel. One of the other knights took station on his left and the other two fell in behind. Mikel rode into the Karien camp, not in triumph as he had dreamed, but a barely disguised prisoner.

"They offer peace," Prince Cratyn announced, throwing the parchment Mikel had delivered onto the long table in the command tent. Smoking torches threw tall shadows on the canvas walls, which made Mikel's eyes water. The braziers did little to warm the big tent.

"They offer nothing!" Lord Laetho corrected, pointing at the document with scorn. "They ask us to pack up and go home! They offer no compensation! They do not even apologise for murdering Lord Pieter!"

Mikel could not read, but even if he had been able, he had not been given an opportunity to examine the contents of the sealed document he had delivered. He wondered at Lord Laetho's interpretation of the offer. Sister Mahina had been quite hopeful that a peaceful solution might be reached.

"I wouldn't go quite that far," Lord Roache corrected. "But you're right, in that it is somewhat arrogant in its tone. The Medalonians appear to think they might prevail."

The full war council had convened upon hearing of the letter from the Defenders, even though it was the middle of the night. Mikel had spent the day being questioned by Lord Laetho and now stood just inside the flap of the command tent, chewing his bottom lip nervously. In his dreams, when he faced the war council, he had not been nervous, or cold, or afraid. Mikel glanced around, rubbing his eyes and trying not to yawn. The movement caught the eye of the tall Fardohnyan captain who stood opposite him on the other side of the tent, near the Princess Adrina. The man winked at him solemnly. The small gesture gave Mikel a much needed morale boost.

Princess Adrina had obviously dressed in a hurry. Her long dark hair was tied back with a plain blue ribbon and she wore a simple dress of fine gray wool, covered with a warm fur cloak. Mikel watched her, thinking that she was just as pretty as the Lady R'shiel, which was only proper, since she was married to Prince Cratyn. But she did not look at Cratyn the same way Lady R'shiel looked at Tarja. There was no warmth in her eyes at all, except when she addressed the fair-haired Fardohnyan captain. And Prince Cratyn's gaze did not linger on Adrina, the way Tarja's lingered on R'shiel.

No, he decided, his prince and princess knew how to behave in public. Nobody would ever come upon *them* kissing where anybody could see them. The princess was far too well bred to lean back suggestively against her husband, while she talked of war to her council, or dress in skin-tight leathers, or ride astride like a man. It was comforting to be back among people who acted with decorum and restraint.

"It is a sign of their weakness," Earl Drendyn announced, leaning back in his chair. "They have seen the force we have gathered and are afraid!"

"Even the lowest creature can fight savagely when it's frightened," Duke Wherland reminded them. His eye-patch looked decidedly ominous in the sputtering light. "I learnt that in the navy."

"It may be a ruse," Duke Palen agreed, scratching at his graying beard thoughtfully. "A delaying tactic, perhaps?" He turned in his seat, his gaze falling on Mikel, who gulped nervously. "What say you, boy? Laetho tells me you were there when they decided to make this offer."

Mikel swallowed again, his mouth suddenly dry.

"The boy knows nothing useful," Duke Ervin scoffed, pulling on the ends of his waxed moustaches. "I don't know why you bothered to bring him here."

"My Lords," the princess intruded cautiously, her eyes lowered demurely. She was such a perfect lady. "Children, like women, are frequently overlooked in a war camp. You may find he knows more than the Medalonians realize."

Prince Cratyn looked up sharply as the Princess spoke, but it was Lord Ciril who answered her. "Her Highness shows remarkable insight for a woman. Come forward, boy!"

Mikel stepped forward hastily, although his throat was so dry it felt as if somebody had sandpapered it. "My . . . My Lord?"

"You were there when they composed this message?" Duke Roache asked.

Mikel shook his head. "No, my Lord. But I heard them discussing it."

"Well? What did they say, boy?" Duke Ervin demanded impatiently.

"Sister Mahina, she said we could win . . ."

"There! What did I tell you!" Drendyn laughed. He took a long swig from his wine cup. He looked very pleased with himself. "They know we will defeat them!"

"Shut up, fool!" Palen snorted, before turning his ruddy peasant's face to Mikel. "Carry on, boy."

"But she said it would be an expensive victory," he finished, gaining a little confidence in the face of the elder Duke's support. "Lord Jenga . . . he said it might . . . give you pause. He said an attack in winter . . . in the mud or the snow . . . would be hard for armored knights."

"Any fool knows that," Roache muttered.

The Fardohnyan captain said something Mikel could not understand, and the others turned to the princess expectantly. "My captain asks if the child heard what the Hythrun Warlord had to say."

Eleven heads turned to look at him expectantly. Mikel suddenly remembered all the horrible things Damin Wolfblade had said about the lovely princess and paled. He couldn't repeat that!

"He said . . . he said that if you accepted the peace offering he would be very disappointed. He said you have too much at stake to withdraw now." The princess smiled at him before she translated the answer for her captain and his heart fluttered. This was how a true lady should look and behave. Decorous, elegant and modest. And Damin Wolfblade said she had the heart of a hyena! How dare he!

"The Medalonians don't appear to be suffering under too many false illusions," Lord Wherland remarked, "if what the boy says is true."

"Aye," Lord Palen agreed, "and they are correct about the snow. It would seriously hamper the knights."

"Then we need to attack before it snows, gentlemen," Prince Cratyn announced. Mikel's heart swelled with pride as he watched the young prince. He was so noble and serious. He did not joke about death or make lewd comments about women. He was renowned for his piety. And he would *crush* the Defenders, Mikel thought fiercely. The Overlord was with him and he had the most beautiful, well-mannered princess in the whole world by his side. Nothing could defeat them.

"Aye," Palen agreed. "We've sat on our backsides too long. It is time to teach these atheists a lesson. Only a fool would wait until winter to attack. Do you have anything else to tell us, boy?"

Mikel faced a moment of indecision. Should he mention the Harshini? Should he say he had seen a demon? Lots of demons? If he did, would they believe him? Or would they send him to the priests for Absolution Through Pain for lying? Should he tell them that Jaymes would only be released if they agreed to the peace offering? It had all seemed so clear when he was a prisoner among the Defenders. But now, faced with the war council and their stern expressions, his courage deserted him.

"My Lords, the child is exhausted," Princess Adrina said, saving him from having to answer. "It is the middle of the night and he is almost falling over with fatigue, as am I. Perhaps I could take the child and see him settled for the night while you make your plans? After all, a war council is no place for a lady," she added, bringing nods of agreement from the men. Mikel thought she was beyond perfect. She was the embodiment of Karien femininity. "Once he's rested, I am sure he will remember more. In fact, I would be happy to take it upon myself to interview the child, thus freeing my Lords for more important business. It would be my small contribution to your war effort." The gathered Dukes nodded, as impressed by her words as Mikel was. "Do I have your leave to depart, your Highness?"

Prince Cratyn waved his agreement with a furrowed brow, as if something concerned him, but he was probably just worried about the princess. She should not have been dragged from a warm bed at this hour of the night.

"Then I bid you goodnight, my Lords," she said, rising gracefully from her seat. "May the Overlord be with you as you make your plans, so that your victory is quick and decisive. Come, child."

She held out her hand and Mikel took it in wonder. He did not notice the cold as they walked from the tent. He barely even noticed the tall Fardohnyan following them outside. The princess said something in her own language to the captain, who nodded and disappeared into the darkness, then she turned and looked down at him.

"You must be the bravest young man in all of Karien," she said with obvious admiration. "To have spent all that time in the heart of the enemy and remain so true to your faith. I want to hear about every single moment of the time you spent with those nasty Defenders."

"I'll try to remember everything, your Highness," he promised her. For the Princess Adrina he would walk to the Sea of Despair and back.

chapter 25

ou are out of your bloody mind!"

R'shiel met Brak's anger with a wall of serenity that she did not entirely feel as she dismounted beside him. It was a little bit like having her emotions suppressed by Korandellan, except this time the calm was self-imposed. She was learning.

"There is no other way, Brak."

"You will never get away with it!" he insisted, pacing the uneven ground. The magnificent sorcerer-bred horses loaned to them by the Hythrun wandered off to graze. R'shiel could the feel the touch of their equine thoughts as they munched contentedly on the fresh grass. The air was cool and still, as if autumn were trying to decide if it should move over and let winter in, or if it should linger on the plain for a time. They had ridden south a ways onto the vast grassland, out of sight of the camp, Brak insisting he had to speak with her alone. She understood the reason for his caution as soon as he opened his mouth. He did not want the humans to hear him chastise her like an errant child. Or perhaps he was hesitant to reveal any limits to their Harshini power. It was far easier to keep up the illusion of invulnerability if others were not aware you *had* limitations.

"One thing! Just one little thing goes wrong and the whole ludicrous illusion will fall apart. You can't just waltz into the Citadel with a demon meld and expect to confront the Gathering—let alone convince them that the meld is really Joyhinia!"

"It convinced everybody here," she pointed out.

"And it lasted for a mere five minutes before it fell apart! The Gathering goes on for hours. The meld won't hold that long."

"Dranymire says it will. With practice."

"Practice? Do you have any idea how long the demons need to *practise*? A dragon is the result of a thousand *years* of practice, R'shiel! Garet Warner is leaving for the Citadel the day after tomorrow and he'll barely make it in time for the Gathering. Even if you could get there in time, you would have to convince at least some of the Quorum to support your case for re-appointing Mahina as First Sister, and that could take weeks in itself, even assuming the meld was sufficiently cohesive to do anything so complex."

R'shiel sighed patiently. She had given this a lot more thought than Brak gave her credit for.

"I can cast a glamor over myself. Nobody will recognize me."

"Well, that changes everything!" Brak snorted. "Now it's just impossible, whereas before it was inconceivable! I can't believe you talked Dranymire into this!"

At the mention of his name the demon popped into being at her feet. He looked up and frowned at Brak. "You are letting your human temper get the better of you, Lord Brakandaran."

"I'm letting my human *common sense* get the better of me," Brak snapped. It was a measure of his fury that he spoke so bluntly to the demon. Brak was usually more circumspect around them, particularly Dranymire. "How can you let her do this?"

Dranymire pulled himself up to his full height, making him nearly as tall as R'shiel's knee, and glared at Brak. "Lord Brakandaran, there are some things more important than individuals. Karien priests gather beyond the border, even as we speak. The Harshini must be able to protect themselves, and to do that, they need access to the Citadel. Sanctuary was built as a retreat—not a defense—and it will not stand a concerted attack if the Karien priests cross the border and discover its location. The Harshini need the protection and the power of the Citadel."

R'shiel looked down at the little demon in surprise. It had never occurred to her that the Citadel might hold power for the Harshini.

"It will do no good if I protect R'shiel from the danger of entering the Citadel, if in the long run the Harshini are destroyed. Xaphista is aware of the demon child's existence, just as any other god would be."

Brak took the demon at his word, it seemed, nodding reluctantly.

"Then let me go in her place. Let me call on the demons bonded to my bloodline to create the meld. I'm expendable. R'shiel is not."

"No," R'shiel said with utter certainty, although she had no idea where it came from. "I have to do this, Brak. I need your help, but ultimately, the task is mine."

He shook his head. "You need me? For what? To bring home your body?"

"I need you to help me convince the Quorum," she explained.

Years of being raised on the schemes of Joyhinia had prepared her for this, more than Brak knew. She had been fed politics for breakfast, manipulation for lunch and treachery for dinner for most of her life. Brak, on the other hand, was more Harshini than he cared to admit, for all that he had killed Lorandranek.

R'shiel took a deep breath, knowing the reaction to her next suggestion was likely to be even more extreme than the idea of the demon meld. "As you said, we need to convince the Quorum, and that could take weeks. So I don't plan to convince them. I plan to coerce them."

Brak was aghast at the suggestion. "*Coerce* them?"

"We will take Joyhinia to the Gathering and when she stands to speak, there will not be a voice raised in protest. Not if we cast a coercion over the whole group."

He took a deep, calming breath before he spoke. "R'shiel, I know you weren't at Sanctuary long, but *somebody* must have mentioned the prohibition on coercing humans to act against their natures. It's . . . it's on a par with *killing*, as far as the Harshini are concerned."

She looked at him evenly. "I am the demon child. I was created to destroy. Coercion seems to pale a little compared to that."

"And when the coercion wears off?" he asked. "What then? What happens when the Sisters of the Blade wake the next morning, wondering why in the Seven Hells they voted Mahina back into power?"

"We'll have to stay in the Citadel long enough to ensure that doesn't happen. If anybody makes too much fuss, Mahina can send them away—post them somewhere remote where nobody will listen to them. A leader always removes the loudest opposing voices upon attaining power. It's a time-honored tradition. It was also the mistake Mahina made the first time she was elected. I doubt she'll be so trusting this time."

"And what of the real Joyhinia? What do you plan to do with her?"

"Not long after the election, Joyhinia will be struck down with a terrible fever that will leave her incapacitated," she explained. "It will destroy her mind, unfortunately. She will be moved to the villa at Brodenvale where the sisters who are too old and infirm to look after themselves are cared for. She will live out her days in comfort and peace, as befits a retired First Sister, blissfully unaware of the events going on around her."

Brak let out a long slow whistle. "Gods, no wonder Xaphista fears your coming. A té Ortyn Harshini who schemes like a Sister of the Blade."

She smiled faintly. "I'll take that as a compliment."

"It wasn't meant as one," he snarled, turning his back on her. He walked to his mount and patted its graceful neck. R'shiel wondered if he was sharing his disapproval with the horse.

"Brakandaran will help you," Dranymire assured her.

"I suppose. But what did you mean when you said the Harshini needed the power of the Citadel? I thought the Citadel was just a bunch of temples?"

Dranymire shook his head. "It is more than that, child. The power is there for anyone to see, even humans."

"What power?" There was nothing she could recall from the Citadel that reeked of Harshini power. And if there had been, she was certain the Sisterhood would have destroyed it long ago.

"You call it the Brightening and the Dimming, I believe," the little demon explained. "It is the pulse of the Citadel."

R'shiel's eyes widened. The gradual brightening of the Citadel's walls and the eventual dimming each evening had been so much a part of her life that she had rarely given it a second thought. The idea that it was proof of the living Harshini magic enthralled her. *The pulse of the Citadel.*

"Can I tap into that power?" she asked. If she could access that, if there was some way to leave her mark on the Citadel, to impose the order they needed to be able to fight the Kariens single-mindedly, she was determined to use it. Another lesson learnt at Joyhinia's knee: use whatever and whomever it takes to achieve your goals. The end always justifies the means.

R'shiel felt so little for the childlike husk that was now Joyhinia, that it was impossible to regard her as the same woman. She felt nothing. No resentment. No burning desire for revenge. The Joyhinia who had raised her, and then cast her adrift to suffer, the woman who had scorned her and ultimately tried to kill her, was dead. The shell that remained was not worth the effort it took to hate. It was strange, though, that after all this time and everything Joyhinia had done to her, it was her foster mother's influence she felt most. The serenity of the Harshini had healed her. But it was Joyhinia's brutal practicality that would enable her to survive. There was something vaguely disturbing in the idea.

"Don't you have power enough?" Brak replied sourly. She had been too engrossed in her thoughts to notice his return. He led his horse toward her and swung into the saddle. His expression was bleak.

She shrugged and glanced up at him.

"I guess we won't know that until I face Xaphista and we see who is left standing once the smoke clears," she said.

chapter 26

They rode back in silence, Dranymire sitting atop the pommel of R'shiel's saddle until they neared the camp. He vanished as the vast followers' camp came into view. R'shiel glanced at Brak, but his expression was still as sour as it had been when they rode out this morning.

"Stop fretting."

"I'll stop fretting when you start demonstrating some sense."

"We have to do this, Brak. Have you seen the size of the Karien army? We need every Defender on the border. We need Mahina in charge."

He shook his head, but did not answer her.

When they reached the corrals on the southern side of the camp, they dismounted and walked their horses forward. The smell was pungent, with so many animals so close, and she could feel. Wind Dancer's thoughts as the mare sensed the nearness of her kin. Two Hythrun hurried forward as they neared the corral where the sorcerer-bred mounts were kept, a little way from the more ordinary Medalonian cavalry horses. R'shiel waved them away, preferring to unsaddle the beast herself.

Wind Dancer's thoughts lingered wistfully on fresh hay. R'shiel enjoyed the touch of her equine mind. Everything was so simple. So uncluttered. Brak moved on a little farther, apparently preferring solitude to her company.

"We have men aplenty to tend your horse, Divine One."

R'shiel hefted the saddle clear of Wind Dancer and turned toward the voice in the gathering darkness. "Please don't call me that, Lord Wolfblade."

"A compromise, then. You call me Damin, and I'll call you R'shiel."

"Done!" She lifted the saddle over the rail and turned to him. "Damin."

"Did you enjoy your ride?"

"Very much. She's a beautiful horse."

"Then she is yours. A gift."

"I couldn't accept anything so valuable, Lord . . . Damin."

"Why not?" He moved closer, stroking Wind Dancer's golden withers as she removed the bridle. "I've already told Tarja I planned to make you a gift of her. He didn't seem to mind."

"I don't need Tarja's permission to accept a gift," she said, ducking under Wind Dancer's head, which put the bulk of the beast between them. She began rubbing the horse down with more force than was absolutely necessary. "I'm just afraid you'll read more into my acceptance than is warranted."

"I see. You think I'm planning to use my association with the demon child for my own political ends, is that it?"

"Aren't you?"

He laughed. "You and my sister would make a great pair. Kalan thinks as you do. I offer this gift because I like you, R'shiel. If it helps my cause some day, then fine, but I would make the offer even knowing it might harm my cause."

She stopped brushing Wind Dancer and stared at him. "Why are you here, Damin?"

"Lord Brakandaran asked me to come."

"So you dropped everything and left your own province vulnerable to attack, to help an enemy? Just because Brak asked you? I find that hard to believe."

"You were raised by the Sisterhood, R'shiel. Perhaps if you'd been raised among people who place their gods above all else, you'd understand."

"Perhaps," she muttered, unconvinced. Damin Wolfblade seemed too sure of his own place in the world to care much about the gods. But it was to him that Zegarnald had delivered Brak and her. The War God had a high opinion of this human Warlord. Maybe that was why she did not entirely trust him.

"R'shiel, I will be the first to admit that my association with you will give the other Warlords pause. If I can call the demon child my friend, my position will be almost unassailable. I might even find out what it feels like not to fear an assassin's blade. But that's not the reason I came. The Karien army has to be stopped before it reaches Hythria. If not, my people face a war on a scale you cannot imagine. Hythria is a large nation, but the Defenders are a much more coherent force than any my people can muster. They are trained to act as one army. My nation has seven Warlords with seven different ideas as to how a battle should be fought, even if you could get them to agree to fight on the same side."

"You sound so plausible, I almost believe you."

"I do, don't I? I've been working on that little speech for a while, although I hadn't planned to use it on you. I wrote it in a letter to my brother Narvell."

"Your brother?"

"He's the Warlord of Elasapine. I hoped to appeal to his better nature and use his forces to block any Fardohnyan incursion into southern Medalon."

"Did he listen to you?"

"Oh yes, he did as I asked. I also hinted in my letter that I would deny him my permission to marry the girl he's been lusting after since he was fifteen, if he didn't."

The darkness had fallen swiftly as they spoke, and the night was lit by cold starlight; their breath frosted as if their words were things of substance. R'shiel opened the corral gate and Wind Dancer trotted through happily to join her companions. She gathered up her bridle as Damin lifted the saddle from the rail and together they headed toward the tent where the tack was stored.

"I think I would rather have you as a friend than an enemy, Damin."

"I could say the same about you."

"You've nothing to fear from me, I—" R'shiel stopped in her tracks as a prickle of magic washed over her. It was faint, but unmistakable. The feeling was unpleasant, as if someone was channelling magic through a filter of slime and filth.

"What's the matter?"

Brak reached them at a run. "Call your men out, Damin. The Kariens are getting ready to attack."

Damin looked puzzled, R'shiel even more so. "Is that what I can feel?"

Brak nodded. "The priests are calling on Xaphista. What you feel is them working a coercion, R'shiel."

She shuddered, thinking this was what she had planned for the Gathering. She hadn't known it would feel so unclean.

"When will they attack?" Damin demanded.

"Not for a while yet. But they'd only be doing this if they planned to move soon."

Damin did not need to be told twice. He dumped the saddle at R'shiel's feet and ran toward the Keep.

"Can't we do something, Brak?"

"If you want to reveal your presence to Xaphista, by all means, stop his priests from calling him."

She glared at him before picking up the saddle, lugging it toward the tent. "What's the use of having all this power if you can't do anything with it?"

Brak held back the tent flap for her as she shouldered her way in. She dumped the saddle and bridle on the racks and then pushed past him as she stepped outside, looking toward the crumbling old fort. Distant shouts reached them on the cold air as Damin raised the alarm.

"You can do anything you want, R'shiel," Brak said, following her gaze. "The trick is knowing when it's going to cause more harm than good."

"Like coercing the Gathering?"

He nodded. "You think what you can feel now is unpleasant. Wait until you're channelling it yourself. The Harshini prohibition on coercion isn't some altruistic principle. It's dangerous, R'shiel, and you are still a babe in arms when it comes to magic."

R'shiel glanced at him, but he wasn't looking at her. His gaze was fixed on the rousing army.

"Then what should I do?"

He turned to her finally and shook his head. "If I knew that, R'shiel, I'd have told you."

chapter 27

rak's timely warning proved its worth and the Defenders were in position long before the Karien army advanced the follow-ing morning. As dawn lightened the sky, Tarja rode behind the lines to Lord Jenga's position on a small knoll overlooking the battlefield, frost crackling under Shadow's hooves.

Ditches filled with sharpened stakes would force the battle down a V-shaped corridor, pushing the Kariens into an ever-narrowing field of fire. The Jagged Mountains to the east, and the Sanctuary Mountains to the west, formed a natural barricade to any flanking maneuvers. The mountains were both a blessing and a curse. The Kariens could not get past them, but neither could the Defenders. The only way to flank the enemy was to wait until they had crossed the border and were well into Medalonian territory.

Damin's mounted archers had been split into two companies: one under the command of the Warlord and one under the command of Cap-tain Almodavar. They were positioned on the arms of the V-shape and would harry the enemy flanks as the Kariens advanced. Their mobility and their astounding accuracy with their short bows meant they would remain relatively safe from counterattack, as the Kariens would have to break ranks and cross the stake-filled ditches to pursue them.

At the apex of the V-shape waited the longbowmen. They were the only hope of halting the Karien advance. The longbow could outrange any weapon the Kariens could bring to bear on the Defenders, and their defense lay in the rain of arrows that should decimate the Kariens before they got close enough to use their own weapons. Behind them stood the infantry, ready to advance if the Kariens got so close that the archers were endangered.

Tarja commanded one of the units of light cavalry. His job was to come at the enemy from behind, once the Kariens were committed to the battle. The deadly trenches had been carefully measured and dug to ensure a cavalry mount could clear them, as it was a safe assumption that a Karien warhorse, weighted down by the knight he carried, would have no hope of achieving the same feat. What worried Tarja was the Fardohnyan cavalry. They had dug the trenches before they learnt they would be facing Fardohnyans as well.

The killing ground was pockmarked with treacherous holes, dug to trap the charging destriers of the mounted knights. Tarja wondered if it was a measure of his character that he felt more sympathy for the horses that would die this day than for the men.

He reached the command position and dismounted, as a trooper hurried forward to hold his mount. Jenga waited under the shelter of a wide pavilion, talking to Damin and Nheal Alcarnen, who had command of the reserves. To his surprise, R'shiel and Brak waited with him.

R'shiel looked pale in the dim light. Brak's expression revealed nothing of what he was thinking.

"It's stopped," she told him as he entered the tent, pulling off his leather gauntlets.

"What's stopped?" Jenga asked, glancing over his shoulder.

"The magic. Whatever the Karien priests were doing, they're not doing it any more."

"Is that a good sign?"

Brak shrugged. "Depends on how you look at it. At the very least, it means you won't have long to wait."

Jenga frowned, uncomfortable with this talk of magic. Tarja warmed his hands over the brazier for a moment before turning to Brak and R'shiel.

"Just exactly what were they doing?"

"Coercing their troops, Brak thinks," R'shiel told him.

"What does that mean?'

"It could mean they won't stop attacking, regardless of what you throw at them," Brak warned. "A coercion makes men act against their natural instincts. Don't count on them breaking, even if faced with impossible odds. They'll just keep on coming until it wears off. That could be hours or days."

Damin looked across the tent at them and nodded. "We have legends of battles fought by men under a coercion. They didn't stop attacking until every last man was dead."

Jenga listened to the discussion with growing alarm. "This is madness! Isn't there something you can do?"

"Zegarnald will be with us," Damin said.

Jenga turned on him impatiently. "Bah! Your gods! I need practical solutions, not flights of fancy."

"Actually, Zegarnald might be more help than you imagine, my Lord," Brak said. "Coercing men in a battle is sort of breaking the rules. It might be worth appealing to him."

Before Jenga could answer the faint sound of a horn reached them. *The Kariens signalling their advance.* Jenga turned toward the sound and frowned.

"You speak to your damned gods, Lord Brakandaran. I have a battle to fight." He strode from the pavilion with Nheal close on his heels.

Damin pulled on his gauntlets and turned to them with a grin. "I'll see you later, my friends. Try not to get yourselves killed."

"Be careful, Damin," R'shiel called after him as he strode out of the tent to his waiting mount, held by a black mailed Raider. Raising his hand in salute, he swung into the saddle and rode at a canter toward the coming battle.

Tarja looked at R'shiel curiously. "You and the Warlord seem to be getting on well."

"Jealous?"

"Should I be?"

"Oh for god's sake!" Brak muttered impatiently.

Tarja smiled, realizing how foolish he sounded. "I have to go. You take care of her, Brak. I don't want her anywhere near the battle."

"I can take care of myself, thank you, Captain," she declared. "But I know what *you're* like, Tarja, so just remember this is a battle, not a border skirmish. You stay where you're supposed to be and don't go getting heroic on me, or you'll wish the Kariens *had* killed you by the time I get through with you."

She knew him better than he realized. Tarja had never fought in a battle on this scale; nobody had in living memory. He would far rather be in the thick of the fighting than standing back, issuing orders while his troops died at his command. Even harder, it was Jenga directing the battle. Tarja respected the Lord Defender, but he had grown used to being the one in command. In this battle he had his orders and no leave to do anything more.

With R'shiel's warning ringing in his ears, Tarja walked out to his horse. He could feel the ground trembling faintly as the Kariens advanced. Calm settled over him like a warm cloak. It always did before a fight. Before the bloodlust stirred in him. He glanced over his shoulder and saw her watching him, her expression grim and her arms crossed, and wondered if he would ever see her again.

Inexplicably, the Kariens sent their infantry to lead the attack. Rank on rank of motley peasants marched across the border, armed with short swords and rough wooden shields, which were painted a riot of colors to declare the province of each man. They moved erratically, not disciplined enough to march in unison. Tarja grimaced as he watched them, wondering if they had been given even basic training. He glanced down the line at the wall of Defender infantry—men who held their shields steady with their pikes upright, like a forest of thin bare trees. The cavalry reserves waited behind, near two thousand men, ready to move forward at the first sign of a breach.

But it was the longbowmen who would fight this battle. Each one was surrounded by a wall of steel that would protect him until the last man had fallen. Buckets of arrows sat behind each man, and beside him, a young man, drawn from the ranks of the rebels, whose job it was to ensure the buckets never emptied.

Tarja could feel the tension building around him as the Kariens approached, but Jenga held off giving the order to attack. Markers had been set up on the killing field, and the Defenders waited, discipline overriding their apprehension as the attackers neared. The Lord Defender did not intend to waste a single arrow. Every man knew and understood that. The war cries of the Kariens reached them long before they passed the markers, and still they did not move.

Jenga waited until nearly half of the Kariens were past the markers before he finally gave the signal. The air hissed as five hundred bowmen let their arrows fly. The raw troops advancing on them were either too inexperienced or too blinded by the coercion laid on them by their priests to react. More than half of them made no attempt to raise their shields against the deadly rain. Another hiss and the sky blackened as the next volley was loosed. More Kariens fell. More arrows found their target. The archers kept loosing their arrows, almost at a leisurely pace. There was no need to aim. In the confined area of the killing field, every arrow hit something. Tarja wanted to scream at the hapless Karien horde to do something, *anything*, to defend themselves. But they simply marched on, stepping over the bodies of their fallen comrades, walking into the arms of death as if it was calling to them.

"Founders!" Nheal swore as he rode up beside Tarja. "Are they brave—or just plain stupid?"

"You heard what Brak said about them being coerced."

"I'm almost at the point of believing him," Nheal admitted with a frown. Like Jenga, he had trouble dealing with the concept of magic. "Jenga wants you to move your men to the eastern flank. He fears the Kariens will try to break through there."

Tarja nodded and turned his attention back to the battlefield as the sound of drums reached them. The infantry were almost completely decimated, but on their heels Karien pikemen marched—five thousand or more men, pikes held before them, moving forward like an implacable spiny hedge. Tarja swore softly. These men were even less well armored than the first wave had been. Where were the knights? And the Fardohnyans?

"This is going to be ugly," Nheal remarked as he watched them.

"I can't understand what they hope to achieve," Tarja agreed. "We've not lost a man, yet still they come. This is insane. Who in the Founders' name is in charge of the Kariens?"

"Whoever he is, he appears to be on our side."

It was a poor joke, but Nheal was called away before Tarja could tell him so. He turned back to watching the Karien pikemen as they passed the markers and met the shower of death sent by his archers. They kept moving forward. Nothing could stop them, short of death.

He glanced up at the sky and realized with a start that the battle had been going on for less than an hour, if one could call it a battle. It was more like systematic extermination. He watched as wounded Kariens fell atop the dead and was sickened by the sight. No bloodlust surged through him to take the edge off his sensibilities. No battle frenzy stole away his conscience. As he turned his horse toward his troops to move them into position he was left with nothing but a hollow feeling of disgust.

And still they kept coming.

Tarja was waiting on the eastern flank with his cavalry when the Fardohnyans finally joined the battle. Although Damin had spoken of their prowess, he saw little sign of it as they charged forward, no more careful of the hail of arrows they rode into than the foot soldiers had been.

The sun had climbed high in the sky but shed little warmth over the battlefield. The Fardohnyans neared the treacherous, pot-holed field almost at the same time as the arrows hit them. Tarja had never seen their soldiers in battle and their speed and discipline impressed him, although their tactical stupidity left him speechless. There were half a thousand of them perhaps, keeping to a tight formation as they rode toward the killing ground. Tarja watched them advancing with a frown. They wore boiled leather breastplates and metal helms, but other than that, were unarmored. Their raised swords caught the rising sun like flashes of starlight in the dim morning. Their captain rode in the van, although Tarja could make nothing of his features, except that he had fair hair and rode well enough to be a Hythrun. They thundered forward past the markers, but Tarja held off a moment longer, watching their advance closely. He did not wish to risk his own mounts on that dangerous terrain. The fair-haired Fardohnyan captain rode through the hail as if protected by an invisible shield, and his men, those that were still ahorse, followed him blindly. The air was filled with the sickening squeals of wounded horses and the cries of dying men. Damin's Raiders were picking off their flanks with the same careless ease they demonstrated on the practice field shooting at melons.

"Enough of this! Charge!"

Tarja spurred Shadow forward at a gallop and cleared the trench with ease, coming up behind the Fardohnyans. His men followed and ploughed into their rear with swords flashing. The Fardohnyans realized too late that they were being taken from behind. With thrust and parry,

Tarja sliced his way though the Fardohnyans, their glazed eyes register-ing little more that vague surprise as he cut them down.

It took only minutes to slash his way through to their captain. The man turned at Tarja's cry, his expression confused. He looked as if he wasn't certain how he came to find himself in the middle of this battle. But he was better trained than most, and instinct took over. He parried Tarja's attack with unconscious ease, although he seemed not to have the wits about him to press home his advantage.

Tarja found himself fighting a real opponent for the first time since entering the fray. He countered the Fardohnyan's strike and let the man counterattack, turning the blow with a flick of his wrist so that his adver-sary was forced to over-correct to maintain his balance. Tarja rammed his blade into the man's side, through the gap in his leather armour as soon as he saw the opening, jerking the sword free as the Fardohnyan cried out in agony.

The young captain let his sword slip from his hand, clutching his side, blood spilling over his fingers as he toppled from his saddle. Glanc-ing around, Tarja was surprised to discover that most of the Fardohnyans were down. Then the sound of a horn reached him: three long, mournful notes calling the Karien retreat. They had given up, he realized, although the decision puzzled him. They had won nothing, lost thousands of men, and had not even tried to throw their knights into the battle.

"Sir!"

Tarja turned at the voice and discovered it was the Fardohnyan captain calling to him. He dismounted and knelt down beside the man. His wound was fatal, as Tarja knew it would be, but there was a light of intelligence in his eyes that had been missing before. Perhaps the shock of impending death had broken through whatever spell the priests had laid on him.

"Captain."

"A . . . message," he panted through the pain, speaking in heavily accented Medalonian. He was already pale from loss of blood. He would not last much longer. "To . . . my sister . . ."

"Of course," Tarja agreed, although he had no way of knowing who this man was, let alone how to get a message to his sister in Fardohnya. But the man was dying. It would not hurt to let him die thinking his last words meant something.

"Treachery . . ." he gasped. "Priests . . . tricked us . . ."

"I'll tell her," Tarja promised as he made to stand up.

The man grabbed his arm with a final burst of desperate strength. "You must . . . warn her . . ."

"I will," he said soothingly. "I'll see if I can get a letter to her."

The young captain shook his head. "No . . . *warn* her . . ."

"Warn her," Tarja agreed. "What's her name?"

The Fardohnyan closed his eyes and for a moment, Tarja thought he was dead, but then his chest heaved and he coughed a stream of bright blood, as his sword-pierced lung tried to cling to life. He muttered something, a name Tarja could barely make out. He leaned closed as the young man tried to speak with the last breath left in him.

"Adrina."

The name took all his remaining strength and with a gasp, the light went out of his unusual golden eyes.

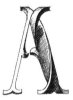drina woke to the sounds of battle. Or perhaps it was more accurate to say the silence woke her. The Karien camp, which was, even at its quietest, a bustling and noisy place, was ominously still. She lay in bed for a time; listening to the silence, wondering what it meant. As sleep gave way to wakefulness, she sat up with a start and pushed back the heavy embroidered curtains around the bed.

"Your Highness?"

Mikel looked up sleepily from his pallet near the brazier when he heard her moving about. The boy had been a permanent fixture since she had rescued him from the war council. Laetho had long replaced him as a page, so Adrina had considerately taken him on. He adored her, although he was obviously suffering under the misconception that she was some sort of living saint. It suited her to let him think that. He was a veritable fountain of information about the Medalonians and she figured she knew more about them than any other person in the Karien camp.

The child had given her some remarkable intelligence, which she fed the war council piecemeal to ensure her continuing presence. Sooner or later, Cratyn was bound to give in to the Dukes' pressure to exclude her, agreement or no agreement. Adrina was not one for relying on others when she could do the job better herself. If all it took to ensure Mikel's continuing trust was letting him think she was the walking embodiment of Karien holiness, then she would bestow her blessing on him cheerfully. Besides, he reminded her of her youngest half-brother, Kander. Sometimes it was nice to have somebody around who loved you, just because you were you. She had actually grown quite fond of the boy. Tamylan, with her usual lack of tact, had rudely accused her of using him as a replacement for her lost dog.

"Mikel, go ask the guard why it's so quiet," she ordered, rubbing the sleep from her eyes.

The boy scrambled from his pallet, pulled on his boots and disappeared outside with a hasty bow. Adrina stretched luxuriously, rather glad she had insisted on the huge feather bed being dragged to the front. She could have done without the heavily embroidered star and lightning bolt on the curtains, she thought sourly, but they did keep out the cold. Perhaps the Overlord *was* looking after her. In a roundabout, materialistic sort of way.

"They're fighting!" Mikel burst out, running through the tent flap, his eyes burning with excitement. "We attacked at dawn!"

Adrina frowned. She had been invited to no war council last night. Nobody had mentioned attacking the Medalonians this morning. "Fetch Tamylan and then find us some breakfast. I want to get dressed."

Mikel bobbed his head and raced outside again. He obviously considered war a grand pursuit. She wondered if he would be quite so enthusiastic once the casualties started coming in.

Tam was quick to respond, although when she entered the tent, her expression was grim. But she had obviously been up and about for a while.

"They left before dawn," Tam explained, before Adrina could frame the question. "Tristan and his men went with them."

Adrina was stunned. "Tristan? How? He's *my* captain! Cratyn can't order him anywhere."

"Vonulus came for him," Tam told her as she helped Adrina pull her gown over her undershift. "I didn't hear what he said to Tristan, but it was enough to get him moving. He told me to tell you he'd report to you tonight."

"What in the Seven Hells could Vonulus say to him that would make him follow Cratyn?" she wondered aloud.

"He didn't say," Tam shrugged. "With Vonulus just outside the tent, I don't think he wanted to give away my presence, but all the troops were gathered to pray to the Overlord for hours before the battle."

Adrina looked at Tam curiously. "He didn't want to betray you to

Vonulus? That's remarkably considerate of him," she said. Tamylan actually blushed. "Oh Tam, please tell me you're not falling in love with him!"

"Don't be absurd!" Tam scoffed, turning Adrina around with more force than was absolutely necessary to lace her gown. "You ordered me to become his lover. I simply do as I'm told. Slaves have a tendency to act that way."

Adrina looked over her shoulder. "A duty you have carried out with great attention to detail, I see."

Tam pulled on the laces so hard, Adrina grunted. "I am your loyal servant, your Highness."

"You know my father is likely to legitimize him if he fails to get an heir, don't you?" she asked. News had reached them in Yarnarrow that Hablet's eighth wife had delivered another tiresome girl child. "He's always been one of Hablet's favorites and the more trouble he gets into, the more Father likes him. Tristan could never marry you, of course, but you could have a very rosy future as a favored *court'esa*, if you play your hand right. Quite a step up for a slave girl."

"You are reading far too much into this. Tristan and I . . . we are simply doing your bidding."

"Of course," Adrina agreed with a smile.

For some reason the idea of Tristan and Tamylan falling in love made her very happy. She loved Tam, as much as one could love a slave, and Tristan was perhaps the only person in the world she loved unreservedly, with no thought for what he could do for her, or she for him. It was the curse of her birthright.

Adrina knew she was always going to be a stepping stone for others. Every suitor Hablet had ever proposed had been a grasping fortune hunter, although some had disguised it better than others. Cratyn had been the first suitor who matched her for title or position, but even he had plans to use her.

As a child, Adrina had prayed to Kalianah, the Goddess of Love, for a man who would fall madly in love with *her*, not her position, or the wealth she could bring him. She had realized the futility of her prayers soon enough, once she understood that as Hablet's eldest legitimate child, she had no equal in Fardohnya. No equal in the world perhaps, with the exception of the younger Prince Cratyn in Karien and the heir to the throne in far away Hythria, who was undoubtedly as corrupt and perverted as his uncle, the High Prince Lernen. No, her prince would never come for her, she knew. Instead, it was a grubby line of lordlings each dreaming of the prestige attached to making her his wife. He'd be dreaming of the wealth, the land and the titles that Hablet would bestow on him for taking her off his hands.

She had adroitly avoided such a fate by being a harridan. Considering how greedy some of her would-be suitors had been it had taken quite an effort on Adrina's part for them to finally decide that no amount of money or titles could compensate them for having to live with her. Eventually, the offers had dried up. Hablet had plenty of other daughters who were much more amenable than the dreaded Adrina.

Until Cratyn.

Until, through her own recklessness, she had left herself vulnerable.

She sighed, pleased that at least Tam had found love. Being a bastard gave Tristan more freedom than she had ever had. And being a man. That annoyed her even more than the fact that every man who had ever expressed an interest in her was looking over her shoulder at the wealth and power that came with her hand.

"Well, I suppose I'll just have to wait until they get back," she said, taking the small stool so Tam could fix her hair. "Cratyn has obviously gone out of his way to prevent me being involved in this. Would you like to make a small wager on the reaction of the guards if I ask for my horse, so I can watch the battle?"

"No need," Tam replied. "They told me on the way in that you would be keeping to your tent today."

"He'll pay for this," she muttered. Her list of things Cratyn was going to pay for was growing so long that she would need to remain married to him for a lifetime, just to make certain he suffered sufficiently.

Mikel arrived back before Tam could offer a reply, brimming with news at how well the battle was going. Adrina paid him little attention. There was no way the child could know for certain. It was his loyalty to Karien speaking, but she let him prattle on as they ate breakfast. His mindless chatter filled the silence and kept her mind off other things.

The day dragged on interminably. Mid-morning the Ladies Hope, Pacifica, Grace and Chastity arrived, suggesting that they pray to the Overlord to protect their men in battle. Adrina agreed absently. On her knees praying to the Overlord was actually preferable to trying to engage her ladies-in-waiting in intelligent conversation. Mikel gave her a look that bordered on worship as she knelt. Poor child. If only he knew she was silently asking Zegarnald to protect Tristan. And inflict a festering wound on Cratyn, while he was at it. Preferably a horribly disfiguring wound that offered a lingering, pain-filled death . . .

After an hour of kneeling, conversation didn't seem such a bad idea after all. She glanced around at the small circle of young women, at their pious faces, and inwardly groaned. *Gods, these girls are pathetic!*

"Ladies, perhaps we should cease our prayers for the moment," she suggested. "The Overlord has a battle to watch over. I am sure he has heard our pleas for victory this day. I think we presume much to distract him so."

The Ladies Hope, Pacifica, Grace and Chastity agreed with her wise words and climbed stiffly to their feet. Adrina ordered refreshments, and as the cold sun climbed higher and higher she listened to their boring talk of inconsequential things—while a battle raged a few leagues away. She could not understand how they did it.

It was late afternoon before they learnt anything useful, and the news was not good. When the guard on the tent was changed, the newcomers spoke of a dreadful battle, of casualties too numerous to count. Adrina frowned, but she was unsurprised by the news. Mikel had told her of the hours the Defenders spent training, of the extensive earthworks the Kariens would have to breach. Defending a position was always easier than attacking. All the Medalonians had to do was sit and wait for the Karien forces to throw themselves over the border and pick off the attackers at their leisure. She hoped Tristan had the sense to stay clear of the battle. It was unlikely Cratyn would try to use her men in battle, she reasoned. He wanted the glory of this victory for Karien and the Overlord. It just would not do to have a bunch of heathens do the work for him.

Just on sunset, Adrina discovered how wrong she had been. Second Lanceman Filip, a young man assigned to her Guard, arrived at the entrance to her tent seeking an audience. He was bloodied and exhausted, his eyes hollow, his expression bleak. He fell to one knee, from exhaustion as much as respect when he saw Adrina. Her heart lurched at the sight of him. Tristan must have taken vast casualties to send a Second Lanceman to report.

"What happened?" Fear clutched at her stomach and her throat was dry.

"It was . . . we were slaughtered, your Highness," he told her, his voice rasping with shock and fatigue. "The Medalonians had archers. Thousands of them. The arrows didn't stop falling for hours. When they did, the rocks started falling out of the sky like hail. The priests . . . they did something to us. It was as if . . . we just couldn't stop, your Highness. It was like . . . we'd lost our wits. We'd lost most of the force before we even saw a red coat, and then they took us from the rear."

Adrina nodded, calling on all her reserves of strength to maintain her regal posture. The man needed to see her strength. In truth, she wanted to scream. "How many of the Guard were lost?"

"There's barely thirty of us left, your Highness."

Adrina staggered. *Barely thirty left!* There were five hundred men in her Guard this morning. Cold anger overwhelmed her grief. "What exactly did the priests do, Lanceman?"

"I couldn't say, your Highness. We gathered on the field . . . they prayed over us, I think. After that, it gets a bit hazy . . . The next thing I remember for certain was the horns sounding the retreat."

"Thank you, Lanceman. Go now and find some rest. I will commend your report to your captain."

The young man looked up at her with eyes full of grief. "Captain Tristan is dead, your Highness. He died bravely, though . . . fighting a Medalonian. I'm . . . I'm sorry."

For a moment, Adrina was numb. She felt nothing. Saw nothing. Did nothing. But slowly, grief crept over her like a sheath of ice that clutched at her fingers and toes and worked its way through her body until it settled around her heart. In the background, faintly, she heard Tam sobbing. She even had time to notice Mikel standing near the entrance, his eyes wide with shock.

"Has Prince Cratyn returned from the battlefield?" she asked. Her voice was ice wrapped in anger.

"I . . . I believe so, your Highness."

"You are dismissed, Lanceman. Tell the other Guards that I will address them later. And tell them I honor their sacrifice and share their grief."

Filip rose wearily to his feet, bowed and backed out of the tent.

"Fetch my cloak, Mikel," she said calmly. The boy nodded and hurried to do her bidding. Adrina did not move. Her anger was like a solid, tangible thing. Had it been a sword, she could have killed with it.

"Your Highness?" Mikel ventured, holding out her cloak. She took it from him and swept it over her shoulders.

"See to it that Tam gets some hot tea, Mikel. She was very fond of the captain."

At the sound of her name, Tam looked up. She wiped her eyes and looked at Adrina suspiciously. "Where are you going?"

"Nowhere you need to concern yourself with."

"*Adrina*!"

Tam's anxious cry followed her as she strode through the camp to the command tent. Her grief was so overwhelming that she could not breathe, could not think. She pushed her way into the tent, ignoring the startled looks of Lord Roache and Lord Palen. The ice shattered as her rage flared. She marched straight up to Cratyn, pulled him out of his chair and delivered a stinging backhanded slap across his face.

"You unbelievable, despicable *bastard*!" she screamed as he picked himself up from the table, gingerly fingering a small trickle of blood from the corner of his mouth. "What did you do to my Guard? What evil-spawned spell did your perverted priests cast on my men? You *knew* what would happen to them! You and your pathetic, craven knights sat back and waited in their damned tin suits while my brother and his men were slaughtered like cattle!"

Cratyn barely managed not to cower under her rage. He glanced at the two shocked dukes, taking a step back from her before he spoke.

"The princess is distraught at the news of her captain's death," he explained warily.

Adrina's anger turned white hot. "*I'm* distraught? You disgusting, impotent, little moron, don't you realize what you've done?"

"In war, hard decisions are necessary, your Highness," Lord Roache said. "When you've had time to consider . . ."

"Time to consider *what*?" Adrina spat. "You *lost*! And what's worse, you fed my men into the fray like they were meat being fed into a grinder to do it!"

"At least they died in honor of the Overlord," Cratyn told her, rubbing his face where she'd slapped him, her handprint stark against his pale skin.

Adrina turned on him angrily. "They died, *Cretin*, because nobody in this whole damned war camp has anything remotely resembling even a passing acquaintanceship with basic military tactics!"

"We have no need of such worldly skills when the Overlord is with us, your highness," Lord Roache replied, quite offended. "His hand was guiding the battle."

"Then your damned Overlord is an even bigger moron than you, Lord Roache. Did you think all it would take to assure victory was some sick spell dreamed up by your priests that forces men to march willingly to their doom?" When they looked at her in surprise, she smiled coldly. "Oh yes, I heard about your priests praying over the troops—and my troops—during the night. And the effect it had on them."

"Then you must be relieved to know your men died in a state of grace."

"There was no need for them to die at all!" she yelled at Cratyn furiously.

"Our priests simply helped the men by removing the fear that lurks in the heart of all those facing battle," Roache explained, stepping forward as if he feared Adrina might attack his prince again.

"You robbed them of the ability to think for themselves!" she shot back. "You took away any chance they had of winning by making them advance into battle like mindless idiots. Your Overlord didn't help you, my lord. He was on the side of the Defenders!"

"If we failed today, then it was because it was part of the Overlord's greater plan," Cratyn insisted. "It is certainly not a woman's place to question his will."

"Then perhaps you might take the time to question my *father's* will," she suggested, holding back her rage by sheer willpower.

"Need I remind you, Princess Adrina, your father is supporting this war," Lord Roache said.

"Forget your stupid war! You've killed one of Hablet's sons! He was planning to legitimize his eldest baseborn son and name him heir. You just murdered the heir to the Fardohnyan throne!"

Oddly, her news seemed to strengthen, rather than frighten Cratyn. "Then it is as the Overlord wills. The heir to the Fardohnyan throne will be of Karien blood. A true believer."

"*Heir!* What *heir?* That limp dick of yours hasn't got the lead to produce an heir, has it, Cretin? Is that why you want to go to war so badly? Because a banner is the only thing you're capable of raising?"

They must have heard the rumors, but both Roache and Palen looked startled by the news. Cratyn, she was viciously pleased to note, was mortified that she had exposed his impotence so brutally. She would have severed his useless organ and marched through the camp with it mounted on a pike at that moment, had someone given her a knife.

"Your Highness! This is not an appropriate place to discuss . . ."

"Your precious prince's manhood? Or rather, his *lack* of it. Don't worry, Lord Palen, the prince's impotence is no longer an issue because I am going home to Fardohnya, where I plan to inform my father that his son was *murdered* by a boy prince who defied every law the gods hold sacred by coercing his men in battle. You can forget this damned alliance. There will be no aid, no cannon, no invasion of southern Medalon. You'll be lucky if Hablet doesn't invade Karien!"

"Attempting to return to Fardohnya would be extremely foolish, your Highness," Roache told her, his voice dangerous.

"Don't you dare think you can threaten me, Lord Roache," she warned. "I will do as I please. I will escort my brother's body home where he will be laid to rest on Fardohnyan soil and my father can mourn his loss."

"Guards!" Roache called. Cratyn looked afraid to take his eyes from her. She could not tell if her threats scared him. Did not care.

"Escort her Highness to her tent," the Duke ordered as soon as the guards appeared. "She is beside herself with grief and not aware of what she is saying. She is not to leave her quarters unless Prince Cratyn or I expressly order it. Is that clear?"

The guard saluted smartly and waited for Adrina. A small worm of sanity tunnelled through her grief reminding her of where she was. It was only then that she realized the enormity of her error. Roache was a very dangerous man. She had forgotten that in her anger.

"Have a care, your Highness," he advised. "It would be most unfortunate if we had to advise your father that he had lost a daughter, as well as a son."

chapter 29

s she was escorted back to her tent, Adrina cursed her temper. With a few careless words she had destroyed months of hard work convincing the Kariens she had converted to their cause. Roache's threat was very real. Would they tell her father she had died of grief for her lost brother? Killed herself in despair? Blame a disease caught in the camp?

Whatever the reason, Adrina knew she had to leave this place, and the only hope of escape was across the border into Medalon and the waiting army of Defenders.

Adrina stopped before she entered her tent and took a deep breath. She wanted nothing more than to throw herself down and sob uncontrollably for the loss of her brother. The tragedy of his death staggered her. That such a bright light could be extinguished so easily for the sake of Karien ambition was more than she could bear. But there would be time to grieve for Tristan later. Now was a time for clear thinking. She took another deep breath and entered the tent, a plan half-formulated over the last few weeks slowly taking on a firmer shape in her mind.

Tam and Mikel both leapt to their feet as she stepped inside. Tam's eyes were red and swollen. Mikel looked very uncomfortable. He did not know how to deal with grieving grown-ups. For a moment, Adrina wondered if he knew how lucky he was that his brother was still a prisoner with the Hythrun. He would not grieve tonight as she would.

"Your Highness?" he said expectantly.

Adrina looked over her shoulder rather dramatically and waved the two of them closer. "I have just met with Prince Cratyn," she said in a low, conspiratorial voice. "I have grave news."

"About the battle?"

"Worse! There is a spy in the camp."

Tam looked at Adrina suspiciously, but Mikel's young face was a portrait of shock.

"A *spy*!"

"Sshh!" Adrina urged. "No one must know!" She moved further into the tent, to ensure they were out of hearing of the guards outside. "It is the reason for the massacre today. The Medalonians knew we were coming!" As she watched Mikel lap up every word she uttered, she had time to think that the Medalonians would need to be blind, deaf and completely witless *not* to notice an army the size of the Karien advancing on them. "Prince Cratyn needs my help. *Our* help."

Mikel straightened his shoulders manfully. "What does he want us to do, your Highness?"

She glanced up at Tam, who was looking at her doubtfully. There would be time to explain things later. "I have to deliver a message to my father, the King of Fardohnya. Prince Cratyn needs my father's cannon to help him defeat the Medalonians."

Mikel took her at her word. "But how?"

"We must go to Fardohnya," she explained in a whisper. "We must leave tonight, while both sides are still in confusion after the battle. We will cross into Medalon and make for the Glass River. We should be able to secure a Fardohnyan trader to see us safely back to Talabar from there."

"Shall I tell the guards to fetch your horse, your Highness?"

"No! Nobody must know about this, Mikel. As I said, there is a spy in the camp. If they learn of this mission, our lives would be in danger!"

"*Would* be in danger?" Tam asked with a short, bitter laugh. "I'd say they'll be in danger anyway, traipsing through Medalon in the middle of a war."

Adrina rolled her eyes. She would never convince Mikel if Tam did not support her. "I do this for my prince," she declared. "I know there is danger, but who else can convince my father to send the cannon? Cratyn needs my help. How can I refuse my husband?"

Mikel laid a comforting hand on hers. "You are so brave, your Highness. But the Overlord will be with us."

"That gives me such strength," she agreed sincerely. "Now you must listen to me carefully, Mikel. Prince Cratyn and I have worked out a plan to see us safely over the border, but it needs your assistance. Will you help me?"

"Of course!"

"And you must guard this secret with your life," she warned. "We do not want the spy to learn of Prince Cratyn's plans."

"I cannot believe that any Karien would betray his countrymen," Mikel protested.

"You have been among the enemy, Mikel. You have seen how they can eat away at a man's faith. Not all the Overlord's subjects are as loyal as you." She ruffled the child's head fondly. "Now listen carefully. Prince Cratyn pretended to place me under guard, so that the spy will not note my absence. I need you to seek out a Fardohnyan Lanceman named Filip and give him a note from me. He will see that we have horses. The battlefield will be a busy place tonight, with both sides looking for wounded and the camp followers picking over the dead. We should be able to slip through unnoticed. Once we are past the battlefield, Tam and I will pose as Hythrun *court'esa* returning home. Nobody will question us if we are careful."

"What's a *court'esa*, your Highness?"

"An entertainer," Adrina told him blandly. "They are very popular in Hythria and Fardohnya, so nobody should think it odd."

"I will protect you, anyway," Mikel assured her. "I'll not let any harm come to you, your Highness."

"I know, Mikel. That's why I insisted Prince Cratyn allow you to accompany me. You have been in the enemy camp and you speak their language. I cannot think of a better protector." No need to disillusion the child and tell him she spoke Medalonian fluently.

Mikel swelled with pride. "The Overlord will protect us all!"

"I certainly hope so," she agreed. "Now go and find some warm clothes. It will be cold tonight. I will write the message for Filip. We must leave as soon as it's dark."

As soon as the boy had left the tent, Tam turned on Adrina. "Are you mad!"

"Probably, but it's preferable to the alternative. Did you pack any of my clothes from home?"

"I packed every stitch you own," she grumbled unhappily.

"Good. Find us something to wear that would pass as a *court'esa's* costume. The more bare flesh the better. Once we reach the border, we'll need to look the part if we are stopped by the Hythrun."

"And if the Defenders stop us?"

"Then we shall distract them with our feminine wiles," she said impatiently. "Men are men, Tam. Oh! Make sure you pack my jewellery, too. I'm not leaving it so Cretin can sell it to finance his damned war."

"How do you intend to get out of here?"

"I'll wear your clothes and leave the tent on an urgent errand for the princess before the guard changes," she said. "Once the new guards are on duty, you do the same, making sure they have instructions not to disturb me. We'll meet Filip and Mikel on the edge of the camp."

"Do we have to take the boy?"

"I need him to get a message to Filip and he's been in the Defenders' camp. We can leave him once we find a boat on the Glass River."

Tam still looked miserable, but Adrina thought her grief was still too raw for her to object much. She wanted out of here as much as Adrina did.

"We'll never pass as *court'esa*, your Highness. Even if you could act humble enough to convince anybody you weren't a princess born and bred. We have no collars. The Defenders might accept the ruse, but no Hythrun would."

"We have collars," she said. "Fetch my jewelry box."

Tam did as she asked and watched curiously as Adrina unlocked the small, beautifully carved chest. She lifted out the top tray, ignoring the wealth that lay scattered on its velvet surface and reached into the bottom. She lifted out two exquisitely worked necklets, one silver, the other gold. Both were in the shape of snarling wolves, with emerald-set eyes and a fiery line of rubies tracing their twisted spines.

"Where did you get *these*?" Tam breathed in astonishment.

"In Hythria. You remember when I visited Greenharbour? High Prince Lernen attended a slave auction while we were there and invited me along for the sport. It was an awful day. He spent the whole time complaining about the poor quality of Hythrun slaves these days, not even bidding on them, when two of the most beautiful young men I have ever seen were brought to the block. They were identical twins, not more than fifteen, I suppose. Lernen took one look at them and just had to own them. He paid a fortune for them—said he wanted to make a gift of them to someone, probably his nephew.

"But I knew he planned to taste the fruit before he shared it around. Gods, but the Wolfblades are a degenerate lot.

"Anyway, Lernen insisted they ride back to the palace with us in his carriage. He couldn't take his eyes off them. As we were climbing out of the carriage back at the palace, one of the boys grabbed my sleeve and begged me for help. They looked innocent enough, but they knew what was in store for them." Adrina hesitated for a moment, not at all certain she wanted to relate the rest of the tale.

"What did you do?" Tam asked.

"I gave him my knife."

"Gods! Did Lernen find out?"

Adrina shook her head. "I saw them later that night at dinner, all powdered and primped and ripe for the plucking. They were wearing these collars—and not much else—and Lernen was crowing over them like a child with a couple of new dolls to play with. The next morning they found the boys dead in Lernen's bed. They slit their wrists and bled to death beside him while he slept."

"That's dreadful! Adrina, why didn't you tell me about this before? If the Hythrun realized it was your knife the boys took to Lernen's bed, you could have been hanged."

"I thought of that. I claimed I lost it before dinner."

"But how did you get the collars?"

"Lernen gave them to me. Once he'd stopped screaming and they'd cleaned the blood off him, he sent for me. I found him sitting in his private courtyard just staring at the collars. They were lying there on the edge of the fountain, still stained with the blood of the boys. Lernen asked me to get rid of them. Told me he never wanted to see them again. I'm not sure why I've kept them. Maybe to remind me why I agree with father when he says Hythria should be invaded and the Wolfblade line destroyed."

"What about his nephew? What was his reaction?"

"I've no idea," she shrugged, fingering the gold collar idly. "I never met him. He probably wasn't sober enough in the entire month I was there to present himself to me. I was never so glad to leave a place as I was when I left Greenharbour. Until now. Leaving here is going to feel even better."

Tam picked up the open silver collar and studied it thoughtfully. "Where are the keys?"

"I don't have them. Once we put them on they'll have to stay there until we get home and can have them cut off. If I can put up with it, so can you, Tam. I'd happily cross Medalon in chains if it means I never have to lay eyes on Cretin again."

As if to prove her point she slipped the collar around her neck and heard it faintly snick closed, as the wolf swallowed its tail. The gold was cold against her skin, the sensation odd. She had never wondered if *court'esa* objected to being collared. They were always such beautiful works of art. The more elaborate and expensive the collar, the more the *court'esa* was worth. Tam had been born and bred a slave and her reluctance seemed a little strange. Perhaps being nominally free since arriving in Karien had sparked a little rebellion in her. "Put it on, Tam. We're running out of time."

By the time Mikel returned, Adrina had written a short note to Filip and packed everything she planned to take with her. Considering the style to which she was accustomed to traveling, it was a pitiful bundle, but it contained her riding habit, her jewels and the small, sharp Bride's Blade. She sent the boy on his way with the note and changed into the costume Tam had selected. It had a thin silver bodice and a split emerald green skirt. It left her midriff bare and pimpled with gooseflesh in the chilly air. Over that she pulled on Tamylan's high-necked gray woolen tunic, and then Tam's serviceable woolen cloak. The rest of her belongings she wrapped in the linen bag Tam used to take her laundry to the camp washerwomen. Tam was still dressing when she left the tent with the hood of her cloak pulled up to shadow her face. She hurried past the guards, who barely glanced at her. They had orders to stop the Princess Adrina leaving. Nobody had mentioned a servant hurrying off with her mistress' laundry.

It was dark by the time she worked her way through the camp to rendezvous with Filip. It had been the most nerve-racking hour of her life as she stumbled over the uneven ground, around groups of soldiers, too bloodied and exhausted to challenge her right to be there. By the time she slipped away from the edge of the camp into the small copse of trees where Filip should be waiting, she was afraid she was going to be sick. Fear was not an emotion Adrina had much experience with, and she prayed fervently to whatever god might be listening that she would not experience it again for a long, long time.

"Your Highness?" Filip's voice was a questioning whisper. She followed the sound and was relived to find Mikel waiting with the young Lanceman, his eyes burning with the excitement of his adventure.

"You've done well, Lanceman," she said as she made out the three dark shadows picking at the sparse dry grass between the trees. "Mikel, go and keep an eye out for Tam." The boy dutifully scurried off and left her alone with Filip.

"You are leaving, your Highness?" Filip asked as he led the horses forward. It was hard to tell from his tone whether he approved of the idea or not.

"I'll not be a party to this monstrous slaughter any longer," she told him. "Fardohnya has shed enough blood to satisfy the Kariens."

"And what of the Guard, your Highness? When the Kariens discover you are missing . . ." He did not need to finish the sentence. She knew their fate as well as he did.

"I want you to cross the border tonight. Take every Fardohnyan in the camp with you who is still breathing. If they can't ride, tie them to their saddles. When you reach Medalon, surrender to the Defenders."

"*Surrender?*" Filip sounded horrified, but it was hard to make out his expression in the darkness.

"The Defenders will keep you prisoner for a time, but I doubt they'll harm you. And you'll eat far better there as a prisoner than as a free man on this side of the border. Tell them your religious beliefs prevent you from taking part in any further fighting. The Defenders have little experience with the gods. They should believe you."

"And what if it is the Hythrun who find us first?"

"Then tell them Zegarnald ordered you to surrender," she told him impatiently.

"The War God would never—"

"It doesn't matter, Filip," she snapped. "Just get your men away. I would rather have you alive and in the custody of the enemy than put to death by Cretin because I ran away. Do this for me and I will see every one of you rewarded when we get back to Fardohnya."

"As you command, your Highness." He sounded reluctant, but there was little more she could do. If they chose to disobey her, that was their decision.

She turned sharply at the sound of scuffing feet and was relieved to find Mikel returning with Tam. As the Karien boy watched in amazement, she shed the cloak and tunic to reveal the Fardohnyan costume underneath. Shivering so hard her teeth were chattering, she pulled out the fur-lined cloak and wrapped herself in it with relief. Tam shed her own woolen tunic to reveal a costume almost as decorative and just as flimsy as Adrina's.

They were *court'esa* now, and the collar felt cold against her skin as she swung into the saddle and turned her mount south toward Medalon.

chapter 30

drina's escape from the Karien camp proved surprisingly easy. The troops were either too stunned or too tired to challenge them, and it was doubtful Cratyn had even thought to post sentries. They rode across the no-man's land between the camp and the border without incident, chilly starlight illuminating their path.

From a distance, the battlefield looked like a surreal, alien landscape. Dark humps littered the ground as far as the eye could see, as if mad sappers had tunnelled the field, leaving countless mounds of black earth in their wake. It was only as they drew nearer that Adrina realized they were bodies, thousands of them, scattered across the landscape like discarded, broken dolls.

The smell hit them even before they reached the fallen soldiers. The heavy stench of blood and excrement hung in the still air, making her gag. Shadowy figures moved among the corpses. Men looking for fallen companions, camp followers looking for loot, women searching out missing loved ones, grim-faced Defenders seeking dying horses, ending their suffering with a quick sword thrust. Others searched for living bodies, friend and foe alike, for the life they might save or the hostage they might take. Huge bonfires on the far side of the battlefield threw a pall of black smoke over the whole nightmarish vista.

"We'll have to lead the horses," Adrina said as they reached the first of the fallen Kariens. "We can't ride through this."

Tamylan and Mikel complied silently and they began to pick their way forward, holding cloaks across their faces against the smell. The ground was treacherous, pockmarked with deep holes, dead soldiers and broken horses. There was not a red coat among them. The Defenders had either taken few casualties or their wounded had already been removed.

The battlefield covered a vast area. As they doggedly trudged on at a snail's pace, seemingly for hours, Adrina began to wonder if it would never end. She stumbled along and tried not to think about the death surrounding her, or the grief that she had dammed up inside, for a time when she would have the luxury of giving it voice. Instead she pressed on, thinking only of placing one foot in front of the other, ignoring the soldiers who reached out to her, crying for help, or the lifeless eyes that stared accusingly at her as she passed by. This was not her war. It was not her fault.

The night went on forever and the smoke grew thicker as they neared the bonfires. Mikel was yawning, wiping streaming eyes, when Tamylan suddenly gasped. Adrina looked back and discovered the slave had stopped walking. She was staring at the fires, her expression horrified.

"What's wrong?"

"They're burning the dead!"

She had heard of the barbaric Medalonian practice of cremation, but had never seen it practised. The sight disgusted her. But she needed to be strong. Their survival depended on it.

"There are too many men to bury, Tam. Anyway, what do you care if they cremate a few Karien corpses?"

"It's not right!"

"No, but neither is it our concern. Now keep moving."

Adrina tugged her horse forward and did not look back to see if Tamylan was following.

Sometime later, they reached the first Fardohnyan corpse. It was a young man with vaguely familiar features, although Adrina could not put a name to him. He lay on his back, his foot still trapped in the stirrup of his dead horse who had fallen beside him. A long, red fletched arrow was embedded in his boiled-leather breastplate. His eyes were wide open and he stared at the sky, as if engrossed in the strange constellations of the northern sky.

"Oh, gods!" Tamylan breathed as she drew level with Adrina. "Lien Korvo."

"Was that his name? I didn't know. I hardly knew any of them."

"And yet they died for you."

Adrina looked up sharply. "They didn't die for me, Tam. They died for Cratyn. A debt I intend to make him pay."

Tamylan looked around with a shake of her head. "If we survive this."

"We'll survive."

"The Overlord will watch over us," Mikel added.

Adrina resisted the temptation to turn on the boy. If this was the Overlord's work, she wanted no part of it. But she needed the child. They still had to get past the Defender's camp, and he knew its layout.

"I'm sure he is, Mikel. Come on. We have to keep on."

The closer they came to the edge of the field, the more Fardohnyan bodies they encountered. Adrina did not look at them, afraid of what she would see, afraid of who she would find. Tristan was here, lying dead on this foreign plain, killed by a godless Defender. Her anger increased with each step, divided equally between the Kariens, who had condemned her brother to death, and the Medalonians, who had carried out the sentence. She would have vengeance for this slaughter, although how or when she did not know. But one day, she vowed, Karien, Medalon and even Hythria, would pay for the life of her brother and those of her Guard.

"Here! What are you after?"

Adrina stopped and turned her head toward the voice. It was a red-coated Defender although, as she knew nothing of their insignia, she did not know if he was a private or a commandant.

"We were just looking for loot," she said, in her best Medalonian. "A girl has to look out for herself, y'know!"

"Who are you? What are your names?" the man demanded. He peered at them suspiciously.

"We're *court'esa*. From Hythria. I am Adrina, and this is Tamylan. The boy is our servant."

"Aye, I've heard of your kind. Fancy whores is all you are," he said, sounding a little disgusted. The man stared at the jeweled collar. "I'd have thought that trinket 'round your neck would be enough for you, without you needing to loot the dead, as well."

"Don't you touch her!" Mikel cried as the Defender reached out to touch the collar. Adrina could have slapped the child. Now was not the time for bravado.

The Defender laughed sourly but made no move to come any closer. "Quite a bodyguard you ladies have. Now clear off! Lord Jenga has ordered all the looters off the field."

"Don't worry, sir, that's exactly what we planned to do."

The Defender nodded and watched them as they pulled their mounts forward. Mikel glared at the man defiantly, but held his tongue. Adrina's heart was pounding as they walked away, expecting him to call them back. She risked a glance over her shoulder and discovered the man had moved away toward another group of looters. She let out a breath she had not realized she was holding and glanced down at Mikel.

"That was very noble and very foolish. In future, try to curb your enthusiasm for protecting me."

"But your Highness, I—"

"Don't call me that!" she hissed. "You must call me Adrina. At least until we are away from here. We are trying to be inconspicuous!"

"I'm sorry, your . . . Adrina."

"That's all right. Just be on your guard."

"Seems a bit rough," Tamylan said, as she trudged along beside Adrina.

"What do you mean?"

"You just told an enemy officer your real name, yet you chastise the boy for trying to protect you."

Adrina stared at the slave for a moment, not sure what surprised her most—Tam's blatant criticism or the fact that she could have been so stupid.

"I never thought . . ."

"Not thinking is what got us into this mess," Tam pointed out grumpily. "First you don't think if you can sail a ship. Then you don't think about threatening the Karien Crown Prince. Then you drag us across a battlefield in the dead of night—"

"That will be enough, Tamylan. You forget yourself."

"Not as often as you do," the slave muttered under her breath, but loud enough that Adrina could hear her.

It was almost dawn by the time they passed the last of the bodies, but Adrina's relief was short lived. At least the men on the battlefield had been mostly dead. Now they would have to get through the Defenders and the Hythrun who were alive and on their guard.

They swung into their saddles and moved off toward the scattered crowd heading away from the field. With luck, they could mingle with the other camp followers and go unobserved. A few people glanced at them enviously. They were mounted on Fardohnyan horses, but Adrina had decided she would claim they had rescued the beasts from the battlefield if they were challenged.

Daylight finally turned the sky the color of pewter as Adrina and her companions left the battleground behind. They rode at a shambling pace amidst the looters and the walking wounded, tired, hungry, thirsty and emotionally drained. The war camp and the tent city lay before them, and beyond that, another two or more weeks to the Glass River. Perhaps there, with luck, a Fardohnyan trader would be waiting, making the most of the profits of this war, before Hablet joined the fray and turned the Medalonians into enemies.

Nobody challenged them, or even cared about them, it seemed. The only time anything caught the interest of the people around them was when a man and a woman galloped past on glorious golden horses. Both were tall in the saddle and rode with the ease of those born to ride. The young woman wore dark leathers, much as the old tapestries depicted the Harshini. She had a thick long braid of dark red hair, and both she and her companion wore grim expressions. At their passing, several civilians fell to their knees, but the pair did not notice.

She looked at Mikel, who was on the verge of falling asleep in his saddle.

"Mikel, do you know who they are?"

"Who, your . . . Adrina?"

"That man and woman who just rode by."

Mikel looked in the direction of the rapidly dwindling figures of the horses and shook his head. "I'm sorry, your . . . Adrina. I didn't see."

"No matter."

Adrina put the pair out of her mind and allowed herself one glance over her shoulder before fixing her eyes forward. She did not need to be reminded of the past hours. The images of the battlefield would stay with her forever.

chapter 31

In the cold morning light, Damin Wolfblade surveyed with disgust the carnage that was the remnants of their first serious engagement with the Kariens. It was not what he expected at all. The air stank of smoke and death. Even the sky was gray with low, sullen clouds that gazed with disapproval over the battlefield. Like Tarja, he had never faced a battle on such a scale, and the aftermath left him strangely unsettled. Although he could not fault the tactics of the Defenders, this had not been a real battle. It was like killing cattle in a corral. There had been no opportunity for personal glory, no chance to fight for the honor of the War God. He had lost one man to injury and that through a fall. The Defenders had lost a dozen men and perhaps fifty were injured. It had been a thoroughly unsatisfying affair.

Lord Jenga was well pleased, though. He had faced down a numerically superior enemy and not just prevailed, he had triumphed. The Defenders were in a buoyant mood. The Kariens were decimated, the Fardohnyan contingent destroyed. Of course, the Kariens still had countless men to throw at them, but they might think twice before launching such a suicidal frontal assault again.

Damin suspected the reason for the victory lay as much with the coercion laid on the enemy by their own priests, as with the brilliance of the Medalonian defense. Even when the odds were hopeless, the Kariens did not have the wits about them to retreat. All they could do was keep moving forward into the arms of certain death.

"My Lord."

Damin turned to his captain wearily. He had not slept in two days and it was starting to tell on him. "What is it, Almodavar?"

"Lord Jenga wishes to see you. There's some disagreement over your orders regarding the Fardohnyans."

Damin nodded, not surprised by the news. He turned his mount and rode toward the command pavilion at a canter. The sooner this was sorted out, the better.

"Lord Wolfblade, is it true you ordered the Fardohnyans buried?" Jenga demanded as soon as he appeared in the entrance. The tent was crowded with Defenders, most of them congratulating themselves over their victory.

"I did. They are pagans, my Lord. It is sacrilege for them to be cremated. You may do as you wish with the Kariens, but the Fardohnyans deserve better."

"They fought with the Kariens," Jenga retorted. "They deserve nothing. In any case, I've not the men or the time to spare burying anyone. I'll have an epidemic on my hands if that field isn't cleared soon."

"Then my men will bury them, my Lord. And I've no doubt there are plenty of pagans in your camp who would aid us."

Jenga snorted something unintelligible and turned to an officer seeking his signature. He signed the document before turning back to Damin.

"Very well, bury them if you must. I've broken enough laws lately for another to mean little. But do it away from here. And don't use my Defenders. Not that there are many who would countenance such a barbaric practice."

"Your respect for our religious customs is touching, my Lord."

Jenga frowned but did not reply. Annoyed, Damin strode from the tent. His men had fought as long and hard as the Defenders. They would not be pleased with an order to bury nearly five hundred Fardohnyans in this cold, hard ground.

"Damin!"

He stopped and waited as R'shiel caught up to him, surprised to find her here. He had expected her and Brak to be long gone. "I heard what you said to Lord Jenga. You did the right thing."

"Then perhaps you could persuade him to lend me some assistance."

"I doubt it. Burial is outlawed in Medalon, Damin. You're lucky he agreed at all."

"I know. But sometimes I wonder about this alliance. I have more in common with the Fardohnyans and the Kariens than I do with these people. Were it not for the gods . . ."

"Were it not for the gods, none of us would be in this mess," she finished with a frown.

Not sure what she meant, Damin shrugged. "You would know better than I, demon child."

"Please don't call me that."

"I'm sorry. Although I'm a little surprised to see you here. I understood you were leaving for the Citadel."

"I'm looking for Tarja to say goodbye. Brak and I are leaving this morning."

"With Garet Warner?"

She nodded. "You don't like him much, do you?"

"Not in the least. Nor do I trust him. Be careful, R'shiel."

She slipped her arm through his companionably and walked with him. Damin found her easy familiarity disconcerting. This girl was a living legend; the embodiment of a myth he had grown up with. He had never expected to find himself counted among the demon child's friends. When they reached his horse R'shiel let go of his arm and patted the stallion fondly.

"What's he thinking?" Damin asked curiously.

"He's thinking it's too cold to be standing around gossiping. He wants his breakfast."

"So do I."

She looked at him with a shake of her head. "How can you even think of food, at a time like this?"

"Armies fight on their stomachs, R'shiel. Starving myself won't bring anybody back to life."

"I feel sick just thinking about it."

Before he could answer her a Defender lieutenant approached them, saluting Damin smartly before turning to R'shiel. His uniform was grubby and soot-stained from a night collecting and burning the dead.

"Captain Tenragan said to ask you to wait for him, my Lady. He'll be along once he's taken care of the last of the looters."

"He's wasting his time," Damin remarked. "Looters and war go together like sand and sea."

The young lieutenant drew himself up and glared at him. "I understand it's a common practice in Hythria, my Lord. Even your *court'esa* aren't above it. In Medalon, however, such a practice is considered to be barbaric and disrespectful."

"This from a man who burns his dead," Damin muttered, then he glanced at the young man curiously. "What makes you say my *court'esa* aren't above it? There are no *court'esa* here."

"Perhaps they belong to one of your men, sir, but I stopped two of them last night. Laden down with bundles of loot they were. All dressed up too, with those jeweled collars and dresses that left nothing to the imagination."

"No man of mine could afford *court'esa* like that. Are you certain?"

"Aye. I spent time on the southern border. I've seen them before. There was no mistaking them."

R'shiel looked at him expectantly as he pondered the news. "What's the matter?"

"Probably nothing. Did you get their names, Lieutenant? Where they were from?"

The man thought for a moment. "One was called Tam-something, I think. The other one said her name was Madina, or something like that. I didn't really take much notice of them once they moved on . . ."

"Which way were they headed?"

"South, with everyone else, I suppose."

"Of course. Thank you, Lieutenant."

He saluted again and headed toward the command pavilion.

"What's bothering you, Damin?" R'shiel asked with a faint smile. "That there were Hythrun *court'esa* looting the battlefield, or that you don't own them?"

"It just seems a bit strange, that's all. *Court'esa* as valuable as that don't roam battlefields unescorted."

"What's all this about *court'esa*?" Tarja remarked as he walked up beside R'shiel. His eyes were bloodshot, no doubt from supervising the funeral pyres through the night, and his shoulders were slumped with fatigue. Damin wondered for a moment if he looked as haggard.

"One of your men stopped two *court'esa* looting the battlefield last night. Hythrun *court'esa*, complete with court collars, he claims."

"You didn't bring any *court'esa* to the front, did you?" Tarja asked.

"No." He shrugged. "It's probably just your men confusing some whores from the followers' camp. Besides," he added with a laugh. "What selfrespecting *court'esa* would call herself Madina? They usually give themselves far more exotic names."

"Assuming he got the name right," R'shiel added. "She could have said her name was Adrina, for all we know."

Tarja's eyes narrowed. "Adrina. . . . Damn!"

"What?"

"The Fardohnyan captain I faced yesterday. He begged me with his dying breath to warn his sister that they'd been betrayed. In the heat of battle, it never occurred to me . . ."

"What are you talking about?" R'shiel asked impatiently.

"Let me guess," Damin said. "His sister's name was Adrina?"

Tarja nodded. R'shiel looked first at Tarja and then Damin with growing annoyance. "So?"

"Hablet's bastards are usually sent to serve in the army as officers once they're old enough," Damin explained.

"So Tarja killed one of Hablet's bastards?" she said, throwing her hands up. "What of it? This is war."

"He wanted me to warn Adrina that they'd been betrayed," Tarja reminded her.

Damin glanced at R'shiel then turned to Tarja with a frown. "And suddenly there are two *court'esa* crossing the battlefield from Karien? Something bothers me about this. I think we should look into it."

Tarja nodded thoughtfully. "Perhaps we should, at that. If Adrina is attempting to send a message back to her father, and she thinks the Kariens have betrayed her, she couldn't risk sending the message by normal means."

"Well, that's nice!" R'shiel declared. "You ask me to wait around so you can say goodbye, then as soon as my back is turned, you're off chasing a couple of floozies in see-through dresses on the off-chance they're Fardohnyan spies."

With a tired smile, Tarja put his arm around her and pulled her close. "I'm only going along to keep Damin out of trouble."

"I think you need someone to keep you both out of trouble!" she complained unhappily. "You look terrible, by the way. Both of you."

"Speaking of trouble, here comes your watchdog," Damin warned, as Brak strode across the field toward them.

R'shiel glanced at the approaching figure and then turned to Tarja. "I have to go. Promise me you'll take care."

"I'll take about as much care as you will, R'shiel," he said, so softly Damin could barely make out the words. Damin turned away, to give them at least the illusion of privacy.

"It's time we were gone, R'shiel," Brak said when he reached them.

R'shiel drew away from Tarja with some reluctance. "I know."

"Keep her safe, Brak, or you'll have me to answer to."

The Harshini laughed sourly. "You, Tarja? There's more than a few gods who I'd have at me, if I let anything happen to the demon child. You'd have to line up for a chance at what was left of me, I'm afraid."

R'shiel frowned. "I wish you would all stop treating me like a fragile doll. I can take care of myself, you know."

"He's knows that, R'shiel. Go and save us all from the Sisterhood, while we stay here and skewer Kariens like fish in a barrel, and when you get back we can all tell each other what heroes we've been."

She smiled at Damin and leaned forward, kissing his cheek lightly. "You are just as bad as he is. You take care of yourself, too. And don't go leading him astray when you find your *court'esa*. The captain is already spoken for."

"What *court'esa?*"

"Don't ask, Brak. Let's just get out of here before Garet decides to leave without us."

With a final kiss for Tarja and a wave for Damin, R'shiel followed Brak to the horses he had waiting for them. He glanced at Tarja.

"Don't worry. She is the demon child. She has forces watching over her that you cannot imagine."

Tarja nodded and seemed to force himself to shrug off his apprehension.

"I'm not worried. Anyway, I thought we were going to investigate some floozy in a see-through dress?"

Damin nodded and swung into his saddle. "Meet me by the arrow-makers' tent. I have to see about burying some Fardohnyans first, then we'll find out what two very expensive *court'esa* were doing looting a battlefield full of dead Kariens in the middle of the night."

chapter 32

hat time is it, Tam?"

The slave looked up at the heavy, overcast sky and shrugged. "Breakfast time."

Adrina's tummy rumbled in agreement. She was rather disgusted that she had not thought to ask Filip to pack any food. Adrina had never had to worry about where her next meal was coming from. It had not occurred to her to think of such mundane things when she planned her desperate flight from Karien. Perhaps when they reached the tents of the camp followers, there would be a stall or a tavern where they could purchase a meal. And supplies for the journey south. As she rode, Adrina tried to calculate what they might need and what it would cost, but she really had no idea. She had never had to buy her own food, either.

They had made little progress since leaving the battlefield, hemmed in as they were by the other travelers on the makeshift road. Adrina fretted at the delay, but knew the crowd was her best protection. Among these peasants she was just another looter returning home from a long night robbing the dead. Once they reached the followers' camp and had equipped themselves for their journey, they could make up for lost time.

She wondered if Cratyn had discovered her missing yet. Even if he had, she realized with some relief that she was safe from him now. He could not follow her into Medalon, and would not suspect it had been her destination, in any case. More likely he would send troops searching the road back toward Yarnarrow. By the time he realized where she was, she would be in Cauthside, perhaps even on a boat, sailing the Glass River south for home. The knowledge invigorated her and some of her exhaustion fell away.

She was free of Karien.

Nothing would ever entice her to go back.

Adrina glanced at Tamylan and smiled encouragingly. Mikel slept in her arms and Adrina led his riderless horse. The poor child was exhausted and Tamylan had offered to hold him while he slept, for fear he would fall from his saddle.

Adrina was not certain what to do with the child. He was a sweet boy, but he was so fanatically devoted to his damned Overlord, he was liable to do anything. She felt a twinge of guilt over her plans to abandon him. Perhaps she could find some Medalonian peasant who would take him in. She could pay for his keep—she had enough jewellery on her to buy him a commission in the Defenders, for that matter.

The thunder of hooves brought her out of her musing and she glanced over her shoulder as a dozen Hythrun Raiders rode by them with a red-coated Defender in the lead.

Probably off to celebrate their victory, she thought sourly.

A little further on the riders slowed and then wheeled their mounts around, heading back the way they came. With a stab of apprehension, Adrina stared steadfastly forward, as if by refusing to look at them they would not notice her.

At a sharp command the Raiders reined in beside her, expertly cutting her and Tamylan out of the crowd. With no choice but to do as they indicated, she turned her mount off the road to confront the Defender and a grubby, unshaven Raider who wore nothing to indicate his rank.

"Ladies," the Hythrun said as they approached. "What a pleasure to find members of your profession out here."

Adrina glared at him with all the withering scorn she could muster, which was considerable. "Don't even *presume* to think I would entertain the likes of you!"

The man seemed more amused than offended by her answer. "Why not? We have plenty of money. And that *is* what you're doing out here, isn't it? Looking for financial advancement? There's a dozen of us here, and at, say ten rivets a turn, you could make quite a tidy sum."

Adrina flushed angrily, not certain what insulted her most—that this barbarian would dare proposition her, or that he would offer a measly ten rivets for the privilege.

"How dare you!"

"*Adrina*," Tamylan hissed beside her, warningly. Mikel stirred sleepily.

"My deepest apologies, madam. Fifteen rivets, then, although for that price, you'd better be good." The dark-haired Defender who rode at the Hythrun's side seemed to find the exchange highly entertaining.

Adrina forced her temper down. She had to talk her way out of this. Adopting an air of extreme disdain, she looked down her nose at the Hythrun and the Defender, both of whom would have benefited considerably from a bath.

"Fifteen, or fifty rivets, it makes no difference, sir. I am a bound *court'esa*. I am not at liberty to accommodate you. As you can see, I wear a collar."

"So you do," the Hythrun said, as if noticing it for the first time. "A wolf collar, at that. Am I to understand that you are the property of House Wolfblade?"

"Naturally," Adrina agreed, with a bad feeling it was a mistake to admit such a thing. These mercenaries worked for House Wolfblade. They might take such an admission as proof that they were entitled to her services.

"I don't recall Lord Wolfblade bringing any *court'esa* to the front, do you, Captain?"

"I'm sure I would have noticed," the Defender agreed laconically. "Perhaps we should take them to him?"

Adrina blanched at the thought. She did not want anything to do with Lernen Wolfblade's degenerate nephew. "No thank you. We can find our own way."

Mikel woke and wiggled around in Tamylan's arms to stare open-mouthed at the Hythrun surrounding them. Adrina threw him a warning glance, hoping the child would have the sense to remain silent.

"But we insist," the Hythrun said, with a dangerous smile. "Lord Wolfblade will be most anxious to see you. He's been a long time out here in the field and these Medalonian women are all dogs."

"My Lady . . ." Mikel whispered urgently. She ignored him.

"Thank you, but no. Now get away with you! I'm sure Lord Wolfblade didn't send you out here to harass innocent people going about their business. I will be speaking to him about this, I can assure you!"

"*Your Highness!*" Mikel's whisper was verging on panic-stricken.

"You know his lordship then?" the captain asked.

"Of course, you fool! Now get out of my way or Lord Wolfblade will have you whipped!" Adrina did not know if that was the case, but it seemed a fair assumption, based on what she knew of the family.

"Your Highness! That *is* Lord Wolfblade!" Mikel cried.

Adrina suddenly felt faint.

Her mouth went dry as Damin Wolfblade rode up beside her, so close his stirrup touched hers. He was nothing like the powdered courtier she imagined. He was big and dirty and unshaven and looked meaner than King Jasnoff's most vicious hunting hound.

For a fleeting moment, she wished she had never left Karien.

Damin Wolfblade looked at her closely. He did not look surprised to discover her identity. She realized with despair that they had suspected all along who she was. That nonsense about ten rivets a turn was obviously his misguided idea of a joke.

"Your Highness." He bowed with surprising grace, but it was the short bow of an equal, not a mere Warlord greeting a royal princess.

"Lord Wolfblade." Adrina marvelled at how steady she sounded.

"Tarja, allow me to introduce Her Serene Highness, Princess Adrina of Fardohnya, or is it Her Royal Highness, Princess Adrina of Karien, these days? It's so hard to keep track of these things."

"Move away from me, sir," she said in a voice that was colder than the Fourth Hell.

Wolfblade smiled. "What do you think, Tarja? Will we get more by selling her back to the Kariens or her father?"

"I'll kill you if you touch her!" Mikel screamed.

"*You!*" The Defender glared at the child and Mikel cowered under his scrutiny. "Founders, how did you get here, boy? I thought we'd seen the last of you!"

"You coward! How dare you pick on a helpless child! As for you," she added witheringly to the Warlord, "I refuse to be your hostage!"

"You *refuse* to be my hostage? I don't recall asking your permission, your Highness."

"Don't take that tone with me, sir. I am a Fardohnyan princess of royal blood!"

"Quite a step up from a *court'esa*," the Defender remarked, not in the least impressed by her declaration.

This was not going well at all. She could not afford to be a hostage. The first thing they would do was send a message to Cratyn demanding the gods alone knew what in return for her release. At that moment, Adrina did not care if the war raged on for another hundred years.

She was not going back to Karien.

"I refuse to be your hostage, my Lord, because I am seeking asylum," she announced, the plan formulating in her mind as she spoke.

The Warlord made no effort to hide his astonishment, or his disbelief. "*Asylum?*"

"But, your *Highness* . . ." Mikel began with a horrified gasp.

"Be quiet, child!"

"You expect me to believe you are running away?"

"I am not *running away*, my Lord, I am altering the terms of the Karien-Fardohnyan Treaty. The Kariens have not kept their side of the bargain, therefore I do not feel compelled to keep mine."

"I'd call that running away," Tarja chuckled.

Damin Wolfblade shook his head, clearly not believing a word she said. "And what is it you want in return for asylum, your Highness?"

"Safe passage to Fardohnya in a manner befitting my station."

"Is *that* all?" Tarja asked with a sceptical laugh.

"Safe passage to Fardohnya? So you can get together with your father and stir up even more trouble? I don't think so, your Highness. Do we look that foolish?"

"You question my word, sir? How dare you! I am a princess!"

"You're Hablet's daughter," he corrected. "That makes every word you utter suspect."

She was going to have to put this man in his place, sooner rather than later. "I will not sit here and be insulted by a barbarian! I insist you take me to the Lord Defender this minute, so that I may present my case to someone with a better understanding of protocol than a savage, such as yourself!"

Damin Wolfblade laughed at her. Adrina loftily ignored him and turned to Tarja Tenragan.

"The boy is under my protection and so is my slave. They will remain with me, so that I may have some basic level of service. You will agree to consult me regarding any offer of ransom made on my behalf. And under no circumstances, will I agree to return to Karien. Is that *quite* clear?"

Her list of demands seemed to startle him. Wolfblade exchanged a glance with the Medalonian before turning to her. "You may keep your slave, your Highness. As for the boy, his fate will be up to Captain Tenragan."

"And the rest of my demands?"

The Warlord laughed. "*Demands?* You are our prisoner, your Highness. You're not at liberty to make demands. But I'll promise you one thing. Give us any trouble at all, and I will see that you learn what it is to wear the collar of a bound *court'esa*. Is *that* quite clear?" He turned his horse away from her before she could frame a suitable retort. "Put the boy on his own horse. He's old enough to ride without a nursemaid."

A Raider rode forward and snatched Mikel from Tamylan's arms. Other hands took the reins of her mount, leaving her nothing to do but cling to the pommel as, surrounded by the Hythrun, she rode toward a crumbling ruin that must be their command post.

Adrina chewed on her bottom lip and wondered if she'd done the right thing, admitting she was trying to get home. Damin Wolfblade clearly did not believe her, but Tarja Tenragan was hard to read. Perhaps he would champion her cause? Surely the Medalonians would see the benefit in letting her go? Her arrival in Talabar was bound to destroy the treaty.

On the other hand, returning her to Karien would be almost as effective. They could demand any number of concessions from Cratyn. She stared at the backs of the two men in whose hands her fate now rested, and realized her only protection lay in making them *want* to shield her from Cratyn's wrath.

Adrina realized that she was going to have to change her tune.

She was going to have to be *nice*.

She wondered, for a moment, if she remembered how.

chapter 33

hat in the name of the Founders are we supposed to do with her?"

Jenga paced the hall, hands clasped behind his back, his brow furrowed with concern. He had hoped for sleep on his return to the Keep. He had not planned on the discovery that Tarja and Damin had captured a *court'esa* who turned out to be the Crown Princess of Karien.

"My suggestion is that whatever you do, you do it quickly. You don't want her around causing trouble, my Lord, and believe me, she *will* cause trouble." Damin spoke from the heart, never more certain of anything.

"She's well guarded," Tarja pointed out.

Damin laughed sceptically. "Then make sure you change them often. In a week, she'll have every man she comes in contact with eating out of her hand. A week after that they'll be helping her escape. It's a good thing we searched her saddlebags. There's enough here to buy more than a few men's souls." He glanced at the fortune in jewelry scattered on the rough wooden table. The blue diamond alone would feed a small village for a year.

"You claimed she was a shrew," Jenga said, stopping his pacing for a moment to glance at the gems. The torches painted dark shadows over his lined face.

"She is," Damin agreed. "But she's also as sharp as a new sword. Now we've deprived her of her purchasing power, she'll resort to more direct methods. She's *court'esa* trained. That may not mean much here in

Medalon, but trust me, it makes her more dangerous than you can possibly imagine."

"What do you mean, *court'esa* trained?" Tarja asked. "She's a princess."

"Your definition of a *court'esa* and ours is very different, Tarja. What you call *court'esa* in Medalon are merely common whores. In Fardohnya and Hythria, they are highly trained specialists, worth a small fortune to those who can afford them. Adrina was probably given her first one around the age of sixteen. He would have been a skilled musician, an artist maybe or a linguist. But first and foremost, his job would have been to make Adrina more valuable as a wife by teaching her the art of giving pleasure in the marriage bed."

"So our princess is a whore?" Tarja asked with a grin.

Damin shook his head impatiently. "You're missing the point. She's Hablet's daughter. She's been trained by the very best and if she thinks it will help her cause, she'll use every skill at her disposal to get her own way. And in case you hadn't noticed, she's not exactly hard to look at. If you don't believe me, go up there now and spend an hour in her company."

"No thanks, I've seen all of Her Serene Highness I want to."

"You two can argue the lady's finer points some other time," Jenga snapped. "Right now, I have to decide what to do with her."

"We could ransom her back to Cratyn," Tarja suggested. "Surely he will sue for peace if it means the return of his wife."

"I'm not so sure," Damin said with a shake of his head. "She seemed very determined not to go back to Karien. And if that Fardohnyan you killed was to be believed, then the Kariens have betrayed them."

"But Adrina never got the message. There has to be another reason she left."

"What of Hablet?" Jenga asked. "Perhaps knowing his daughter is our hostage will stay his hand?"

Damin shrugged. "He's a treacherous bastard. He could just as easily abandon her to her fate as try to get her back." He smiled sourly. "We've more chance of trading the jewelry, I fear."

"Maybe we should consult her Highness on the matter?" Tarja suggested. "She did, after all, demand to be informed of any negotiations regarding her ransom."

"You jest, surely," Jenga said.

"If only he *was* joking," Damin sighed.

"Well, I'll leave it up to you, Lord Wolfblade. You captured her, so I'm making her your responsibility. You may use whatever men you need to keep her guarded, but I don't have time for this distraction. Give me your recommendation when you've decided what to do. And put those gems somewhere safe. Now, if you gentlemen will excuse me, I'm going to bed."

Damin watched the Lord Defender leave with an unfamiliar feeling of despair. He turned to Tarja, who seemed more amused than concerned. The captain wrapped the jewels in their velvet cover and tucked them into his belt.

"You've a fortune there, you know." Damin finished his wine with a grimace and then glared at Tarja. "Don't look at me like that, you have no idea what she's like."

"Oh, I got an inkling today. You're welcome to her."

Damin rose from his seat by the fireplace and poured himself another cup of wine. He drank it in a gulp.

"She tried to kill my uncle, you know."

"Adrina?"

Damin nodded. "Hablet sent her to Greenharbour for Lernen's birthday, a couple of years ago—the same year you were recalled to the Citadel, as I remember. Adrina had obviously been well briefed about my uncle's various weaknesses before she arrived and she pandered to them very effectively. She dragged him along to the slave auction and coaxed him into buying a pair of twin boys. The cunning little bitch even made the boys ride back to the palace in his carriage, no doubt hoping to whet his appetite. That night they slit their wrists in my uncle's bed and bled to death while he slept. The blade they used was Adrina's table knife. She must have slipped it to them in the carriage. I wonder how she sleeps knowing they killed themselves rather than do as she demanded."

"I'm surprised you didn't go to war with Fardohnya over an attempt on the High Prince's life."

Damin shrugged and poured another cup of wine. "Nothing definite could be proved. I was out hunting that day, and didn't return until late, but I was told Adrina claimed at dinner that she had lost her knife. We could never connect the boys to her afterward, and we tried every avenue of investigation. In the end, we had no choice but to let the matter drop." He swallowed the wine and thumped the cup down on the table. "You know what really irks me?"

"What?"

"That bitch and her slave are wearing the collars Lernen gave those two dead boys. I'd recognize them anywhere. Lernen and I had quite an argument over their cost. It's how my mother met her gem merchant, incidentally. Adrina no doubt kept them as a souvenir."

Tarja frowned, as if he could not conceive of anything so callous. "So take them back."

"No, I think I'll leave them right where they are for now. Another thing you may not understand about Fardohnyans and Hythrun, Tarja, is that for a noblewoman to be collared like a slave is the worst kind of insult. Her Serene Highness could well do with a little humiliation. Anyway, she thinks I need a key to open them. I can keep her collared for quite some time, while I'm waiting for the keys to arrive from Hythria."

"Have you sent for them?"

"No need. There's a concealed clasp. But the idea that her good behavior will earn her release might keep her tractable for a time."

"I could always offer to dismember her slave," Tarja suggested with a grin. "It worked on the Karien boy."

"Adrina would probably tell you to go right ahead and then ask if she could watch," he predicted sourly. "Speaking of the boy, he is your responsibility. I don't want him anywhere near her. He'd probably run one of us through if she asked him."

Tarja nodded, his expression suddenly glum. "I miss R'shiel already. She seemed to be able to get through to the child. And I'd be happier if Mahina were here to deal with Adrina."

"So would I," Damin agreed. He poured a cup of wine, then poured another for Tarja and pushed it across the table to him. "Here. If I'm going to get drunk, then you'd better join me. It has been a thoroughly unsatisfactory day. That battle was as glorious as a cattle cull."

Tarja took the wine and sipped it as Damin downed his in a gulp. They were silent for a while, only the crackling fire and the hissing torches disturbing the silence. Damin filled his cup again.

Tarja glanced at him curiously. "You said it was common practice among Hythrun and Fardohnyan nobility to have their sons and daughters trained by *court'esa*. Does that mean you were?"

"Absolutely!" Damin could feel the wine making his head spin. It was a rough blend, too young to be drunk with such determination. He drank it anyway. "Her name was Reyna. I was fifteen when she came to Krakandar."

"It beats fumbling around in the stables with a nervous Probate, I suppose."

"Having never fumbled around in a stable with a nervous Probate, I'm not in a position to comment on the comparison, but I imagine you're correct. Drink up, Captain. I'm getting very drunk here and you haven't finished your first cup."

"Perhaps you should get some sleep, Damin. It's been a long day."

"Yes, mother."

"I only meant—"

"I know what you meant." He studied the bottom of his cup for a moment. "You know, we call rough wine like this 'Fardohnyan courage' in Hythria."

Tarja smiled. "We call it Hythrun courage."

"I shall ignore such a heinous insult, Captain, because I like you." Suddenly, he hurled the cup at the fireplace where it shattered into thousands of clay shards. "Dammit! Why couldn't she stay on her own side of the border?"

"You really should get to bed, Damin. You're drunk and you're not thinking straight."

"I'll grant you that I'm drunk, Tarja," he conceded. "But as for thinking straight, I've never been surer. Shall we pay her Highness a visit?"

"It's the middle of the night."

"All the more reason to wake her up. Her Royal Sereneness tried to kill my uncle and she allied herself with the Kariens. She sent her men to be slaughtered and then fled the scene of her crime like a cur in the night. I intend to rattle that bitch until her teeth come loose."

Ignoring Tarja's pleas for reason, Damin took the crumbling stairs to the chambers so recently vacated by Joyhinia, two at a time. Voices filtered up to him, as someone entered the hall at a run. Damin ignored them, his eyes focused, (as much as they could focus in his present state), on the door at the end of the landing, guarded by two red-coated Defenders. He had no clear idea what he would say to Her Serene Highness, but he was going to say something, by the gods!

"Damin!"

Tarja's voice held an edge of urgency that made him pause just before he reached the door. He leaned over the balustrade and looked down into the torchlit hall.

"Forget the princess! The Fardohnyans have surrendered!"

Sobriety returned quickly as the cold night air caught Damin unawares. The camp surrounding the Keep was surprisingly busy, considering the lateness of the hour. Men normally well abed by now were sitting in small groups discussing the battle, dissecting its every nuance with varying degrees of expertise, depending on how much ale they had consumed. Morale in the camp was high. Nobody had expected to weather the first attack with so few casualties. Laughter and the off-tune baritone of men singing victory songs filled the air. Fires blazed with little thought to the fuel they were consuming. Thunder rattled in the distance and a light rain had fallen while he was in the Keep, dampening the dusty ground. Soon enough, these men would be forced to take shelter. There would be no frost tonight with this cloud cover, but if it got much colder it would snow, which should slow the Kariens down somewhat.

This morning's battle had been a desperate attempt to break the Medalonian defenses before winter set in. Damin was rather proud of himself for working that out. Maybe he wasn't as drunk as he thought.

The young man in command of the Fardohnyans was a Second Lanceman named Filip. He wore an expression of defeat along with his battle-stained uniform. His eyes were dull, and his exhaustion seemed to be warring with an emotion that it took Damin a little time to identify: self-loathing. The thirty or so Fardohnyans stood in a loose group, surrounded by Defenders, their torches hissing as the occasional tardy raindrop vanished into the flames.

"Lord Wolfblade." The Fardohnyan bowed low, obviously relieved to see someone who might speak his language. The Defenders who had taken their surrender had disarmed the men behind him. A few were wounded and four lay on the wet ground, too seriously injured to stand.

Tarja, who always seemed much better organized when it came to these things, ordered the wounded removed to the Infirmary Tent and the sleek Fardohnyan steeds moved to the corrals, leaving Damin to deal with the prisoners.

"I've seen many a strange sight in my time, Lanceman," he said in the young man's native tongue, "but Fardohnyans surrendering is not among them."

The lad's expression clouded. Surrender did not sit well with him. "We were ordered to surrender, my Lord."

"What did he say?" Tarja asked, coming to stand beside him.

"He says they were ordered to surrender."

"By whom?"

"Who ordered you to surrender?" he asked in Fardohnyan.

Filip hesitated, glancing over his shoulder at the men behind him before answering, rather reluctantly. "Princess Adrina, my Lord."

Tarja did not need that translated. "Ask him why."

Damin turned to Tarja impatiently. "You don't think I might have thought to ask that by myself?"

"Sorry."

"Did her Highness give a reason?"

The Fardohnyan shrugged. "She was beside herself with grief, my Lord. She said she did not want any more Fardohnyan blood shed for Karien."

"Pity she didn't decide that *before* she sent her men to be slaughtered," he muttered as he turned to Tarja and translated the young soldier's words.

"Grief for whom?" Tarja asked, his sobriety allowing more clarity of thought than Damin was capable of.

"Captain Tristan, my Lord," Filip replied when Damin translated the question. "The captain was the princess's half-brother. They were very close."

"And where is her Highness now?" He was curious to discover if this surrender was part of a plan, or if the young soldier was an innocent pawn in some devious game that Adrina was playing. Damin desperately wished his head was clearer.

"With her husband, of course!" Damin would have known he was lying, even if Adrina was not currently being held in the Keep behind them.

"I see." He turned to Tarja questioningly. "What do you want to do with them?"

"That'll be up to Jenga. For now, I suggest we find some place to hold them until morning." Thunder rumbled louder as another storm rolled in. Tarja glanced up at the sky with a frown. "Put them in the Keep. They'll be out of the rain, at least. We can make more permanent arrangements tomorrow."

Tarja began issuing orders to his men. Damin watched them being herded toward the Keep, wondering about Adrina's paradoxical behavior. The woman had cold-bloodedly plotted the murder of the Hythrun High Prince, yet she'd ordered the remainder of her troops to surrender, rather than see them come to harm. Suddenly he was very glad that he had not made it to the princess's door.

He had a feeling the only way to face Her Serene Highness, Adrina of Fardohnya, and survive, was stone cold sober.

chapter 34

A lthough discovery by the Medalonians had been a risk, Adrina had not really expected it, and was therefore unprepared for her sudden change of circumstances.

For two days, she paced her prison cell impatiently, waiting for something to happen. Meals were delivered regularly by silent, grim-looking Defenders, but they refused to answer her questions. A wan, desperate smile—the precursor to establishing a rapport with her guards—was a wasted effort. Each shift was made up of different men entirely, and once they had left she never saw them again. Nor was Tamylan allowed to leave the chamber, although the slave did not seem nearly as bothered by captivity as her mistress. The waiting began to wear on Adrina's nerves, and she found herself reassessing the intelligence of her captors. They were smarter than she had given them credit for.

The only advantage her isolation provided was the chance to consolidate her plans to deal with the Medalonians. Her first problem, she acknowledged readily, was Damin Wolfblade. She had always imagined him to be something of a dandy, powdered and spoilt, as used to having his every whim indulged as his uncle was. She had known he was a Warlord, of course, but she had pictured him as a figurehead. A gloriously armored fop who sat astride his decorative stallion while others did the work for him. That assessment had been wildly inaccurate. He was a damn sight more ambitious than his uncle, and all together too certain of his place in the world. But he was still a man, she reminded herself, and a Wolfblade at that. The family was too inherently degenerate for the differences to be more than skin deep.

Tarja Tenragan, on the other hand, had been a pleasant surprise. Dark-haired, handsome and remarkably well mannered, his worst fault, she decided, was his attitude to poor Mikel. He obviously commanded a great deal of respect in the camp, and his opinion would carry a lot of weight with the Lord Defender when it came time to decide her fate. If she could engineer a meeting with him alone, she was certain she could entice him to see things her way. She might even enjoy it.

There were good reasons for avoiding such a dangerous game with Damin Wolfblade. He was a prince of Hythria, for one thing, and while it was perfectly acceptable to entertain oneself with the lower classes, frivolous liaisons between members of the nobility were frowned upon. Such a complication between the heir to the Hythrun throne and the Fardohnyan King's eldest daughter did not bear thinking about. The most compelling reason, however, was that while Tarja might be seduced by her *court'esa*-trained skills, Damin would more than likely see straight through them. He probably had a *court'esa* as a nursemaid.

No, she would not play that game. She would pick the easier target. If only someone would please put the target where she could reach it . . .

Adrina plotted and planned and rehearsed her story a thousand times, but day after day she was left alone with nothing but Tamylan and her own anxiety for company.

By the time they finally came for her, Adrina was seething. Nothing was going according to plan. She had been locked up, her possessions stolen, her demands ignored and her imagination had had time to devise all sorts of dreadful fates in store for her. When finally a sergeant opened the door, without knocking, to escort her downstairs, she turned on him, fully prepared to give him a piece of her mind.

"I demand to see someone in authority!"

"Certainly, your Highness," the man replied calmly, although he did not bow. Hardly surprising. These Medalonian peasants had no experience with royalty. "I'm here to take you to Lord Wolfblade."

"I want to see the Lord Defender!"

"That will be up to Lord Wolfblade, your Highness. You'd better wear this. It's raining and you'll ruin that fur."

Adrina snatched the plain, but serviceable woolen cloak from the man and threw it over her shoulders. She still wore the flimsy *court'esa* costume and it was ill suited to the bitterly cold chamber. The fur cloak she had brought with her from Karien was the only thing that had kept her from freezing to death.

"If Lord Wolfblade had any manners he would come to me!"

The man smiled, as if her posturing amused him and led the way down into the main hall. Two more Defenders fell in behind as they crossed the hall and stepped outside into a torrential downpour. Even wrapped in the Defender's cloak, Adrina was drenched in seconds.

She stumbled along beside the Defenders as they walked through the camp, her sodden skirts hampering her steps. The slave collar was cold against her skin and her hair was plastered to her head, the braid slapping wetly against her back with every step. The hem of her skirt was splattered with mud and she was shivering uncontrollably by the time they reached the edge of the neatly laid out Defenders' tents and crossed the open ground between the two camps. She squinted through the rain, trying to pick out any tent that looked as if it belonged to a prince, but there were no banners flying, no obvious declarations of rank. When they finally reached their destination, it proved to be a plain tent, larger than those surrounding it, but bearing nothing to indicate its occupant was of noble blood.

"Wait here," the Defender ordered as he stepped inside, leaving Adrina standing in the rain.

Adrina fumed, but did as she was told, certain this little expedition was nothing more than an attempt to humiliate her. For the first time in months Adrina found there was someone she hated more than Cratyn.

"Your Highness." The sergeant reappeared and held back the tent flap for her. Adrina stepped through, glaring at the man to make certain he was aware of her displeasure. The man smiled in return and left her alone with the Warlord.

Damin Wolfblade sat at a small desk, writing something that seemed to take all his concentration. Adrina waited, dripping onto the thick carpet that covered the floor of the tent and looked around. An inviting brazier stood in the center of the tent and she itched to step closer, but refused to give him the satisfaction. A thick tapestry, of exquisite Hythrun geometrical design, divided the tent in two, concealing the sleeping quarters. Besides the writing desk there was a large table covered in maps against the far wall, and near the brazier, a pile of thick cushions surrounding a small, low table. The Hythrun were fond of sitting on the floor.

She turned her attention to the Warlord then and tried to study him without being obvious. He was a typical Hythrun: tall, blond and well muscled from hours spent in the saddle. But that was the limit of her favorable impressions. He had the distinctive Wolfblade profile and an air about him that reeked of arrogance.

He looked up finally and frowned. He apparently had as low an opinion of her, as she had of him. "Your Highness."

"My Lord."

He put down his quill and stood up. "I'm sorry. Is it raining? Please, give me that cloak. You must be freezing."

Is it raining? She could barely hear herself think over the downpour pounding on the taut, oiled canopy. She shed the cloak, dropping it on the floor behind her, hoping it ruined his damned carpet, and stepped closer to the brazier. Adrina found herself looking up at him. That was disconcerting. She had been able to look Cratyn in the eye.

"Don't take me for a fool, my Lord. You probably waited until it was pouring before you sent for me! You might find such mindless games amusing, but I merely find them a sign of your inability to grasp the finer points of courtesy regarding the treatment of prisoners of rank."

Damin looked her up and down, making her very aware of the flimsy, sodden outfit, then shrugged. "I suppose it won't serve my purpose if you catch pneumonia and die." He pushed back the tapestry dividing the tent and pulled a woolen shirt and trousers from a trunk. "Get out of that ridiculous costume. It ill suits a woman of your rank, in any case. You can get changed in there."

Adrina snatched the clothes from him and walked behind the tapestry. She peeled off her wet skirts, deliberately dropping them on the center of the bed before emerging into the main part of the tent. Her shivering stopped once she was wrapped in the warm shirt, and although it was clean, the faint smell of him lingered on it. The golden collar was icy around her throat.

"Please, sit down."

Adrina did as he suggested, taking the cushion closest to the fire. Steam rose off her hair as the brazier warmed her. Damin offered her a cup of mulled wine, which she stared at warily.

"It's not poisoned. We've already established that it won't serve my cause for you to die."

She took the cup and sipped the wine, the welcome warmth flooding through her. "Your gallantry is overwhelming, sir."

"Don't flatter yourself, Adrina. I'm being practical, not gallant."

"You will address me in a manner befitting my station, my Lord. I did not give you leave to address me so informally."

Damin lowered himself onto the cushions opposite with surprising grace for one so tall. "I'll address you any way I please, madam. You'll find few in this camp who care about your station. Your only value at present is your worth as a hostage. That requires that I keep you alive. It does not require me to bow and scrape and cater to your every idiotic whim."

"In Fardohnya, good manners are not considered an 'idiotic whim'," she pointed out frostily.

"I'll bear that in mind when I next visit Fardohnya. In the meantime, I suggest you curb your tendency to think every person you meet is beneath you. The Medalonians have little patience with nobility. They judge people by their actions, not an accident of birth."

"Ah! And that's what you're doing here, I suppose? You so impressed these atheist peasants with your heroic actions that they could not wait to welcome you into the fold?"

"What I'm doing here is not the issue. The question is, what are *you* doing here, your Highness."

"I was going home."

"You were betraying the Kariens?"

"Don't be absurd. It is simply that . . . there are a number of conditions of the Karien-Fardohnyan Treaty that have not been met to my satisfaction."

"Call it what you like, your Highness, I imagine Cratyn will consider it treason." Damin drank his wine thoughtfully. "That's what they call this place you know—Treason Keep. Rather appropriate, don't you think?"

Nice, Adrina reminded herself. *I have to be nice. He'll send me back to Karien in a heartbeat unless I can convince him to protect me.*

"I . . . I cannot return to Karien, my Lord." She lowered her eyes as she spoke and made sure she added a touching catch to her voice.

"Why not?"

"My life there was intolerable."

"So you fled to Medalon dressed as a *court'esa*, accompanied by nothing more than a slave and a child?"

"I just wanted to escape. I didn't really stop to think." Now that was the truest thing she'd ever said. If she'd stopped to think, she wouldn't be in this predicament.

He obviously didn't believe a word she said. "There are those who think this alliance is merely a ruse, that your father is simply aiding the Kariens so he can cross into Medalon and then turn south into Hythria."

"Well, if he is, it's news to me." Adrina sipped her wine to hide her alarm. *Was Hablet's treacherous nature so famous that a Hythrun could read him so easily?* She composed her features before continuing. "The Defenders don't have the troops to fight a war on two fronts. If you release me immediately, when I reach Talabar, I will speak to my father. I should be able to stay his hand."

"Perhaps," Damin said doubtfully.

Adrina wasn't sure what else she could do to convince him. "I've no love for Karien, my Lord. I just want to go home."

"Does Cratyn know you were planning to leave him?"

"No. After I discovered what had happened to my troops I made some rather foolish threats. It was then that I decided I should leave."

"Are you with child?"

"Of course not! What a stupid question!"

"Oh? If you were with child, and Cratyn has his eye on your father's throne, you might simply be taking the shortest route home, to ensure the child is born on Fardohnyan soil."

Damn him! Where had he gotten that idea? How could some ill-bred warlord from a thousand leagues away see things so clearly?

"Cratyn had some . . . difficulty . . . in fulfilling his conjugal duties."

To her surprise, he laughed with genuine humour. "Poor Cratyn. An inexperienced Karien princeling is no match for a *court'esa*-trained Fardohnyan princess."

"No match at all, I fear."

For a fraction of a second, they were not enemies, but conspirators, sharing laughter at the expense of a hated adversary. The moment lasted just long enough for an uncomfortable silence to descend between them.

"I don't trust you, Adrina. You're trying to play both ends against the middle. You claim to be running home, yet a week ago you were standing at Cratyn's side, throwing your troops into battle for him. You are allied in marriage with Karien on one hand, while offering to hold back your father's troops with the other. You expect me to believe Cratyn doesn't know where you are. I know he's inexperienced, but nobody is that stupid. Your story is so full of holes I could use it as a fishing net."

"Perhaps the intricacies of politics are beyond you, my Lord," she suggested with saccharine sweetness, forcibly hiding her annoyance. Her tale had sounded quite reasonable when she'd tried it out on Tamylan. She never expected a Hythrun to have even a basic grasp of politics.

"I understand you better than you think. You're Hablet's daughter. Treachery has been bred into you."

"Don't make the mistake of judging me by my father."

"I'm not likely to. I have a feeling you are far more dangerous."

For some contrary reason, his comment pleased her. "You can't keep me here forever, my Lord. Eventually you will have to release me."

"Not until I'm good and ready, your Highness. And not until I can see a profit in it."

"I do not intend to sit here and wait upon your mercenary pleasures, my Lord," she retorted, silently cursing her temper. *Be nice.*

"I suggest you rethink your position, your Highness. Right now, you can wait on my mercenary pleasures, or you can go back to your husband. Neither prospect bothers me unduly."

Adrina did not answer. She sipped her wine to hide her expression, afraid that Damin Wolfblade meant exactly what he said.

Nice, she said silently. *I have to be nice to him.*

"I have asked for your protection, my Lord," she said with a demure smile. "Is that too much to ask?"

"The Kariens are prepared to go to war over the death of an Envoy, your Highness. I hate to think what they'll do over their crown princess."

"But you could protect me," she suggested with wide-eyed admiration. In her experience, there were few men who could resist a woman who believed in him so ardently.

Damin Wolfblade was apparently one of them.

"Protect *you*? And while we're protecting you from the wrath of the Kariens, your Highness, who's going to protect us from you?"

chapter 35

Mounted on sorcerer-bred Hythrun horses, R'shiel and her companions reached the small village of Lilyvale in time for dinner on the first day. Joyhinia, Mahina and Affiana rode in a covered wagon, one Garet suggested they replace with something more auspicious as they neared the Citadel. Although the wagon slowed them a little, Joyhinia was incapable of sitting a horse safely, so they sacrificed speed for the assurance that the First Sister would reach the Citadel in one piece.

R'shiel rode with Brak for most of the way, letting the horse set its own pace as she listened to him explain the dangers of drawing on her power to bend others to her will. If he was trying to scare her, he succeeded, but he said nothing to change her mind. There simply wasn't enough time to reach the Citadel and convince the Quorum to accept Joyhinia's resignation and Mahina's appointment any other way.

Garet Warner rode with them for a time. He had, somewhat reluctantly R'shiel thought, agreed with her plan, despite Tarja's objections. The discussion regarding this trip to the Citadel, held hastily and heatedly as the Medalonians prepared for the coming battle, had been strained. R'shiel was fairly certain that if she had waited until after the battle, Jenga and Mahina would have objected, and certainly Tarja, with Brak's assistance, would have found any number of ways to prevent it. As it was, everyone was so distracted by the knowledge that the Kariens were on the move that her desperate plan was spared close scrutiny.

"The gods' power is the power of all things natural," Brak was saying, sounding just like Korandellan. "It's at its most effective when used to enhance a natural occurrence."

"A convenient way of getting around the facts," Garet said.

"The gods are a natural force, Commandant."

"So anything can happen, and you blame a god for your misfortune. Don't you people have free will?"

Brak appeared to be enjoying the conversation with the atheist Defender. He seemed to forget about R'shiel. "Kalianah can make two people fall in love, but not against their will. Dacendaran can encourage a thief to steal, but he could not easily make a thief of an honest man."

"You truly are adept at seeing miracles in the mist," Garet remarked.

R'shiel listened to the men and realized Brak had not forgotten about her at all. He was trying to remind her of the dangers of what she was planning to do. The gods could amplify a yearning or bring about an event that might occur eventually without their help, but to use their power to force an unnatural event was akin to swimming upstream against the river of magic. In doing so, all the slime and filth that had sunk to the bottom of the river was stirred up and brought to the surface. That was why she had been nauseous when she felt the Karien priests working their coercion. She noticed Garet's sceptical expression and turned to him.

"You don't believe any of this, do you, Commandant?"

"I believe that *you* believe every word. I never cease to be astonished at the facility of humans to rationalize perfectly natural events and award them divinity."

"You've seen demons, yet you refuse to believe in them," Brak pointed out. "Isn't that your way of rationalizing away something you don't understand?"

"I've seen creatures I cannot explain and illusions that are masterful, but that is hardly enough to turn me into a pagan. Watch even a moderately talented illusionist in the markets of the Citadel and you will be convinced that a woman can be cut in two and then put together again. Believing a thing doesn't make it real."

"Yet you're going to help us," R'shiel said. "If you think this is just trickery, why bother?"

"My decision is based on logic, not faith, R'shiel. Medalon is facing an enemy that the Sisterhood is not in a position to deal with. I support

Lord Jenga because we are more likely to survive with him in charge than a committee of selfish women grasping for their own political survival."

R'shiel frowned, but Brak seemed more than satisfied with the commandant's answer. "Assuming we succeed, how soon can the rest of the Defenders be mobilized?"

"Fairly quickly," Garet assured him. "I'll get things moving in anticipation of your success at the Gathering. If you achieve your goal, I can have the first of them under way in a matter of hours."

"And if we fail?" R'shiel asked.

"Then I will turn those same men on *you* and claim I was simply playing along with you to gain your confidence and learn your plans," he replied calmly.

"No wonder Joyhinia always thought you were dangerous."

"Dangerous?" he shrugged. "I doubt that, R'shiel. But I am a survivor, and all the heathen trickery in the world cannot alter that." Garet kicked his horse forward to the head of their small column, leaving R'shiel to stare after him thoughtfully.

"Now there's a rare creature," Brak remarked.

"What do you mean?"

"I think Garet Warner is the only truly honest human I have ever met."

It was mid afternoon some days later when Dacendaran appeared. They were traversing the open plain, on a road that slowly wound its way south toward Cauthside, and the ferry that would take them across the Glass River. The day was overcast and chilly, with the sharp smell of impending rain hanging in the still air. R'shiel, with Brak and Garet on her heels, had ridden ahead of the wagon. The weather was making Wind Dancer nervous and she wanted to give the mare a chance to stretch her legs.

She found Dace waiting by the side of the road, sitting cross-legged atop a large gray boulder. He waved as she neared him, his fair hair tousled, his motley clothing as mismatched and ill-fitting as R'shiel had ever seen it.

The God of Thieves had not been much in evidence while R'shiel was at Sanctuary. There was little amusement in those peaceful, hallowed halls for a god who thrived on larceny. Dacendaran preferred the company of humans. Although she knew he was a god—could sense it now that she knew what to look for—she found it hard to think of him as anything but the impudent lad who had befriended her in the Grimfield. She smiled as she reached the boulder, genuinely pleased to see him.

"Dace! What are you doing here?"

"I came to see how you were faring out in the big wide world. Hello, Brakandaran." Brak reined beside her, followed by Garet who glared at the boy suspiciously. The wagon and its attendant guards were still some way back.

"Dacendaran."

"Who's that?" Dace asked, pointing at Garet.

"Commandant Garet Warner, meet Dacendaran, the God of Thieves," R'shiel said, smiling at Garet's expression.

"*This* is one of your gods?"

Dace clapped his hands delightedly. "He's an atheist!"

"And you shouldn't be here," Brak scolded. "Go away, Dace."

"But I want to help! There are noble deeds afoot and I want to be a part of them!"

"If you really want to do something noble, go steal a few of Xaphista's believers," Brak suggested. "You are *not* going anywhere near the Citadel with us."

Dace frowned. "Brakandaran, at some point in the past few centuries, someone *must* have mentioned that mortals do not dictate to the gods. I will go where I please!"

"Will someone please explain who this child really is?" Garet demanded.

"Ah, how I do like a non-believer!"

"Dace, listen to Brak, please," R'shiel pleaded. "Do something to annoy Xaphista if you must help, but there is nothing you can do here."

The god sighed melodramatically. "I suppose. I'm *obviously* not wanted here."

"Stop being such a baby," R'shiel said.

The god grinned. "I make a poor substitute for the God of Guilt, don't I?"

"The God of *what*?" Garet asked incredulously.

Even Brak smiled. "Commandant. I suggest you either ignore this entire exchange or start believing in the Primal gods."

"I think I'll ignore it," he said with a frown. He turned his mount and rode back toward the wagon.

"Did I upset him?" Dace asked innocently.

"No more than you usually upset people," Brak said. "Why did you let him see you?"

"All humans should have the opportunity to look upon a god every now and then. It's an honor."

"Not when they don't believe you exist," R'shiel pointed out.

"Well, now that he's seen me, he'll have to believe in me, won't he?"

"Don't count on it," Brak warned.

"You always look on the dark side of things, Brakandaran. I was going to give you some news, but now I'm not so sure. You're bound to think the worst."

"What news?"

"I'm really not certain that I should . . ."

"Dace," R'shiel cut in impatiently. "Stop teasing. If you have something important to tell us, then out with it!"

The god pouted. "You have been spending far too much time with Brakandaran, R'shiel. You're beginning to sound just like him."

"Come on, R'shiel," Brak said, gathering up his reins as he glanced over his shoulder at the approaching wagon. "He obviously has nothing important to tell us, and the others will be here any moment. Goodbye, Divine One."

"Xaphista has believers in the Citadel!" the god blurted out.

R'shiel stared at Dace with concern. "Believers? Who?"

"I don't know," Dace shrugged. "All I know is that the Citadel can feel them and he doesn't like it one bit!"

Confused, R'shiel turned to Brak for an explanation. "What does he mean? He speaks as though the Citadel is alive."

"It is, sort of," Brak answered before turning to Dace. "Has anything happened yet?"

"No. You know what he's like. It takes him a century just to remember his own name. But he can feel Xaphista's taint and he's not happy about it."

Brak nodded slowly. R'shiel had absolutely no idea what they were talking about.

"Brak, has this got something to do with the power in the Citadel that Dranymire spoke of?"

Before he could answer, the wagon creaked to a stop behind them. Garet rode forward and frowned at Dace.

"I see your god is still with us. Are you two planning to sit here in the middle of the road blocking the way, or can we proceed? In case you hadn't noticed, it's going to rain soon. I'd like to reach Malacky before then."

"These atheists really are an impatient lot, aren't they?" Dacendaran remarked loftily. With that, he vanished, leaving Garet wide eyed.

R'shiel looked at Garet and wondered how the commandant would explain Dace's sudden disappearance to himself, but after a moment's stunned silence, he waved his men and the wagon forward as if absolutely nothing untoward had happened.

part three

—⁓—

THE POLITICS OF SEDUCTION

chapter 36

ikel was separated from the princess and placed in the custody of the Defenders' Master of Horse, a small, slender man with dark hair and an affection for the creatures in his charge which bordered on obsession. Captain Hadly had endless patience with his horses and none at all for defiant Karien boys. When one of Lord Wolfblade's Raiders delivered him into Hadly's care, he had glanced at the note Tarja had hastily scribbled, then looked disdainfully at Mikel.

"Captain Tenragan says you are to be placed in my care. He says that if you try to escape, or give me any bother at all, I am to inform him immediately. He also says to remind you about your brother. Do you know what he means?"

Mikel nodded sullenly. He had hoped Tarja might forget about Jaymes.

"Good, because I've no time to waste on infants. I've damned near two thousand horses here, boy, and now there's the Fardohnyan mounts to take care of. Go find Sergeant Monthay. He'll find something useful for you to do."

With little choice in the matter, he did as he was told.

Besides being sick with worry over the princess, Mikel was desperate to discover his brother's fate, but there seemed little chance here among the horses. The Hythrun mounts were corralled away from the Medalonian horses—something to do with the purity of the Hythrun breed that Mikel didn't really understand—so there was no chance to question anyone about the Karien boy they held prisoner. Sergeant Monthay set him to distributing hay, an endless task with so vast a herd. He spent all day lugging haybales from the cart into the corrals, then running to catch up as Monthay moved the wagon on to the next enclosure. It was backbreaking work, but it kept him from thinking too much, and at night he collapsed into the bedroll Monthay had found for him in the tack tent, asleep almost before his head hit the saddle he used for a pillow.

On the fourth day of his captivity, the rain cleared and the weather grew even colder. The sharp smell of snow lingered on the wind and Hadly fretted at the lack of protection for his horses. He had commandeered a large force of workers from the followers' camp and had them erecting canvas-covered shelters in the corrals in anticipation of the coming inclement weather.

Mikel shivered as he went about his chores. Monthay was anxious to finish for the day and get back to the warmth of his tent. It was almost midday when they reached the corral where the workers were tying canvas over another sapling framework. The cold sun did nothing to warm the day. There was a small fire burning just outside the corral, and several women were doling out hot soup as the workers took a break from their labor. Monthay glanced at Mikel, ordered him to keep working, and went to join them.

He lugged another bale from the cart and dragged it along the ground toward the corral, cursing Medalonians in general, and Monthay in particular. He muttered a prayer to the Overlord, asking his god to strike down the men enjoying the hot soup with dysentery. It seemed only fitting.

"Xaphista's far too busy to answer, you know."

Mikel looked up and discovered a boy of about fifteen sitting on the top rail of the corral. He was dressed in an odd collection of clothes that looked like cast-offs from some bygone era. Mikel was not aware that he had spoken aloud.

"You should not speak the name of Xaphista. You're an unbeliever."

"Not at all! I know Xaphista personally! Can't say that I speak to him much myself, mind you, but he does exist."

Mikel straightened and stared at the youth, a little surprised to hear

such an admission from an atheist. He supposed the boy was one of the
workers erecting the shelters.

"What do you want?"

"Nothing."

"Then leave me alone." He grabbed the twine holding the bale
together and grunted with the effort of dragging it over the rough ground
toward the corral.

"What are you doing?"

"What does it *look* like I'm doing?"

The fair-haired youth laughed. "That bale is near as big as you are!"

"Then why don't you help me?"

"Ah, now that would mean work. I don't do work."

Mikel let go of the bale and glared at him. "What *do* you do, then?"

"I'm a thief."

The news did not surprise Mikel. The lad looked dishonest. "Thiev-
ery is a sin."

"Don't be absurd! Who told you that? Ah! Xaphista did, I suppose.
Cheeky sod."

"You shouldn't blaspheme! That's a sin too!"

"There is no such thing as sin . . . what's your name?"

"Mikel."

"Well, Mikel, let me put your mind at ease. There is no such thing as
sin. A thief is not doing something wrong, he is honoring Dacendaran,
the God of Thieves."

"There is only one true god!" Mikel insisted.

The boy frowned and jumped off the rail. "You really believe that,
don't you? Are all Kariens like you?"

"Yes! Now go away and leave me alone!" Mikel made to reach for
the bale, but the youth sat himself down on it and looked at him
closely.

"Mikel, the only reason Xaphista invented the concept of sin was to
stop his believers honoring the other gods."

"There *are* no other gods!"

"I can see I'm going to have to educate you, young man." The
youth sighed heavily, then suddenly brightened. "I know, I shall
become your new best friend and lead you to the truth about the Primal
gods!"

"I already know the truth. Xaphista is the Overlord."

"Xaphista is a pompous old windbag, actually, and I shall delight in stealing you from him."

"Come on, boy! We'll still be here at midnight at this rate! Get a move on!"

Mikel started as Monthay yelled at him. He turned back to the boy sitting on the bale and was even more startled to discover he was gone.

"Don't just stand there talking to yourself like a fool," Monthay scolded as he drew near. "Go get some soup, but be quick about it."

Mikel ran toward the fire and the enticing smell of the hot soup, wondering where the youth had gone so abruptly. Then he remembered his rash prayer and hoped that the Overlord had not heard his request about the dysentery.

Mid-afternoon, two Defenders appeared in the corrals and told Monthay that Captain Tenragan wanted to see the Karien boy. Monthay muttered a curse and surrendered him reluctantly, glancing at the hay still to be distributed. The two Defenders took Mikel into custody and walked him back toward the Keep. They said nothing, even to each other, leaving Mikel plenty of time to imagine the worst.

When they reached the old keep, they took him into the main hall where Tarja was waiting near the huge fireplace. Damin Wolfblade was sitting at the table, stabbing the tabletop with his dagger as if something vexed him. Captain Almodavar stood near Tarja and next to him, to Mikel's astonishment, was his brother.

"Jaymes!"

Mikel ran the length of the hall, skidding to a halt a few steps from his brother, taking a quick inventory to check he had all his fingers. Jaymes grinned and crossed the small distance between them, hugging his younger brother warmly.

"They told me you were back, but I wanted to see for myself!"

"Oh Jaymes! I've been so worried about you! Are you well? Have they harmed you?"

"Of course not!" Jaymes laughed. "I'm the one who's been worrying about you! What happened when you went back to Lord Laetho?"

Mikel glanced at the men and then back at Jaymes. His brother was taller, as if he had grown from a boy into a young man while in captivity. He looked well; much too well for a prisoner. "I'll tell you later."

"There won't be a later, lad," Almodavar warned. "Jaymes has work to do."

"He's right. I have to get back. My training keeps me pretty busy. But I'll try to see you now and then, if I can get away."

"Training?"

"I'm learning to be a soldier."

Mikel took a step backwards. "With the Hythrun?"

"Of course, with the Hythrun."

"You're a *traitor*?"

"I warned you," Damin muttered to no one in particular, stabbing the table to punctuate his words.

Jaymes sighed. "It's not like that, Mikel . . ."

"Have you turned from the Overlord, too? Do you worship the Primal gods now? How *could* you?"

"The Overlord? What do I care about the Overlord! I want to be a soldier, Mikel! I can't ever be a knight in Karien. I'm a commoner. Good for nothing but a pikeman. But the Hythrun don't care about that. They judge men by their ability, not who their father is."

"Our father is the Duke of Kirkland's Third Steward!"

"Which is worth shit, and you know it!"

Tears of anger and betrayal clouded Mikel's vision. He could not believe what he was hearing.

"What have you done to him?" he demanded of Tarja, although the Medalonian had not had charge of his brother. Tarja had, however, been responsible for most of his woes these past few months so it seemed reasonable to blame him for this, too.

"Your brother made his own choice, boy."

"You've done something to him! Jaymes would never betray Karien! He would never renounce the Overlord!"

"Grow up, Mikel," Jaymes sighed. "The Overlord doesn't care about the likes of you and me. He's the God of Lords and Princes. All he ever did for us was make us work for *them*. You believe in his generosity if you must, but I plan to follow those who can teach me what I want to learn." Jaymes turned to the Warlord and bowed. "May I be excused, now, my Lord?"

"You can go."

Jaymes glanced at Mikel and shook his head. "I'm sorry, little brother . . ."

Mikel refused to look at him. "I have no brother."

"Maybe when you're older, Mikel, you'll understand."

He turned his back as Jaymes and the Hythrun captain walked the length of the hall. When he heard the door shut, he wiped his eyes and looked up at Tarja.

"Can I go, too?"

"No, you may not. You're going to tell us about the princess."

Jaymes' betrayal was suddenly forgotten. He glared at Tarja, drawing himself up to his full height. "If you have harmed one hair on her head . . ."

"Oh for the god's sake, child, settle down!" Damin snapped. "Your precious princess is fine."

"I shall not betray my Lady!"

"Nobody is asking you to," Tarja pointed out reasonably. "We just want to know how you came to be in her company."

"I was appointed her page. By Prince Cratyn himself!"

"I see. That's quite a position of trust."

"Prince Cratyn trusts me."

"He must trust you a great deal, to ask you to escort her Highness through Medalon when your nation is at war with us."

Mikel was still young enough that flattery, even from a man he despised, made his heart swell proudly. "Prince Cratyn knew that I would not betray him. No spy . . ."

"Spy?" Damin asked, glancing up from the tabletop. "What spy?"

Mikel took a step backwards, frowning warily. "I said nothing about a spy."

Damin looked at Tarja and shrugged. "Send him back to the horses, Tarja. Adrina has already told us everything we want to know. She was trying to escape to Fardohnya to get away from Cratyn and stop her father joining in the war."

"That's a lie!" Mikel shouted, horrified that they would think such a thing of the noble princess. "You are making that up!"

"Not at all," Tarja told him. "Adrina told us everything."

"You must have tortured her!"

"If you call mulled wine and a warm fire torture," Damin said with a faint smile, "Quite the opportunist, your princess, Mikel. She changes sides more often than most people change their clothes."

"Princess Adrina is the most noble, pious, beautiful woman in the whole world! She's brave, too!"

"Brave?" Tarja scoffed. "She was running away.'

"She was not! She was going to see her father to get him to send the cannon! So that you would all die!"

Tarja and Damin glanced at each other as Mikel realized what he had blurted out. He wanted to cry. He wished the cold flagstones would open up and swallow him whole. First Jaymes had betrayed him.

Now he had betrayed Adrina.

chapter 37

"Who do you believe? The boy or the princess?" Jenga paced the hearth, rubbing his chin thoughtfully. Gray daylight flooded the hall but the air was crisp, even this close to the fire.

Damin shrugged. "She's lying. She's heading for Talabar to bring her father's cannon into the war. She's not running away."

Tarja nodded his agreement. "I believe the boy is telling the truth, but it's the truth your princess fed him. She could hardly *announce* her intention to run away." He was sitting in front of the inadequate blaze, warming the soles of his boots, obviously pleased that the decision about what to do with Adrina was not his to make.

"Will you stop calling her *my* princess!"

Tarja grinned. "Well, she's your problem. And you're always telling me how much better you understand the Fardohnyan nobility than us poor peasants here in Medalon . . ."

"Very funny."

"I was merely trying to point out that—"

"Enough, Tarja," Jenga cut in wearily. "Lord Wolfblade, would it be fair to say that you really have no idea what she is doing here?"

Damin nodded. "That would be fair."

"And we've had no emissaries from the Kariens seeking her out."

"I'd be surprised if we did," Tarja said. "If she's on the run, the last place Cratyn would look for her is Medalon."

"And if she's telling the truth, then he needs to pretend that nothing is amiss," Jenga agreed.

"You know, we'd get a lot more out of Her Serene Highness if she thought we believed her."

"The rack and a red hot poker would do me just as well," Damin muttered. Jenga threw him an annoyed look before turning to Tarja.

"Explain."

"Perhaps, if her status was one of honored guest rather than prisoner, she might let something slip."

"She won't let anything slip. She's too smart for that." Damin glared at Tarja, not liking the direction this conversation was heading.

"Maybe," Jenga mused. "What are you suggesting exactly?"

"Release her. Give her the freedom of the camp. We should ask for something to prove her story, of course. Some piece of intelligence we can easily verify, as a gesture of good will. And we'd have to put a guard on her—there's no telling what she'd get up to on her own, but we can claim it's for her protection. We can't let her get her hands on her jewels, either, but there is no reason why she shouldn't think we believe her."

"If we believed her, we'd send her back to Fardohnya," Damin pointed out. "She won't fall for it."

"Oh, yes, she will. Because you, my Lord, are going to start acting as if she's an ally, not your sworn enemy."

"The hell I will!"

"I'm afraid you've lost me, Tarja?" Jenga said. "How would that help?"

Tarja sighed patiently. "As Damin keeps reminding us, she's a very smart girl. But she never got the message from her brother and she knows nothing of the Hythrun Raiders stationed in Bordertown. If we release her, at least conditionally, and our Warlord here can keep a civil tongue in his head, she'll come to believe we need her help in holding back her father's troops. I'm not saying she'll believe us right away, but if we act as if we think she's on our side, even if she's lying, she has to play along with it."

"So you think she may end up betraying herself, simply to maintain the illusion of cooperation?"

"Relax your vigilance for more than a heartbeat, and she'll slip a knife between your ribs," Damin warned.

"Ah, but she's *your* princess, remember?" Tarja said with a grin. "I don't plan on getting that close."

Damin glared at Tarja. "Nice plan, my friend, but in case you hadn't noticed, there's a war going on out there. I have too much to do to waste time playing games of intrigue with a Fardohnyan princess. The Kariens could attack again at any moment."

Jenga shook his head confidently. "Not likely. They've still not recovered from the last battle and it will snow any day."

"Besides, your troops seem to get along very nicely without you," Tarja added, taking far too much pleasure in Damin's misery. "Almodavar coped quite well while you were off consulting your god for nearly a month."

Damin considered that an entirely unfair argument. "It's not the same thing. My men knew I was gone to consult with the gods. They're not likely to be nearly as understanding if they think I'm neglecting them for a woman."

"I disagree," Jenga remarked with a rare smile. "From what I've seen of your men, Damin, they'd give that just as much credence."

Damin chose to ignore that one. "It won't work."

"Of course it'll work," Tarja assured him. "Just pray to one of your gods."

Damin gave the captain a withering glare. "We don't actually have a god of Bloody Stupid Ideas, Tarja."

Damin did not bother knocking. He ordered the guards to open the door to Adrina's chamber and marched in unannounced. He was a little disappointed to discover Adrina and her slave sitting on the pallet that served as a bed, apparently engaged in nothing more sinister than idle chatter, their legs covered by a blanket to ward off the cold. Adrina still wore the shirt he had given her in his tent, and someone had given the slave something warmer to wear as well. The women looked up as he entered.

"Out!" he ordered the slave. She responded to the authority in his voice without thinking and scurried from the room, leaving them alone. Adrina did not move. He was quite impressed with the way she managed to look down on him, even though she was sitting and he was standing.

"You have the manners of a barbarian."

"You seem to bring out the worst in me, your Highness."

Surprisingly, Adrina smiled. "I have a feeling I've not seen anything closely resembling your worst, Lord Wolfblade. What do you have there?"

She pointed at the sack he carried which he placed on the bed beside her.

"Jenga ordered your things returned to you. He thought you might be more comfortable in your own clothes."

"That was considerate of him," she remarked as she felt around inside the bag. "However, my jewelry seems to be missing."

"The Lord Defender was concerned about such valuable property lying about unguarded. He will keep your jewels for now. For safe keeping, of course."

"Of course," she echoed sceptically. "Am I to assume this sudden desire to see to my welfare means you have come to a decision about me?"

"In a manner of speaking. Although I, for one, don't believe a word of your unlikely tale." It wouldn't do to completely change his tune. She would see through that in an instant. "The Medalonians, unfortunately, are much more naive. Jenga believes your story and has ordered that you be treated as an honored guest from now on."

"Then I am to be released?" Damin could detect the glimmer of hope in her voice.

"I said they were naive, your Highness, not stupid. The Lord Defender wants proof. Once he is convinced, then he will endeavour to have you returned to Fardohnya. In return for an assurance from King Hablet that he won't step foot outside his own borders, naturally."

"And if my father refuses such an assurance?"

"Then you'd best learn to like Medalonian cooking, your Highness, because you won't be going anywhere without it."

Adrina thought for a moment, but Damin could not tell what was going on behind that lovely face. She was like some exotic piece of coral that grew on the reefs south of Greenharbour—glorious to look at, deadly to touch.

"What sort of proof does he require?" she asked eventually.

"Information. Something he can corroborate from another source."

Adrina nodded. "I'm not certain I know anything of strategic value, my Lord, but I will try to think of something."

"Just let the guards outside know, when you think of it. They'll see the message gets to the Lord Defender."

He gave her a short bow, out of politeness rather than respect, and turned to leave, a little surprised that he had managed to remain so calm.

"My Lord?"

He turned back. "Was there something else?"

"May I leave this chamber, now that I'm a *guest*, as opposed to a prisoner?"

"Only under escort, I'm afraid. You are in the middle of a war camp, your Highness. The Lord Defender would not wish any harm to come to you."

"You wouldn't mind a bit, though, would you?" She met his eye evenly, her gaze a blatant challenge. Damin almost let his desire to strangle this woman get the better of him, before he swallowed his annoyance and forced himself to smile.

"I am also a guest here, Adrina, and I'm compelled to abide by the wishes of my hosts. The Lord Defender wishes to see you treated well, and I will see that you are. But don't mistake my cooperation for weakness. If I can prove you are lying, I will cheerfully slit your throat myself."

If his declaration frightened her, she gave no sign. Her gaze never wavered; her expression did not change. "I find your honesty a refreshing change in a Wolfblade, my Lord. Perhaps there is hope for your family yet."

"Unlike the Fardohnyan Royal Family, we Wolfblades strive for quality, not quantity." Damin almost enjoyed her refusal to cower in the face of his unveiled threat.

Adrina's eyes glittered; they were quite a remarkable shade of green. "Ah, quality. Is that what you call it? One can only hope your striving for *quality* has been more successful in your case than it has been in your uncle's."

Damin was far too aware of his uncle's peculiarities for her barb to have much impact, but he admired her courage. You did not trade insults with a Hythrun Warlord, or impugn the character of the High Prince, unless you were very, very sure of yourself. Then she unconsciously touched her hand to the glittering wolf collar, reminding him sharply of her true nature. His momentary admiration withered and died in an instant.

"Perhaps, if you live long enough you'll find out, your Highness." He turned from her again, unsure how much longer he could keep his temper.

"I'd like to get out of here. Out of this keep. I want to go riding."

Damin stopped with his hand on the latch. "I'll see what I can arrange."

"And I want this collar off."

He shrugged. "It will take time, your Highness. I don't make a habit of carrying court collars and their keys to war."

"Not even for your own *court'esa*?"

"I don't make a habit of bringing *court'esa* to war, either."

She smiled maliciously. "I suppose you hardly need them, with all these big handsome soldiers around."

He was across the room, his hands around her throat, before he realized what he was doing. The collar was warm to the touch, and ironically, was the only thing stopping him from squeezing the life out of her, there and then.

"Don't push me too far, Adrina! I could *kill* you for even having possession of this collar!"

"Get . . . your . . . hands . . . off . . . me!" Her voice was fury coated in ice.

He let her go with a shove and strode from the room, shaking with anger, slamming the door behind him.

Tarja was waiting for him at the bottom of the stairs. "How did it go?"

"Wonderful!" he growled as he walked past without stopping.

"So you didn't try to kill her, then?" Tarja called after him with a laugh.

"Only once."

It took Tarja a few moments to realize he wasn't joking.

chapter 38

The next time Mikel met Dace, he had a little girl with him. She was a pretty little thing and looked to be about five or six. She had bare feet and wore nothing but a flimsy, sleeveless shift, despite the cold, although she hardly seemed to notice the weather. The child examined him with a slight frown, then looked up at the older boy.

"He's so *sad*!"

"What do you expect?"

Mikel glared at the pair, annoyed that they spoke as if he wasn't there. "What are you doing here? Have you come to steal something?"

Dace grinned. "In a manner of speaking. This is Kali. She's my sister."

The little girl smiled up at him. "Do you love me?"

"I don't even know you!" Mikel retorted, a little taken aback by the odd question.

She sighed. "Oh well, once you get to know me, you'll love me then. Everybody does."

Mikel frowned and wondered what sort of home this odd brother and sister came from, that Dace would proudly claim to be a thief and Kali would expect everyone to love her on sight. He glanced around, expecting Monthay to yell at him, but the sergeant was talking to another Defender and seemed oblivious to the fact that Mikel had stopped to talk to the children.

Dace noticed the direction of his gaze and grinned. "Don't worry about him."

"Easy enough for you to say," Mikel grumbled.

"Did you want to come and play with us?" Kali asked.

"I can't. I'm a prisoner."

"What did you do?"

"I didn't do anything. I'm a prisoner of war."

"But you're just a little boy!" Kali sounded quite upset. She turned to Dace and tugged on his sleeve. "Go and make that man in the red coat let him go. For the afternoon at least. Then we can have some fun."

Dace pulled a face at her. "I don't do that sort of stuff."

She let out an exasperated sigh. "Think of it as *stealing* him away, Dace."

"Oh, well if you put it like that," the older boy said with a grin. "That's easy."

Almost as soon as he spoke, Monthay suddenly turned to Mikel.

"Hey! Boy! Take the afternoon off. I don't want to see you until dinner time!"

Startled, Mikel looked at the children with wide eyes. "How did you do that?"

"Magic," Dace replied. "Come on!" The boy began to walk away, his sister at his side. "What shall we do, Kali?"

Mikel hesitated for a moment, then ran to catch up.

"I don't know. Did you want to visit with your friends?"

"I have no friends here," Mikel told her glumly as he fell into step beside them.

"What about your brother?" Dace asked. "Isn't he with the Hythrun, or something?"

"How did you know . . ." he began, then he remembered what Jaymes had become and shook his head. "I have no brother."

Kali looked up at him curiously. "Why are you lying?"

"I'm not lying."

"Yes, you are!" she insisted. "We should have brought Jakerlon," she added to her brother.

"Well, if I'd known he was a liar, I would have," Dace replied.

"Who is Jakerlon?"

"The God of Liars," Kali explained, giving him an odd look. "He doesn't know much, does he?"

"That's Xaphista for you," Dace shrugged. "He pretends the rest of us don't even exist."

"What do you know about Xaphista?"

"We know lots about Xaphista," Kali announced stiffly. "We know he's a bully."

"And arrogant."

"And rude! You wouldn't believe how rude he can be!"

"Stop it! You mustn't say such things! The Overlord will strike you down!"

"Not likely," Dace laughed. Then he glanced at Mikel and noticed his distress. "I'm sorry. You don't have to get so upset, you know. He really isn't listening to us. He's got far too many problems to care what we're saying about him."

"Serves him right," Kali said. "If he wasn't so busy trying to rule the world he'd have time to listen to his believers instead of ignoring them."

Mikel stopped walking, unable to tolerate their blasphemy any longer. "Stop it! You have no idea what you're talking about! The Overlord loves us. He listens to every prayer!"

"Ah, but does he answer them?" Dace asked.

"Of course, He does!"

"Very well, prove it," Kali said.

"How?"

The little girl thought for a moment. "I've a better idea. I'll prove he doesn't listen. Did you pray to the Overlord to watch over you during the war?"

"Yes."

"Then what are you doing here?"

Mikel couldn't immediately think of an answer to that one.

Kali laughed at his hesitation. "There! What did I tell you?"

"The Overlord works in mysterious ways," he retorted, falling back on a favorite saying of the priests. "He has a reason for everything He does!"

"Nonsense!" Dace scoffed. "You're here because Xaphista hasn't the time to spare for one insignificant little boy. Your brother has the right of it, although he shows a distinct lack of sense by choosing to follow Zegarnald. Still, Zeggie never was that discerning—any soul who wants to pick up a sword will usually do for him."

"Jaymes is now a follower of Zegarnald?" Mikel asked in horror.

Kali looked at him with narrowed eyes. "I thought you didn't have a brother?"

"Leave him alone, Kali. Come on, we were going to find something to do. Did you want to learn how to be a thief?"

"No!"

"Why don't we pay Tarja a visit?" Kali suggested. "He's your friend, Dace, and he owes me a big favor, although he doesn't know it yet."

"I hate Tarja," Mikel muttered. Kali and Dace both turned to stare at him.

"But why?" Kali asked. "He's really nice. Well, for a non-believer, at any rate, even though he knows the gods exist. I think he just hasn't decided who he should worship yet."

"Well, it won't be you," Dace said. "Not when he finds out what you did."

"Oh? And I suppose *you* think he'll follow you? Just because you met him first?"

Mikel looked from brother to sister in complete confusion. "What are you *talking* about?"

They abruptly stopped arguing and smiled at him guilelessly.

"Nothing," Dace shrugged.

"I know, let's go visit Adrina!" Kali suggested brightly. "You like her, don't you, Mikel?"

"Of course I like her! She's the most noble princess in the whole world!" The prospect of seeing the princess raised Mikel's spirits considerably, although he could not imagine how these two could arrange to get anywhere near the closely guarded keep. "And besides, she's a true believer," he added, just to remind these pagans who had the most worthy god.

"Adrina? Believe in the Overlord? What rubbish!" Kali laughed delightedly at the very idea. "She follows Kalianah, the Goddess of Love. She used to pray to the Goddess all the time."

"*Used* to," Mikel pointed out triumphantly. "Now she prays to Xaphista."

"No," Kali said with a sorrowful sigh. "I think she just gave up. It's hard to find love when your father is so powerful. I always meant to find someone nice for her when she was old enough, but then she stopped asking. I wonder why?"

"What do you mean, *you* were going to find someone for her?" Mikel asked. "The princess is married! She's in love with Prince Cratyn!"

"Don't be silly! Of course she's not in love with him."

"How do you know?"

Kali pouted. "I just do, that's all."

"Why don't you just ask her?" Dace said, pointing toward the corrals.

Their walk had taken them past the Medalonian corrals and closer to the enclosures where the beautiful Hythrun horses were mustered. Unlike the Medalonians, each Hythrun was responsible for his own mount and every morning the Raiders would come to the corrals to feed their mounts, groom them and talk to them as if the horses could understand every word. There were no ramshackle canvas-covered shelters here. The Hythrun had actually built stables, which were almost completed, on the other side of the field. Mikel had heard Hadly complaining about the waste of precious timber, while staring wistfully in the direction of the sturdy Hythrun stalls.

Mikel followed Dace's pointing finger and spied Adrina, mounted on a Hythrun steed, in the company of the Warlord. Damin Wolfblade was talking to the foreman in charge of the construction team, and Adrina sat patiently beside him, waiting for him to finish. She was dressed in her dark blue riding habit, her long fur cloak draped over her shoulders. She sat astride her horse, rather than sidesaddle, as was proper for a lady. She looked remarkably well, and when the Warlord turned and spoke to her, she nodded and replied with a faint smile. The foreman bowed to the princess and returned to his duties. Adrina and Damin wheeled their mounts around and headed south at a canter.

"He'd better not hurt her," Mikel muttered, to himself as much as his companions.

"He won't," Kali assured him. "Pity he's one of Zeggie's favorites . . ."

"Don't even think about it, Kali," Dace warned. "He'd be so mad at you if you did anything."

"I know. But they do make a nice couple."

"Kali . . ."

"Oh, don't worry Dace, I'm not that silly." She turned to Mikel and smiled brightly. "Your princess seems to be enjoying herself. You'd think she'd be a prisoner too, if she believed in the Overlord."

Mikel had been thinking the same thing. He watched the riders as they dwindled into the distance, saw them pick up the pace until they were galloping across the plain. The faint sound of Adrina's laughter lingered on the breeze. His heart constricted as he watched her. She was his princess. She was married to Prince Cratyn. She shouldn't be out riding alone with a man like Damin Wolfblade.

And she damned well shouldn't act like she was enjoying it, either.

chapter 39

drina gave the sorcerer-bred mount its head, relishing the
feel of the cold wind in her face and the sure-footed beast
beneath her, unable to stifle the laugh of sheer joy that
escaped her as the horse thundered across the plain. She'd
heard tales of the fabled breed, had seen them when she
visited Greenharbour, but until Damin Wolfblade had first taken her riding a week ago, she had never been allowed close to one. She suspected
Damin had provided her with a Hythrun mount, rather than her own
Fardohnyan steed, to intimidate her. Adrina had taken to riding the
notoriously difficult breed like a Hythrun born and bred.

Their first outing had been a strained affair. Damin was still angry
with her and she was in no mood to put up with such an unpredictable
brute. Three hours in the saddle had done much to ease the tension.
Horses were a safe subject and Damin appeared genuinely impressed by
her ability. They had finished the day not quite friends, but at least on
speaking terms.

Since then Damin had taken her out every day, and for the most part
he was tolerable company. He usually allowed her to accompany him as
he did a round of the vast camp, taking care of the myriad problems that
cropped up in the course of the day with remarkable patience. Twice
Tarja had accompanied them for part of their ride. He treated Adrina
with respect but kept glancing at Damin as if something amused him
greatly. It was proving onerous to be civil to Damin Wolfblade on a continuing basis. Tarja was a much more likely prospect.

Mindful of her need to learn as much as possible about him, she decided to question Damin. Her tactful and entirely innocent question regarding Tarja's marital status had Damin roaring with laughter.

"Don't waste your time even thinking about it!"

"I'm sure I don't know what you mean," she declared loftily.

"Oh yes you do! I know exactly what you're thinking. He's young and good looking, in a position of authority, and you think he'll be no match for your *court'esa* trained powers of seduction."

"I thought no such thing!"

"Trust me, Adrina, nothing you could offer Tarja Tenragan could compare with what he's already got."

"You think I couldn't steal him away from some rustic Medalonian peasant girl?" Adrina was insulted at the mere thought.

"I think you couldn't steal him away from the Harshini demon child, your Highness."

Adrina stared at him. "*The* demon child?"

"In the flesh. And rather nice looking flesh it is too."

"I don't believe you! The Harshini are gone. The demon child is just a legend!"

"The demon child is very real, Adrina. Her name is R'shiel té Ortyn, and she left the camp the same day you arrived. She'll be back in a few weeks. You should find it an enlightening experience, meeting someone who is not in awe of you."

Adrina was tempted to comment that he didn't seem to be particularly in awe of her, either. But she held her tongue and wondered why, if the Harshini really had returned, the demon child would be fighting on the side of atheist Medalon.

Her plans for Tarja having met an unexpected hitch, Adrina turned her attention, somewhat reluctantly, to Damin Wolfblade. The more she saw of him, the more she realized she had misjudged him badly, a fact she found worrying.

He was not a younger version of his uncle. Nor was he a spoilt, figurehead Warlord. He was intelligent, surprisingly well educated, far too astute for her liking, and obviously enjoyed the respect of his men and the

Defenders in equal measure. Not a man to underestimate. She needed to learn as much as she could about the Hythrun prince. She needed to discover what he liked, what he loathed, whom he admired and whom he despised, and, more important, why he was angry with her.

That she had done something to enrage him was obvious. The day he came to her room to announce she was to be given the freedom of the camp, he had come close to killing her. Her snide remarks had not been enough to provoke such a reaction. She had seen enough of him since that day to know that he was generally even-tempered, at least around everybody else. But nothing she had done since her capture warranted the anger she felt simmering in him, even when he was making an effort to be civil. It puzzled her. Until she discovered its source, she had no hope of escaping this place.

They rode far south of the camp, toward a distant line of trees. She wondered what would happen if she turned her horse and tried to make a break for it, then glanced at Damin. He would run her down in a heartbeat and the fragile trust she had fostered among her captors would be destroyed. She sighed and let her mare follow Damin's stallion.

They slowed to a walk as they entered the small copse of thin poplars. There were stumps littered about, the crude result of the Defenders' need for shelter for their horses. The thick carpet of fallen leaves muffled their horses' hooves and the sound of running water was the only thing that disturbed the silence. Adrina rode up beside Damin, assuming an air of nonchalance. It was time to start working out what made this man who he was, and she was never going to do that arguing with him. *Be nice*, she reminded herself.

"It must be hard for you, being Lernen's Heir."

He shrugged. "It can be a little trying."

"You're not much like him."

He turned and looked at her. "Gods! Was that a compliment?"

She smiled. "Actually, I think it was. I must be slipping."

Damin laughed. The first genuine laugh she had heard from him since their embarrassing conversation about Tarja. "Don't worry, Adrina, we're alone. I won't tell if you don't."

His laugh was infectious. She began to understand what others saw in him. He was very hard to dislike in this mood. It made him doubly dangerous.

"Do you miss your family? So far from home?"

"Sometimes," he admitted, which surprised her a little. "Medalon can be . . . trying at times, too."

"I miss my family." Perhaps empathy would work where sarcasm had failed.

"From what I hear, there's quite a lot of them to miss."

"My father is prolific, if nothing else. Do you have brothers and sisters?"

"In abundance. Although not quite as many as you can claim. You met my half-sister in Greenharbour, I believe."

"Did I?"

"She's the High Arrion."

"Kalan is your sister?" She wondered why that nosy little toad, Lecter Turon, had never mentioned that the leader of the powerful Hythrun Sorcerers' Collective was the High Prince's niece. "I didn't know."

"She's a couple of years younger than me. My father was killed in a border raid when I was only a year old, and my mother remarried with something close to indecent haste. Even more indecent when you count the months from the wedding date until Kalan's and Narvell's arrival," he added with a grin.

"Narvell?"

"Kalan and Narvell are twins."

"You mean your mother had a lover while she was married to your father?" The idea did not shock her—many noblewomen took lovers— but she was a little surprised that Damin seemed so complacent.

"She probably had several. It was an arranged marriage—Lernen's idea—and there was little affection between them."

"My father made an offer for the Princess Marla once."

"I know. I think that's why he married her to my father, just to annoy Hablet."

"My father still hasn't forgiven Lernen for that," Adrina remarked.

"And you wonder why I don't trust you?"

She was sorry she ever brought the subject up. Now was not the time to remind Damin of the conflict between their monarchs. She ignored the remark and smiled brightly. "You were telling me about your sister."

Damin looked at her oddly for a moment, then continued his tale.

"Kalan's father was the Warlord of Elasapine's son. Mother returned to Greenharbour after he died, leaving Kalan, Narvell and me in Krakandar. But Marla kept finding husbands—and losing them. Every few years she would breeze in, introduce us to our latest stepbrother or stepsister, then vanish again for years at a time. I think Almodavar raised us more than Marla did."

"That's dreadful!"

"On the contrary, I had a wonderful childhood. We had a whole palace to play in, no parents to interfere and a staff that we chose ourselves for the most part."

"*You* chose the staff? The children?"

"It was more a process of elimination," he laughed. "If we didn't like somebody we had ways of getting rid of them. Half a dozen children can be very inventive when the need arises."

With a twinge of envy, Adrina recalled her own closely guarded childhood in the nursery of Hablet's court in Talabar. Such freedom was almost beyond her ability to comprehend.

"Did your mother not fear for you? Alone like that?"

"We weren't alone. Almodavar was my father's closest friend and some of the people in Krakandar have been there since my grandfather's time."

"You're lucky. At least you knew your mother. Hablet had my mother beheaded."

It was Damin's turn to look startled. "Why?"

"My mother was his first wife; a princess from Lanipoor, from a very ancient and noble line. He never loved her—he only married her for the prestige she brought him—and her very large dowry. He loved a *court'esa*, a Hythrun actually, named Welenara. She and my mother fell pregnant within days of each other. It was bad enough that my mother had to endure Welenara so blatantly carrying Hablet's child, but then, to add insult to injury, it was Welenara who produced a son, while the best my mother could do was a daughter. She was rather put out, by all accounts. When Tristan was only a week old, she hired an assassin to poison him and his mother. The assassin failed, my father learnt of the attempt and had her beheaded." Adrina shut her mouth abruptly, stunned that she had told him so much. She was supposed to be trying to draw him out, not regale him with *her* life story. She never discussed her mother with anyone. It was a forbidden subject around Hablet.

"I'm sorry. I didn't know."

"Pity is the last thing I need from you, my Lord."

Her sudden change of mood had him shaking his head, but he said nothing. He rode on a little further and then dismounted beside a leaf-strewn pool. There was steam rising off the still water and the air tasted faintly of sulphur. Adrina dismounted beside him and looked around in surprise.

"The water's hot!"

"Almost too hot to swim in," he agreed. "It's a thermal spring. The timber cutters discovered it. I hear Lord Jenga has already had an approach from some enterprising soul who wants to build a tavern here. For medicinal purposes, of course."

"Of course," Adrina agreed. She knelt down, peeled off her riding glove and dipped her hand into the pool, snatching it out quickly as the water seared her cold fingers.

"Your brother Tristan was killed in battle, wasn't he?" Damin asked behind her.

Adrina stilled warily. *How had he known that?* "Yes."

"And that's the reason you ran away?"

She stood up and turned to face him. "One of them."

"I see," he said thoughtfully. He was standing by his horse, a good five paces from her, but she still felt as if he was crowding her. "So the Karien boy was lying. You weren't trying to sneak through Medalon to ask your father for his cannon."

Mikel was lucky he was nowhere in reach at that moment. Adrina could have cheerfully strangled the little brat. "He's a child. I told him that to keep him quiet. He would have run straight to Cratyn if he thought I was leaving for any other reason."

Damin gathered up his reins and swung into his saddle. "I'm curious. Why did you order your troops to surrender?"

"Cratyn would have executed them when he discovered I'd left. I couldn't think of anything else."

He nodded, as if she had confirmed something he already knew. "A noble gesture, your Highness. Not something I would have expected from someone like you."

Adrina remounted, glaring at him. "What's that supposed to mean?"

But he didn't answer her. He nudged his horse forward, leaving her to ponder his words. She had a feeling that if she could figure out what he meant, she would understand the reason he despised her so much.

Still, she had made progress. It was the first conversation of substance they had ever had that hadn't ended with him threatening to send her back to Karien. Or to kill her.

chapter 40

drina woke with a start, aware that something was different, although she could not pinpoint exactly what it was. She was sweating, her palms moist, her heart pounding. She had dreamed again, the same nightmare that had plagued her since she had left Karien—that Cratyn had found her, dragged her back across the border and forced her to dine with him on a meal that frequently turned out to be her dead dog. With a shudder, she pushed the memory away. It was a stupid dream. She refused to be cowed by an over-active imagination.

The chamber was filled with gray light—and silence. It reminded her of waking in the Karien camp the morning of the battle. The air had that same eerie quality, the same stillness, the same feeling of anticipation. Cautiously, she climbed out of bed. Shivering in the icy chamber, Adrina snatched up her cloak from the bed where it served as an extra blanket and threw it over her shoulders. She walked to the arrow-slit window and looked out, but as far as she could make out, the world had turned white. It took her a moment to realize what she was seeing.

When it hit her, she gasped, and hurriedly dressed in her riding habit, ignoring Tam's sleepy question from the other pallet in the corner of the room. She pulled on her boots and was out the door, startling the guards with her sudden appearance. Running past them, down the stairs and through the deserted hall, she jerked open the heavy door to the Keep and stepped out into a wonderland.

There were a number of mounted Defenders in the yard and the men on the wall-walk stamped their feet against the cold, but Adrina took no notice of them. She hurried to the gate and looked out over the snow-covered camp in astonishment. The landscape had completely changed. Where there had been the panoply of war yesterday was now a silent, white vista as far as the eye could see. It was barely dawn and the soldiers were only just beginning to rouse. Thin smoke rose from the cookfires. The vast plain had been transformed from a war camp into a thing of beauty.

"You've not seen snow before, have you?"

Adrina turned at the voice to find Tarja riding up behind her with a sergeant and a number of troopers in tow. He dismounted, amused by the expression on her face.

"It's . . . glorious!"

"Well, it is for now. Give it a few hours and most of this will have turned into slush," he warned with a wave of his arm. "It's too warm for it to last long and too early in the year for a decent fall."

"Oh," she said in disappointment.

Tarja seemed to take pity on her. "Would you like to take a good look while it's still in all it's pristine glory?"

"Don't you have something better to do?"

"I've got plenty to do, but nothing that can't wait. Besides, It's Founder's Day. It's supposed to be a holiday." He waved a red-coated defender forward. "Sergeant! Her Highness would like to borrow your horse. Tell Hadly I've been delayed, then go find some breakfast. I'll be back in an hour or so."

The man saluted and retrieved his mount for Adrina, holding it for her while she mounted. Tarja swung into his saddle and walked his horse forward.

"Ready?"

"This is very noble of you, Captain."

They moved off at a slow walk, letting the horses pick their own way through the camp.

"Being noble is vastly preferable to discussing the riveting topic of horse feed with Hadly, your Highness."

She smiled at him, wondering if Damin had lied to her about Tarja. He seemed anxious for her company. Maybe he was feeling the loss of the absent demon child. A lonely man was a vulnerable one.

"Well, I still think you're being noble, Captain. You have rare good manners."

"For a Medalonian?" he teased.

"That wasn't what I meant. I just meant that compared to some people around here . . ."

Tarja laughed. "Ah! You speak of our Warlord. I thought you two were starting to get along quite well."

Adrina frowned and reminded herself that this man was Damin's friend. It would be inadvisable to tell him what she really thought of the Hythrun.

"Lord Wolfblade can be tolerable, when he's not trying to be abrasive."

He looked at her oddly. "Well, you can't really blame him, can you? Not after what you did."

"What did I do?"

He refused to answer her question. Instead, he kicked his horse into a canter.

"Captain!" she called as she raced after him. "I believe that statement demands an explanation!"

"The sun will be fully up soon," he remarked as she caught up with him, admiring the scenery with determination. "Most of the snow will be melted by midday." They had ridden past the northern edge of the camp and crossed into the deserted training grounds.

"Don't ignore my question! What did you mean by, 'not after what I did'?"

He glanced at her and shrugged. "I'm sorry, I shouldn't have said that. It's none of my business. You and Damin should sort out things between yourselves."

"I'd be happy to," she snapped. "If I had any idea what you were talking about!"

"You really don't know?"

"I wouldn't be asking if I did!"

Tarja reined in his mount and turned to face her. "He claims you tried to kill the High Prince of Hythria."

"That's ridiculous!"

Tarja shrugged. "I'm just telling you what he told me. He said you hired some boys to do the job, but they killed themselves rather than carry out your orders."

Adrina felt her fury rising like a volcano. All her plans to be nice evaporated in the face of such a terrible accusation. "That arrogant, lying . . ."

"I take it you have a somewhat different opinion?"

"How dare that . . . that . . . degenerate . . . even think such a thing! Let me tell you about your pet Warlord, Captain! He's a savage, unfeeling monster who doesn't deserve to breathe! I never tried to kill his damned uncle, although I wish I had! I gave those boys my knife to spare them from the twisted lust of a depraved old man."

Tarja was taken aback by her fury, but seemed determined to believe his friend's version rather than hers. "Yet you kept the collars as a souvenir. Why?"

"To remind myself why his whole damned family should be destroyed!"

He frowned, then suddenly wheeled his horse around. "Come on, there's something I want to show you."

He led her north toward the battlefield. Adrina urged her horse to follow, wishing for a sorcerer-bred mount, rather than this sturdy, but uninspiring beast. She no longer felt the cold. Her anger warmed her better than any cloak, better than any fire. As they neared the snow-covered mangonels, he veered right, away from the field. The soldiers manning the front paid them little attention as they rode by, their attention focused on what lay north of the border. This was the closest she had come to the border since escaping from Karien and she allowed herself a moment to wonder what Cratyn was doing. He and that damned Hythrun would have made quite a pair.

Tarja led her east, away from the field until they reached a low stone wall that encircled a large snow-covered mound. Adrina looked about in puzzlement.

"You brought me here to show me this?"

"It's a grave."

"Whose grave?"

"Your Fardohnyans. The men who died on the battlefield."

Adrina swallowed an uncomfortable lump in her throat. It was so *big*. *Had there been so many?* She wiped away bitter tears that suddenly stung her eyes.

"I thought Medalonians cremated their dead?"

"We do. Burial is illegal in Medalon but Damin refused to allow the Fardohnyans to be cremated. He had his own men dig the grave. He buried them with their weapons, to honor your War God. Your captain was buried separately because he was of royal blood."

"Tristan! Where? Where did they bury him?"

Tarja pointed to a small rock cairn on the southern side of the mound. Adrina flew from the saddle and ran to it, no longer caring if Tarja saw her crying.

Tristan! Oh, Tristan!

Tarja dismounted and followed her slowly, leading her mount with his. He waited patiently as she knelt by the cairn, not caring that her knees were being soaked by the snow, her face in her hands, as she let go of the grief she had so tightly controlled until now. She sobbed until her throat was raw. She sobbed until she had no more tears to shed.

Finally, she had no idea how long, she sat back on her heels and wiped her eyes, the scabbed-over wound of her grief lanced and washed clean by her tears. It was then that she noticed the position of the cairn in relation to the mound. It was facing southwest. Toward Fardohnya.

"They buried him facing home."

"That's your savage, unfeeling monster for you."

She turned and looked at him sharply. "Don't try to tell me this proves anything! Cratyn is the most devout man that ever lived, but it doesn't stop him from being a bastard!" She sniffed inelegantly and climbed to her feet. "I'll grant you I'm surprised, but it hardly makes Wolfblade a saint."

"Perhaps not," he conceded. "But I think you do him an injustice."

"I'm the one falsely accused of attempted murder."

"Then take it up with Damin, your Highness," Tarja said wearily. "We should be getting back. Hadly's waiting for me."

He handed her the reins of her borrowed horse before swinging into his own saddle. Adrina stared at the mound for a moment, marking the place in her memory, before mounting the dun gelding.

"How did my brother die?"

Tarja hesitated for a moment before he answered. "He died in battle, your Highness. Isn't that all you need to know?"

"I want to know who killed him."

"To what purpose?"

Tarja's reluctance to give her a straight answer made her suspicious. "It was Wolfblade, wasn't it? That's why you're looking so uncomfortable. Damin Wolfblade killed my brother, then buried him here as some sort of barbaric boast, so he could come and gloat over his grave."

"No," Tarja replied, looking even more discomforted. "Damin didn't kill your brother."

"How can you be certain?" she demanded. "You said yourself, he died in battle. How do you know this burial mound isn't some sick Hythrun ritual to mock the dead? How do you—"

"He died by my hand, Adrina."

His admission stunned her into silence. He met her accusing eyes with genuine regret.

"I'm sorry, Adrina. But this *is* war and he *was* trying to kill me at the time. If it's any comfort, his last thoughts were of you."

Tarja gathered up his reins and turned his mount toward the camp. She stared at his retreating back wishing she could somehow take vengeance on this man who had robbed her of her beloved brother. But she had not expected this. Not his confession, nor the pain it had cost him to make it. Confused and troubled, Adrina followed Tarja back to the camp in silence, not even seeing the glorious snow-covered plain.

When they reached Treason Keep Tarja helped her dismount without a word and turned to lead her horse away.

"Tarja?"

He looked at her over his shoulder.

"Why did you tell me? Why not let me think someone else had killed him?"

"A Defender is honour-bound to speak the truth, your Highness."

"You could have said nothing."

"I could have," he agreed. "But you are determined to think the worst of Lord Wolfblade. We could have sued for peace weeks ago. Were it up to me or the Lord Defender, you would have been ransomed back to your husband the day we found you. Damin is the only thing standing between you and the husband you seem so determined to desert. It didn't seem right to let you blame him for that too."

Tarja led the horses away and left her standing there. She wondered for a moment why she felt no burning urge to avenge Tristan. The man who killed him was right here, within reach.

Then the reason came to her. It was not Tarja who was responsible for Tristan's death. He may have wielded the blade, but it was Cratyn who had killed him. Cratyn and his sick priests.

Cratyn was the one who would pay.

chapter 41

The news that the First Sister was on her way home caused a flurry of activity in the Citadel. Everyone seemed intent on sprucing up their own little patch of the city and even the Defenders were not immune. Loclon found himself facing an empty arena day after day, as the cadets were called away to other duties. Learning swordcraft was all very well, but the First Sister was due and she was bound to insist on an inspection. One had to get one's priorities right.

Left to his own devices, Loclon sought amusement in the Blue Bull, but even that worthy establishment was suffering the effects of the First Sister's impending return. There was nobody drinking in the tavern and the benches were stacked on the tabletops as fresh rushes were laid out. Loclon slammed the door in annoyance and headed back to his rooms.

When he arrived back at Mistress Longreaves' Boarding House he discovered a note pinned to his door. He looked around before opening it, but at this time of day, the hall was deserted. *I want to see you*, the note said. It was unsigned, but he needed no name to know who had sent it. He went into his room, threw the note on the fire, and exchanged his red jacket for a nondescript brown one. It would not do to be seen entering Mistress Heaner's in broad daylight in his uniform.

Lork opened the door for him and stood back to let him enter. He pointed wordlessly to the hall. Loclon frowned. He did not like meeting Mistress Heaner in the basement; did not like to be reminded that he was serving the Overlord.

When he reached the bottom of the stairs, he discovered Mistress Heaner was not alone. The narrow altar was ablaze, the symbol of Xaphista glittering malignantly in the candlelight. The old woman was on her knees, chanting softly. Beside her was a man wearing a brown cassock, his tonsured head so polished it reflected the candles. *How in the name of the Founders had a Karien priest managed to get into the city?* He waited as they finished their prayers and the priest helped the old woman to her feet before retrieving his jeweled staff from the altar. Mistress Heaner studied him with predatory eyes and turned to her companion.

"This is the man I spoke of. Captain Loclon, this is Garanus."

Loclon nodded warily in the direction of the priest, then looked at Mistress Heaner. "You said you wanted to see me. I can come back later when you're not busy."

"It was I who sent for you," the priest said. His voice was accented and oddly rasping, as if his throat had been burned. He laid the staff gently on Loclon's shoulder, waiting for a moment before withdrawing it with a faint nod of satisfaction. "Mistress Heaner tells me you have something of a history with the demon child."

At the mention of R'shiel, Loclon's doubts vanished. "Do you know where she is?"

The priest nodded. "She will be here within a day. She accompanies the First Sister."

Loclon burned with the heat of his need. "Then I will kill her as soon as she arrives." *Kill her, yes, but slowly and oh-so-painfully—and only after she begs for mercy.*

"You will do no such thing!" the priest snapped.

"Isn't she destined to destroy your god? I'd have thought killing her would be the first thing you'd want."

"She was *created* to destroy him, Captain. That's not the same thing as destiny. The demon child lacks commitment. She has not accepted the task, or she would be heading for Karien, not the Citadel."

"So . . . what . . . you think you can turn her to your cause?"

"Xaphista is the one true god," Mistress Heaner reminded him. "The demon child will become his ally and destroy the Primal gods. He has decreed that it will be so."

Loclon thought it unwise to point out the flaw in her argument. If Xaphista really was the only god, then who had created the demon child?

And if the Primal gods did not exist, as the Overlord claimed, what need for someone to destroy them?

"Your task will be to bring her to us," Garanus explained. Then he added with a slight frown, "Whole and unharmed, Captain."

"I was promised vengeance."

"And vengeance you shall have," the priest assured him. "Once the demon child has embraced the Overlord, she will turn on our enemies, and yours, and destroy them."

That wasn't quite what Loclon had in mind. "What did you want me to do?"

"You will be taking part in the Founder's Day Parade, yes?"

He nodded. Nobody got out of *that* duty.

"The First Sister will arrive toward the end of the parade. She has no doubt timed the event to maximize the impact of her return."

"The First Sister is fond of making an entrance," Mistress Heaner added scornfully.

"You will assign yourself to her party and stay close to her."

"Assign myself? You don't know much about the Defenders, Priest. One doesn't assign oneself to anything."

"If you are nearby when she arrives, and volunteer for the duty, I am sure you can manage something."

"And what about R'shiel?"

"It is likely you will not recognize her. She may be using a glamor to conceal her identity. But that is not your concern. There is a man with her. A Harshini half-breed named Brakandaran. You must kill him."

He shrugged. "And then what?"

"Once you have brought proof that Brakandaran is dead, we will discuss the best way to handle R'shiel."

Loclon was not very happy with the arrangement. "Are you sure you know who you're dealing with? There is no *best way* to handle R'shiel. She's a murderous bitch."

"The demon child can be controlled, Captain. Her strength is also her weakness." He reached inside his cassock and withdrew a thin silver choker with a jeweled clasp in the shape of the star and lightning bolt of the Overlord. "This will ensure her cooperation."

"You think she's going to change sides for that little trinket?" he scoffed.

"With this 'little trinket,' as you call it," the priest informed him with a malicious smile, "the demon child will do anything you want of her. The more she tries to use her power to fight it, the worse it will be for her."

Loclon took the choker and examined it thoughtfully.

"She'll do *anything*, you say?"

The priest nodded. "Anything."

Founder's Day dawned overcast and dull, with low clouds threatening rain and a cold, blustery wind that groped through any gap in clothing with chill fingers. The crowd was thick around Francil's Hall as the citizens gathered for a glimpse of the returning First Sister, but their mood was subdued. It was too cold to stand around waiting and as the parade passed by, many thoughts were turned to the bonfires and the warm food waiting in the Amphitheater. If she did not arrive soon, hunger was likely to win out over curiosity.

Loclon had volunteered for crowd duty, rather than riding in the parade. He had managed to get himself placed in command of the guards around the Hall and was well positioned on the steps, just below Sister Harith and the remainder of the Quorum. Thunder rumbled overhead and the clouds seemed low enough to touch. Loclon fretted at the time it was taking the noisy floats to move down the street. There was no sign of the First Sister.

The last float was rounding the corner of the Administration Hall when the skies opened. The Quorum hurriedly moved back under the shelter of the entrance to the Hall while the crowd dived for whatever cover they could find. Many simply turned and fled, running with cloaks held over their heads to escape the downpour. Loclon stayed at his post, drenched by the icy rain, barely even noticing it in his impatience. *Where is she?*

There was a moment of anticipation as the crowd waited, but the rain was a significant deterrent. If the First Sister's carriage did not arrive soon, there would be nobody left to greet her. Loclon watched the crowd thin with dismay. He had hoped to get to the half-breed in the crush, but soon there would be nobody left but him. He glanced at his men who looked desperate to find shelter, warning them with a look, of the consequences should anybody presume to break ranks. Sister Harith and the Quorum were conferring under the meager eaves of the Hall. With another glance down the street in the direction of the Main Gate, they vanished inside.

The departure of the Quorum signalled the end of the festivities as far as the rest of the citizens were concerned. Within minutes the street was all but deserted and Loclon no longer had an excuse to keep his men standing in the rain. He muttered a curse and turned to dismiss them as the First Sister's retinue arrived.

His men hastily stood to attention as the outriders appeared, followed by a closed carriage with the shutters pulled tight against the downpour. Loclon could feel his heart beating faster as the carriage drew to a halt, waiting to catch sight of her. His hand caressed the hilt of his knife, ready to draw it in an instant to kill the half-breed. He had no fear of the consequences. Once a dead Harshini lay at the First Sister's feet, he would be a hero.

"Loclon! What in the name of the Founders are you doing out in this! Get those men out of here!"

He started at the anger in Garet Warner's voice.

"We were waiting for the First Sister, sir! To see if we could be of any assistance!"

The commandant was as sodden as Loclon as he dismounted, but he didn't seem bothered by it. "Don't be absurd! The First Sister has her own men. Dismiss your men, Captain."

"But sir . . ."

"I said, dismiss your men!"

Loclon did as he was ordered and watched helplessly as Joyhinia's guard gathered around the carriage to help the First Sister down. One of them held a cloak over her head, to shield her from the rain as another sister disembarked. Although the deluge obscured his vision, Loclon could have sworn it was Mahina Cortanen. He waited for a moment longer, but a dark-haired woman and Lord Draco seemed to be the only other passengers.

He looked about desperately, but there was no sign of R'shiel, or the half-breed he was supposed to kill. The First Sister was hurried inside and the remainder of the Defenders headed gratefully for the stables with the carriage and the horses.

Loclon stood in the rain, cursing softly.

Where is she?

chapter 42

Brak and R'shiel waited in the shelter of the gatehouse for the better part of an hour before following the First Sister into the Citadel. Brak had drawn a glamor over them and their horses, so that the guards sheltering from the rain did not notice their presence. It did not make them invisible, but the guards' attention slid off them like water off an oiled cape. R'shiel braided and unbraided her reins nervously as the rain hammered down and they waited on Bhren, the God of Storms, to finish the task R'shiel had asked of him.

Brak had never had much luck communicating with the Storm God. Bhren was a solitary spirit with cares on a global scale. The insignificant problems of humans seldom touched him. But he had come when Lorandranek had called him and had responded just as promptly when his daughter had asked his help. Brak glanced at the water sheeting down from the low clouds, then looked at R'shiel with concern.

"You did tell him we just wanted a storm, didn't you, not a global catastrophe?"

"It'll stop soon," she assured him, although she did not sound convinced.

The rain had been Lord Draco's idea, conceived five nights ago in Cauthside while they waited on the ferry to take them across the Glass River. Their method of gaining entrance into the Citadel, without Joyhinia being immediately overwhelmed by the long list of people who required an audience with her, had been a matter for hot debate.

Garet Warner insisted that if Joyhinia was thought to be sneaking back into the Citadel, suspicions would be immediately aroused. She had to enter in a manner befitting her station. It was expected. But they could not risk someone speaking to Joyhinia. Her response was likely to be a childish giggle. And they certainly could not risk her in front of a crowd.

R'shiel had wanted to use the demon meld, but even Dranymire had balked at that suggestion. The demons had been practising their meld, but it took a lot out of them and the Gathering was still to be faced. Brak had suggested a glamor, but that did not solve the problem of Joyhinia being seen publicly. A glamor would conceal her and that brought them back to the problem of sneaking into the Citadel.

It was Draco who had remarked that it was a pity they couldn't arrange for it to be raining. No matter how important the personage, nobody would hang about, cold and wet, for a glimpse of the First Sister—and neither would they expect the First Sister to stand about waving to them. R'shiel had glanced at Brak with that dangerous light in her eyes that he was coming to associate with the demon child having an idea he knew he wouldn't like.

"You could ask Bhren."

"The Storm God is not like Dacendaran, R'shiel. He spends little time worrying about the Harshini, and even less time thinking about humans. The only Harshini I knew who could get any sense out of him was Lorandranek." He regretted saying it the moment he uttered the words.

"Maybe I could ask him?"

"Ask who, what?" Garet demanded.

"Ask the God of Storms to make it rain the day we arrive at the Citadel."

Garet stared at her for a moment, then shook his head. "I don't want to know about this." He rose from the table in the Heart and Hearth tavern and took the stairs to his room two at a time.

Draco watched him go and then turned back to Brak and R'shiel. "He is uncomfortable with your gods."

"And you're not?" R'shiel shot back. She did not like Draco. Tarja's father had been Joyhinia's creature for thirty years. He had ordered the murder of R'shiel's family and the village where she was born, and he had been quite prepared to put his own son, R'shiel, and three hundred rebels to the sword at Joyhinia's command. But the man reeked of regret.

In many ways he was like Lord Jenga—honorable to the point of foolishness. One mistake had set him on a path so far from his original destination that he was almost completely lost. The man was trying to claw his way back, to somehow make amends, but neither Tarja nor R'shiel was ready to forgive him. Brak trusted him more than Garet Warner. Garet had his own agenda. All Draco wanted was redemption.

"I've seen enough to believe your gods exist, R'shiel, although I do not worship them."

"You're more adept at turning on your own kind, you mean," R'shiel snarled. Brak laid a restraining hand on her arm.

"Stop trying to pick a fight, R'shiel."

Surprisingly, she did as he asked. Deliberately excluding Draco she turned to him questioningly. "How do I speak to Bhren?"

"Very carefully," Brak had replied, only half jokingly.

"See, I told you it would stop!"

Brak forced his attention back to the present to discover the rain had eased to a light drizzle. "Thank you, Divine One," he said under his breath, although it was unlikely that Bhren was listening.

"We should get moving," R'shiel advised, glancing warily at the guards. Brak nodded and followed her into the street, still holding the glamor tightly around them.

It was nearly two hundred years since Brak had been in the Citadel, and the changes wrought in that time depressed him. Once this had been his home, before the Sisterhood had snatched it from the Harshini. As a child, he had played with demons among the vast gardens that were now replaced by cluttered housing. He had gone exploring in the ancient woods surrounding the Citadel that had long been cleared to meet the voracious human appetite for firewood and lumber. Humans had obliterated all the beauty of the Citadel, all the elegant hallmarks of Harshini architecture. Only the temples and the Halls of Residence remained of the original city, but they too had been corrupted, their artwork painted over, their graceful lines distorted by later additions to their structures. Brak was glad the Harshini could not see the Citadel now. It would bruise their souls to see what had been done to their home.

"I can feel it," R'shiel breathed in wonder. "I can feel the Citadel."

"He's reacting to your presence."

She frowned, trying to reach out with senses not yet mature enough to identify what she was experiencing. The Citadel was welcoming her home, just as it had watched over her for most of her life. Until now, she had not been aware of the power that enabled her to feel his presence.

"I thought only gods could tell what I am?"

"The spirit of the Citadel is a god," Brak explained. "An Incidental god, not a Primal god, but a god nonetheless."

"You mean he's like Xaphista? He's a demon that grew powerful enough to call himself a god?"

"No, the Citadel is unique. He came into being as the complex was built. He is the essence of the place. Its soul if you like."

R'shiel digested the information silently as they approached the Temple of the Gods. Brak did not know what the humans called it now, but once it had been the center of Harshini life—the place where any god, no matter how powerful or insignificant, could be called into being. He had played with gods and demons in that Temple, back in a time when life held a great deal of promise. Back in the days before he understood what it was to be half-human. Back in the days before he had killed Lorandranek.

"What did Dranymire mean about the Harshini needing access to the Citadel to protect themselves?"

"You can't kill a Harshini here, R'shiel. The Citadel won't permit it."

She looked at him, her violet eyes wide with astonishment. "You're kidding?"

"No. But don't get too exited. That protection doesn't extend to half-bloods. You and I are just as mortal as anybody else, here."

"So if the Harshini could come back to the Citadel, they would be safe from the Kariens? Even if they cross the border?"

"It's the only protection they have, other than remaining hidden. Their inability to kill is painfully real, R'shiel. There's a story I heard once about the First Purge. A mob of humans attacked a Harshini family trying to flee the carnage. They raped the women, butchered the children and then handed the last Harshini standing a sword. They knelt in front of him and offered him their exposed throats, taunting him to kill them. He dropped the sword and threw himself on the ground, hoping

they would take his life too. He couldn't ask them to do it, the prohibition against violence includes suicide." He did not realize how cold his
voice had become until R'shiel looked at him with genuine concern.

"It's not just a story, is it, Brak?" she asked softly.

"No."

"What happened?"

"We arrived too late to save him. But the humans who attacked them
never lived long enough to gloat about their deeds."

"You *killed* them? How, if the Harshini can't kill?"

"There were a lot more half-bloods in those days. Before the Sisterhood, mixed marriages were not that uncommon. We were young and
hot-headed and didn't take the Purge lying down."

R'shiel thought about that for a moment. "Where are the other half-
bloods now?"

"One half-blood was more dangerous to the Sisterhood than a dozen
pure Harshini. They made a special effort to eradicate us." They had
ridden past the Hall of the Gods without stopping. Brak was very sorry
he had ever mentioned the First Purge. Although centuries old, the
memories still burned like acid.

"You're the only one left."

"Until you came along."

R'shiel did not ask anything further on the subject, for which Brak
was grateful. He glanced at the low, gray sky and realized that R'shiel
had been correct in her assertion that rain would force the Gathering
indoors and that the Hall was the only other possible venue.

She was still insisting they coerce the Gathering into accepting Joyhinia, but Brak had held off showing her how to do it, until the last possible moment, hoping she would change her mind. He lacked the power
himself, to coerce a large group of people, but he knew the technique,
although working it left him sick to his stomach. Since her stay at Sanctuary, under the careful guidance of Korandellan and her Harshini tutors,
R'shiel had learnt much about her ability. But she was still a babe-in-
arms by Harshini standards. A babe who was acquiring knowledge she
lacked the judgment to use wisely, at a frightening rate. So frightening
that Brak found himself being very careful about what he did in her
presence.

She had come a long way since Shananara had tried to teach her simply how to touch her power. That day by the Glass River, more than a year ago, seemed to be part of a much more distant past.

If the Citadel's desecration had cut him to the core, then Tavern Street was like rubbing salt into the wound. The whole cluttered street, which had once been a wide, tree-lined avenue, wore an aura of shoddy greed. With the rain, the feast in the Amphitheater had been washed out and the tables laden with food had been moved to the verandahs outside the taverns. The street was packed with people venturing out into the fading drizzle to avail themselves of the Sisterhood's generosity. Red coats mingled with gray-robed Probates, green-robed Novices and the more varied colors worn by ordinary people. There were only a few blue Sisters in sight. Most of them had chosen to stay indoors, rather than fight the crush in the rain. Of the white-robed Sisters of the Quorum, there was no sign at all.

"Isn't there somewhere else we can go?" Brak asked, eyeing the crowd uneasily. They had planned to take rooms in a tavern close to the Hall of the Gods and stay out of sight until the Gathering at sundown.

"But we were supposed to meet Affiana here."

"She'll wait for us."

R'shiel thought for a moment, then nodded. "The Amphitheater will be deserted with the food moved down here. The caverns should be quiet enough."

R'shiel turned her horse and led the way, although Brak could have found his way blindfolded. The caverns had been stables once, built to house the ancestors of the Hythrun sorcerer-bred horses. They rode into the torch-lit tunnel and dismounted, leading their horses deep into the caverns where they were unlikely to be disturbed. Brak looked around the empty, hollow rooms with a sharp sense of loss.

He shook off the feeling and turned to R'shiel. "Are you sure you want to do this?"

"There's no other way, Brak." The darkness hid her expression, but it could not hide her excitement. Since returning to the world of humans, the differences between the demon child and mere mortals were more evident each day. Those differences were beginning to make her feel a little too superior for Brak's comfort. He could remember feel-ing the same way, when he was her age, and he discovered how much his power set him apart. But that kind of arrogance was dangerous to R'shiel and everyone around her. She needed to be brought down a peg or two, as he had been, and soon.

"What you want to do is wrong, you understand that, don't you?"

"It is necessary."

"Are you prepared for the consequences?"

"What consequences?" For the first time, she didn't sound quite so certain.

"Coercing humans is easy, R'shiel," he explained. "People do it to each other all the time. They don't use the same sort of power as we do, but they have other methods which work just as well."

"I don't understand what you're getting at."

"You remember when you were fighting with the rebellion? I saw you coerce those young hot-heads any number of times and you didn't know anything about the Harshini power you had access to. Tarja convinced three hundred rebels to attack a full Company of Defenders in Testra with nothing more than rhetoric. Every mother who cajoles her child into eating stewed turnips is using coercion."

"What's your point, Brak?"

"The point is that you could bully the heathens into fighting because, deep down, they wanted to. Every rebel who attacked Testra at Tarja's behest secretly dreamed of victory. Even the child who eventually succumbs to the stewed turnips has hunger giving him a push. Coercing people to act against their will, is an entirely different matter. You have to get past their natural inclinations and then force them to move in a different direction. You are robbing them of any vestige of free will, and free will is something that runs so deep in the human soul it's like trying to get the Glass River to flow backwards."

"You think I don't have the power to do it?" she asked, sounding rather alarmed. "The Karien priests can do it."

"R'shiel, you could level a mountain if the mood took you. Your power is not the issue. As for the Kariens priests, their ability is an abomination. Remember that Xaphista was a demon once. During their initiation ceremony they drink his blood. And it's not some slaughtered animal's blood they're drinking either, it really is Xaphista's. The blood links them to their god in the same way we're linked to our demons. Through that link they can call on his strength to weave the coercion."

"But the link must be pretty tenuous," she said. "Where did they get the power to coerce a whole army?"

"Individually they're weak, but as a group they can be devastating."

"You're not worried I'll start worshipping the Overlord, are you?" she asked with a grin.

Brak could have slapped her for being so flippant. She wasn't listening at all. "It's what will happen to these people afterward, that worries me. If you coerce them into believing Joyhinia wishes to retire in favor of Mahina, then that's exactly what they'll do. But tomorrow, or the week after, or a year from now, when you're not around to suppress their natural feelings, they will begin to wonder why. They'll know they've been tricked. Mahina's reign is likely to be even shorter than the last time. One dissenting voice will turn into two, which will turn into ten which will turn into an avalanche."

"I've already told you, we'll send the most likely dissenters away . . ."

He shook his head in exasperation. "It won't matter. You have no way of knowing who is susceptible and who isn't. The ones you think most likely to object may take to the coercion like it was mother's milk. But there will be others, people you don't even suspect, for whom the coercion will last less than a day. There will be nearly a thousand Sisters in that Hall, R'shiel. You can't watch them all."

"Then we'll do something to keep them quiet. It only has to last long enough for Mahina to issue the orders sending the rest of the Defenders to the front. She can resign after that and they can hold another election—"

"Do what?" Brak cut in.

"I don't know," she snapped. "Maybe if they all got sick, or something . . ."

"You mean you'd create an epidemic just to keep the Sisters occupied?"

"I suppose. Nothing serious, just something that keeps them close to the garderobes for a few days."

"I see. And when this epidemic spreads to the general population, as it will, what of the young, too weak to fight it? The old, too frail to withstand it? Are you ready to kill innocent people to keep your coercion from falling apart?"

"Then what do you suggest we do? We have to get the rest of the Defenders to the border!"

"Fine. Have Joyhinia issue the order. Have her resign, too, if you must, but the more complex the coercion, the more chance there is of it blowing up in your face."

"But we need Mahina in charge."

"Then put her in charge, but let her take control herself. If you impose an artificial control, the results could be catastrophic. Trust her to know what she's doing. She got caught out once. I don't think she'll be so foolish this time."

"What are you suggesting? That we get through the Gathering and then walk away?"

"Actually, I was thinking of running, not walking. One of the hall-marks of maturity for a Harshini is knowing when *not* to use your power, R'shiel."

"I'm not Harshini. Not completely."

"You're not completely human, either, but that's no excuse for acting like an idiot. Consequences, R'shiel. I ask you again. Are you prepared for the consequences?"

She was silent for a moment, considering her answer carefully.

"The consequences of not acting are liable to be worse," she said finally.

"You don't know that for certain."

"No," she agreed, then she sighed. "Alright, I'll grant you that letting Mahina establish control in her own right is probably safer than imposing it artificially. But I will have to coerce them into accepting her appointment at the Gathering."

"And then we leave?"

"I suppose."

"Good. I'll be waiting outside the Hall with our horses. It's too damned dangerous for you here, R'shiel."

"Dangerous? Compared to what? The border, where there's a war going on?" She smiled wearily at him. "Show me how it's done, Brak. We're running out of time."

Brak silently admitted defeat. He had done all he could to deter her, short of refusing her the knowledge outright. But she had felt it once before, the night before the battle. If he did not instruct her properly, he knew that she would simply try to copy what the Kariens' priests had done, and the result might be disastrous.

The irony was, using simple human tactics, she was coercing him into showing her something he thought far too dangerous for her to learn. At least she had agreed to leave, once the deed was done. Brak couldn't put his finger on it, but he had a feeling of impending danger and it had been growing steadily stronger ever since he had entered the Citadel.

He wished the Citadel was easier to read, easier to understand. He could feel its anxiety and it was making him very nervous.

chapter 43

oclon waited until almost sundown before finally accepting that R'shiel and her half-breed companion were not going to appear. Cold, wet and thoroughly disgusted, he made his way to the Blue Bull tavern to meet with Garanus and report his lack of success.

Loclon had thought the tavern an odd choice for a meeting place. It was far too public for his liking, and a Karien priest would stand out like a red-coated Defender in a snowstorm. Garanus had shrugged off his concerns. He had private rooms available, he said, and had paid the tavern keeper well to ensure her silence. Besides, it was Founder's Day and the Citadel was full of strangers. A few more would barely rate a mention.

The rain had dwindled to a light drizzle about an hour after the First Sister arrived and had completely stopped an hour or so after that. Not wishing to be seen defying Garet Warner's orders, he had paid an urchin to watch Francil's Hall, and another to keep an eye on the Main Gate. It had proved a waste of good coin. Nobody even remotely fitting R'shiel's description had entered the Citadel since the parade. She had either arrived early, or the priest was wrong.

Tavern Street was still crowded when he arrived, the revellers determined to get full value from the public holiday, particularly now the rain had stopped, although the air was bitterly cold and many of the party-goers stood hugging the small fires that lined the street. He pushed through them impatiently into the crowded taproom of the Blue Bull, where he spied Lork standing guard outside the door to one of the private dining rooms. The big man wore an expression that turned away the curious, simply by its ferocity. When he reached the door, Lork barred his way with a low snarl.

"I'm expected," he said. Lork glared at him for a moment before dropping his thick arm. Loclon opened the door and pushed past him.

He froze in shock as the door snicked shut behind him. He was expecting Mistress Heaner and Garanus to be waiting for him, not five more Karien priests and a tall man with hooded eyes, who by his bearing just had to be a Karien nobleman, despite his unremarkable clothing.

"Ah, Captain," Garanus said, looking up at the sound of the door closing. "You bring us good news, I trust?"

For a fleeting moment, Loclon wanted to run. This was getting out of hand. His desire to see R'shiel suffer had not included treason. He had been able to convince himself for months that his association with Mistress Heaner was simply a ploy. He had made himself believe that information he passed on was not critical, that *he* was using *them* rather than the other way around. Confronted with incontrovertible proof of Karien involvement at the highest level, what was left of his conscience gave a dying cry of protest. He ignored it.

"Your information was wrong. R'shiel was not with the First Sister."

The Karien Lord glanced at Garanus, frowning. "You claimed you could feel her."

"I could," Garanus assured him. He glanced at the other priests, who nodded in agreement. Their tonsured heads and pale skin made it hard to tell one from the other. "We all could. Our captain here may have missed them, but the glamor the demon child and her lackey wove to conceal themselves is like a beacon to those of us who are close to the Overlord. Trust me, Lord Terbolt, she is here."

Loclon studied Terbolt guardedly. The name meant nothing to him, he had little interest in Karien politics, but he was bound to be a personage of some note. A man whose good will he needed to foster if he was to continue on this path.

"They must have arrived earlier, before the parade."

Garanus shrugged. "When they arrived is not important. The fact that they are here is all that counts."

"So what now? I can hardly kill this half-breed if I can't find him."

Lord Terbolt nodded in agreement. "Nor can we expose this ungodly Harshini alliance with the Sisterhood, with either of them on the loose. Can't you use your . . . powers, or whatever it is that you do, Garanus, to track them down?"

"What Harshini alliance?" Loclon asked, before the priest had a chance to answer.

Lord Terbolt turned to him. "The Sisterhood has been secretly allied with the Harshini for years, Captain. The demon child was raised under their protection. Now they have openly allied with the Hythrun, and the Harshini, whom the Sisterhood claims have been extinct for more than a century, begin to reveal themselves once more. We already have reports of Harshini appearing again in Greenharbour. Before long, they will overrun the entire continent with their insidious heathen gods. We are here to put a stop to it."

Loclon wasn't sure that he believed the Karien, but it made sense. Until she had run away with Tarja, R'shiel had been training for the Sisterhood. Her mother was the First Sister. The thought that his career had been destroyed by a Harshini bitch who was secretly working to destroy Medalon burned like acid in his gullet.

"What do you want me to do?"

"I think we should pay a visit to the First Sister," Terbolt said.

The Sister's Hall was all but deserted. Every Blue Sister in the Citadel was heading for the Gathering. Getting past the guards was easy. Loclon knew the effect a barked order had on men conditioned to follow their officers without question. He and Gawn had led Lord Terbolt, his priests, and the silent Lork to the main residential wing of the Sister's Hall quite openly. With their heads covered by hooded cloaks, and their staffs hidden in their folds, the Kariens looked as ordinary as any other visitors to the Citadel.

Gawn's inclusion was not part of Loclon's original plan. The captain had appeared on the verandah of the Blue Bull as they were leaving, looking for some entertainment with a willing Probate. Now that he was a widower, he spent a great deal of his off duty hours entertaining willing Probates. They were safer than tavern-keepers' daughters. As a rule, if you impregnated one, you were not required to marry her.

Gawn's eyes had widened at the sight of Loclon's companions, but he was even further along the road of treason than Loclon, these days.

He acted as if he really did believe all that nonsense about the Over-lord. A thing made easier, no doubt, by the fact that the Overlord had answered his prayers and his slut of a wife lay buried these past few weeks, dead from a fatal dose of heckleweed that she unfortunately mistook for seasoning. Loclon had grabbed his arm and dragged him along, explaining the situation in a low voice as they made their way toward the Sister's Hall. Gawn had fallen in with them willingly.

The guards at the entrance were easily dealt with. One did not question a captain without very good cause. The men on the upper levels were just as efficiently disposed of. Loclon ordered them downstairs, accusing them of hiding inside the building to escape the cold. The men saluted sharply and hurried outside.

The guards in the hall outside the First Sister's apartments were a different matter. These were Garet Warner's men. Loclon could order them about until he turned green without any noticeable effect. He stopped just out of sight on the landing of the broad, carpeted staircase and motioned the Kariens to silence.

"What do you think, Gawn?"

"I think we're going to have to fight," the captain replied softly.

"There is no need to fight," Terbolt informed them in a low voice. "Lork, take care of it."

Before Loclon could protest, the big man stepped into the hall and walked toward the two Defenders standing either side of the First Sister's door. The men looked up at his approach, hands on the hilts of their swords as they challenged him. Lork did not answer them. He just kept walking. As soon as he was in reach of the Defenders, who, by this time, had begun to draw their weapons, he grabbed a man with each of his plate-sized hands and smashed their heads together so hard Loclon could hear their skulls cracking. He hurried forward as the men collapsed at Lork's feet.

"You fool! You've killed them!" he hissed.

"They were agents of evil," Garanus announced as he came up behind them with Lord Terbolt and the other priests. "Their deaths will please the Overlord."

"Well, they won't please anyone around here! We have to get the bodies out of sight!"

"We can move them inside," Terbolt said, turning to face the bronze-sheathed door. "Should we knock?"

Gawn muttered something as the Karien pounded on the door. It was opened a few moments later by Lord Draco, who took in the fallen guards and the tonsured priests with a glance, reaching for his sword with a speed that belied his age. Lord Setenton was prepared, however. He plunged his dagger into Draco's breast while the older man's blade was still in its scabbard. The Duke of Setenton shoved him backward into the room. Draco slid off the blade and collapsed on the expensive patterned rug, his red jacket darkening with blood. He cried out an unintelligible warning but there was nobody around to heed it.

Loclon stood frozen in shock, as Lork dragged the bodies of the guards into the room and locked the door behind him. They had killed two Defenders. They had killed the Spear of the First Sister.

He was damned whichever way he looked at it.

"Find the First Sister," Terbolt ordered. The priests spread out, checking the numerous doors that led off the main hall of the First Sister's apartments. Loclon stared at Draco who lay groaning softly, hand clutched uselessly over his punctured chest.

"Finish him, Captain," Terbolt ordered brusquely. "His moaning offends me."

"But he's . . ." Loclon began uncertainly.

"I'll do it," Gawn offered, drawing his sword. He walked to where Draco lay dying and barely even hesitated as he plunged the blade into him, over and over again. Draco was long dead before he stopped.

Loclon watched Gawn mutilating Lord Draco and discovered, somewhat to his embarrassment, that rather than repulse him, the smell of the blood was arousing him. He turned away to hide the evidence of his excitement.

"Can't bear to watch, eh?"

Loclon composed himself before turning back, trying to sound nonchalant. "A bit excessive, don't you think?"

Gawn shrugged. "I thought you'd be pleased."

"Pleased? To watch you hack an old man to death?"

"He's not just an old man, Loclon. I thought you knew. Lord Draco is Tarja Tenragan's father."

Before that startling news had time to register, one of the priests cried out from a room up the hall. They hurried to the door and pushed their way through.

Across the threshold lay the body of a statuesque middle-aged woman, blood pooling beneath the knife wound in her chest. Her dark hair partially covered her face, but could not hide the startled look in her dead eyes. Loclon stepped over the body and stared, open-mouthed at the sight before him.

They had found the First Sister.

She was sitting on the floor, dressed in a simple gray tunic, her long, gray streaked hair undone and hanging limply over her shoulders. In her hands was a tattered rag doll with one eye missing. She was rocking back and forth, humming tunelessly.

Joyhinia Tenragan, the most ruthless First Sister in living memory, the woman who had ordered a Purge that had killed thousands of Medalonians, looked up as they crowded in her room and smiled at them.

"Do you want to play with dolly?" she said.

chapter 44

Since befriending Dace, Mikel rarely spent a full day among the horses. Whenever Dace appeared, Sergeant Monthay would suddenly turn to Mikel and dismiss him, along with the warning that he did not expect to see him again until dinnertime. Mikel had no idea why Dace had that effect on the Medalonian and finally decided to stop questioning his good fortune. Perhaps it was the Overlord's way of sparing him a life of forced labor.

Sometimes, Kali would join her brother on their daily jaunts. Every time he saw the barefooted little girl, she would stare at him closely and demand, "Do you love me?"

Mikel thought it the strangest question, and it seemed to annoy Dace too, but he had begun answering yes, simply because Kali would sulk if he answered any other way. An answer in the affirmative left her beaming for the rest of the day. She would hold his hand, and smile at him a lot, and not say blasphemous things about the Overlord, which Mikel found something of a relief.

Dace pouted a lot when Kali was with them, and he argued with her all the time. But he seemed incapable of refusing her anything. If Kali had been *his* sister, Mikel thought, he would have ordered her to stay at home and expected her to comply. These Medalonians really did lack the proper understanding of the place of a female.

When Dace and Mikel were alone, they spent hours exploring the Medalonian camp. They were never challenged by the Defenders, never asked what they were doing, never in trouble. The followers' camp was even more interesting. Dace had a knack for smiling at people so charmingly that they never thought to question his right to be there. Mikel had no success trying to emulate his companion's winning smile. The one time he had tried it on a Defender, hoping to sneak into the Keep to find out how the princess was faring, the Defenders on guard had sent him packing with a blistering reprimand.

Of course, one had to be on their guard around Dace. He was always trying to coax Mikel into stealing things. He did not seem to care what Mikel stole, just that he stole *something*. Its value was irrelevant, it was the act that mattered. But Mikel had been true to his faith and had not fallen to the dangerous charms of his new friend. If anything, he felt he was a positive influence on the young thief and was certain that he had saved the youth from sinning on more than one occasion.

Today however, Dace had finally suggested they steal something that even Mikel could not resist.

There was, according to Dace, a blue swallow's nest in the tower of the old keep. The mother swallow must have gotten her seasons mixed up because it was almost winter, and the chicks would die if they hatched at this time of year. Dace's noble plan was to steal the eggs from the nest and take them somewhere warmer, where they could incubate safely. Once hatched, they could dig up worms for the chicks and nurse them through the bitter weather. By spring, they would be ready to make it on their own and the boys could release them.

Try as he might, Mikel could find no fault with Dace's plan. Saving the chicks from a freezing death was a good deed, and brave too, when one considered where the nest was located. Although Dace insisted on calling their rescue mission "stealing" he joined in the escapade willingly. His enthusiasm pleased the young thief enormously. He acted almost as happy as his sister Kali, the first time that he had agreed he really did love her.

Strange people, these Medalonians.

"How are we going to get into the Keep?" Mikel demanded as he hurried alongside Dace toward the old fort. Dace had been disturbingly vague on that point. The ground was slushy underfoot from a light snow-fall the night before which had turned to mud almost as soon as the sun touched it. Mikel hated this Medalonian weather. He fervently wished it would snow properly, like it did in Yarnarrow or Kirkland, not this half-hearted mucky stuff that fell from the skies every few days with no other purpose than to make everything muddy and damp.

"They change the guard just before sundown," Dace explained. "We'll sneak in then."

Mikel had not been inside Treason Keep since the day he had been interrogated by Tarja and Lord Wolfblade. He tried hard not to think of that day. The memories still hurt too much for him to be able to recall them willingly. Even the Keep's unofficial name seemed to taunt him.

"But aren't there guards on the tower?"

"Lord Jenga says it's too dangerous up there and not worth repairing. The guards stay on the wall-walk. Once we get inside, we'll be fine." Mikel could hardly question such a confident assurance, so he trudged alongside the thief and prayed to the Overlord that Dace was right. "Besides," Dace added cheerily, "It's Founder's Day. Lord Jenga declared a holiday. There won't be many guards on duty."

"What's Founder's Day?"

"It's when the Medalonians celebrate the day they stole Medalon from the Harshini." Dace suddenly stopped walking and grinned at Mikel. "Now that was an interesting time, let me tell you! The others were steaming mad. Of course, a theft on that scale made me stronger than Zegarnald for a time, but then the Sisterhood launched their purge and the fighting started and I went back to being just plain old me. It was fun for a while, though."

"Dace, what are you talking about?"

The thief shrugged. "Nothing. Come on, we'd better hurry. It's almost sundown and we won't be able see the nest in the dark."

Shaking his head, Mikel hurried after Dace. The boy had a habit of wandering off like that. It was very disconcerting.

As Dace predicted, they were not challenged as they passed through the gate into the Keep. The Defenders barely even glanced at them. Mikel followed as he walked boldly across the muddy yard to the dangerously crumbling steps that led to the tower. As they carefully climbed the broken stairs, Mikel understood why Lord Jenga had condemned the tower. The masonry wobbled under even his slight weight.

The sun appeared to be resting on the steep peaks of the Sanctuary Mountains as they reached the top of the tower. It was a blocky, square structure but the merlons had crumbled and in one corner there was nothing but a pile of fallen rubble, almost as tall as Mikel. It was to the pile that Dace led him, squeezing in through the narrow opening between the rubble and the wall. It smelled musty in the tiny cave formed by the ruined masonry, but the mother swallow had picked her location well. The nest was protected from the wind and from the eye of any roving hawk looking for an easy meal.

"See! Five eggs!" Dace declared.

"I can't see a thing!" he complained. It was so dark inside the little cavern he could only make out Dace from his glittering eyes.

"Look, it's over . . ."

"Sshhh!" Mikel froze as the sound of footsteps reached him. He turned slightly, so he could see outside.

It was Princess Adrina. He bit back a cry of surprise as a man joined her on the tower. The Hythrun Warlord's profile was sharp against the setting sun.

"I trust you have a reason for this perilous expedition?" the princess demanded as she turned to stare out over the plain.

"I thought you might enjoy the view, your Highness."

Damin Wolfblade really should learn to speak to the princess with more respect.

"It's lovely. Can we go now?"

"Tell me what you see."

"I see nothing, and I'm freezing. Is this really necessary?"

"You see nothing," Damin repeated thoughtfully. "Interesting, don't you think?"

"You find nothing *interesting*? Well, that's hardly surprising for a man of your limited intellect."

Mikel grinned in the darkness of his hidey-hole. *That's telling him!*

"Adrina, a few leagues from here, your husband's army sits and waits. They do nothing. They don't attack. They don't train. They don't even run away. They just sit there, waiting for something. I want to know what they're waiting for."

Adrina turned north, her expression puzzled. Rather than the biting retort Mikel was expecting, she shrugged. "I have no idea."

"Were they planning something, before you left? Something that would account for their willingness to hold an army of that size immobile for so long?"

"I'd tell you if I knew. Their war council did little more than argue, and you've already seen their idea of battle. The Dukes of Karien are not renowned for their tactical genius. When you have countless troops to throw into battle it isn't really necessary."

Mikel wasn't sure he believed what he was hearing. They sounded so . . . friendly.

"Could one of the Dukes have advised him to wait?"

"Lord Roache may have," Adrina shrugged.

"What did the Duke of Setenton advise?"

"Lord Terbolt? He's not there. He sent his brother Ciril in his place."

The warlord frowned. "Terbolt isn't there? He's Jasnoff's most trusted commander. Where is he?"

"I don't know. Cratyn didn't seem surprised by his absence, though. Perhaps Jasnoff had other plans for him."

"What other plans?" Damin asked, the concern in his voice obvious even to Mikel.

"I was permitted to join their war council rather begrudgingly, my Lord. They weren't in the habit of discussing anything of import while I was present."

Damin laughed softly. "Not an unwise precaution, in light of recent events."

Adrina turned on the Warlord. "That remark was uncalled for, my Lord."

Damin sighed. "That's right, I forgot. You aren't committing treason, you just want to be free."

"Free! Get this damned collar off my neck, then I might remember what the word means!"

As Damin moved closer to her, Mikel wanted to leap to the defense of his princess, but Dace held him back.

"No!" the thief whispered.

Burning with frustration and not at all certain why he remained hidden, Mikel turned back to watch, thinking the Warlord was much too close to the princess to be proper.

Damin was fingering the golden collar Adrina wore with surprisingly gentle fingers. It reflected the setting sun, making the wolf's ruby eyes glitter malignantly. Adrina's rigid posture betrayed more than she imagined.

"What would you give to be free, Adrina?" he asked softly.

"Unhand me, sir!"

Damin dropped his hand. "I can see why your marriage was never consummated, your Highness."

Mikel swallowed a horrified gasp. He knew what "consummated" meant.

Adrina laughed. She sounded genuinely amused. "You don't like me much, do you? Is that why you take so much pleasure from tormenting me?"

"Ah, now there's the tragedy, your Highness. If you weren't such a treacherous, conniving little bitch, I'd probably be quite taken with you."

Adrina turned away from him, to study the red streaked clouds. The sun was almost completely set. "You presume to know an awful lot about me, considering the short time of our acquaintance, Damin Wolfblade. How much is your own opinion, and how much is hearsay, I wonder?"

"I make my own judgments. I've no need to listen to hearsay."

"I beg to differ, my Lord," she retorted, turning to face him. "You told Captain Tenragan I tried to kill the High Prince. You weren't there. How could you possibly know what happened, unless you listened to hearsay?"

"He told you that, did he?"

"Yes, and it's a damned lie! I did no such thing! Your uncle is a perverted monster, and if those boys would rather die than let him touch them, I don't blame them!"

"So you did give them the knife?"

"Yes!"

Damin was silent for a moment. "Why did you take the collars?"

"I didn't take them. Lernen gave them to me. I kept them as a remembrance of two children destroyed by a debauched old man. Somebody owed them that much."

He took a step back from her. "It's cold, your Highness, and I know how anxious you are to return indoors. Shall we go?"

Adrina planted her hands on her hips angrily. "That's it? No apology? No admission that you were wrong? How dare you, sir!"

The Warlord shrugged. "For all I know, you're lying about that, just as you lie about everything else."

"I am *not* lying!"

Damin closed the gap between them with frightening speed. "Then prove it, Adrina. Tell me the truth! Why did you leave Karien?" Although he was looming over her, Adrina held her ground. Mikel watched help-lessly, wanting to kill Damin Wolfblade almost as much as he wanted to stay hidden and watch this strange scene unfold.

"I've told you a thousand times! I left because Cratyn is a miserable, cowardly, little cretin! The day we were married he hit me and called me a Fardohnyan whore and told me all he wanted was a Karien heir to my father's throne. It went downhill from there."

Tears misted Mikel's eyes to hear such words coming from his princess. *She is lying to protect herself,* he reasoned anxiously.

She walked to the other side of the small tower and leaned against the crumbling merlons, turning her back to the Warlord. The darkness was settling rapidly, making her features hard to distinguish.

"Was it that bad?" Damin asked, in a surprisingly sympathetic voice.

"Worse than you could possibly imagine. The bastard even killed my dog."

She's making it up, Mikel told himself, over and over. *She's making it up.*

"Does your father know what it was like?"

"Even if he did, he wouldn't care. Hablet has his own plans."

"To invade Hythria, no doubt." Adrina looked around sharply, but Damin smiled. "Don't worry, Adrina. I won't overtax your ability to admit the truth any further, this night. Your father's worst fault is his pre-dictability. His plans are easy enough to fathom. It's the Kariens who have me worried at the moment."

"I told you, I don't know what they have planned."

"And oddly enough, I believe you. Come on. The sun has set. If we stay up here much longer they'll be able to decorate their damned Founder's Day banquet with a couple of ice statues."

He held out his hand to help her down and, to Mikel's disgust, she accepted it. But she halted at the top of the steps and leaned toward him in a most unladylike manner. "Tarja showed me the graves, Damin. That was a noble thing to do for an enemy."

"Careful, your Highness, you might actually get me believing there's a heart hidden beneath that rather impressive bosom."

She snatched her hand from his angrily. "You are an intolerable bas-tard! I was trying to be gracious!"

"Gracious?" he laughed softly. "That wide-eyed look? Those slightly parted lips? That eloquent sigh? What's next? 'Oh Damin, won't you

please let me go'? Gods Adrina! I've been around *court'esa*-trained noblewomen all my life. You'll have to do better than that."

"You flatter yourself, my Lord," Adrina said, her voice colder than
the rapidly darkening night. "In the unlikely event I ever turn my skills
on *you*, you won't even know what hit you, until you lie whimpering at
my feet, begging for more!"

"Don't try playing that game with me, Adrina. You might find the
rules a little different this far from Fardohnya."

"Rules?" she laughed softly, savagely. "In this game, my Lord, there
are no rules."

Adrina vanished from Mikel's sight as she descended the stairs, followed closely by Damin. Mikel's breath came out in a rush and he discovered he was trembling. He wished he could make sense of even half
of what he had seen and heard. The princess must be very upset to lie
about Prince Cratyn like that. What were they doing to her?

"Psst!"

Mikel glanced in the direction of the thief who sat squashed in the
dark cavern.

"What?"

"You have to steal the eggs!"

Annoyed, Mikel reached in and snatched the fragile speckled eggs
from the nest.

"There! Satisfied?"

Dace nodded, grinning broadly. "You have honoured the God of
Thieves."

"If you say so," he agreed distractedly. It was a measure of his distress that he did not bother to correct the youth. Normally such a statement received a sharp denial of the existence of any other god.

"Your soul belongs to me now, Mikel," Dace said, sounding enormously satisfied with himself.

"My soul belongs to the Overlord," he replied mechanically.

"That's what you think," the God of Thieves smirked.

chapter 45

The Medalonians celebrated Founder's Day with a degree of abandonment that Adrina considered rather inappropriate for men in the middle of a war. Admittedly, there wasn't much of a war going on at present, so they might as well take this opportunity to enjoy themselves. Even the Hythrun Raiders joined in as if it were a festival of the gods. They didn't care much for Founder's Day, she suspected, but they weren't going to ignore an excuse for a party. There was precious little else to do. One senseless battle and now Cratyn was sitting on the other side of the border with his vast army doing precisely nothing.

The hall was filled with people, as Jenga had declared an open house and many of the officers whose wives and lovers were in the followers' camp had brought their women to the party. Someone had managed to find a quantity of blue linen and had made a hopeful attempt to decorate the crumbling walls, but there had not been enough to go around. The decorations had a forlorn, unfinished look. The only source of heat was the abundant torches and the huge fireplace near the far end, but the heat of so many bodies pressed together seemed to take the chill off the air.

There were quite a few *court'esa* present as well, although Adrina thought the term a rather misguided one, when applied to these ill-bred, uneducated whores, whose only feature in common with real *court'esa* was their willingness to trade sexual favors for coin. A small band of musicians was playing in the corner, enlisted men mostly, whose skill with an instrument had got them invited to the officers' party. They weren't bad either, considering their first calling was killing people and musicianship was merely a secondary talent.

With his hand on her elbow, Damin guided Adrina through the crush toward Lord Jenga, who stood by the stairs that led up to her quarters, talking to Tarja Tenragan.

Adrina studied him curiously. She had never been able to crack that calm certitude, even when he admitted to killing her brother. And it was not for lack of trying. The captain showed no interest in her—or any other woman present, she noted, slightly mollified. Perhaps Damin was right. Perhaps there was nothing any woman here could offer him that compared with what he already had.

"I'm so glad you could join us, your Highness," Lord Jenga said as they approached.

"I wasn't aware that I was given a choice in the matter, my Lord. Good evening, Captain."

"Your Highness. Damin."

"I thought you'd be taking part in the festivities, Captain. I'm sure there are any number of young ladies here who would be delighted to keep you company."

Tarja shook his head with a faint smile. "I'm sure there are, your Highness, if I was willing to spend the coin and didn't mind what diseases I caught. May I get you some wine?"

"Thank you," Adrina replied, a little startled by his blunt answer.

Damin caught her look and leaned forward to whisper in her ear. "You deserved that."

She glared at him for a moment, then turned to Lord Jenga. "So what is this party in honor of, my Lord?"

"Founder's Day, your Highness. It's the day we celebrate the foundation of the Sisterhood's rule over Medalon."

"And you find that worthy of celebration?"

"It's tradition, your Highness," Jenga replied. "I'm sure you have many such traditions in Fardohnya."

"Of course, my Lord. I apologise if you took offense."

"Don't listen to her, Jenga," Damin warned. "She's not in the least bit sorry." He ignored the look Adrina gave him, and gave her no chance to defend herself. "Her Serene Highness did tell me something though, that she's conveniently neglected to mention until now. The Duke of Setenton isn't with Cratyn."

Jenga's weathered brow furrowed. "That would explain their tactical stupidity. Is he out of favor with Jasnoff?"

"Not that I'm aware of," Adrina told him.

"Why did you wait until now to tell us?"

"I didn't realize you would consider it so important, my Lord."

"Tell us what?" Tarja asked, returning with a cup of wine for both Damin and Adrina. She took the tankard and swallowed the wine with a gulp. How was she supposed to know Lord Terbolt's absence was such a big issue?

"The Duke of Setenton isn't in the Karien war camp."

"Then where is he?"

"That's a question I'd like answered," Damin replied, looking pointedly at Adrina.

"I told you! I don't where he is."

"You've told us a great deal, your Highness, half of which is probably outright lies, and the rest of which is doubtful."

"If we were in Fardohnya, sir, you would be put to death for insulting me so."

"If we were in Hythria, your Highness, *you'd* have been flogged for being—"

"Damin!" Tarja warned.

Fortunately, the Warlord didn't finish the threat. Adrina smiled at Tarja gratefully, but it was time to escape the company of such an intolerable man.

"Do you dance, Captain?"

"Only when I can't avoid it," Tarja replied with a grimace.

"Consider this one of those times. I feel the need for some entertainment and I find the company in this part of the hall quite dull."

Much to her annoyance, Damin laughed aloud at her comment. She thrust her wine cup at Lord Jenga and all but dragged Tarja to the center of the Hall where a lively jig was in progress. She had no idea of the steps involved, and did not particularly care. She took her place in the line and followed the steps of the girl beside her, a young thing of about sixteen with a pretty face that was ruined by a missing tooth she displayed when she smiled. The dance was fairly simple and repetitive so it didn't take long before she got the hang of it. She glanced across the hall and saw Damin watching her. She quite deliberately turned her head away and smiled winningly at Tarja.

"You don't have to keep looking at him," Tarja told her when the dance brought them together for a turn.

"Looking at whom?" she asked, feigning innocence.

"You know who I mean. Are you trying to make him jealous?"

"Don't be absurd! That would imply I care what he thinks."

"And you don't, of course."

"Of course not."

They parted then and broke into two lines, men on the right, women on the left. The steps changed and Adrina found herself having to follow the toothless peasant girl for a time. When she looked up, she couldn't see the Warlord, but she could feel his eyes on her. The dance took her back to her partner and she found herself confronting Tarja's infuriatingly calm expression.

Was he really immune to her charms, she wondered? *Is R'shiel so enticing that even when she is hundreds of leagues away, he can resist what is right under his nose?*

The lines of dancers moved together. When Tarja took her in his arms for the next part she leaned into him and smiled, meeting his eyes with an open invitation. There weren't many men who could deny her when she chose to be irresistible. Cratyn and Damin Wolfblade being rather notable exceptions, she recalled sourly.

Tarja's reaction was not at all what she expected. His expression grew serious. "Damin wasn't kidding when he said you were dangerous, was he?"

"Do *you* think I'm dangerous?" she teased.

"I think you're a spoilt brat, actually," he replied pleasantly. "I think that's why you really left your husband. You're so used to getting your own way that you ran away, rather than be denied."

"And what would you know about it?"

"I'm something of an expert on spoilt brats, your Highness. R'shiel is fairly famous for it in some circles."

Adrina's anger evaporated in the face of such a startling admission.

She had never heard Tarja speak of R'shiel before. She was more curious about the demon child than she cared to admit.

"Is she very beautiful?"

"Very."

"More beautiful than me?"

Tarja laughed. "I'm afraid I'll have to say yes, but I'm hardly what you'd call objective. Damin could probably give you a more accurate answer."

"Thank you, but I'd rather not ask him anything. Tell me more about R'shiel. Is she truly the demon child?"

"So the Harshini claim."

"Don't you believe them?"

"I'm an atheist. I'm supposed to devote my life to eradicating the Harshini."

"Yet you have a Harshini lover? A curious way of carrying out your orders, Captain."

"I have a talent for complicating my life far more than is necessary, your Highness. And you are a complication I don't want or need, so quit rubbing up against me like that, or I'll end up doing something we'll both regret, and when R'shiel gets back she'll turn you into a toad and me into something that looks like a smudge on the road."

Adrina smiled. "I like you, Captain. I've even forgiven you. Is the demon child really so fearsome?"

"No, just very certain about her territorial boundaries."

"And I'm crossing them?"

"You're getting close."

Adrina stepped back a little, her ego somewhat appeased. She had been beginning to wonder if she was losing her touch. The dance ended with a round of applause and Tarja led her back to the stairs. The Lord Defender had moved on and was talking to the officer who had charge of the horses. The musicians struck up another tune and the hall echoed to the stamping feet of the dancers. Damin was sitting on the stairs sipping his wine. He did not bother to rise as she approached. His manners were appalling.

"I see her Highness dances with the same flair she spins fanciful stories," Damin remarked. "You survived, Tarja. I'm proud of you."

"Only just," Tarja admitted with a smile. "Your Highness, it's been a pleasure, but I have duties to attend to. I'm sure Lord Wolfblade would be delighted to keep you entertained." He bowed and walked away, leaving her standing there. His abrupt departure left her speechless.

"Don't worry, Adrina, you didn't drive him off. He's waiting for a bird from the Citadel. Tonight is more important to the Medalonians than you know."

She turned to Damin curiously. "What do you mean?"

"Tonight is their annual Gathering at the Citadel. R'shiel is planning to make some changes in the Sisterhood and Tarja's very nervous about it. Here, have a seat and drink up. I'm sure you'll find me much more agreeable company if you're drunk."

Adrina accepted the cup and sat beside him on the stairs, drinking her wine thoughtfully. It was a surprisingly strong blend. "He told me about R'shiel."

"I'm not surprised. You weren't being very subtle, you know. I was half expecting you to start tearing his jacket off, right there on the dance floor."

"Do you always have to be so crude?"

"I'm being suitable to the occasion, your Highness. If you act like a whore, you shouldn't be surprised when you get treated like one."

Adrina had taken just about all she intended to from this barbarian. He had done nothing but taunt her and torment her. It was time to put him in his place. Time to wipe that superior smirk off his face.

"You're jealous."

"Of *you*? Don't flatter yourself."

"Of course, you are," she laughed. "I've misjudged you badly, my Lord. All this time I thought you were a degenerate pervert like your uncle, when in fact, you fancy yourself Kalianah's gift to women. You don't even like me, yet you can't bear the thought that I might find Tarja attractive. How pathetic!"

"Your attempts to sleep your way to freedom are far more pathetic than anything I can come up with, Adrina."

"If I'd been trying to 'sleep my way to freedom,' as you so crudely put it, I would have been out of here weeks ago," she assured him confidently.

"You're that good, are you?"

She finished the wine in a swallow, surprised at how potent it was. She had heard that the drier the climate the stronger the wine, but she hadn't realized until now the difference between the sweet blends of Fardohnya and the hardy Medalonian vintages.

"Well, that's something *you're* never likely to find out, is it?"

Damin refilled her cup from a jug he had on the step by his feet. "Ah, now that would imply that I would want to find out, Adrina. Thank you, but I prefer to sleep with women who aren't likely to try slipping a knife between my ribs."

"I imagine that's all you *can* do, Damin. *Sleep* with women." She downed the wine recklessly. She was enjoying this. To the Seven Hells with being *nice.*

"This from the woman who couldn't even coax a virgin boy into her bed," he said. "I wonder what Cratyn's doing at the moment? Praying to the Overlord for the return of his beloved wife, or thanking him for getting rid of her?"

"You're a pig, Damin Wolfblade!" She stood up—far too quickly, she discovered with alarm—and gripped the rough stone wall. "I'm not going to sit here and listen to your drunken insults any longer."

"Giving in so easily, your Highness? You disappoint me. I thought you'd be good for another hour at least."

"You're drunk!" she accused, turning to climb the stairs to her room. She misjudged them and stumbled, but Damin caught her before she fell.

"Actually, I'm disappointingly sober," he corrected. "You, on the other hand, are well and truly under the weather. How much did you have?"

"Let me go!" she demanded, shaking free of him. "I am not drunk. I had two cups, that's all."

"They weren't cups, they were tankards, and the wine you're used to is like mother's milk compared to this Medalonian stuff. Come on, let's get you upstairs before you really do something to embarrass yourself."

"Take your hands off me!" she hissed. Gripping the wall, Adrina took the steps carefully, grateful, but not willing to admit it, that Damin was behind her. Her head was starting to spin alarmingly.

By the time they reached the door to her room, Adrina felt a little better. She took a deep breath and turned to Damin, feeling almost gracious enough to thank him for his assistance. Until she saw the smirk on his face.

"You're insufferable! How dare you laugh at me!"

"You really should learn not to take yourself so seriously. You'd be much more bearable, if you did."

"I've no interest in making myself bearable to suit you."

"I doubt you could even if you tried, Adrina."

A small part of Adrina—that part that was still reasonably sober—warned her to let the comment go. But for some reason, she felt compelled to rise to the challenge. She was sick to death of this man.

"I've told you before. In the unlikely event I ever decide to entertain myself with you, Damin Wolfblade, you won't know what's hit you."

"So you keep telling me. You're not quite game to put it to the test, though, are you?"

"You think I couldn't?"

"I think you're afraid of me."

"I'm not afraid of anyone, least of all you!"

"Brave words from a cheap drunk. Go to bed, Adrina."

She laughed softly. "You're afraid of *me*, that's the truth of it. You even warned Tarja that I'm dangerous."

"He told you that?"

"Yes."

"He really does have a bad habit of repeating the most inconvenient things, doesn't he?" He reached across and opened the door to her chamber. "Goodnight, Adrina."

"I'm right, aren't I? You're afraid of me." Adrina wasn't sure why she was being so insistent. It just seemed that the world would be a much better place if Damin Wolfblade admitted that he feared her. Even a little bit.

"Terrified," he agreed, as if he were speaking to a small child. "Now go to bed."

"You're just saying that to get rid of me."

"You noticed? Maybe you're not as drunk as I thought."

"I know why you're afraid."

"Why?"

"Because of this," she said, and then she kissed him.

Adrina had intended to bestow one blazing, breathtaking kiss on him and leave him gasping for more. He would never get any more, of course, but that was the whole point. Let him have a taste of the forbidden fruit and then deny him the sweetness forever more.

But she didn't count on Damin's reaction. She didn't count on him kissing her back. Didn't count on finding herself pushed against the wall with strong arms holding hers pinned against her body while her pulse pounded in her ears, blocking out all other sensations. Adrina had kissed plenty of men before, but no *court'esa* in her service would have dared such unbridled lust. Her grand plan evaporated in a heartbeat. For a fleeting, dangerous moment, she gave herself up to the sheer, unexpected pleasure of it.

"Your *Highness?*"

Tamylan's startled greeting brought her back to her senses and she pushed Damin away with a shove, gasping for air. Her slave stood in the open doorway to her chamber, her expression a mixture of astonishment and horror.

"Are you alright, my Lady?" she asked with concern, glaring at Damin.

"I'm fine, Tam. Go back to bed. I'll be in shortly."

The slave nodded warily and moved away from the door. Only then did Adrina feel composed enough to meet Damin's eye.

"I think I've proved my point, don't you?"

Damin's expression was far too smug. "You think so?"

"I hope you enjoyed it, my Lord. You'll never receive another. From now on, you'll just have to dream about what you're missing."

Adrina still had enough of her wits about her not to wait for his answer. She turned on her heel and slammed the door behind her with a resounding, and most satisfactory, thump.

"What are you playing at, Adrina?" Tamylan demanded as soon as the door banged shut. "Have you completely lost your mind?"

"You forget your place, Tamylan."

"So have you, your Highness," the slave retorted. "Have you forgotten where we are? Who he is? *What* he is?"

"Be silent!"

Tamylan shook her head in disgust and left the rest of it unsaid.

chapter 46

For the second time in her life, R'shiel entered the Great Hall to attend the annual Gathering of the Sisters of the Blade, although on this occasion she did not have to scale the outside of the building in the rain.

This time she walked through the main doors quite brazenly, concealed by a glamor that made her unnoticeable. She broke from the crowd at the entrance and made her way to the narrow stairs leading to the gallery. Once she had climbed the stairs, she walked along the gallery to almost the exact spot from which she had watched the Gathering two years ago with Davydd Tailorson. It was odd, and a little disconcerting that she could barely remember his face. Davydd had died trying to help her and Tarja escape the Citadel. He deserved to be remembered more clearly.

R'shiel watched the Hall filling with blue-robed sisters, fidgeting nervously. She wanted to call Dranymire, to ensure the demon knew what was expected of him and his brethren, but she could not risk them being noticed before she took control of the Gathering. She wanted to know where Mahina was. She wanted to get a message to Affiana, concerned that the woman had not been at the pre-arranged meeting place. It could simply be that she had not waited around. R'shiel and Brak had been late arriving at the tavern. R'shiel was worried. Affiana had not even left a message for them.

She leaned on the balustrade, watching the growing crowd. Garet Warner, the ranking officer in the Citadel, stood off to the left of the dais with two other officers, where Lord Jenga and Tarja had stood the night

Joyhinia had been appointed First Sister. She wished she could tell what he was thinking. Wished she knew how far he could be trusted.

R'shiel also wished Brak had come with her, but he had insisted he wait outside with the horses, ready for a quick departure. He wanted her away from this place with a determination that bordered on obsession. Brak was a hard man to read. The only thing R'shiel was certain of was that he would stay by her, regardless of how he felt about what she was doing. She wasn't even sure that Brak liked her very much, but he took his responsibilities seriously. He had killed the Harshini King to ensure her survival. To desert her now would make that act meaningless.

The doors closing with a hollow boom signalled the start of the meeting and every eye turned forward as the white-robed members of the Quorum filed on to the dais from the door at the back of the Hall. Traditionally, the First Sister entered last, a custom R'shiel was extremely grateful for. She sent out a mental call for Dranymire. The demon responded instantly, popping into existence beside her, his too-large eyes glittering in the gloom.

Are you ready?

May the gods be with us, Dranymire responded before he disappeared again.

"Be careful," she whispered to the vanished demon.

She turned her attention to the dais, as Francil began reciting the ritual thanksgiving to the Founding Sisters. On the edge of her awareness, she could feel the demons forming the meld that would be Joyhinia. She pushed aside the distraction and reached inside herself, feeling the glow of the Harshini magic that nestled in her mind. She drew on the power carefully, as Brak had shown her, and formed the thoughts she wanted to impose on the Gathering although she held back releasing them. Her eyes darkened until they turned completely black, the whites of her eyes consumed by the power she gathered to her. As Francil's dry voice finished the litany, the door leading from the small anteroom opened and the demon meld stepped onto the dais.

Dranymire and his brethren had done an impressive job. The Joyhinia they had formed was a little too tall perhaps, and her eyes had never been quite that shade of blue, but one would be hard pressed to tell her from the genuine article. Joyhinia stepped up to take her place with a commanding air, nodding in acknowledgment to the Quorum before turning to face the Gathering. It was against protocol, R'shiel knew, but she did not want to risk the meld for a moment longer than she had to. Joyhinia would stand up, make her announcement and then leave. R'shiel could not pick out Mahina among the sea of blue-robed sisters, but she trusted the old woman to be in place.

She held back the coercion with difficulty. The power, once tapped, did not like to be restrained. Sweat beaded her forehead and her eyes burned as she gripped the balustrade. Unconsciously, R'shiel mouthed the words of Joyhinia's rehearsed speech, as the demon meld addressed the crowd.

"Sisters! It is good to be back among you, in these trying times." The voice was too low, almost masculine, but it was so long since any of the sisters had heard Joyhinia speak, R'shiel doubted anybody would notice. "I have been on our northern border, supervising our efforts to repel the insolent Karien invasion of our sovereign nation." The Gathering was silent as they listened to the First Sister, more curious than concerned. "Medalon will be safe in the hands of the Defenders and we must press all our efforts in that direction."

"From what I hear, it was a Defender who got us into this mess!" a voice called from the back of the Hall.

R'shiel grimaced. She had not coached Dranymire to trade taunts with hecklers. The coercion labored to be released. Her knuckles were white with the effort of holding it in. Dranymire ignored the comment and carried on, oddly enough, making the meld seem more like Joyhinia than ever.

"The single most important issue facing Medalon is our survival. Everything else is insignificant in comparison to this. Personal ambition, feelings and prejudices must be put aside." That actually drew a spattering of applause. There were many Sisters who were more concerned with their duties than their careers. Having grown up in Joyhinia's shadow, R'shiel had to occasionally remind herself of that.

Joyhinia waited a moment before she continued. R'shiel fervently hoped it was Dranymire pausing for dramatic effect, not fighting for control over the meld.

"To this end, I plan to step down from the position of First Sister and nominate the woman who I believe is the only one among us strong enough to see us through this: Mahina Cortanen."

Pandemonium erupted in the Hall at Joyhinia's announcement. R'shiel let go of the coercion, almost gagging as it descended on the Hall, forcing down the opposition like a wet blanket thrown on a fire.

R'shiel had known it would be uncomfortable, she remembered the feeling on the border when the Karien priests had coerced their troops, but she was not prepared for the wave of debilitating nausea that washed over her. Her knees buckled as she forced the women below to accept what they could not accept, to believe the unbelievable. She gritted her teeth, waiting for Mahina to step forward to accept the mantle of First Sister. The crowd settled as their thoughts were turned from rebellion to compliance, but there was no sign of the old woman. Joyhinia looked up toward the gallery uncertainly.

"I call forth Mahina Cortanen!"

Where is she? R'shiel forcibly held back the suspicions of the crowd, fighting the sickening feeling with all her strength. A movement at the back of the crowd caught her attention and she spied Mahina moving toward the dais with relief. It would be over soon. It was almost done.

Mahina finally stepped up to the platform and turned to face the Gathering. R'shiel could not imagine what she was thinking. As First Sister she was sworn to destroy all vestiges of Harshini magic, yet her appointment this night could not happen without it. She faced the Gathering with an unreadable expression as R'shiel forced the thousand or more Sisters present to accept her reinstatement.

"Do you accept my nomination?" Joyhinia asked.

"Yes!" came the unanimous, if somewhat muted reply. R'shiel needed them to agree. She did not have the skill to inspire them with enthusiasm.

"Then I declare Mahina Cortanen First Sister!"

There was no accompanying cheer, barely a murmur, in fact. Mahina did not wait for the customary accolades, in any case. The demon meld wobbled for an instant and R'shiel knew they could not hold it together much longer.

"Commandant, as the ranking officer of the Defenders in the Citadel, will you take the oath on behalf of the Lord Defender?"

"I will, your Grace," Garet replied, stepping forward into the small clearing at the foot of the dais.

R'shiel fought off the crippling nausea as Garet drew his sword and laid it at the feet of the new First Sister. *Not much longer,* she told herself, understanding now why Brak had insisted she work the coercion and then leave immediately. She wanted to vomit and she wasn't sure how much longer she could stay on her feet.

Garet knelt on one knee and began the oath in a voice that rang clearly through the Hall. A commotion at the edge of the crowd distracted R'shiel for a moment, but she ignored it. It was almost over. The demon meld shimmered but Dranymire managed to hold his brethren together. As soon as the Defenders were sworn to Mahina, Joyhinia could leave. It didn't matter if the meld disintegrated the moment they were out of sight. The important thing was to prevent it falling into a puddle of little gray demons in full sight of the Gathering. R'shiel was coercing the Sisters into accepting Mahina's appointment. If she were forced to cover for the demons, she would have to let that thought go. Even if she had the skill to perform such a task, she doubted she had the strength left.

R'shiel's black eyes watered with the effort of forcing down the natural opposition of the Sisters in the Hall to this blatant breach of protocol. It was like trying to hold a surging ocean back with nothing more than a fishing net. As Brak had warned, for some the coercion settled on them with barely a flicker of protest, while other minds rebelled against the thoughts she imposed on them. That opposition surged up like a stormy sea. No sooner had she quieted one mind than another screamed in protest. The mental strength it took surprised her. Physically, she was on the point of exhaustion.

It seemed to take Garet forever to complete the oath. Time slowed as her vision narrowed to a pinpoint, fixed on the dais. It was all she could see, all she cared about. As the power consumed her, every sense not immediately involved in holding the coercion together seemed to shut down. She could no longer feel her fingers gripping the balustrade. She could no longer hear anything. The odor of damp wool cloaks that had permeated the Hall faded into nothing. She was isolated in a bubble of total concentration that allowed no room for any distraction.

"Stop this abomination! You are being deceived!"

The voice rang out from the back of the Hall, a male voice that startled the Sisters with its harsh Karien accent. R'shiel felt the Sisters' resistance to the coercion surge in response to the sudden cry and it slipped from her grasp. At almost the same instant, Dranymire lost control of the meld.

Screams filled the hall as Joyhinia fell apart, leaving nothing but a writhing mass of wrinkled gray gnomes who blinked out of existence as soon as they realized they were exposed. All except one. The little demon who had attached herself to R'shiel in Sanctuary, who sought warmth in her bed, cowered behind the lectern on the podium, unseen by the humans surrounding her, trembling with fear.

R'shiel did not see the demon. She had no idea what was happening. She collapsed against the balustrade and brought up everything she had eaten for the past week. Her eyes watered so hard she could not see, could not find the source of the pounding feet on the narrow stairs that led to the gallery. She wiped her mouth and glanced up, barely had time to notice the tonsured man standing over her as a jeweled staff landed on her shoulder, tearing a scream of unbearable agony from her.

She quivered on the gallery floor as rough hands held her down and something cold and hard was snapped around her neck. As soon as the clasp snicked shut, R'shiel felt the last remnants of the Harshini power vanish, as if a door had been slammed shut on it.

Dazed and barely able to walk, she was dragged to her feet, pushed down the winding stairs, then half pulled, half carried to the front of the Hall. The men holding her threw her to the floor. Simply letting her go would have had the same effect. Her head cracked against the bottom step, but she barely noticed the pain or the blood that spurted from her forehead. She pushed herself up onto her elbows and wiped her eyes.

More screams filled the hall as the little demon spied R'shiel and flew at her, chitterring in terror. She wrapped her arms around R'shiel's neck. As soon as the demon came in contact with the collar, she squealed with pain and fell to the floor, quivering, temporarily robbed of every vestige of power, too stunned to disappear and save herself. R'shiel tried to catch the creature but she was pushed away roughly. One of the priests pinned the demon to the floor with his staff.

R'shiel cried out in protest as the little demon squealed in agony. Someone knocked her down. By the time she had pushed herself up again, the demon was being hurried from the hall by two of the Karien priests. She looked up then and caught sight of the First Sister.

Joyhinia looked down at her. The real Joyhinia. Savage intelligence burned in eyes that should have been filled with childish innocence. She smiled with malicious glee, then held her arms wide to address the Gathering.

"What has happened here is sorcery, my Sisters! Only with the help of Lord Terbolt and the Karien priests have I been able to expose this treachery. I have not resigned. I do not surrender my position to any woman." She spared Mahina a glance, then turned to Garet Warner. "Arrest the usurper!"

Garet did not even hesitate. Mahina was being led away before she could protest—before anyone could protest. The Commandant had changed sides without a whimper. Angrily, R'shiel forced herself to concentrate and reach for her power, but all she got in return for her trouble was a vicious burning sensation around her neck that wrenched an agonized cry from her lips.

Joyhinia glanced down at R'shiel. She was gloating. Her eyes were filled with vengeance waiting to be sated. The aura that surrounded her was black streaked and tantalizingly familiar. She held her arms wide again and addressed the Gathering.

"Behold, Sisters! Let me present the author of this treasonous plot. I give you the reason for the Purge. I give you the result of relaxing our vigilance. I give you a Harshini sorcerer! I give you the fabled demon child!"

chapter 47

onsciousness returned slowly. It crept up on her like a thief in the night, so slowly that it took time for her to realize she was awake. It took even longer for her to realize where she was.

R'shiel lay on the floor, her head throbbing from the shallow cut she received when she had hit the marble steps leading to the dais. Cold morning light from the highset windows checkered the expensive rug where she lay. Her neck ached as if it had been burned; the icy collar that circled her throat a grim reminder of the foolishness of trying to reach for her power. Her mouth tasted like the floor of a pigsty. Her hands were tied behind her back, the ropes so tight that her fingers were numb. She was in a bedchamber, rather than a cell, but she could not recall how she got there. Her last clear memory was Joyhinia staring at her with savage, lucid eyes as she destroyed everything R'shiel had been working toward.

"You're awake, I see."

R'shiel turned her head in the direction of the voice. The man who spoke was a Karien.

"Can I have some water?" she croaked.

The Karien nodded and R'shiel felt other hands pulling her up into a sitting position. A cool tankard touched her lips and she swallowed the water gratefully. The man who held her head was Karien too, with the tonsured head and fanatical expression of a priest. Fear stabbed at her like a knife. She had been the victim of a Karien priest before. It was not an experience she wished to repeat.

"You failed in your attempt to subvert the Sisterhood. You realize that, don't you?"

"Who are you?"

"I am Lord Terbolt, the Duke of Setenton, Personal Envoy of King Jasnoff III and the anointed representative of Xaphista the Overlord."

"Is that supposed to impress me?" she said, pushing away the tankard. Too late now to wonder if it had been drugged.

The Karien frowned. "You would do well to show some respect, demon child. I can have you put to death with a word."

R'shiel stared at him, trying to gather her wits. She ignored the pain with an effort. Now was not the time to give into something so distracting. "I'd be dead already if you were planning to kill me."

Lord Setenton nodded slowly, as if reluctant to admit the truth of her statement. "You live because the Overlord wishes it, demon child. He is liable to change his mind quite rapidly, should you fail to do as you are told."

"Then kill me now," she suggested. "I'd rather die than do anything Xaphista demanded of me."

The Karien frowned at her blasphemy. The priest actually gasped.

"No, Garanus!" Terbolt ordered. He was standing behind her, so R'shiel could not see what the priest intended.

"She blasphemes, my Lord!"

"She doesn't know any better."

"But, my Lord . . ."

"No Garanus, his Majesty was quite specific. She is not to be harmed. The Overlord has plans for the demon child."

R'shiel struggled to sit up and glared at the Karien. "Look, I don't know where you got the idea that I'm the demon child, but you're gloating over the wrong catch. The Harshini are extinct. I am human."

"You are a liar," Garanus countered.

"Let her be, Garanus. Her denials are meaningless. Go find Gawn and see if there is any word on the half-breed."

So they hadn't caught Brak. The news gave her hope. The priest followed the Duke's orders with some reluctance, closing the door behind him. As soon as he was gone, Lord Terbolt rose from his chair and crossed the room. He untied the ropes holding her, then helped her to her feet. R'shiel winced as the blood returned to her numb fingers.

"Thank you."

"I am not a vicious man, R'shiel. I have no wish to see you harmed. I have orders to deliver you to King Jasnoff in one piece. I would appreciate it if you gave Garanus and his ilk no reason to harm you."

"You mean, if I cooperate, I'll be safe until you hand me over to Xaphista so he can kill me himself? What a tempting offer."

"As I understand it, the Overlord wants your cooperation, not your death, demon child. I believe he seeks an alliance, not your destruction."

"An alliance? With me? Now I really *have* heard everything."

Before Terbolt could answer, the door opened and R'shiel felt the room sway momentarily as Joyhinia stepped into the room. It was impossible, she knew, for Joyhinia to have regained her wits. Dacendaran had stolen them and Tarja had destroyed them. How could she be standing there? So sure of herself? So obviously aware?

"Did you want something, Captain?" the Duke asked, addressing the First Sister with ill-disguised impatience.

R'shiel stared at him in confusion. *Captain?*

"Garanus wishes to speak with you, my Lord. In *private*." Joyhinia turned her frighteningly lucid eyes on R'shiel and smiled unpleasantly. "I'll watch the prisoner for you."

"She is not to be harmed," the Duke warned.

"As you wish."

Joyhinia closed the door behind the Duke, then leaned against it, studying R'shiel with contempt.

"Your sorcerer's tricks didn't help you much this time, did they?"

"I don't know what you're talking about."

"Oh yes you do! You may have fooled everyone else, but these Kariens know what you are. And I've seen your evil first hand. Only this time Tarja's not around to save you, is he?"

It slowly dawned on R'shiel that this was not Joyhinia. The body was hers, certainly, but the words were not. She knew the aura surrounding Joyhinia, and this did not belong to her foster-mother. Neither did the memories. Joyhinia had never seen her use anything remotely resembling magic. Nobody in Medalon had, with the exception of her friends still on the northern border and the Fardohnyan crew of the *Maera's Daughter*. The only other person was . . .

"Loclon!"

The name evoked a flood of memories she had thought long forgotten. Nightmares she hoped she would never revisit suddenly threatened to overwhelm her. R'shiel's mouth went dry and she took an involuntary step backwards, wishing Korandellan had never removed the block on her emotions. For a brief, sickening moment the pain, the humiliation she had suffered in this man's hands tried to swamp her. She fought a wave of nausea as bad as the one that had almost crippled her when she tried to coerce the Gathering.

"In the flesh," Joyhinia agreed. "Well, in the First Sister's flesh actually. Ironic, don't you think?"

"How?" she managed to ask, her head reeling from the implications of such a dreadful combination.

Joyhinia shrugged. "I'm not sure how. The priests did it. They called on their Overlord, or something. I wasn't too thrilled to begin with, until it occurred to me what I could do as First Sister. By the look on your face, I'd say it's occurred to you, too."

Actually, R'shiel was still struggling to come to grips with the dreadful specter of the man she loathed and feared most in this world controlling the body of the woman she hated almost as much. Her mind had not had time to deal with the wider implications of all that sadistic megalomania trapped inside the woman who ruled Medalon.

"You won't get away with this, Loclon. You can't make people believe you're the First Sister."

"That's where you're wrong, demon child. I *am* the First Sister."

"Where's Mahina?"

"The usurper? Safely under lock and key. She'll be tried and hanged for treason, along with the Lord Defender and Tarja, when I get my hands on them. I may even keep you alive long enough to watch them swing."

"You've no say over what happens to me, you deluded fool. You're a Karien puppet. You're dancing to their tune."

"Only while it suits me."

"Don't kid yourself," she warned. "They'll only keep you alive long enough to do what they want. And you won't be able to deny them. Where's your own body, Loclon? Somewhere safe? Being tended by Karien priests? Did they promise to watch over you while your mind inhabits Joyhinia's body? How long do you think you'll last if they slit your unresisting throat?" R'shiel had no idea if her prediction was accurate, but Loclon didn't know that.

Joyhinia's face paled a little, small satisfaction though it was. It was obvious the Kariens had not explained much about the mechanics of transferring his mind into Joyhinia's body. That could work in her favor. Loclon was many things, but first and foremost, he was a coward.

"You console yourself anyway you want, R'shiel," the First Sister retorted. "Just remember, I'm the one in control now."

R'shiel had to keep reminding herself that this was Loclon, not Joyhinia, and that she needed to deal with *him*, not her. "You're not in control of anything, Loclon, least of all me. I don't care whose face you wear, you're still nothing but a craven, petty, insignificant, little man. The only difference is that now you're wearing a skirt."

Loclon took a step toward her, reacting as he always did to her taunts. R'shiel tentatively reached inside herself and tried to touch her power, but even that delicate probe caused the collar to burn. She understood why the Duke had untied her, why Loclon did not fear her. They had cut her off from the source of the Harshini magic.

"I intend to make you suffer until you beg for mercy!" Joyhinia's voice hissed, but it was Loclon's vengeful mind that supplied the words.

"You'll be doing nothing of the sort," the Duke of Setenton corrected.

Joyhinia spun around in annoyance to find the Karien standing by the open door wearing a look of intense displeasure.

"R'shiel is a wanted criminal, my Lord. She belongs to Medalon."

"She belongs to the Overlord, Captain, and if I see any evidence that you intend to interfere with the Overlord's wishes, you may find the penalty life-threatening. Your usefulness is limited. There are other, more cooperative minds who could serve our needs just as easily."

Loclon's eyes burned with anger in Joyhinia's face. She strode from the room, pushing past Setenton. The duke watched her leave and then turned to R'shiel.

"You will be confined here until we leave. There are a number of things that need to be taken care of first. But we should be able to leave in a few days. If all goes well, we should be in Karien by the end of the month."

"Then you plan to travel overland? A bit risky, don't you think, in the middle of a war?"

Lord Setenton smiled coldly. "War? What war? Of course, you left the Gathering early, didn't you? Your nation is no longer at war with Karien, my dear. The First Sister has already dispatched the order to your forces on the border. Medalon has surrendered."

chapter 48

Surrender?" Damin leapt forward and snatched the note from Tarja's hand. "The hell we will! This is a trick!"

Tarja looked haggard, as if he hadn't slept for days. "The note carries the correct authentication seal from the Citadel. It's genuine."

"Who sent it?"

"The First Sister," Jenga told him grimly.

"But *which* First Sister?"

"Mahina would not betray us," the Lord Defender objected.

"Well, somebody did! Probably your precious Garet Warner. I told you he wasn't to be trusted."

Tarja sagged against the edge of the long table near the hearth. "You're both missing the point here. This message means that R'shiel failed. Their demon meld didn't work."

Damin glanced at the Medalonian captain sympathetically. "I'm sure she's fine, Tarja. Perhaps they didn't arrive in time."

"If they hadn't arrived in time, then things would have simply gone on as they have for months. Something went wrong." He stood up and squared his shoulders determinedly. "I'm going to the Citadel."

"No you're not, Captain. I need you here."

"R'shiel needs me."

"There is nothing you can do for her, Tarja," Jenga reminded him with cold practicality. "It would take you weeks to reach the Citadel and for all you know she's already dead."

Tarja's eyes blazed defiantly, but he could not deny Jenga's logic.

"That's it then? We just roll over and die? Shall we send an emissary to the Kariens with our surrender, or were you planning to do the honors yourself, my Lord?"

"I don't think we should do anything just yet," Damin advised. "Who else knows about this?"

"Just the three of us at present."

"Then let's keep it that way for a little bit longer. I want to have a word with Her Serene Highness, first."

"What can she tell you that we don't already know?" Jenga asked. He did not balk at holding off carrying out his orders, Damin noticed with relief.

"I'm not sure. I just have a funny feeling about this. I'll tell you after I've spoken with her. Can you have her brought to my tent?"

"She's right up those stairs, Damin," Tarja pointed out. "Why not just go up and ask her now?"

"I want this discussion to take place on my territory, not hers."

It was a measure of his distress that Tarja didn't even smile. An hour or so later, two Defenders arrived in the Hythrun camp escorting Adrina. Damin had spent the intervening time mentally rehearsing what he was going to say.

He had not quite recovered from their last encounter. Adrina had caught him unawares, and that irked him no end. What really annoyed him was that he had been expecting her to try something like that ever since he first laid eyes on her and had steeled himself against it. He knew her background too well. Knew that if she couldn't get her own way by demanding it, she would eventually resort to using her body. But she took him by surprise and he'd reacted exactly as she'd wanted him to. His only comfort was that she seemed to have been as unnerved by the incident as he was.

When she arrived, Adrina was dressed for warmth, rather than effect, wrapped in the woolen shirt he had given her and a warm Defender's cloak. Her skin was flushed from the walk, her dark hair piled loosely on top of her head. Gods, she was stunning. He wondered why he'd never noticed how green her eyes were. Dark lashes almost too long to be real framed eyes the color of cut emeralds. Damin mentally berated himself for a fool as she shook off the cloak and stepped up to the brazier to warm her outstretched hands.

"You wanted to see me, my Lord?"

"I thought we might continue our discussion from the other night."

"Which one?" she asked calmly. "The one about Cratyn's intentions, or the one about us?"

"There is no *us*, your Highness, so I guess that leaves Cratyn."

"I've told you everything I know."

"Then tell me again."

"I don't see the point."

"You don't have to."

Adrina's eyes narrowed cannily. "Something's happened, hasn't it?"

"I'm sorry, I'm being very remiss as a host. Can I offer you some wine?" He turned his back, reaching for the jug on his writing desk.

"Don't avoid the question, Damin. What's happened?"

He poured the wine and turned back to her. "The Medalonians have been ordered to surrender."

Now *why* had he told her *that*?

Her face was a portrait of shock. He doubted even Adrina could fake such a genuine reaction. "In the name of Zegarnald, *why*? They're *winning*!"

"I don't know if I'd go so far as to call this stalemate winning," he said as he handed her the wine. "But they certainly aren't in danger of imminent defeat."

"I don't understand it."

"Neither do I. That's what I wanted to see you about. Could this have anything to do with Setenton's absence from the front?"

"It might," she nodded thoughtfully. "I thought it a little odd that Jasnoff sent Cratyn to the border without Terbolt. But the Kariens are very big on honor and distinguishing themselves in battle. I always supposed he wanted to give Cratyn a chance to prove himself to the Dukes."

"If he's behind this sudden turnabout, that would explain it. What about the treaty with your father?"

Adrina hesitated for a moment, then sighed. "What I told you before was the truth, or most of it. Father agreed to invade Medalon from the south come summer, and to supply the Kariens with cannon."

"Cannon? Are they really as devastating as they claim?"

She nodded grimly. "The truth? They're proving more trouble than they're worth. They blow up when you least expect it, only work sometimes and we still haven't found the right sort of alloy that won't split after a few shots and kill the men manning the guns. My father's cannon are as much the result of clever rumors as they are fact."

"I see. And what does Hablet get in return for all this?"

"Gold and timber. Lots and lots of it."

"I know your father's greedy, Adrina, but there has to be more to it than that."

"The prize is Hythria, Damin," she said softly. "I thought you'd already worked that out for yourself."

He stared at her for a moment, wondering why she had chosen this moment to reveal Hablet's plans. "Hablet doesn't need the Kariens to invade Hythria."

"No, but he needs the Defenders occupied. You know as well as I do how futile it's been, trying to attack Hythria over the Sunrise Mountains. There are only a few navigable passes and they can be defended by a handful of men against the entire Fardohnyan army. A naval invasion would be just as futile. Your ports are too well defended. Hythria's only vulnerable point is the border with Medalon. If the Medalonians had territorial ambitions, you'd have been overrun a century ago."

"So Hablet plans to turn south, once he reaches Medalon."

"And you've made the job even easier for him. Your province borders Medalon. You're supposed to be Hythria's first line of defense."

Damin really didn't need Adrina pointing out his tactical error at that point. He was more than capable of punishing himself for being so arrogant.

"Did your father know anything about the Karien plans for Medalon?"

"If you mean, was he expecting them to surrender, of course not. His entire strategy is based on the Kariens keeping the Defenders off his back. Hablet doubts the Defenders would care if he invaded Hythria, one way or the other, but they're likely to take a very dim view of him marching through Medalon to do it, particularly since they allied themselves with you, Damin."

That was the second time today she had called him by name. He wondered if she realized that she was doing it.

"And if Medalon surrenders?"

"Jasnoff will have time to wonder what my father is up to. The Kariens are religious fanatics. It's bad enough the entire southern half of the continent is devoted to pagan worship. They certainly don't want it united under one crown. Hablet will invade Hythria and Karien will follow to stop him. Either way, Hythria will lose. Your only hope is to keep me safe from the Kariens."

Damin smiled. It was amazing the way she could twist any situation to her advantage. "Exactly how would that make a difference?"

"Any child of mine by Cratyn would have a claim on Hablet's throne. With Medalon defeated, if Hablet ruled Fardohnya and Hythria, the Kariens would own the entire continent on his death."

"A death that would be sooner, rather than later, knowing the Kariens." Damin shook his head at the vast scope of the Karien plans for world dominance. Or perhaps they were Xaphista's plans.

And the demon child, the only one who could stop him, was probably dead.

"An heir and a spare—and I too become surplus to requirements," she reminded him grimly.

He studied her for a moment, wondering if he was seeing the real Adrina for the first time. The woman whose life depended on staying one step ahead of the men who controlled her. Her father. Her husband. Even him. Every one of them was trying to use her to further their own ambitions.

"Is there anything else you haven't told me, Adrina?"

She sipped her wine, looking at him over the rim of her cup. "Haven't I told you enough?"

"That depends on what critical piece of information you're holding back."

She lowered the cup and smiled. "You're the most suspicious man I've ever met."

"With just cause, around you."

"Well, I hate to disappoint you, Damin, but you know just about everything I do."

"It's the 'just about' that concerns me."

"I've nothing to gain by lying to you. If Medalon surrenders, I will be returned to Karien. I would rather die."

Oddly, he believed her. If what she had told him was true, the Kariens would allow her to live long enough to produce the requisite heir—and not a moment longer. She had already betrayed them once. They wouldn't be so lax in their vigilance a second time.

Then something else occurred to him, which changed his opinion of her rather radically.

"Cratyn's impotence was all your fault, wasn't it? You didn't want to give him an heir to your father's throne."

The question startled her at first, then she smiled smugly. "As you pointed out the first time we spoke, my Lord, an inexperienced Karien princeling is no match for a *court'esa*-trained Fardohnyan princess."

"It seems I've misjudged you, your Highness."

"Something else I warned you about."

He refused to acknowledge her reprimand. "More wine?"

"Thank you, no. I've learnt the folly of consuming too much Medalonian wine on an empty stomach." She held out her empty cup. "I should be going. Was there anything else you wanted?"

He took the cup from her outstretched hand. "Untie your shirt."

"*What?*"

Damin smiled. "Untie your shirt."

"You have *got* to kidding."

"I've never been more serious. Untie your shirt, or I'll do it for you."

She glared at him, but to her credit, she didn't back away. "You lay one finger on me and I'll—"

"What? Scream?" he finished with a laugh. "You're in the middle of my camp, Adrina. Who's going to come to your rescue?"

"I'll gouge your eyes out if you touch me."

He shrugged and turned his back on her, replacing the empty cups on the desk. "As you wish. I was under the impression you wanted that slave collar off. I must have been mistaken."

He waited with his back to her. She was silent for a very long time.

"You could have said that's what you were planning."

"And miss seeing you squirm like that?" he asked with a grin as he turned back to her. "I don't think so. So, shall we start again? Untie your shirt. I can't get to the thing with you bundled up like that."

"Just give me the keys and I'll do it myself."

"No. And for being so uncooperative now you're going to have to say please."

"You are the most unbelievable bastard."

"I know."

She stepped around the brazier and the cushions, unlacing the shirt as she went. By the time she reached him the shirt was open far enough to expose the collar and a tantalising glimpse of pale throat—and not a thing more.

"There! Just take the damned thing off!"

"Say please."

"Please!" Her eyes burned with fury.

Getting that much out of her was something of an achievement, so Damin decided not to push his luck. She might still try to gouge his eyes out, just on principal.

He took her hand and pulled her closer, then slid his fingers under the collar. Lernen had only shown him once how the catch worked, and he wasn't at all certain he could find it. The jeweler who had designed the collars was a craftsman and they were manufactured to prevent a clever slave finding the means for their emancipation. Adrina closed her eyes rather than meet his. It was very distracting, holding her so close. He could feel her hot breath on his face, smell the faint perfume of the soap she used to wash her hair.

He found the catch and heard it open with a faint snick. Adrina heard it too. She opened her eyes, a little surprised to find herself so close to him. She looked up, met his eyes.

Later, Damin couldn't say who moved first. One moment she was staring at him with those impressive green eyes. The next he was kissing her and she was kissing him back. The collar tumbled forgotten to the floor. It was almost as if she wanted to devour him. He cursed the layers of winter clothing they both wore as she tore at the lacing on his shirt. There was no logic to this, no rational thought.

"This is insane," Adrina gasped between kisses, as she fumbled with the buckle on his sword belt. "I hate you."

The sword belt dropped to the floor with a clatter. "I hate you too."

"We shouldn't be doing this," she added as she pulled the shirt over his head.

"We'll talk about it later," he promised as her shirt fell away, exposing her glorious pale breasts. Damin fell onto the scattered cushions beside the brazier. Adrina landed astride him. Her hair had come loose and it fell about them in an ebony wave that cut off the rest of the tent so that it was only Adrina that he could see. It was only Adrina that he wanted to see, in any case.

"Damin?"

He pulled her down and kissed her, but she pulled back impatiently.

"Damin!"

"You're not going to ask me to be gentle, are you?"

She smiled wickedly. "No. I only want one thing from you, my Lord."

"Name it, your Highness."

Her smile faded, replaced with a look of unexpected savagery. "Make me forget Cratyn."

The request did not surprise him nearly as much as her vehemence. But he understood it. "Say please."

"Go to hell."

He laughed softly and drew her down again. Before long it was doubtful if either of them could recall their own names, let alone the name of Adrina's husband.

chapter 49

"You did *what?*"

Tarja wondered if he'd mis-heard the warlord. He glanced across at Damin and feared he hadn't.

They were supposed to be riding out to inspect the border troops, but Tarja realized now that Damin's suggestion had merely been a ruse. He wanted to break the news to Tarja out of the hearing of the rest of the camp. The Hythrun was looking rather shame-faced with all of the things that had gone wrong in the past few days. This was one complication they could have done without.

"You heard me."

"Founders, Damin, she's the wife of the Karien Crown Prince!"

"I'm aware of that."

"I thought you couldn't stand her?"

"I can't. Look, it's . . . complicated. It's hard to explain."

"Well you'd better think of something," Tarja warned. "I imagine Jenga's going to want a fairly detailed explanation when she complains that you raped her."

"I never raped her!" Damin declared, offended by the very suggestion. "Her Serene Highness was a very willing participant, I can assure you."

Tarja shook his head doubtfully. "Even so, when she's had time to think about it, she might change her mind. Just because you didn't throw her on the ground and tear her clothes off, doesn't mean she won't claim you did."

"Perhaps I should get in first," Damin suggested with a grin. "She was the one tearing at my clothes, after all."

"Be serious!"

The Warlord sighed and reined his stallion in. He studied the snow-dotted plain for a moment before turning to Tarja. Their breath frosted in the early morning light. The sun had risen over the rim of the Jagged Mountains, but the day was overcast, threatening more snow.

"Is Jenga planning to surrender?"

Tarja shrugged. "I wish I knew. He's torn between duty and reason at present."

"I have to leave, Tarja."

"I expected as much," he agreed without rancor. "It's the Defenders who are being ordered to surrender, not the Hythrun."

"I'd have to go in any case," Damin told him. "Hablet's planning to invade Hythria. I need to be in Krakandar."

"Adrina told you that?"

He nodded. "She confirmed it, but I've suspected that was his ultimate goal ever since I first heard of the Karien–Fardohnyan Treaty. If the Defenders surrender to Karien, there'll be nothing stopping him."

"Did Adrina tell you this before or after she tore your clothes off?"

Damin looked at him and smiled sourly. "I deserved that, I suppose. But I'm the Hythrun Heir, Tarja. I can't sit here minding your border while the Fardohnyans pour over mine."

"I understand, and so will Jenga."

"I didn't doubt that, Tarja, but are you going to be so understanding when I tell you Adrina is coming with me?"

In light of the Warlord's recent admission, the news did not surprise him. However, that didn't make it any more palatable.

"Don't be ridiculous, Damin. If we surrender to Karien, the first thing they'll do is demand her return. And if we don't surrender, she'll make a very useful hostage."

"I won't allow you to return her to Karien, Tarja."

"You slept with her once, Damin. I hardly think that warrants throwing her over your saddle and riding off into the sunset with her."

Damin grinned. "Poetic as it may seem, Tarja, my reasons are far more pragmatic. Should Adrina and Cratyn have a child, it would have a claim on both the Karien and Fardohnyan thrones. I don't intend to let that happen."

"As opposed to a child with a claim on both the Fardohnyan and *Hythrun* thrones," he pointed out. "Or had that minor detail escaped you?"

Damin looked so surprised that Tarja realized that he probably hadn't considered that possibility.

"It's not the same thing."

"It's *exactly* the same thing, Damin. A child who can unite Karien and Fardohnya is a threat, I'll grant you that, but a child who could bring Hythria and Fardohnya together is even worse. The Kariens will hunt you down like a criminal. I can't even begin to guess what the other Hythrun Warlords will do when they discover you've run off with Hablet's daughter."

"I'm not running off with her," he objected. "I'm averting a potential catastrophe."

"You're *creating* a potential catastrophe. Founders, man, think about this! How do you think the Kariens are going to react when they find out? Taking a lover might not be cause for concern in Hythria or Medalon, or even Fardohnya, for that matter, but it's a *sin* in Karien and they take their sin very seriously."

"I'm not her lover!"

"If you didn't take her by force, then what else do you call it? I'm sure the Kariens will see it that way. They tend to be very black and white in their thinking."

"All the more reason not to send her back to Karien. She'd be stoned if they found out."

"A few weeks ago, that prospect wouldn't have bothered you one whit."

Damin didn't look pleased at the reminder. "All right, I'll concede that my opinion of her has . . . softened . . . somewhat."

"*Softened*? That's one way of putting it, I suppose."

"I won't send her back, Tarja. Even if what you say is true, the fact is we *know* the Overlord wants a Karien heir to the Fardohnyan throne. The rest of it is just speculation. I'll deal with the known threat and face the rest of it *if* and *when* it happens."

"Jenga's not going to like this."

"I wasn't planning to ask his permission. I'm an ally, not a subordinate."

"Have you told Adrina?"

"Not yet."

"What if she objects? She might prefer to go back."

"She'd kill herself before she agreed to return to Karien."

"She doesn't strike me as the suicidal type."

"Ask her about Cratyn sometime."

Tarja reached forward to pat Shadow's neck. The mare was restless, no doubt picking up his apprehension. "When are you planning to leave?"

"The sooner the better. Jenga will have to act on that order soon, one way or the other. If he surrenders, this plain will be crawling with Kariens any day, and if he refuses the order you'll be fighting Karien on one side and your own people on the other. I don't want to get caught in the middle of it. Besides," he added with a frown, "when we crossed into Medalon we had Brak's help. We're going to have to make our way home by more ordinary means. If I don't leave now, Hablet will be in Krakandar before me."

At the mention of Brak, Tarja's brow furrowed with concern. Brak was supposed to be looking after R'shiel. But the Sisterhood had betrayed them. R'shiel would never have let that happen willingly.

"If you're so damned worried about R'shiel, do something about it," Damin said, guessing the direction of his thoughts.

"That would mean deserting my post."

"Well, you've done that before," the Warlord pointed out rather tactlessly, "so it should be easier the next time round. Anyway, if Jenga surrenders, how long do you think your head is going to stay attached to your neck, my friend? You're responsible for the death of the Karien Envoy, remember? I'll bet you any sum you care to name that your head on a platter was a condition of the surrender."

"That doesn't give me the right to abandon Jenga at the first sign of trouble."

"Think of it as saving the world, Tarja. The demon child is the only one who can destroy Xaphista. There's something of a moral imperative involved in going to her rescue."

"She might already be dead."

It pained him to admit it. With Brak watching over her and with the power she commanded, she could achieve anything. R'shiel had been so determined that Tarja was certain nothing short of death could have stood in her way.

"Somehow, I doubt it. The gods have gone to a lot of trouble to get her this far. I don't think they'd stand by and let her be destroyed out of hand. She hasn't done what she was destined for yet."

The reminder did little to ease Tarja's worry. Being assured that R'shiel lived so that she could eventually confront a god was hardly a comforting thought.

"I wish there was some way of being certain."

"Ask Dace, he should know."

"I recall having this discussion with you once before. You said he wouldn't come if I called him."

"And he probably wouldn't," Damin agreed. "But you don't need to call him, he's here. I saw him hanging around with that Karien boy the other day."

"What's he doing here?" Tarja asked suspiciously. He mistrusted these creatures that the pagans called gods.

"The God of Thieves, by his very nature, is bound to be up to no good, but that doesn't necessarily mean he's doing your cause any harm." Damin laughed suddenly. "I wonder how that fanatical child of the Overlord is coping with the idea that his new friend is a pagan god?"

Tarja smiled in spite of himself.

"Tell you what, Tarja, let's go back to the camp. You round up your little Karien friend and ask him where Dace is, and I'll speak to Adrina. I promise I'll only take her with me if she wants to come. I haven't the time to waste dragging her to Hythria by force, at any rate. After that we'll talk to Jenga. Who knows, if you can prove R'shiel still lives, he may even sanction your heroic dash to her rescue. I'm sure he'd like to know what really happened at the Gathering and it may stay his hand on the surrender for a time."

"Make sure that's all you do when you see Adrina. *Speak* to her."

"You show a disturbing lack of trust in me, Captain," Damin turned his stallion toward the camp and managed to look quite offended.

Tarja shook his head and followed him. "I thought we were going to check on the border troops?"

"They'll keep. Besides, if Jenga surrenders, it doesn't really make much difference how they're placed, does it?"

Tarja could not deny the Hythrun's logic and in truth, he would much rather find Dace and learn of R'shiel's fate than conduct an inspection. He stared at the border thoughtfully, then kicked his horse into a canter and headed back to the camp with the Hythrun Warlord.

chapter 50

Brak watched the scene between Joyhinia and R'shiel unfold with growing frustration.

R'shiel's recovery from her suffering at the hands of Joyhinia and Loclon was too fragile to be tested so soon. He could almost taste her fear. To face Loclon in the body of her foster mother was testing her to the limit. One she feared; the other she loathed. It was like a nightmare come to life. It could push her over the edge. His futile efforts to reach out to her, to contact her, to somehow let her know that he was with her, brought a frown to the War God's stern face.

"I have already explained to you, Brakandaran. She cannot see you. She cannot hear you."

"I have to go to her."

"And you shall," Zegarnald promised. "In time."

Brak turned on the god impatiently. "Why are you doing this? They'll kill her!"

Zegarnald did not answer for a moment. He waited as the First Sister left the room and Lord Terbolt explained his plans to R'shiel, then nodded slowly.

"The Karien human speaks the truth, Brakandaran. Xaphista wants the demon child for himself. Her ability to destroy a god is quite indiscriminate. She could destroy me just as easily as Xaphista."

"Oh, I *see*," Brak retorted, his voice laden with sarcasm. "That's a good plan. Hand over the only person who can destroy you to your enemy. Now why didn't I think of that?"

"Your disrespect wears on my nerves, Brakandaran."

"Not half as much as your scheming is wearing on mine, Zegarnald."

"I agreed to humor you, Brakandaran, by allowing you to assure yourself that the demon child lives. I did not agree to listen to your whining."

Brak watched helplessly as the Karien duke left the bedchamber where R'shiel was being held. As soon as she was alone, R'shiel threw herself on the bed and stared at the ceiling, cursing softly. After a while, she gave up that futile pastime and began pacing the room. She checked the door first, but it was firmly locked. Then she went to the window and threw it open, looking down with despair at the six-storey drop to the courtyard below. Finding no joy in that escape route she sat on the edge of the bed and tentatively reached for her power, drawing back hastily as the silver collar she wore began to burn.

"Let me out of here, Zegarnald. I have to help her."

Here was a hard place to define. The War God had Brak trapped between the world R'shiel inhabited and the world the gods called home. He was powerless here—at Zegarnald's mercy. He could move around freely, but he could not be seen, nor could he affect anything that happened in the ordinary world of humans.

He could have kicked himself for walking into Zegarnald's trap so blindly. He should have known the War God's sudden appearance in the alley beside the Temple of the Gods meant trouble. Zegarnald probably hadn't walked the halls of the Citadel for two centuries. Brak knew the gods well enough. He should have suspected *something*. And he should *never* have accepted Zegarnald's uncharacteristic offer of a handshake. Touching the god had been his undoing. Once Zegarnald had a hold of him, he was powerless to resist being drawn into this gray limbo.

"She must help herself."

"How? She can't even touch her power. That collar is as bad as those damned staffs Xaphista's priests lug around."

"She can touch it. But the pain will be intolerable. If she wants to escape badly enough, she will find a way to bear it."

"This is another of your tests, I suppose? Another part of the 'tempering' you're so fond of? What happens if she doesn't want to play your game, Zegarnald? Suppose she throws her lot in with Xaphista?"

"Then I will release you and you will destroy her."

Brak glanced at the god warily. "You trust me to do that?"

"If the demon child joins with Xaphista, what is left of the Harshini will be destroyed. I have no need to trust you. I trust your determination to remove a threat to your people."

The worst of it was that the War God was right. Should R'shiel give in to Xaphista he would not hesitate to kill her. He turned back to watching her, feeling like a voyeur.

"You're taking a big risk, Zegarnald."

"Perhaps. If the demon child is too weak to face down Xaphista, if she is willing to become his disciple, I would rather find out now than wait until she has matured."

"The finding out could kill her."

"Xaphista will try to win her over. He'll not resort to force unless he has to. He wants the demon child to believe in him, Brakandaran. She is no good to him if she despises him."

"I can't imagine she'll be too thrilled by *your* efforts," he pointed out. "If you ask me you're playing right into his hands."

"I do not recall asking you."

Angrily, Brak drew on his power and tore uselessly at the restraints that bound him to this place. Zegarnald didn't budge. His efforts were trivial in the face of the god's implacable will.

"Control yourself, Brakandaran. Such undisciplined behavior ill becomes a member of your race."

"I'm half human, Zegarnald. I'm doing my human ancestors proud."

"Stop fighting me. You will harm no one but yourself."

"Then let me out of here."

"In time."

Brak cursed and let go of the power. Fighting a god was a fruitless effort. Fighting Zegarnald was a *complete* waste of time. He thrived on it. Brak's efforts were only making him stronger. The realization brought another thought to mind and he decided to change his tactics. If he couldn't force Zegarnald into releasing him, then he had to make him want to do it.

"Medalon has surrendered."

"So it would seem," the god agreed, a little wary at Brak's sudden change of heart.

"You're taking it pretty well."

"What do you mean?"

"The war is over. That's going to seriously affect your standing among the other gods, isn't it? I mean, now that the Kariens and the Medalonians aren't fighting any more, things are going to get very cosy. Before long they'll be shaking hands, then they'll start making friends. Before long they'll be falling in love . . . Kalianah's going to be very happy. And considerably stronger, unless I'm mistaken."

Zegarnald frowned. "The Defenders will not surrender."

"You think so? You haven't been keeping up to date, Divine One. The Defenders are the most disciplined army in the world. If they were ordered to dress up like chickens and run around clucking, they'd do it without blinking. They won't ignore an order to surrender."

"Then I will have to content myself with the Fardohnyan invasion of Hythria," the War God told him smugly.

Brak bit back another curse. He hadn't known about that. Zegarnald needed wars to keep him strong, but he didn't really care where they happened. A conflict between those who worshipped him would serve him just as well as one between those who didn't.

"I suppose you're right. Of course, you're assuming that Kalianah won't interfere."

"There is nothing she can do to prevent a war."

"Don't be so sure. All she has to do is make the right people fall in love and your war is done for." Brak wondered if Zegarnald knew how desperate he was. He was certain he sounded desperate.

"If you know something of her plans, then you should tell me, Brakandaran."

He shrugged. "I merely speculate, Divine One. If Kalianah's got something up her sleeve, you'll have to ask her about it."

Zegarnald's dark eyes narrowed suspiciously. Trust was not a commodity the gods owned in any great quantity and they tended to take things rather literally. They were jealous creatures and were more conscious of rank than the most snobbish Karien nobleman. It dawned on Brak then that Zegarnald was afraid of R'shiel. He was afraid of what they had created. That's why he was determined to prove that she could be trusted, before her ability developed beyond the point where the gods could take action.

Brak looked at R'shiel with new respect. It took a lot to frighten a god.

The knowledge did little to help him out of his current predicament, however. Perhaps divine jealousy would work where reason had failed. Brak had no idea if Kalianah even cared that there was a war going on. For all he knew, she was off making a hive of bees happy, somewhere. But he was certain she would not approve of Zegarnald's plans to test the demon child's fortitude by throwing her to Xaphista's priests. If he could taunt Zegarnald into seeking her out, he might be able to prevail upon the Goddess of Love to release him. Kalianah was a happy-ever-after sort of god. She didn't like her plans being disrupted and she had gone to a fair bit of trouble to keep R'shiel and Tarja together. He was clutching at straws, but at this point anything was worth a try.

"Of course, if Kalianah was up to something while you're at the Citadel making certain the demon child has a spine, you're not going to know about it until she's standing over you, smiling that annoying little smile, asking you if you love her."

"Kalianah would not dare interfere. She knows what is at stake."

"She made R'shiel and Tarja fall in love. That's interference where I come from. If Kalianah gets the better of you, R'shiel won't be *tempered*, she'll be mooning about like a lovesick cow."

One of the advantages of trying to manipulate a god was their total inability to comprehend anything other than their own natures. Zegarnald knew what love was in a theoretical sort of way, he even tolerated it, but he didn't *understand* it. Brak's prediction sounded quite plausible to him.

"I will put a stop to her interference at once!"

"You do that, Divine One. In the meantime, let me out of here and I'll make certain R'shiel doesn't fall for Xaphista's devious—"

"Don't push me, Brakandaran. You will stay here until I have dealt with Kalianah. And don't bother to call any of my brothers or sisters. They will not hear you unless I will it."

The War God vanished, leaving Brak alone in the half-world between reality and dreams. He looked down on R'shiel and found her sitting on the bed, her knees drawn up and her head resting on them, her whole posture radiating abject misery. He tried reaching out to her again, but he knew it was useless. Until Zegarnald released him there was nothing he could do to help her.

The demon child was on her own.

chapter 51

oclon stood before the full-length mirror in the First Sister's apartments and studied Joyhinia's naked body curiously. It was a pity she was so old, he mused, although he supposed the body was quite well preserved for a woman approaching late middle age. The once full breasts sagged disappointingly. The hips and thighs were thickened by age, and her skin was showing signs of decay.

There was little joy to be had from this body in any case. Pleasures that normally had him stiff with anticipation seemed like far-away memories. He recalled the desire but did not really feel it. The woman's body he inhabited seemed to dampen his maleness. It was as if such thoughts could not thrive in this female form.

But if sexual pleasure was denied him, there were other compensations. The power he wielded as First Sister left him breathless. Of course, there was a limit to what he could achieve at the moment. Lord Terbolt and his priests hovered around him like vultures over a fresh corpse, but that would end soon. He would toe the line for now, but once the Kariens left the Citadel, *he* would be in control. Loclon smiled coldly. If they thought the old Joyhinia had been a tyrant, the citizens of Medalon would lack the words to describe the new one.

He had a long list of victims who would suffer at the First Sister's hands once he had a free rein. Men who had slighted him; women who had scorned him; all of them would pay.

He would start with Tarja Tenragan.

Fortunately, this coincided with the Kariens' plans and the order would be issued today, under the First Sister's seal. A courier would take it to Lord Jenga in the north as soon as the ink was dry. It would demand that Tarja Tenragan be arrested immediately and handed over to the Kariens to stand trial for the murders of Lord Pieter and the priest Elfron. Loclon would have preferred to take a more personal hand in Tarja's demise, but the Kariens were planning to burn him alive. It was a very satisfying thought; his pleasure diminished only slightly by his being unable to witness the event.

There were others too, who would feel his wrath, but they could wait. With Tarja accounted for, he must take care of R'shiel. Unfortunately, his chance at her had a deadline.

When Terbolt left the Citadel, R'shiel would go with him, willingly or not. He felt betrayed by the Kariens' plans for R'shiel. They had promised him revenge and then denied him. R'shiel was a prisoner, granted, but she was hardly suffering. She was fed regularly and well, and treated with cautious respect by Terbolt and his priests. The collar that circled her neck caused her pain only if she tried to touch her Harshini power, and she appeared to have learnt that lesson very quickly. All in all, her incarceration was remarkably comfortable and not at all what Loclon had in mind. If he was going to do something about the bitch, he would have to do it soon.

Conveniently, the Kariens were creatures of habit. Xaphista was a demanding god, and every day at sunset, when the mysterious Dimming began in the Citadel, they would gather in the apartments Lord Terbolt had seconded and pray for at least an hour. For that hour, R'shiel was guarded by only two Defenders and as First Sister, he could order them about with impunity. He sighed contentedly. It was almost sundown. By the time he was dressed Terbolt, Garanus and their companions would be on their knees at their devotions. He knew the folly of killing R'shiel, but for an hour at least, he could take the revenge he felt he so richly deserved.

She was standing by the window when he arrived, her exquisite profile limned by the sunset. Her glorious dark red hair was loose. It hung past her waist and had obviously been brushed until it shone—she had little else to fill her days. She wore dark, supple leathers that hugged her lithe body. Had he still been a man, the very sight of her would have aroused him. That had always been his mistake in the past. He had let his lust for this woman rule his head. But not this time. This time he inhabited a woman's body and the desire that had betrayed him in the past was nothing more than a shallow echo.

R'shiel turned at the sound of the door and stiffened at the sight of him.

"What do you want?" She sounded annoyed rather than fearful. That would have to change.

"I've come to ask you some questions," he said, placing the large covered birdcage he carried on the floor beside him.

"Ask them from there," she said, crossing her arms defensively.

"You're hardly in a position to be giving me orders, R'shiel."

"And you're hardly in a position to defy your Karien masters. Does Terbolt know that you're here? No, of course he doesn't. He's at prayer, isn't he? You're too craven to dare anything if you thought he might catch you at it."

Loclon bit back his fury at her scorn. "I've no care for what Terbolt thinks."

"You should have. Have you been to check on your body, Loclon? Are you sure it's well? Are they feeding it? Turning it frequently so you don't get bedsores? Do you really trust them that much?"

"Stop it!"

She smiled, which was a big mistake. Loclon did not take well to being laughed at. But he would have his fun. Instead of responding to her taunts he pulled the cover from the cage.

R'shiel gasped in horror. The little demon cowered in the center of the cage, crouched into a tangle of arms and legs, her large black eyes filled with terror.

Loclon saw R'shiel's expression and knew he had found the perfect way to torment her.

"Funny little creature, isn't it?"

"Let her go."

"You know I can't do that. Aren't you going to ask how we caught it?"

"I know how you caught it. How are you keeping her there?"

Loclon shrugged. "I've no idea. The priests tied the top of one of those staffs to the top of the cage, here . . . you see . . . and it does something to the bars. Did you want to see?"

"No."

"Oh, but you must," he insisted with a malicious smile.

He poked the creature and it jerked away from him instinctively, but the cage was too small and the movement pushed it back against the metal bars. The creature cried out with pain and jerked back from the bars, only to come up against the bars on the other side, where the agony was waiting for it. The high-pitched screams were most gratifying. It took the creature two or three attempts to curl back up into the ball that kept it away from the bars. When it finally settled down, it was trembling uncontrollably, with tears spilling silently from its liquid black eyes.

"Want to see it again?" he asked.

"Stop it!" She crossed the room in a few paces and grabbed him by the hair, forcing him to his knees. Loclon did not cry out, or even struggle against her.

He simply reached out with his foot and kicked the cage, which set the demon off again.

R'shiel let him go and ran to the cage, but she could no more touch the enchanted bars than the demon could. The priests' magic worked best on those who could channel the power of the gods. R'shiel had no hope of freeing the terrified creature. All she could do was kneel on the floor and watch it suffer.

Loclon climbed to his feet, laughing. Her attempts to open the cage were useless, even touching the latch was agony. She heard him move and turned to look up at him. The pain in her eyes was all he could have hoped for.

"Go ahead, let it go. If you can."

R'shiel glanced back at the cage which had fallen on its side. The demon was screaming in agony. There was nothing she could do to help it. She couldn't even right the cage to save the demon from the pain of contacting the bars.

As if she had realized the same thing, she climbed slowly to her feet.

"Giving up so soon?" he taunted.

Without warning, she turned and kicked the cage with all the force she could muster, lifting it clear off the floor. The cage clattered against the wall and landed with a thud. As it did, the base of the cage popped open and the demon gratefully scrambled clear of the trap.

"Be gone!" she cried urgently, as Loclon grabbed her.

The demon winked out of existence with a startled squeal.

Loclon punched her, then pushed her onto the floor and held her there with his knee while he looked around the room for something to hurt her with. There was nothing handy. Terbolt had stripped the room of anything remotely resembling a potential weapon. He wished for his male body. R'shiel was physically stronger than Joyhinia. Fighting her with his bare hands was not an option. Lacking anything more substantial than his fists, he wrapped his hand tighter through her hair and slammed her forehead into the floor, over and over, until she was almost senseless.

He stopped himself just in time. He would be in enough trouble for letting the creature escape. Killing R'shiel could easily cost him his life.

"Get up!"

She did not respond.

"I said, get up!" He kicked her in the stomach and she grunted involuntarily, confirming his suspicion that she was faking unconsciousness. "Get up, you inhuman slut!"

R'shiel rolled over slowly and stared at him with defiant eyes, a little dazed.

"Get up, I said!"

She pushed herself up onto her hands and knees. The wound on her forehead had opened and the blood flowed freely, obscuring her vision. Impatient with her slow response, he kicked her again, throwing her backwards against the wall. He laughed. This was what he wanted. What he needed.

R'shiel collapsed against the wall and for a moment she lay still, but when she looked up there was no submission in her eyes. Instead there was an expression of such hatred that he took a step back from her. Her eyes began to darken ominously. As she drew on her power the collar around her neck began to glow in response. She pushed herself up as her eyes turned black. The collar grew so bright it was almost painful to look on it.

Truly fearful of what he might have provoked, Loclon backed away from her. The sickening stench of burning flesh reached him as R'shiel gathered her power to her and the collar punished her for her efforts. She grabbed the windowsill and pulled herself to her feet, her eyes as black as night, the collar like a thousand candles burning under her chin.

With a visible effort she steadied herself and prepared to hurl her fury at him. The stench of burning flesh grew stronger. Loclon marvelled at her tolerance for the pain she must be in, but his own fear prevented him from taking any pleasure in it. If she broke through the constraint of the collar, he would not leave this room alive.

"*Die!*" she hissed.

Loclon expected his life to end at that moment, but the collar flared as she tried to unleash her power. She screamed and dropped to the floor, tearing uselessly at the burning necklet. Loclon let her drop, shaking with relief as she collapsed.

The screams stopped only when she finally passed out. He waited for a long, long time to be certain she really was unconscious this time.

When Loclon finally stopped shaking he was appalled to discover his bladder had let go and for the first time was grateful for Joyhinia's long skirts. R'shiel lay under the window, her breathing shallow. He approached her cautiously, half expecting her to be faking again. As he neared her, he realized it was unlikely. Her magnificent long hair tumbled over her face, obscuring the worst of the damage, but blood streamed from her forehead and he could see savage blisters marring her neck above and below the now quiescent collar.

He prodded her experimentally with the toe of Joyhinia's boot, but received no response. A harder kick got the same reaction. He kicked her again, this time for sheer pleasure rather than any attempt to determine her state of consciousness. The kick following that one was just for the hell of it.

He tired of that game soon enough. Bruises and broken ribs would heal in time. Even her scars would probably fade—she was Harshini, not human. He wanted to leave her with a reminder. He stood back and studied her for a while, wondering. Then it came to him. He crossed the room to the door and opened it a fraction.

"Bring me scissors," he ordered.

The guard looked a little startled by the order but hurried to comply. Joyhinia tapped her foot impatiently as she waited for him to return. When he hurried back to his post clutching the scissors, she snatched them from his hand and locked the door again.

Loclon dragged R'shiel to the bed, annoyed by Joyhinia's weakness. If he had his own body, it would have been nothing to scoop her up and throw her onto the bed. As it was, he grunted and struggled to get his hands under her arms and move her across the room. Lifting her was almost beyond him, but he managed it somehow. When he finally got her on the bed, he laid R'shiel out with almost tender care, crossing her hands demurely across her breast. He combed out her glorious mane with his fingers until it spread like a fiery halo around her head, then stepped back to admire his handiwork.

If one was prepared to ignore the blood and the burns, she looked quite stunning. He smiled, thinking he had never seen her quite this way—so peaceful, so . . . vulnerable.

Loclon sighed and picked up the scissors. He moved to the bed and planted a lingering kiss on her slightly parted lips.

Then he took the scissors and cut her hair as close to the skull as he could get. He hummed tunelessly as he worked, stopping only once to stare suspiciously over his shoulder.

He could not avoid the feeling that someone was watching him.

chapter 52

hen Tarja questioned first Hadly, then Sergeant Mon-
thay regarding the whereabouts of the Karien boy, nei-
ther of them could provide a satisfactory answer.
Hadly was too busy, and Monthay sounded genuinely
perturbed. He could recall giving the boy the afternoon off, but not why.

Tarja thanked him for his assistance and went looking for the child
himself. He didn't blame the sergeant. If the God of Thieves had taken
it into his head to lead Mikel astray, there was little Monthay could have
done about it.

He leaned forward and patted Shadow, wondering where a small
Karien boy and a mischief-making god could be hiding in the vast camp.
Nowhere there was work to be done, that was certain. They were
unlikely to have gone north toward the border. Not only was it dangerous, there was no entertainment in that direction. The Keep was just as
unlikely, as was the Hythrun camp, where Mikel's brother was, or the
neat Defender's camp, where surely somebody would question their
right to be there. He glanced south at the follower's camp thinking there
was plenty of trouble to be found there. He turned Shadow and let her
pick her own pace, hoping he was heading in the right direction.

There would be a town here soon if the war dragged on much longer,
he thought as he rode through the vast camp. Already some enterprising
merchants had set up rickety wooden frames to house their commercial
endeavors, between tents that ranged from the ramshackle to the truly
spectacular. The larger tents belonged to the *Court'esa*'s Guild. They had

moved in within days of the Defenders. All these lonely men out here in the middle of nowhere was an opportunity too good to be missed. Half the *court'esa* here could probably retire in luxury by now and those that couldn't would not have long to wait.

Tarja debated stopping by the largest tent to speak to Mistress Miffany. If Jenga surrendered, the *court'esa* were in real danger. Miffany was a generous, rotund little woman who had worked in the Citadel as a *court'esa* when Tarja was a cadet. She had inherited the business from Mistress Lyndah, when the sour old bitch had finally died—making everyone in the Citadel who knew her breathe a sigh of relief—and had set about making life pleasant for as many Defenders as possible since then—at a reasonable price, of course. Tarja liked her and had no desire to see her, or her girls, stoned by the invading Kariens.

On impulse, he turned toward her gaily-striped tent. If he could do nothing to stop the surrender, he could at least save a few lives. That Jenga *would* surrender was a very real possibility. The Lord Defender had stretched his loyalty about as far as it was likely to go. From the moment he had defied Joyhinia in Testra, he had been fighting a losing battle with his conscience. The order to surrender, while unpalatable, was probably easier to live with than treason.

A grubby child ran forward to hold his mount when he arrived. He dismounted and threw the child a copper rivet, before pushing back the flap, bending over to enter the tent. Inside, a number of women looked up hopefully at his captain's insignia, smiling at him with open invitation. Tarja smiled back, but otherwise ignored them. Miffany hurried forward as soon as she recognized him, obviously happy to see him.

"Tarja!"

"Hello Miff," he said, kissing her cheek. "You've lost weight."

Miffany laughed delightedly. She was almost as wide as she was tall.

"You tease! I look like a pudding, and you know it, but it was nice of you to say so. Did you want a girl?" Miffany was never one to beat around the bush.

"No, I wanted a word with you. In private."

Curious, but unconcerned, she turned to her girls. "I'm going to take a turn of the camp with the captain, here. Becca, you're in charge until I get back."

Miffany slipped her arm though his and led him outside.

They headed south between the tents down what could only very loosely be described as a street. The tents had been placed with little thought to the traffic in the camp and they were forced to step over tent pegs and dodge muddy puddles as they walked. Miffany clung to his arm with a smug grin that broadened to an outright smirk as they passed by the tent of one of her competitors.

"There'll be tongues a-wagging in there, soon enough," she predicted.

Tarja smiled. "We could stop outside on the way back while I declare I've never had better."

"You are such a sweetheart," she laughed, squeezing his arm.

"Have you done well since you've been here, Miff?"

"I'll say! I'm rich enough to buy myself one of those posh little villas on the riverfront in Brodenvale. War is good for a business like mine."

"Then perhaps you should think about retiring."

She looked up at him suspiciously. "You're taking a sudden interest in my welfare."

"I care about you."

"You're sweet, Tarja, I've always thought that, but you're a captain. One of Jenga's closest officers. You didn't come all this way to suggest I retire without a damn good reason."

"Isn't caring for you enough?" he asked with a hopeful smile.

"Much as I'd like to kid myself that that is the case, Tarja, I'm not a fool. What's really going on?"

"I can't say, Miff. All I can do is suggest that you quit while you're ahead."

The chubby *court'esa* thought for a moment and then nodded. "How long do we have?"

He could have hugged her for being so astute. "A few days. A week at most. Your profession won't be looked upon kindly after that."

"I owe you for this, Tarja."

"You don't owe me anything, Miff. Consider it a debt repaid."

"What debt?"

"I was fourteen the first time I came to Mistress Lyndah's. You didn't laugh at me."

She chuckled at the memory. "I was a lot thinner in those days. You were a sweet boy then, Tarja, and you still are, in my book. Tell me, do you plan to act on your own advice, or stay here and let them kill you?"

Her blunt question startled him. "I haven't decided yet, but I don't plan on letting anybody kill me."

"Well, that's something, I suppose. You know, I'll need some guards when I leave. I've quite a haul in the chest under my bed. Not looking for a job, are you?"

He shook his head. "Sorry, but I've got other things demanding my attention."

"Ah well, it was worth a try. I'll ask young Dace. He seems to know everybody in the whole damned camp."

Tarja stopped dead, almost jerking Miffany off her feet. "Dace? A fair-haired lad about so high? Wears the worst collection of cast-off clothing you've ever seen?"

"That's our Dace," Miff agreed. "How do you know him?"

"I came here looking for him."

"I thought it was too much to hope that you came here just to see me," she sighed.

"Where can I find him?"

She shrugged. "Who knows? He's a sweet boy too, but every time he appears, something goes missing. He hangs around with a Karien boy. They turn up every now and then, looking for a meal."

"And you feed them, of course."

"Of course."

"Do you have any idea where I can find him? It's really important."

Miffany thought for a moment and then nodded. "Try old Draginya, the herb woman. She lives over by Will Barley's tavern tent. She's a weird old buzzard, always praying to the Primal gods and muttering to herself, but I've seen Dace with her now and then. She might know where he is."

Tarja bent down and kissed Miffany's plump cheek. "You are the best."

"Then how come you're leaving?" she called after him.

Tarja would have found Draginya's tent simply by following the smell, even if Miffany had not described its location. The tent was crammed with dried herbs and a smoking brazier that gave off an aroma unlike anything he had smelled before. The old woman was wrapped in several tattered shawls against the cold and she looked up with rheumy eyes as

Tarja bent almost double to get through the tent flap. He straightened up once he was inside, his head brushing the roof of the tent.

"Captain Tarja Tenragan," the old woman said, as if she expected him.

"How do you know who I am?" The tent was gloomy and he had to squint to make her out.

"You are the demon child's appointed lover. Kalianah has made it so. She told me about you."

Tarja was still atheist enough not to want to know what she meant. "I seek Dacendaran."

"The God of Thieves? An odd companion for a man like you."

"Do you know where he is?"

"The gods are everywhere, Captain."

"I was hoping you could be a bit more specific."

The old woman smiled, revealing toothless pink gums. "Dacendaran said you were unusual for a Defender. I see what he means."

"I need to speak with him," Tarja insisted.

"The gods listen to all our prayers, Captain."

"I don't want to pray to him, dammit, I need to ask him something!"

"Well, there's no need to yell, Tarja. I'm not deaf." He spun around to find the God of Thieves standing behind him. The boy looked unchanged from the last time he had seen him in Testra, but that was hardly surprising. Dace pushed past him and knelt down beside the old woman. "Is he bullying you, Draginya? Shall I turn him into something with six legs that likes to live under a rock?"

"He is young, Divine One, and at the mercy of Kalianah's geas."

Dace stood up and turned to Tarja. "Well, it seems you get to stay in one piece. What did you want?"

"Where's R'shiel?"

"At the Citadel, I suppose." Dace shrugged.

"Something's happened to her."

"I'd know if she were dead. You humans worry far too much."

Tarja glared at the boy. "Jenga has been ordered to surrender."

That news gave the god pause. His grin faded. "That's probably not a good sign."

"Dace, the only way that order could have been issued is if R'shiel failed. Something has happened to her."

"Well, if it has, it's her own fault. I offered to go with them, but did they want my help? *No.* They wanted to do it all on their own. The Harshini are like that you know. They always think—"

"*Dace!*"

"What? Oh, I'm sorry. What did you want me to do?"

"Find out . . . what happened . . . to R'shiel," Tarja explained very slowly and carefully.

"Oh. I suppose that's not a bad idea. If something's happened to her, we'll have to start this whole demon child thing all over again. Now that *would* be a bore."

"How long will it take?"

Dace shrugged. "I don't know."

Tarja clenched his fists at his side, rather than grab Dace around the throat and shake him soundly, which was what he really wanted to do. "When will you leave?"

"You are *so* impatient."

"She could be in danger, Dace."

"She might just be sunning herself beside a pool somewhere, too," the god retorted. "On the other hand, it is winter and R'shiel never was the sort to relax, although it wouldn't do her any harm . . . Oh, stop looking at me like that! I'll go and see what's happening, but I won't cross Zegarnald if he's got a hand in this. He's as strong as he's ever been with this war going on."

"You do whatever you have to, Divine One," Tarja agreed.

Dace grinned. "*Divine* One? Does this mean you're finally coming to believe in us, Tarja?"

"I believe in you, Dace, I just don't happen to want to worship you."

"Ah, well," the god sighed. "Just so long as you never tell Kalianah you love her."

"That's not very likely."

"Glad to hear it. Will you see that Draginya gets away safely?"

Tarja nodded. The boy turned to the old woman and kissed her cheek. "See, Tarja will take care of you. I'd better go see what's happened to the demon child."

Dace vanished without warning, leaving Tarja frowning and old Draginya smiling toothlessly.

chapter 53

ikel was chattering away to Dace about the eggs they had stolen when he suddenly realized that his friend was no longer with him. He looked around the crowded camp, puzzled. Dace was nowhere to be seen.

Mikel sighed, used to Dace's odd disappearances by now. He did that sort of thing a lot. One minute he was there and the next he was gone. Still, it wasn't that important. Mikel knew the way to the old herb woman's place where the eggs were safely nestled in an old shawl in the corner of her tent. He was far more interested in them, anyway. The chicks should hatch any day now and he was as excited as any expectant father.

He turned into the street beside Will Barley's tavern tent and stopped dead as a familiar figure emerged from the old woman's tent. Mikel bit back a startled cry and slipped back between the tavern tent and the tent beside it. *What was Tarja doing in the old woman's tent? Had he discovered the eggs?*

Even Mikel knew that stealing a clutch of swallow's eggs would not warrant the attention of a Defender. *Perhaps he was sickening for something and had gone to see Draginya for a cure?* Then something truly dreadful occurred to him. Perhaps Tarja had discovered that Mikel spent most of his afternoons with Dace and had come looking for him. The only reason Tarja would seek him out was to punish him, Mikel was certain. *What would he do? Would Jaymes lose a finger because of his brother's folly?* That he had disowned his brother as a traitor was momentarily forgotten.

He waited anxiously, filled with trepidation as Tarja moved off between the tents. When he was sure the Defender would not turn back, he hurried to the old woman's tent and slipped inside.

"Did he hurt you?" Mikel demanded as soon as the flap closed behind him.

Draginya sat in her chair by the smoking brazier from where she hardly ever seemed to move; at least in Mikel's company.

"Did who hurt me, child?" She sounded surprised by his question.

"Tarja."

Her face creased into a wrinkled frown. "You speak with too much hatred for a child."

"That's because he's a monster!"

"Your ignorance blinds you, boy. Tarja is the appointed lover of the demon child. He is destined for great things."

Mikel stared at her. "Says who?"

"The gods, of course. Hasn't *your* god explained these things?"

"The Overlord doesn't speak to the likes of me. He only speaks to the priests and stuff."

Draginya nodded sadly. "That is a great shame."

"Anyway," Mikel added, rather put out by the old woman's pitying tone. "Tarja's a Medalonian. That makes him an atheist. Even if *I* believed what you say about the other gods, he wouldn't."

"Tarja knows the gods exist, Mikel. He simply choses not to worship them. The Primal gods like to have believers, but they don't need them. You honored Dacendaran when you stole those eggs. Whether you believe in him or not doesn't enter into it."

"We never stole anything!"

"You removed those eggs from their rightful owner without permission. That defines theft, don't you think?"

"But we wanted to save the chicks," he protested.

"If you kill one man to save another, it is still killing, Mikel. Good intentions don't alter the nature of an event."

"Then I betrayed the Overlord," he concluded, sinking down to the floor beside Draginya's stool. "I'm doomed."

"You're exaggerating," the old woman scolded. "You are a child, Mikel, and far too young to concern yourself with visions of doom and eternal damnation. Live life to the full and follow the god of your heart, not the tired litanies of grown-ups whose desire for power has a lot more to do with their faith than what their god might want."

"That's blasphemy."

"No, it's wisdom. When you're as old as I am, you get to call everything wisdom. Now go check on your eggs and be off with you. I'm tired and I have to start packing."

"You're leaving? *Why?*" Mikel was much less concerned about the old woman traveling in winter than he was about his eggs. If she left, what would he do with them?

"Because your people will be here soon. They'll take one look at me and burn me for a witch, I'm certain."

"You mean there'll be another battle? One that Prince Cratyn will win?"

She shook her head and placed a withered hand on his shoulder. "The battle has been fought and lost far from this place, child. The Defenders have been ordered to surrender."

All thought of eggs fled Mikel's mind as the news sunk in. *The Defenders were going to surrender! Jaymes would be released and brought back into the arms of the Overlord.*

And best of all, he thought happily, Princess Adrina would not have to pretend to hate Prince Cratyn any more.

Mikel hurried back through the camp, his heart lighter than it had been for months. Any day now, Prince Cratyn would cross the border in triumph. Karien had won. Tarja would be hung for the criminal he was. The Overlord had made the Medalonians surrender without another drop of blood spilt. It didn't matter what happened now. It didn't matter what they did to him. The Overlord was truly omnipotent, just like the priests said.

He skirted the edge of the camp and wound his way back through the corrals, taking the route closest to the Hythrun stables. He always took the same route. Dace claimed it was in the hope of catching sight of his brother—a charge Mikel vehemently denied. It was simply the easiest way back, he insisted, ignoring Dace's knowing smirk.

This time, however, he actively searched for his brother. He had to give him the news, quite certain that as soon as Jaymes learnt his own people would soon be here, he would see the error of his ways. Mikel was thrilled by the prospect and burning to share it with someone.

Jaymes was nowhere to be found, but as he stuck his head cautiously around the corner of the first stable block, he spied someone who deserved to hear the news even more.

Adrina was alone, brushing down a gorgeous golden mare, talking to the beast softly as she worked. There was nobody else around, not even a guard. Mikel chose to think of that as a sign from the Overlord, rather than the more obvious conclusion—that she wasn't guarded because they didn't consider her in need of one.

"Your Highness!" he hissed loudly.

Adrina turned and frowned when she caught sight of him.

"Mikel? What are you doing hiding over there?"

He slipped into the stable and ran to her, dropping to one knee as he had seen the Fardohnyan lanceman do after the battle. The gesture had struck him as being terribly noble.

"Your Highness, I have the most wonderful news!"

"Have you now? Do tell."

"Medalon has surrendered, your Highness. Prince Cratyn will be here any day. We are to be rescued!"

Mikel looked up, expecting to see relief and happiness radiating from her in equal measure. He was disappointed to find her taking the news quite calmly.

"And where did you hear this startling piece of intelligence?" she asked.

"From the old herb woman in the camp. She's already packing to leave for fear of the Overlord's wrath."

Adrina smiled. "Mikel, don't you think if Medalon had surrendered, their troops might be told before some old herb woman? I'm sure she's mistaken."

"But she seemed so certain, your Highness. Even Tarja went to visit her."

"Now that's interesting," Adrina agreed. "Do you know why?"

"The old woman said it was to talk to the God of Thieves, but I don't believe her. There is only the Overlord, isn't there?"

"Yes, of course," she agreed absently.

"Aren't you happy, your Highness?"

"I'm delirious with happiness," she assured him. "It's just not seemly that a woman in my position display extremes of emotion."

He smiled with relief. He had forgotten how well mannered she was, how careful she was not to shame herself. It must have been so hard on her, having to pretend to be nice to everyone, while inside she was missing Prince Cratyn so badly.

"It will be alright, your Highness. Prince Cratyn will be here soon."

"I can't tell you what a comfort that is," she said.

Mikel stood up beaming. To have been able to deliver such wonderful news to his lady was more than he could have hoped for in this dreadful place.

Adrina smiled down at him. "I thank you, Mikel, but shouldn't you be getting along? The Defenders haven't surrendered yet, and I'd hate for you to wear a beating on my account."

"It won't be long now, your Highness," Mikel promised with an encouraging smile. He turned and ran from the stable, almost colliding with Lord Wolfblade. He yelped with astonishment and fled past the Warlord, praying he hadn't been recognized.

A few paces from the stable, Mikel stopped and looked back over his shoulder. The Warlord had vanished inside. The princess was in there. Alone. It just wasn't proper. He wavered with indecision for a moment and then headed back to the stable.

Mikel slipped back into the building silently, grateful for Dace's instruction on how to sneak around without being noticed, and hid in the first empty stall he came to. It was close enough to hear what the Warlord said to the princess. The boy smiled expectantly. Now that she knew she was to be rescued soon, he fully expected Adrina to give him a piece of her mind.

"You don't have to do that, you know."

Adrina looked over her shoulder. "When I was a child, the only thing we were ever allowed to do for ourselves, was groom our horses. Hablet thought it would teach us a responsibility."

"And did it?"

She smiled. "Actually, I think it taught us more about the value of bribes. It was more fun trying to avoid the task than doing it."

Damin walked up behind Adrina and placed his hand over hers as she brushed the animal with long slow strokes. He stood so close behind her that their bodies were touching. The princess didn't scream. She didn't even flinch. Damin bent his head and touched his lips to her neck, just below her right ear. She arched her back and leaned into him.

"Stop that."

"Why?"

"There's no future in this, Damin. You know that as well as I."

He slipped his arms around her waist and pulled her closer. "Ah, that's right, we hate each other, don't we?"

She turned in his arms and touched her forehead to his. "You're confusing lust with genuine feeling, my Lord."

As if to give lie to her words, she kissed him. There was no mistaking it for anything else; *she* was definitely kissing *him*, not the other way around. Mikel almost bit through his bottom lip to prevent himself from crying out his outrage.

"If that's your idea of trying to make me stop, then the *court'esa* who trained you needs to be horsewhipped." Damin laughed softly when they finally came up for air.

Adrina smiled. It was the same sort of intimate smile R'shiel saved for Tarja. The sort of smile Adrina had never bestowed on his prince.

"That's all this is, you know. A simple case of two well trained and rather bored people amusing themselves far from home."

"I grant you that we're both well trained," Damin agreed, unwrapping her arms from around his neck. He held her hands for a moment and then turned them over, kissing the palms. "And I've no doubt you're bored. But this is far from simple, Adrina."

She sighed. "I know. So what are we going to do?"

"Well, I don't know about you, but I'm heading home while I still can."

"How noble of you. What happens to me?"

"That's up to you. You have two choices. Stay and face Cratyn, or come with me."

Adrina's eyes widened. "Follow you to Hythria? You're pretty damn certain of yourself, aren't you?"

"I wish I could say my offer was entirely motivated by the knowledge that you'd rather die than live without me, but the fact is, neither you nor I want a Karien heir to your father's throne. The whole *world* will be safer with you in my bed, rather than Cratyn's."

"You are the most arrogant pig I have ever met."

"Probably. Will you come with me, or not?"

"Is sharing your bed a condition of the deal?"

"No. If you want, I'll never touch you again. I'll escort you to Hythria and kill any man who tries to lay a hand on you against your will. Myself included."

"You'd throw yourself on your sword for me? Somehow, I doubt that, Damin."

"It sounded rather noble, though, don't you think?"

Adrina kissed him again. Mikel couldn't tell how long it lasted. He was too busy wiping away tears of anger and disappointment. Adrina knew that Cratyn was on his way to rescue her. The only reason she was doing this was the one he had refused to contemplate until now.

"I have conditions," she said, when they finally broke apart.

"Somehow, that doesn't surprise me." Damin gathered up the mare's lead rope and led her to an empty stall next to the one where Mikel was hiding. He held his breath.

"I'm a princess of royal blood, Damin, not some whore you picked up in the followers' camp. I expect to be treated as such."

"My men shall treat you with the utmost respect, your Highness, or I'll whip them myself." He closed the gate on the stall and walked back to her. The sun had almost set and it was getting hard to see them in the gloom.

"I wasn't referring to your men, I was talking about you."

"I'll ignore that. What else?"

"The remainder of my Guard, those men the Defenders are holding prisoner, are to be released."

"I think I can arrange that."

"And I'm not your damned prisoner, either. If I go with you, I go of my own free will. I'll be free to leave anytime I want."

"Was that all?"

"No. I want it clearly understood where we stand with each other."

"And where is that, exactly?"

"I don't love you, Damin, and I'm damned sure you don't love me. I'll admit that there is a certain . . . physical attraction . . . between us, but that's all it is. I get a thrill out of flirting with danger and you are about the most dangerous thing around. I don't want you mistaking this affair for something it's not."

Damin didn't answer her for a long moment. Then he smiled. "You're a consummate liar, Adrina."

"I assure you, sir, I meant every word."

"That's what makes you so believable. Very well, I agree to your conditions. I'm planning to break camp the day after tomorrow. Be prepared for some hard riding. If your husband should happen to discover where you are, we'll have every Karien on the border chasing us all the way to Hythria."

"Then you'd better hope your Medalonian friends don't tell him. I wasn't planning to leave him a note, you know."

"Now there's a thought," he laughed. He picked up her cloak from where she had thrown it over the railing and held it out for her. Adrina turned and allowed him to drape it over her shoulders. "Let me see, how would it go? Dear Cratyn—"

"Cretin," she corrected. "I always called him Cretin. The Kariens thought it was my accent."

"Very subtle . . . Dear Cretin, sorry I can't be here to meet you, dear, but I've run off to Hythria with a dashing warlord—"

"*Dashing?*"

"Handsome sounded a bit arrogant, I thought . . . Anyway, where was I? I've run off to Hythria with a dashing warlord with whom I've been making wild, passionate love every night for . . . how long has it been?"

"One week and two days . . ."

"Are you counting?"

"Only out of curiosity." She turned to face him, her expression suddenly serious. "We shouldn't joke about this, Damin. He'll kill us both."

Damin kissed her forehead. "It will take more than—what did you call him? Prince Cretin the Cringing—to kill me. And I swear I'll kill you myself before I hand you back to him."

"Well, that makes me feel *so* much better."

Mikel shrank down as they walked past his stall exchanging that odd mixture of intimate secrets and insulting banter that seemed to characterise their conversations, tears of bitter disappointment sliding down his cheeks.

The truth burned in his stomach like a bad meal. He waited in the darkness surrounded by the moist smell of the horses for a long, long time after they were gone. His heart was breaking; his childish illusions well and truly shattered.

By the time he forced himself to move, his fingers were numb with cold. But he had made a decision. When the Karien army crossed the border, Mikel would find a way to gain an audience with the prince.

He was going to have to explain to Cratyn that his beautiful, noble princess was nothing more than a traitorous slut.

part four

—ⵉⵉⵉ—

CONSEQUENCES

chapter 54

The walls of the Citadel defined Brak's prison. He had discovered this annoying detail quite by accident as he had tried to follow Lord Terbolt to a meeting with another Karien agent in the small village of Kordale, west of the city. He had met an invisible wall as solid and impenetrable as the wall that cut him off from his power. Brak had tested its limits right around the Citadel, but could find no weak point. He wondered if it was entirely Zegarnald's doing or if the Citadel itself was aiding the War God, although he could think of no reason why the Citadel would ever cooperate with Zegarnald.

He spent his days watching and worrying over R'shiel. His frustration was a palpable thing and his worry enough to make him physically sick. He had watched Loclon tormenting her and the demon, helpless to intervene. He had watched him punish her then cut off her hair, tearing uselessly at the invisible barrier that separated him from the ordinary world. But worse, he watched as every day R'shiel sank a little lower into despair; a little closer to giving in; a little closer to the day he might have to kill her.

Brak had an odd relationship with R'shiel. Part guardian, part teacher, he had been sent to find the demon child and bring her home to Sanctuary. His first impressions of her had not been good—she was spoilt, manipulative and rebellious. She bore long grudges and tended to be rather single-minded when it came to getting even. Brak had not liked her much in the beginning. It had taken a long time for him to discover how much of R'shiel's behavior was a result of her upbringing as much as her true nature. She carried a lot of hurt inside and those who hurt her would suffer for it. He was also cynical enough to realize that the very qualities that made him distrust her were just the sort of characteristics one needed if one was destined to destroy a god.

When he had first set out to find the demon child, he had vague visions of a noble young man with a pure heart, who would take on his appointed task with a solemn vow and then . . . well, he'd never really got to that bit. He had not expected R'shiel; not expected to find a complicated, troubled young woman, who had been raised by the most ruthless and unloving mother that the Sisterhood had ever spawned.

It wasn't until he learnt how much of her suffering had been sanctioned by the gods, that he truly began to sympathise with her. Zegarnald's "tempering" had been a cruel and rocky road for R'shiel and she was a long way from the end.

If he stood back from it, he understood the logic. Xaphista was a master of seduction, in his own way. He had seduced millions of Kariens into believing him. One half-breed Harshini would hardly be a threat, unless that half-breed was inured to his enticements. R'shiel had to be so determined to destroy him that nothing would stop her. She had to be ruthless enough to stand back and watch everything and everyone she held dear threatened with extinction, and not waver from her purpose. She had survived being raised by Joyhinia, raped by Loclon, imprisoned by the Sisterhood, a near-fatal wound, and the discovery that she was a member of a race that she had been raised to despise. The experience had left her battered and bruised, but it had not even come close to breaking her. Brak was beginning to wonder if her current situation would succeed where everything else had failed.

When she regained consciousness after Loclon left her room, it had taken her a little while to get her bearings. Her face was a mess—her forehead puffy and bruised and covered in dried blood. She lay for a time, staring at the canopy over the bed, as if trying to recall how she came to be there. Then she sat up and ran her fingers through her hair. She stiffened with shock, then looked behind her at the carefully laid-out halo of dark red hair that was left behind on the pillow.

For a moment she did nothing but stare at it in bewilderment, then she leapt off the bed and ran to the mirror hanging over the dresser. Brak winced as she looked at her reflection. Vanity was not a quality he associated with R'shiel—she had always seemed rather unconscious of her beauty—but even the plainest woman would have gasped at the reflection staring back at her. Loclon had hacked off her hair with little care. It stood up in clumps in places; elsewhere it had been cut so close to the scalp that the skin showed through. Her eyes were blackening, the cut on her forehead a red slash across a purple landscape of bruises. Her long neck was livid; white blisters already visible above and below the thin silver collar. Several had burst when she began to move, leaving weeping patches of raw flesh to rub against the metal.

R'shiel stared at her reflection for a long, long time, then she sank down onto the floor and sobbed like a brokenhearted child.

Brak could feel her anguish but could do nothing to relieve it.

He could not imagine what it must be like for her to cope with Loclon in Joyhinia's body. Added to that, she had failed in her attempt to coerce the Sisterhood. Mahina was imprisoned. Affiana and Lord Draco were both dead. Garet Warner had changed sides and the Kariens effectively had control of the Citadel. If that wasn't enough, when the order to surrender arrived at the border, Tarja's life would be forfeit. He had no way of knowing, but Brak suspected R'shiel's tears were as much from failure, as they were from pain.

But while her reactions up to that point had been typical, since that day R'shiel seemed sunk so far in misery, that she no longer cared what happened.

Terbolt had been quite appalled at the state she was in when he returned from his prayers and livid over the loss of the demon. He had chastised Loclon severely, but the Karien still needed a cooperative Joyhinia, so he had done little more than make his displeasure known. He had ordered the priests to treat her wounds and Garanus, in a rare show of compassion, trimmed her hair until it was, if not quite styled, then at least tidy. Once the bruises faded, she wouldn't look too bad, Brak thought. She had that sort of bone structure.

But R'shiel cared no more for how she looked than she did about anything else, at present. She ate only if the priests stood over her, and then it was mechanically, as if she didn't taste a bite. She said nothing unless directly addressed and then answered in a monotone. She washed when they told her, ate when they ordered her, and when she was alone she simply sat where they left her, staring blindly into the distance.

Two days after Loclon's attack some of the blisters under the collar began to fester. She did not even flinch when the priests held back her head, lanced the sores and poured saltwater onto the open cuts. They did not remove the collar, simply worked around it, but even that rough handling got no reaction from her. He remembered how vague she had been after he rescued her from the Grimfield, the night she had tried to kill Loclon. She had been animated then, compared to her present state.

And there was not a damned thing he could do about it.

Two weeks after R'shiel's capture at the Gathering, Lord Terbolt finally announced his intention to leave the Citadel and return to Karien. Brak had been certain he was waiting for something, but could not work out what it was. The arrival of a tall, dour-looking Karien who introduced himself as Squire Mathen was apparently what the duke had been expecting. The two of them remained closeted for hours. When they emerged, Terbolt announced his plans to leave.

Loclon had been fairly panting in anticipation for that moment, and his chance at unfettered power as First Sister. Brak had wondered if Terbolt would be so foolish as to leave Loclon in charge. The Karien Duke was not stupid and Loclon's loss of the demon and his attack on R'shiel had done nothing to foster any trust between them. Brak thought it would be better for everyone if he simply slit the throat of Loclon's senseless body and let his soul wither and die.

They kept Loclon's body in a room in the First Sister's apartments. The priests tended it with businesslike efficiency. Transferring the mind of one person into the body of another was not such a difficult feat to arrange, by Harshini standards. It was just one of those things that was only done if there was a good reason for it—and that was rare. Had they thought about it, they could have done the same to Joyhinia themselves, although considering the way things had turned out, it probably would not have made a difference, given that Zegarnald actually *wanted* to push R'shiel to breaking point.

There were risks, though. If the host body died, then the mind automatically returned to its own body with little more than a nasty shock. But if the vacant body died, the soul had nowhere to go. It would survive a day or two, no longer, before joining its physical counterpart in death. Loclon's transfer was nothing like the subtle removal of wit that Dacendaran had performed on Joyhinia. This was the working of a clutch of Karien priests who lacked the finesse of a god. They had simply taken Loclon's mind—lock, stock and barrel—and dumped it into Joyhinia's unresisting body.

Squire Mathen would remain behind to "assist" the First Sister. Loclon was furious, and could do nothing but agree. Two priests would remain behind also, Terbolt declared, then made a great show of handing Mathen the key to the room where Loclon's body lay. The message was clear, even to Loclon.

Terbolt's announcement of their imminent departure drew no visible reaction from R'shiel. She barely even glanced at him. Loclon waited outside the door, fidgeting with Joyhinia's long skirts. As soon as Terbolt emerged, he began demanding to know exactly who Squire Mathen was. Brak made to follow them, until he spied Garet Warner entering the apartment. He said something to guards on R'shiel's door that Brak didn't catch, then went inside. On impulse, Brak followed Garet.

The commandant seemed shocked at R'shiel's condition, but she was as unresponsive to his arrival as she had been to anything else in the past week. Garet knelt down beside her chair and gently shook her shoulder.

"R'shiel?"

She ignored him, or perhaps she was so far inside herself, she really didn't know he was there.

"R'shiel?"

Finally she turned to him, her eyes blank. "What?"

"You're leaving today. With Lord Terbolt."

"I know."

"They've ordered the troops on the border to surrender."

"I know."

Garet muttered something under his breath that sounded like a curse. "Do you understand me, R'shiel? Do you even know who I am?"

"I know you," she replied tonelessly. "You betrayed me."

He nodded, satisfied with her answer for some reason. "I didn't betray you, R'shiel. I just can't help anyone from a prison cell. Do you understand? Do you know why I did what I did?"

She turned to him, showing some real interest for the first time. "You did what you said you would do. Brak called you an honest man."

"Not a description I'd use myself, but I think I know what he means." He reached into his boot-top and withdrew a thin sheathed blade. "Can you hide this somewhere?"

She stared at the knife uncomprehendingly. "What for?"

"To escape, maybe? Or do you want to go to Karien?"

"I have to face the Overlord. He wants me to join him."

Garet sighed and pushed the knife into the top of her boot. "You do what you have to, R'shiel. The only thing I'm concerned about is Medalon. I've done all I can for you."

The commandant left after that and the guards came in to escort R'shiel downstairs. She let them drape a plain woolen cloak over her shoulders and lead her away without resistance. Brak followed her and the Karien party as they descended the stairs, wanting to scream with frustration. Once they left the Citadel, she would be entirely out of reach.

Garanus handed her into the carriage and then climbed in beside her. As soon as the door snicked shut the carriage moved off toward the Main Gate where Terbolt and nearly a thousand Defenders awaited the order to move out. Brak had never felt more helpless in his entire life.

"*Zegarnald!*"

The gray limbo in which he was trapped seemed to quiver with the strength of his cry.

"*Zegarnald! Let me out of here!*"

The silence he received in reply was absolute.

chapter 55

drina had just finished packing, if throwing her few meager possessions into a sack could be called that, when the door flew open and Tarja appeared.

"If you're leaving, your Highness, you'd better do it now," he warned. "The Kariens are on their way."

"How can that be? Damin said Jenga had agreed not to surrender until we'd gone."

"I don't know. Perhaps they know about the order from the Citadel. They may even have had a hand in it somehow. All I know is that there's a whole troop of knights riding this way under a flag of truce."

Adrina cursed in a most unladylike fashion. "Tam, go and find . . . no, on second thoughts, you'd better stay with me. Someone might recognize you. Are you certain they're heading this way?"

"Yes."

"How long do we have?"

"Not long at all, I'm afraid."

"We'd best get moving then." Adrina snatched up her sack and slung it over her shoulder. Tarja led them onto the landing. The guards were gone now. Lord Jenga had dismissed them days ago, when it became apparent she was no longer using the quarters over the main hall often enough to warrant placing a guard on them.

She followed Tarja cautiously, Tam close on her heels. They were halfway down the stairs when he stopped suddenly and held his arm out to bar her progress. The Hall doors rattled as they were pushed open.

"Back! Now!" Tarja hissed.

Adrina did not need to be told twice. She raced back up the stairs, pushing Tam ahead of her. When they reached the landing, Tarja motioned them down. By the time they were stretched out on their bellies, looking down over the Hall, the first of the Kariens were clattering through the door.

Adrina recognized Lord Roache and Lord Laetho as they raised their faceplates. The other knights she did not know; they were more than likely an escort. The Dukes made their way to the end of the hall as Lord Jenga entered with Cratyn at his side. Following them were a dozen or more Defenders. None of the Medalonians looked very happy.

Adrina studied Cratyn for a moment. He removed his helmet and ran his fingers through his hair as he looked around the Hall. His eyes skimmed over the darkened balcony. He could not see her, she knew, but she held her breath in any case. Jenga ordered wine served and turned to face Cratyn. The two opposing sides had unconsciously arranged themselves on either side of the long wooden table near the fireplace.

"You requested a parley, your Highness, and I have honored your flag of truce. What do you want?"

Cratyn seemed a little taken aback by Jenga's blunt manner. "I'm certain you know exactly what I want, my Lord. I want your surrender."

Several Defenders, those officers who did not know of the order from the Citadel, gasped in surprise. Jenga silenced them with a look and turned back to the young prince.

"What makes you think I'm planning to surrender?"

Cratyn looked at Roache uncertainly. "I was led to believe, my Lord, that you had received an order to that effect some time ago."

"Then you were misinformed, your Highness."

Adrina was quite astounded to hear the Lord Defender lie so blatantly. *Isn't truth supposed to be a virtue of the Defenders?* She glanced at Tarja, but he was engrossed in the scene below and his expression was impossible to read in the gloom.

"He's lying, your Highness," Roache assured the prince confidently.

Jenga turned on Roache. "You impugn my honor, sir?"

Before Roache could reply the doors flew open and Damin burst in, followed by Almodavar and a score of Raiders. Adrina smiled at Damin's theatrical flair—every man with him must have been picked for his size, she thought. They were conspicuously armed and arrayed themselves across the doorway, blocking the exit.

Tarja groaned softly. "Founders, what's he up to now?"

"My apologies for being late," Damin announced as he strode into the Hall. He walked straight up to Lord Roache and bowed extravagantly. "You must be Prince Cratyn."

"I am Cratyn," the prince announced in annoyance. Damin had walked straight past him. It was no accident, Adrina was certain. Roache was old enough to be his grandfather and Damin knew well how old Cratyn was.

"*You?*" Damin asked in feigned surprise. "Gods! You're just a child. Ah, but you're not a child, are you? I hear you're married now. How is your lovely wife, by the way?"

Adrina cringed at the question. *What the hell was he playing at?* Cratyn glared at him, quite appalled by the Warlord.

"Who are you, sir?" Roache demanded angrily.

"I'm sorry, did I forget to introduce myself? I am Damin Wolfblade, Warlord of Krakandar, Crown Prince of Hythria, Prince of the Northern Marshes, and there's another title or two that I can't quite recall. And you would be . . . ?"

"This is Lord Roache and Lord Laetho, my advisers," Cratyn said, not having the wits to announce their full titles.

"Lord Laetho?" Damin asked. "Now *you* I've heard of. What happened to that brat we sent back, by the way?"

"We are here to discuss surrender!" Cratyn declared, sounding more like a petulant child than a statesman.

As she watched Cratyn try to impose his will on the gathering, she could not help but compare her husband to her lover. Apart from the physical differences between the men—even the most objective observer would agree that Cratyn fared a poor second—there was no comparison. Damin commanded authority without even trying. Cratyn had to *demand* it—loudly.

"*Surrender?*" Damin cried, as if it was the first time he had heard the word. "Surely you're not going to quit after one measly little battle, Cratyn? I came here for a good fight and you want to surrender already? Have some balls, man!"

Even Jenga bit back a smile at Damin's deliberate misunderstanding.

"Not me, you fool!" Cratyn snapped. Normally surrounded by men who treated him like rare porcelain, he was floundering in the face of Damin's disrespect. "Medalon is surrendering to us!"

"You are?" Damin asked Jenga. "Since when?"

"No decision has been made as yet, Lord Wolfblade."

"You claimed you knew nothing about this," Cratyn accused.

"An unverified message has been received, your Highness. I do not consider that an order when dealing with an issue of such importance."

"You require verification, my Lord?" Roache asked.

"Naturally. Would you surrender a strategically superior position without some sort of confirmation?"

Roache nodded solemnly. "Of course not. How long will this verification take?"

"I suppose that depends on whether or not the order is genuine." Jenga shrugged. "I imagine the confirmation should arrive within the week, if it is."

"And if the order is proved genuine?"

"Then I have no choice, your Grace," Jenga conceded.

Roache appeared satisfied with the Lord Defender's answer. He was the most experienced of Cratyn's dukes. He understood the Lord Defender's position, even admired his stance.

"Perhaps then, in anticipation of the verification you require, we could discuss the details of your surrender?"

"That is somewhat premature, is it not?" Jenga ventured.

"Not at all, my Lord. Given that we have also been advised of your imminent surrender, one could safely assume that the order is genuine. Given that neither of us wishes unnecessary misunderstanding, such an agreement would seem prudent, don't you think?"

Cratyn had become superfluous in the face of the experience of the Lord Defender and the canny Lord Roache. Even Laetho seemed at a loss for words. But Damin wasn't finished. Not yet.

"Well, I'm sorry, but if you're going to surrender, I can't condone it," he declared. "I have a reputation to uphold."

"The surrender includes all forces currently allied with Medalon," Cratyn pointed out stiffly.

"Then consider our alliance at an end," Damin announced. "I'm not going to surrender to this whelp." He turned on Cratyn, shaking his head. "Did you really marry one of Hablet's daughters? Gods! I can't *imagine* how you manage to keep her satisfied."

Adrina would have thrown something at Damin, had she had a missile handy, but Cratyn did blush an interesting shade of red.

Damin turned to Jenga. "My Lord, I cannot countenance this farce any longer. I shall be leaving immediately. Kindly have my *court'esa* delivered to my tent at once."

The Warlord tossed his head dramatically and marched from the Hall, his savage-looking Raiders in his wake. Jenga purposely kept his eyes downcast.

"Aren't you going to stop him?" Lord Laetho demanded.

"Lord Wolfblade is an ally, my Lord. I do not command him. Short of a pitched battle, I don't see how I can stop him leaving."

"The Hythrun is of no importance," Roache agreed. "There is only one place he can go, and he might find more waiting for him when he gets there than he bargained for."

"There is also the matter of Captain Tenragan," Cratyn added, annoyed that the discussion was slipping from his control.

"Your Highness?"

"Don't play the innocent, Lord Jenga. Tarja Tenragan murdered Lord Pieter and the priest Elfron. He is to be handed over to us for trial."

"There was nothing mentioned about this, even in the unverified order."

"I can assure you, verification is on its way. You must agree to hold him, pending your surrender."

Adrina glanced at Tarja. He was torn between stepping forward and bolting, she thought. Duty warring with survival. She placed a hand on his arm and shook her head.

"Don't do anything stupid, Tarja," she said softly. "There's nothing you can achieve by going down there."

Tarja looked at her for a moment. He nodded slowly, acknowledging her advice, then turned back to watching the Kariens.

"Should such an order be received, then of course I will honor it," Jenga assured Cratyn.

"I should think so," Cratyn replied, rather lamely. He really wasn't handling this very well.

"In that case, gentlemen, I believe this discussion is at an end. I shall have Captain Alcarnen escort you to the border. Should verification arrive, I will send a message, advising my position."

"Your cooperation in this matter is much appreciated, my Lord," Roache agreed, before Cratyn could add anything further.

"Captain!"

Nheal Alcarnen stepped forward and saluted sharply.

"Would you be so kind as to escort our guests back to the border?"

"Sir!"

There was little else Cratyn and his party could do but follow the captain.

As soon as the Kariens had left the Hall, pandemonium broke loose, as the officers demanded an explanation. Tarja waited until Jenga had quieted his men and ordered them about their business. The last man was leaving as they descended the stairs. Jenga looked up at their approach. His face was haggard.

"You'd better get out of here, and soon."

Adrina nodded. "I thank you for not betraying my presence, my Lord."

Jenga shrugged. "A small victory over the Kariens, your Highness, even if there is nobody to share it with. I wish you a safe journey, although I suspect your future is as doubtful as mine." He turned to Tarja. "I want you to go with them, Captain."

"I won't desert you, Jenga. Not this time."

The Lord Defender shook his head. "I want your resignation then. I'm damned if I'm going to hand any man of mine over to the Kariens for some sort of farcical trial with a noose waiting at the end of it. Particularly for a crime he didn't commit."

Adrina looked at Tarja curiously. *If Tarja hadn't killed Lord Pieter, then who had?*

"I won't run away, Jenga."

"Now is not the time to be noble, Tarja. I lied to the Kariens. A courier delivered the orders from the Citadel this morning, signed by Joyhinia. Accompanying the orders was a warrant for your arrest."

"Then you *will* surrender?"

"I have no choice."

Tarja didn't answer.

"Go," Jenga ordered. There was more emotion in that one word than Adrina could ever recall seeing the Lord Defender betray previously.

Tarja hesitated for a moment, then saluted smartly. "My Lord!"

He turned away, his expression determined and even a little disappointed. Adrina impulsively leaned forward and kissed Jenga's weathered cheek before she and Tam hurried after him.

"Captain!"

They stopped and looked back. Adrina could have sworn there were tears in the old man's eyes.

"Take as many men with you as you can. Just be quiet about it."

Tarja nodded in understanding. "As you wish."

"You're the only one I can ask this of, you understand that, don't you? No other man in my command has experience of this type of warfare."

The comment puzzled Adrina. "War is war, isn't it? Besides, you said you would surrender."

"I'm surrendering my forces, your Highness. I have no say over what former officers do once they have resigned from the corps."

"You'll accept my resignation then, my Lord?"

The Lord Defender nodded.

"Make the bastards pay, Tarja," he added. "Make them pay for every league of Medalon soil they claim."

What could one man and a handful of renegade soldiers do, she wondered, to halt an army the size of the Kariens? Then she glanced at the captain and saw the look of quiet determination in Tarja's eyes.

Cratyn was going to find taking Medalon a lot harder than he imagined.

chapter 56

There was no denying the rumors once the Kariens arrived under a flag of truce, and Lord Jenga did not bother trying. On the morning following the meeting with Prince Cratyn word was passed through the camp that Medalon would surrender. The following day a messenger was sent north through a miserable squall to request another meeting with the Kariens—this one to negotiate the details. Mikel heard the news with mixed feelings. The welcome thought that he would soon be back among his own people was soured by the knowledge he carried.

The Hythrun camp was dismantled with remarkable speed. Rather than move out as one large force, Lord Wolfblade dispatched his men in waves, a Century at a time. He was concerned that his fleeing force might prove too tempting to the Kariens. Cratyn would not be able to resist pursuing a thousand Hythrun across Medalon, but it was unlikely he would bother hunting down countless scattered bands of them.

Mikel overheard Monthay discussing the strategic merits of the Warlord's decision with another sergeant. He seemed to admire it. The Raiders left in platoons of one hundred, which would break into smaller groups once they were clear of the battlefield. They had been ordered to make their way home any way they could. Some would ride straight for the Glass River, others would stay on this side until they almost reached Bordertown. It would be well nigh impossible to round them all up.

The Hythrun weren't the only ones departing in haste. The followers' camp was a frenzy of activity as some hastened to leave and others dug in, hoping for even more business once the countless Kariens arrived. Mistress Miffany's brightly striped tent was gone even before the Kariens had paid Lord Jenga a visit, as was old Draginya's tent. Mikel had no idea what happened to his eggs but he cared little for them now. He had more important things to worry about. More adult things. He had not seen Dace or Kali for days and assumed his new friends had left too.

The last of the Hythrun to leave was Lord Wolfblade's party, and the size of it puzzled him. He was certain nearly all of the Hythrun Raiders had left already, yet there seemed far too many men gathered on the edge of the camp waiting for the order to move out. Then Mikel realized that over half the men riding with the Warlord were mounted on sturdy Medalonian horses, not the magnificent golden horses of the Hythrun. There were even men mounted on the captured Fardohnyan steeds. His suspicions were confirmed when Damin appeared with Tarja at his side. The soldiers wore nondescript civilian clothing, but they were Defenders, sure as Xaphista was the Overlord. Tarja was abandoning the field and taking hundreds of his men with him, including the captured Fardohnyans.

Mikel watched from the top rail of the corral nearest the Hythrun stables. He could not see the princess, but she was there somewhere, he was certain. Nor could he spot Jaymes in the milling crowd. He had anxiously studied every troop leaving the field and was sure that his brother was still in the camp. Perhaps Jaymes had seen the light; or perhaps the Hythrun had abandoned him once they knew they were heading home.

It was just on dawn when Tarja gave the order to move out. He and Damin waited off to the side, their heads close together as they discussed something of import, as the men moved off. Several other riders waited behind then, but from this distance, Mikel could not identify them.

"Mikel!"

Jaymes broke away from the host and cantered toward him. He was mounted on a Medalonian horse—he was too raw to be trusted with a valuable Hythrun mount, but his saddlebags were full, his bed roll tied to the saddle.

"Have you come to see me off?" His brother's eyes glittered with the excitement of his adventure. He sat his horse as proud as any Defender.

Mikel glared at him reproachfully. "Traitor."

Jaymes' expression hardened. "You're a child, Mikel. You don't understand."

"I understand plenty. You're betraying your country, your lord and your prince. Just like her."

"Just like who?"

"It doesn't matter." He was not going to share his knowledge with Jaymes. He didn't deserve to know the truth.

His brother sighed. "I have to go, Mikel. Will you give mother and father my love?"

The audacity of the request made Mikel's blood boil. "I'll do no such thing! I'll tell them you're dead. Better they think that than know the truth!"

He jumped off the rail and ran back toward the Keep, ignoring Jaymes' frantic calls for him to return.

When he finally stopped and looked back Jaymes was gone.

The next time Prince Cratyn arrived, a long and frustrating day after the Hythrun had departed, it was with a much larger party and there was no white flag in evidence. The Prince knew he had won and was in no mood to mind the tender feelings of his vanquished foe. He marched into the Keep, his dukes at his heels, with all the assurance of one who knew he had nothing to fear.

Mikel hung around the yard, trying to be inconspicuous. It proved to be a relatively simply task. Neither the Defenders on guard nor the Karien escort spared him a glance. They were too busy eyeing each other warily to be concerned with one small boy.

Mikel had no idea how he was going to get near the prince. He knew none of the knights waiting outside with the horses, and he was fairly sure that he looked like nothing more than a Medalonian urchin. They would not spare him a copper if he was starving, let alone take him to see the prince. The meeting dragged on for hours as the cold sun climbed high in the sky. Mikel missed lunch and his stomach growled in complaint as the sky darkened toward dusk.

His chance came just as he was on the verge of giving up. Sir Andony emerged from the hall to speak to the knights waiting outside. Mikel swallowed his apprehension and hurried forward.

"Sir Andony?"

The young knight glanced at him, his eyes widening in shock.

"Mikel? What in Xaphista's name are you doing here?"

"I have to see the prince, Sir Andony."

"Don't be absurd! What could you possibly need to see the prince for?"

"It's about Princess Adrina."

Andony was not renowned for his intelligence, but even he understood the implications. He nodded slowly.

"Wait here."

Mikel fidgeted impatiently under the scrutiny of the Karien knights as Andony disappeared inside. In a surprisingly short time, Lord Roache appeared. He grabbed Mikel by the collar and dragged him aside, out of the hearing of the knights and the Defenders alike.

"What do you know of the princess?" he demanded without preamble.

"She was here, my Lord."

Roache's expression betrayed nothing of what he was thinking. "Are you certain?"

He nodded. "I fled Karien with the princess and her servant. The Hythrun captured us the morning after we left. The princess has been here ever since."

"And where is her Highness now?"

"I'm not sure. I think she left with Lord Wolfblade."

"I see."

"My Lord? There . . . there is something else you should know."

"What?" Lord Roache sounded impatient, as if his mind was already on other things.

"The princess and Lord Wolfblade . . . they're . . . well . . ."

"Out with it, boy!"

"She was kissing him, my Lord," Mikel blurted out.

Roache's eyes narrowed. "Who else knows of this?"

"Nobody, my Lord! I—"

"Come with me," Roache demanded, not in the least interested in what else Mikel had to say. He pulled Mikel along in his wake and thrust him at Andony.

"Take the boy back to our camp. Now!" Roache ordered. "You are to stop for no one. Nor must you allow anybody to speak to the child. He is to be held in my tent until I return."

Andony nodded, too well conditioned to question his orders. Before he truly understood what was happening Mikel was sitting in front of

Andony on his big warhorse, riding away from the Medalonian camp and heading for home.

It was close to midnight before Roache returned and when he did, he had Prince Cratyn with him. Mikel's determination to reveal the true depth of Adrina's treachery wavered in the Prince's serious presence.

"Tell his Highness what you told me," Roache ordered, waking Mikel from a light doze. The boy jumped to his feet and brushed his fingers through his sleep-tousled hair.

"The Princess is with Lord Wolfblade," Mikel told Cratyn. The young prince's expression was shadowed in the light from the smoking brazier.

"Then she fled to Medalon, not back to Yarnarrow as we thought."

"She told me she was going to Fardohnya, your Highness. To seek aid from her father." Mikel thought it important that he establish his own innocence as soon as possible. "I thought I was following your orders, Sire."

"Lying bitch," Cratyn muttered. "What else?"

Mikel glanced at Lord Roache uncertainly.

"Tell him the rest of it, boy."

"I saw them kissing, your Highness."

"You mean Wolfblade was forcing himself on her?"

Mikel shook his head sadly. "No, your Highness. She was . . . well, she didn't seem to mind at all. She called you . . ."

"What? What did she call me?"

Mikel stared at his boots with determination. "Prince Cretin the Cringing."

"I see. And what else did she say?"

Mikel looked to Lord Roache desperately for help. He did not want to repeat what he had heard, despite his promises to himself.

"The prince must know the truth, boy," Roach said, almost sympathetically. "Tell him."

Mikel nodded and told him everything he had heard. He told him of the meeting on top of the tower. He told him of what he had seen and heard in the stables. He told him everything he knew, although it broke his heart to be the bearer of such dreadful news.

Cratyn swore under his breath and then turned to Roache. "This is intolerable! I will send a party out to hunt her down. By Xaphista, I will see the bitch burn!"

"We'll hunt her down," Roache agreed. "But do you really want it made public that the wife you could not satisfy turned to a Hythrun for comfort?"

Cratyn paced the tent angrily. "She can't be allowed to get away with this!"

"Nor shall she, but there are other things to consider."

"What other things? She has publicly humiliated me!"

"And she will humiliate you even more, should the truth get out. You do *not* want to put her on trial, Cratyn."

The Prince glared at Lord Roache. Mikel seemed all but forgotten.

"You're surely not suggesting that I take her back?"

"Of course not! I am suggesting that you do everything in your power to rescue your wife from the clutches of the barbarian warlord who has kidnaped and raped her. It will be unfortunate, but she will be killed in the attempt."

"We'll have no chance at an heir if she's killed."

"She has been sullied by another man. No heir could come from your union in any case."

Cratyn nodded, savagely pleased with the duke's suggestion.

"I will lead the rescue party, myself."

"That would be most heroic of you, your Highness. Your grief, on the discovery of your wife's fate, will be inconsolable, of course. But I'm sure you will recover. In time."

Cratyn smiled coldly. "I'm sure I will. And what of the boy?"

Lord Roache glanced at Mikel for a moment before turning back to the prince.

"Perhaps he should accompany you, your Highness. He can, after all, give testament to your wife's . . . indiscretions."

The prince nodded. "It would be most unfortunate if something were to happen to him."

"Most unfortunate," Lord Roache agreed.

Mikel studied the prince and the duke, not at all certain he understood.

chapter 57

The darkness into which R'shiel retreated was comforting at first. The memories of the Gathering and everything that had happened since that awful night could gain no toehold here. There was no pain, no unbearable guilt, and no despair. Just blessed emptiness. A nothing place where nobody could hurt her.

She had been here before. She first discovered it on the road to the Grimfield, when Loclon had chosen her as his instrument of revenge on Tarja. It welcomed her the night she had confronted Loclon and almost succeeded in killing him. For a time, on waking to find herself in Sanctuary amid the Harshini, she had fled there again, until Korandellan's magic had suppressed her emotions and made it bearable to face reality. It was a tantalizing, alluring place, and each time she retreated there, it became a little harder to leave.

A part of R'shiel still existed in the real world. A part of her responded when someone spoke to her, ate the meals she was served, and rode in the carriage each day staring blindly at the winter-browned plains as they wound their way north. But it was a small part only. Just enough to pretend she was alive.

Within herself, R'shiel knew that she could not stay here indefinitely. Comforting it might be, but it was her Harshini side that fled from the violence and the pain. Her human side hankered to return, to wreak havoc on those who had caused her suffering.

It was her human side to whom Xaphista spoke.

R'shiel did not recognize his voice at first. The sensuous, soothing tones seemed like a distant echo that she hardly noticed. It took a long time to recognize it for what it was. It took even longer before she bothered to respond.

You run from the pain, demon child. Let me ease it for you.

Calling her the demon child finally evoked a response. She had never liked that name.

Don't call me that.

What would you have me call you?

Don't bother calling me anything. Just leave me alone.

The voice did not reply and R'shiel did not particularly care.

Later, she had no way of judging time in this place, the voice returned. It was stronger, as if by acknowledging it the first time, she had given it strength.

I can help you, R'shiel.

How do you know my name?

All the gods know the name of the demon child.

Are you a god?

I am the only god. At least I will be, with your help.

She laughed sourly. *With* my *help? Why would I want to help you?*

Because I can ease your pain, R'shiel. I can take away the hurt.

Can you turn back time?

Of course not.

Then you can do nothing for me. Go away.

The voice did as she bid, leaving her alone with her thoughts.

The living part of R'shiel vaguely noted the changing scenery as the days grew shorter; saw the silver ribbon of the Glass River draw nearer. For some reason, the sight of the broad waterway sparked a brief reaction in her, as if the thought of crossing it would take her beyond redemption.

You fear crossing the river? the voice asked curiously.

I fear what it represents.

It brings you closer to me.

I can destroy you, Xaphista. Shouldn't you be the one who fears my approach?

You need not destroy me, R'shiel. Together we would be invincible.

Together?

You would be my High Priestess. We could rule the world.

Suppose I don't want to rule the world?

You are half human.

That doesn't mean I crave an empire.

What do you crave, R'shiel?

Sanity.

Xaphista had no answer to that and it was a long time before he spoke to her again.

They crossed the river in a blustery, cold wind that chopped the mirror-like surface of the water into millions of glittering shards. The sun was high in a pale, cloudless sky, offering no warmth. R'shiel stood by the rail on the barge, oblivious to the cold spray that misted over her as the sailors hauled on the thick rope, pulling the barge across the river with grim determination. The current fought them at every turn. Although they professed to be atheists, the ferrymen muttered among themselves about the wrath of Maera, the River Goddess. They had never known a crossing like it. It was as though the Glass River was alive and determined to prevent them landing on the other side.

They made it eventually. R'shiel let Terbolt lead her onto dry ground and waited patiently for the rest of their party to disembark. The barge would be busy for two days or more, ferrying the remainder of the troops across. Aware of this, Terbolt commandeered the Heart and Hearth and settled in to wait. R'shiel paid no more attention to her surroundings at the inn than she had when they camped by the road each night on the journey here.

Garanus came to her at dinnertime and stood over her while she ate. When her meal was finished he sent the tray away and sat beside her. He did the same thing every night. He would talk to her as if she was listening, describing the power of the Overlord, preaching in a rasping, but impassioned voice that R'shiel found more irritating than comforting.

He pleads my case most eloquently.

He's a nuisance. If you truly want to ease my pain, getting rid of Garanus would be a good start.

As you wish. Without warning, Garanus broke off mid-sentence and left the room. *I would give you anything you asked for, R'shiel.*

So long as I promise not to kill you, she added wryly.

That would be a reasonable expectation, don't you think?

You can't give me what I want, Xaphista.

I can give you anything. You have but to ask.

Free me, then. Take this collar from me. Let me feel the power again.

Ah! I'm not certain I trust you that much, demon child.

Then what do I need you for? You are the reason for my pain.

Not I, R'shiel. It is the Primal gods who want you to suffer.

The Primal gods created me.

And they live in fear of their creation. Who do you think allowed this to happen?

It is your followers who hold me prisoner.

For your protection, nothing more. The Primal gods have interfered in your life enough.

What are you talking about?

Can you be so blind, child? They wish to destroy me. Why do you think you were raised in the Citadel? No child raised by the Harshini could contemplate killing, even with human blood.

Brak seems to manage.

He is as much a creature of the Primal gods as you are.

Are you telling me the Primal gods made Joyhinia adopt me?

That's exactly what I'm telling you. They picked the most ruthless, cold-hearted bitch they could find to raise you. How else could they ensure you had the skills to commit murder? They engineered your suffering, R'shiel. They have manipulated you since you were born.

You're delusional, Xaphista, as well as power hungry.

It is you who are deluded. Do you think your love for Tarja is an accident? Or his for you? Of course not! Kalianah made it happen.

Why?

Just to make you suffer. Think what it has cost you. Loclon raped you because Tarja loves you.

The last time I looked, Loclon was on your side. He misjudged her badly if he thought that was going to persuade her to his cause.

You will see the truth eventually, demon child. I pray that it will not be too late.

He left her then, leaving R'shiel with a puzzling thought. Xaphista was a god. To whom did *he* pray?

They left Cauthside and continued their journey north the third day after the river crossing. Outwardly, R'shiel showed no more interest on this side of the river than she had on the other. Garanus no longer came to her each night to aid her conversion, but little else changed. She woke, she ate, she rode in the carriage, then ate and slept where she was told. The routine never varied; it was unlikely she would have noticed if it had.

Her retreat was no longer peaceful, though. Her silent haven had been disturbed by Xaphista's poisonous logic.

Was she really just a pawn, manipulated since birth to become a weapon the Primal gods could use against their enemy? Was Tarja's love for her simply imposed on him? Had the Primal gods sat back and let Loclon do what he had done to her, hoping it would toughen her up? The idea seemed ludicrous at first, but the longer she thought about it, the more credibility it gained.

And what of Xaphista? Was he really so evil? And who was she to judge what was evil anyway? Xaphista had hurt her, there was no denying that; her current predicament was entirely attributable to him, but he was fighting for his survival. Were his actions any worse than those of the Primal gods?

For the first time since retreating into herself, R'shiel began to hunger for release. It was no longer peaceful here. Memories she had no wish to confront began to plague her. Thoughts she had no wish to contemplate refused to go away.

You see? Everything you hold dear is a lie, Xaphista told her seductively. *Tarja's love is no more real than this place. The Harshini secretly despise you, else why would they let you leave Sanctuary? Even the Primal gods fear you. You are a weapon, R'shiel, to be aimed and pointed by whoever holds your heart in his hands. Don't let them use you.*

You would use me just as soon as the Primal gods.

I offer you something in return. I can ease your pain. I can help you.

How? By suppressing my emotions like the Harshini did? That was simply an illusion and it hurt tenfold when they released it. I've no wish to experience it again.

I can do better than that, demon child. I can take away the memories that pain you.

Those memories make me who I am.

Then perhaps you should think about who you would rather be.

I won't be your pawn, Xaphista.

I offer you a partnership, R'shiel, not bondage.

Perhaps, she thought once he was gone. *But when it comes to the gods, who can tell the difference?*

chapter 58

Tarja set a gruelling pace as they fled the border. Jenga had promised to stall the Kariens as long as he was able, but even in Tarja's most optimistic estimate that gave them a start of only a day or two. Adrina kept up and did not complain, despite the fact that her backside felt bruised to the bone and her inner thighs were rubbed raw. They ate cold rations when they stopped each night, and collapsed into their bedrolls under an open sky.

As a child Adrina had been entranced by the bards who sang long, romantic ballads about lovers on the run who spent all day galloping toward freedom and all night making love. What utter nonsense, she thought, dismounting gingerly in the small grove of trees Tarja had chosen for their camp that night. Damin proved to be more human than heroic. He looked tired and haggard and even he walked a bit stiffly, despite a lifetime spent in the saddle. For some reason his discomfort made her feel a little better.

Their numbers had thinned considerably since they left the border. Following Damin's lead, Tarja had broken his men into much smaller groups and dispatched them south with orders to muster at an abandoned vineyard south of Testra, where he seemed to think they would be safe until he could join them. There were barely a hundred men left, and less than half of those were Damin's Raiders. The rest were Defenders and the remainder of her Guard. When they crossed the Glass River at Cauthside, they would split up once more. Tarja and his men would head for the Citadel, while Damin continued south for Hythria.

Adrina knew the reason for Tarja's mission, although he rarely spoke of it.

Something had happened to R'shiel.

Adrina prayed it was nothing serious. Tarja would not rest until he discovered the demon child's fate. It was a pity she would never meet her. Although she was careful not to broach the subject, R'shiel fascinated Adrina. Damin spoke of her in such glowing terms that she might have been jealous, but for two very good reasons. The first was Tarja. He was so completely besotted with the girl, that if he thought Damin's motives were anything but honorable, he'd have killed the Warlord long ago. The second was Damin. Jealousy would imply she had some feeling for the man, and of course she didn't, so there was nothing to be jealous about.

Adrina unsaddled her mount and dumped her gear near the small fire that one of the Defenders had started. Tarja had ordered at least one night with a fire and a hot meal. If he was feeling the strain of the pace he set, then he knew some of the others would be at the point of exhaustion. Adrina had tried not to look too happy when she heard the news, but poor Tam's expression had been pathetically grateful. The slave wasn't accustomed to long hours in the saddle, and Adrina looked a picture of health compared to her faithful companion.

"Can I take your horse, my Lady?"

Adrina turned and smiled wearily at Damin's captain. Almodavar was a fearsome-looking brute, but he was quite the gentleman underneath all that leather and chainmail.

"Thank you, Captain, but it's every man for himself on this journey. I can take care of my horse. You have other things to do."

"Aye, your Highness, but I have a few young studs with more energy than sense. I'll see she's cared for. You take the chance to rest while you can."

Adrina was too tired to argue. "Thank you."

Almodavar led the mare toward the picket line. He had sent someone for Tam's horse too. She turned to find Tamylan by the fire, warming her hands and swaying on her feet.

"Sit down before you fall down, Tam."

"I'll stand, if you don't mind. In fact if I never sit down again, it will be fine by me."

By the time darkness fell completely, Adrina was feeling a little bet-

ter. A hot meal and a warm fire eased her aching muscles. Damin and
Tarja did not join them until long after they had eaten. Tam had already
fallen asleep and Adrina's eyes were drooping. The only reason she was
still awake was her inability to find a comfortable position.

"Come on, sleepy. Time for some exercise."

"Don't be absurd. I can barely keep my eyes open."

"I know, but trust me. If you stretch your legs now you'll be much
better for it in the morning."

Damin reached down and grabbed her hand, hauling her to her feet.

"Leave me alone!"

"Stop complaining. You sound like a spoilt princess."

"I *am* a spoilt princess," she retorted.

"Who am I to argue with royalty? Are you coming, Tarja?"

"No. I have to check on the sentries. Enjoy your walk, your Highness." She couldn't see his face clearly in the darkness, but she could
hear his amusement.

"I'll bet he doesn't laugh at R'shiel," she grumbled as Damin pulled
her along beside him. It was bitterly cold and the uneven ground made
her muscles cry out in protest.

"Would you laugh at someone who could fry you with a look?"

"How can you possibly be in such a good mood?"

"I've still got my head on my shoulders. In this business that's daily
cause for celebration. Take longer strides. The idea is to stretch your legs
out, not mince along like you're at court."

"I do not *mince*, thank you."

"I do beg your pardon, your Highness."

"Don't patronize me either."

"You're in a right temper tonight. I thought you'd be happy to be free."

"I'm cold and I'm tired, Damin. I feel like someone's tied me in a
sack and beaten me with a pole for an hour or two. I don't have the
energy to be happy about anything."

He slowed his pace a little and put his arm around her shoulder. "I'm
tired too. And I'm cheerful because I'm a Warlord and nothing is supposed to bother me."

"I'm not one of your hired hands, you know. You're not morally
obliged to keep my spirits up."

He laughed softly, but did not answer. They kept walking through the darkness away from the fires, although they stayed within the ring of sentries posted around the camp. Adrina could make out the silhouette of a guard every fifty paces or so, their eyes fixed on the open ground beyond the trees.

It was much warmer with his arm around her and after a time her legs seemed to loosen up a little. The respite was temporary, though. Tomorrow they would resume their killing pace.

"How long till we reach the river?" she asked after a long period of companionable silence.

"Seven or eight days, I guess. Tarja could tell you exactly."

"Are we going to keep this pace up for another *eight* days?"

"No. The horses couldn't take it, even if we could. We'll ease up in a day or so."

"You think Cratyn will come after us, don't you?"

He nodded, all trace of his previous good humour gone. "Jenga won't tell him where you are, but there are plenty of people who know you were in the camp. We have to assume he'll hear about it, sooner rather than later."

"What if he catches us?"

"He won't. We've got too big a head start and we're not stopping for anything. Once we've crossed the Glass River, he'll have no chance of finding us." He stopped and pulled her to him, kissing her forehead lightly. "Stop worrying about it."

She laid her head on his shoulder and stood in the circle of his arms, surprised at how comforting it was. It was a real pity he was a Hythrun. She could easily grow accustomed to this. To feel so secure, so . . .

"Hey, don't fall asleep on me," he chided. "I'll be damned if I'm going to carry you all the way back."

She drew back from him, annoyed that he had disturbed her pleasant, if rather unrealistic, daydreams. "You are so rude sometimes! I'm sure you do it just to aggravate me."

"Rude I might be, but I'm still not going to carry you," he said with a grin.

"A true nobleman would."

"That's because most true nobleman are inbred morons with more brawn than brains. I could cite your husband as a prime example."

"I didn't choose him, you know."

"Which says something for your good taste, I suppose. Come on, we'd best get back before Tarja sends out a search party."

Stifling a yawn, Adrina took his hand and they walked back toward the fire and the welcome prospect of a good night's sleep. She glanced at him as they walked back through the darkened trees and reminded herself sternly that Damin Wolfblade might be very disarming when he wanted, but he was, first and foremost, her enemy. His desire to keep her from Cratyn was nothing more than political, and she had better not forget it.

They were on the move by first light the next day. Poor Tam was on the verge of tears as she struggled to mount her horse, but Adrina found she was much better than she expected. Although she would have preferred to ride with Damin or Tarja, she took her usual place in the very center of the column surrounded by Raiders, Defenders and Fardohnyans who had orders to die before any harm was allowed to befall her.

They kept to the road that wound south toward Cauthside, in part because it was the fastest route, and in part to disguise the size of their group. They had left the border in significant numbers and there was no need for any pursuing force to think that had changed. Scouts ranged ahead and behind them, scouring the countryside for signs of pursuit, or unexpected danger. Now that Medalon had surrendered, any Defenders they met heading north would be enemies and both Tarja and Damin agreed that in this case running was more prudent than fighting.

She had heard them discussing their plans late into the night as she lay by the fire, her head resting in Damin's lap and he unconsciously stroked her hair. She drifted into sleep listening to Tarja explain his plans for the men who waited for him in Testra.

She understood now why Jenga had wanted Tarja to resign from the corps, why he wanted him to escape the border while he still could. It had little to do with the Lord Defender's affection for him. Tarja was an expert guerilla fighter and Jenga wanted him to do to the Kariens what he had done to the Defenders when he led the heathen rebellion. He didn't have the men to take on the Karien invaders directly but he would make life very difficult for them.

Adrina fell asleep and dreamed of ambushes, and sabotage, and hit-and-run raids on places she had never heard of.

They stopped just after midday at a small brook that tumbled over moss-covered rocks beside the road. The water was icy, but the horses seemed grateful. Adrina stood by her mare as she drank her fill, munching on a wedge of hard cheese, when one of the forward scouts came thundering through their midst. He skidded to a halt in front of Damin and Tarja, turning his mount sharply to avoid barrelling them over.

"Defenders!" he panted. "A thousand at least. Headed this way."

"How far?" Tarja demanded.

"Five leagues. They're not moving very fast, but if we stay on the road, we'll ride straight into them."

Tarja grabbed his mount and swung into the saddle. "Show me."

The scout turned his mount and galloped off with Tarja on his heels.

"Almodavar!"

"My Lord?"

"Get everyone off the road. Make camp in that stand of trees we passed a league or so back. No fires, no noise. You know what to do."

Damin was mounted and racing down the road after Tarja before Almodavar had a chance to acknowledge the order.

Adrina patted her mare with a weary sigh, then climbed back into the saddle. Almodavar got them organized in a very short time, the urgency of their situation not lost on a single man. They rode back along the road at a canter, until Almodavar called a halt when they neared the trees.

The copse was a fair way back, separated from the road by a broad stretch of long brown grass. The captain studied the tree line for a while, then stood in his stirrups to look over the surrounding countryside. Then he turned and cantered back in the direction they had come from.

"What's the matter?" Adrina asked the guard on her left.

"If we ride through that grass, your Highness, we might as well put up a sign telling them where we are. The captain's looking for a way to reach the trees without leaving any tracks."

Adrina nodded, rather impressed by the Hythrun eye for detail. They waited for another few minutes before Almodavar returned.

"There's a gully back that way that leads toward the trees," the captain announced in Medalonian, for the benefit of the Defenders among them. "But we'll have to lead the horses, it's too treacherous to ride through. Once we clear it, we'll have a bit of open ground to cover, so we'll cross it in single file."

He did not ask for questions, or expect any. Adrina followed her guards and picked her way through the gully after the young man who had told her of Almodavar's intentions. A bubbling stream coursed through the center, perhaps a tributary of the brook where they had stopped earlier. The rocks were slick and the icy water splashed over her boots. She was dressed in trousers and a warm jacket, as was Tam—there was no point in advertising their presence by dressing like ladies—but her feet were starting to numb by the time she led her mare out of the gully and mounted for the ride to the trees.

There was no respite when she reached them, either. Almodavar ordered no fires to betray their presence so she settled down for a long cold wait until Damin and Tarja returned.

Adrina was sitting with her back to a tall poplar, Tam's sleeping head resting on her shoulder, when the sound of galloping horses woke her from a light doze. Expecting to find Damin and Tarja returning, she gently moved Tam's head onto the cloak they were using as a rug and struggled to her feet. She found Almodavar waiting at the edge of the trees as a Defender and a Raider galloped toward them through the grass, making a mockery of his effort to conceal their hiding place.

"That's not Damin and Tarja," she pointed out as the horsemen drew nearer.

"The Raider is Jocim, one of the rear scouts," Almodavar agreed. "I don't know the Defender."

They waited until the men had almost reached the trees before waving them down. Jocim stayed in his saddle, but the Defender jumped down, almost collapsing with exhaustion as he hit the ground. Almodavar reached out an arm to steady him, but he waved it away.

"Where's Captain Tenragan?"

"He's not here."

"Who's the ranking Defender officer then?"

Almodavar looked a little annoyed at the man's insistence on following Defender protocol.

"If you have news, man, out with it."

The Defender looked as if he was going to argue the point, but weariness won out over procedure.

"I have a message from the Lord Defender," he said. "The Kariens crossed the border two days after you left. The Defenders were ordered to throw down their arms. The Kariens have control of the Keep."

Almodavar nodded, unsurprised by the news. "Jenga ordered you to founder a horse just to tell us that?"

He shook his head. "No. He sent me to tell you that two hundred Kariens were dispatched south at the same time. He thinks they know about the princess. Cratyn is leading them himself."

Adrina's heart skipped a beat. Surely they had enough lead on them to escape? The Kariens could not travel as fast as their troop and they were making excellent time.

Almodavar nodded and glanced at Adrina. Her expression must have betrayed her thoughts. "They'll not catch us, your Highness."

"Not if we keep moving," she agreed.

Adrina left the rest of it unsaid. Almodavar knew, as well as she, that a force of a thousand Defenders was blocking the way south.

chapter 59

rom a distance, the northern plains looked as flat and feature-
less as a tabletop. The view was deceptive, though. In reality
the plains were a series of low rolling folds that concealed as
much as they revealed. Tarja, Damin and the Hythrun scout,
whose name was Colsy, dismounted some distance from the
Defenders. They led their horses off the road for quite a way, before
leaving them to fend for themselves as they scrambled up a low hillside,
dropping on their bellies as they neared the summit.

"Gods!" Damin muttered as they reached the top.

Tarja studied the scene below, forcing down a wave of despair. The
column of Defenders was stretched out along the road in a snaking line
that stretched for half a league or more. At its head, rode a Karien knight,
displaying a coat of arms on his shield that he could not make out from
this distance.

"Do you have your looking-glass?"

Damin nodded and handed Tarja the instrument from the pouch he
carried on his belt. Tarja aimed it at the knight's shield. As the three silver pike on a red field slowly resolved into focus he swore softly, then
handed it back to Damin.

"Well, at least that answers the question about the whereabouts of
the Duke of Setenton."

Damin took the looking-glass and followed Tarja's pointing finger.

"And where the order for the surrender came from," Damin agreed.
"What's he doing leading half the damned Defender Corps north?"

Half was a gross exaggeration, but that near a thousand Defenders marched under the command of a Karien knight was cause enough for concern.

"If he was waiting at the Citadel when R'shiel arrived . . ." Tarja did not finish the sentence. He was afraid to put his thought into words.

"I wonder who's in the carriage," Colsy added, pointing at the elaborate vehicle drawn by six matched horses, which trundled along behind the Kariens.

"That's the First Sister's carriage."

"That's all we need," Damin groaned. "Joyhinia Tenragan, in all her vicious glory. I thought you destroyed her wit after Dacendaran stole it?"

"So did I."

Damin returned the looking-glass to its case and rolled onto his back. He put his hands behind his head and stared at the pale sky for a moment, then looked at Tarja.

"They'll be on us by nightfall."

"Or so close it won't matter."

"I've always fancied myself a brilliant warrior, Tarja, but odds of ten to one are a bit much, even for me."

Tarja nodded. "There's nothing to be achieved by engaging them."

"So what do we do? Hide until they ride by? Head overland?"

"If we turn off the road, it'll take a lot longer to reach the river and even more time to find a place where we can cross. Cauthside is the only place with a decent barge this side of Testra." He didn't add that going overland meant turning west. Damin knew it without having it spelled out for him.

"Then it seems we have no choice. We hide until they pass by."

"That may not be as simple as you think. Terbolt might be in command, but the Defenders won't let that interfere with their normal routine. They'll have scouts out, you can be certain."

"I didn't see any," Colsy objected.

"That doesn't mean they aren't out there," Tarja warned.

Damin nodded in agreement. "The reputation of the Defenders is well earned. All the more reason not to take them on."

"If we're careful, we should be able to avoid them," Tarja suggested.

The Warlord smiled wistfully. "Remember the good old days, Tarja? When you and I knew exactly who our enemies were? I miss them."

"I remember them well. You were the enemy, as I recall."

"And you were always one step ahead of me. I always meant to ask you how you managed that."

"I probably shouldn't disillusion you, but it was luck as much as anything."

Damin grinned. "I don't believe you. Nobody could be that lucky."

"Alright, if it makes you happy, it was my sheer tactical brilliance."

"Just as I always suspected," Damin agreed. He rolled over and stared down at the advancing Defenders. "I have to tell you. The sight of those Defenders has completely ruined my day, you know that, don't you?"

"You'll get over it."

"Eventually," Damin sighed. "Let's get back to the others."

"Aren't we going to do *anything*?" Colsy asked, obviously disappointed.

"We are going to hide, young man."

"Hiding is for women."

"And very smart men," the Warlord retorted.

It was late afternoon before they located Almodavar and the rest of their band. The Hythrun captain had done an excellent job of concealing their presence. But for some scattered tracks heading toward the tree-line, there was nothing to indicate that more than a hundred men were concealed among the trees. Tarja looked around the camp with approval. The Hythrun seemed to lack discipline, but when it really counted, they did exactly as they were ordered.

Adrina hurried forward as they rode into the camp. The change in her was quite remarkable, Tarja thought. She seemed to have shed her spoilt outer shell. She had ridden without complaint, as though she was trying to prove she was worthy of the danger they had placed themselves in by offering her protection. Her face brightened at Damin's approach, revealing far more than she meant to.

Tarja was wary of Damin's relationship with Adrina. It was fraught with danger and long-term ramifications that did not bear thinking about. Despite the insistence of both Damin and Adrina that the relationship meant nothing, Tarja could see the danger signs. Adrina never strayed far from Damin and he was prepared to risk his life to keep her by his side. Tarja understood what it was like to be willing to lay down your life for someone you loved. He wondered how long it would be before the Hythrun Warlord and the Fardohnyan Princess worked it out for themselves.

"Cratyn's coming!" Adrina cried as Damin dismounted.

Damin looked over her shoulder at Almodavar who approached them at a much more dignified pace.

"She speaks the truth, my Lord. Jenga sent a messenger to warn us."

Tarja dismounted and let Shadow be led away by one of his own men who had clustered around them, anxious for news.

"How far behind us?"

"A day or two, three at the outside."

"This could make things interesting," Damin remarked laconically.

Adrina punched his arm impatiently. "*Interesting?* Don't you realize the danger we're in?"

Tarja understood Adrina's annoyance. Damin had a bad habit of treating everything as if it was some sort of elaborate game. His refusal to take anything seriously could be frustrating at times. In this case it was downright dangerous.

"She has a point, Damin."

"What's the problem?" he shrugged. "We've already agreed that it would be insane to take the Defenders on. We can't go overland—it will slow us down too much—so we hide. The Defenders will ride by us, none the wiser."

"And run straight into Cratyn," Tarja reminded him. "What do you think will happen then?"

"If we're lucky, they'll wipe each other out," the Warlord chuckled.

"Be serious!"

Damin had the decency to look contrite. "You're right. If Cratyn knows when we left, and we haven't been seen by the Defenders, even *he* should be able to figure out that we're around here somewhere."

"Can't we slip past the Defenders?" Adrina asked hopefully. There was an edge of desperation in her voice.

Tarja shook his head. "Not a chance."

"Then we go overland," Damin said, no happier with the idea than Tarja. But at least this way they would have a chance of avoiding the two forces that were inexorably closing in on them. But it took him away from the Citadel. Away from R'shiel.

"If we start moving now, we can put a few leagues between us and the Defenders by nightfall."

The Warlord nodded and ordered Almodavar to get everyone moving. Tarja's stomach rumbled in complaint, reminding him that he had missed lunch as Damin led Adrina away, his arm around her shoulder.

As he watched the retreating couple he frowned. He should have put a stop to it. That he would have had more chance of stopping the sun rising tomorrow did little to ease his concern. Were it not for Adrina, Cratyn would more than likely have ignored the Hythrun refusal to surrender. What were a thousand Hythrun to a man who could muster a hundred thousand men? If Cratyn was simply chasing down his errant wife, then it was bad enough. If anyone suspected that she and Damin were lovers, and shared their suspicions with the prince, Cratyn would not rest until every last person who knew of the liaison was dead. He was the Karien Crown Prince and his religion demanded the most terrible vengeance he could wreak. Adrina's infidelity could not be forgiven—it could only be washed away in blood.

It was slow going as they picked their way cross country. The terrain was hard on the horses. One minute they were climbing, the next descending, and although the slopes were not steep, the horses had been ridden hard for days now. By the time darkness fell, and with it the temperature, even some of the magnificent Hythrun horses, renowned for their stamina, were stumbling. Tarja called a halt and ordered them to make camp, but refused to allow any fires. The chance of being spotted by a Defender scout was too real to be ignored.

Tarja hobbled his mount and finally got around to eating something long after dark, although hard cheese and jerky barely counted as a meal. He had been spoilt, he decided, living on the border. There was a time when he didn't mind trail rations. Had he been tougher then—or just less discerning, he wondered?

"Tarja?"

He turned, a little surprised to find Adrina weaving her way among the picketed horses toward him. Her breath frosted in the moonlight and she held her borrowed jacket tightly closed against the cold.

"I thought you'd be asleep by now."

"Sleep?" she laughed humorlessly. "That's a joke. Who can sleep with a thousand Defenders over the next hill and the Kariens riding us down?"

"You need to rest, then, even if you can't sleep. The last few days are going to seem like a picnic compared to what lies ahead."

She reached up and patted Shadow's forelock. The mare nuzzled her hopefully for a moment, then returned to her feedbag when she decided the princess had nothing better to offer.

"Can I ask you something, Tarja?"

"I suppose."

"If I wasn't here, you wouldn't be doing this, would you?"

She knew the answer as well as he did. He wondered what was really behind the question.

"Cratyn probably wouldn't be on our tail, but we'd still be hiding from the Defenders. You can't blame yourself for that."

She smiled. "Actually, I'm a little surprised at myself. Taking the blame for things is not my style. I've never been known for my selflessness."

Tarja found that very easy to believe.

"I keep thinking I should just go back to Cratyn and be damned."

"What good would that do?" He hoped he hadn't let his astonishment show. Such an offer from Adrina verged on the miraculous.

"R'shiel is missing, Tarja. You should be helping her, not saving me from my own stupidity." She smiled self-consciously, as if she was startled to have made such an admission. "I have a feeling that the demon child is more important in the general scheme of things than one disgruntled princess."

"She's right, Tarja."

Brak appeared out of nowhere a pace behind Adrina. The princess spun around, startled by the unexpected voice. A thousand questions leapt to Tarja's mind at the sight of him, but one question overrode every other, even his astonishment at Brak's sudden return:

"Where is R'shiel?"

"Closer than you think," Brak replied, then he bowed to Adrina. "You must be Hablet's girl. Adrina, isn't it? The one who married Cratyn?"

"Who are you?" she demanded. "Tarja? Who is he?"

"Brakandaran," Tarja told her, fighting to keep an even temper. *What in the name of the Founders had happened to R'shiel? How did Brak get here?* "He's Harshini. He was supposed to be looking after R'shiel."

"You can't blame Brak, Tarja, it wasn't his fault."

Tarja started at the new voice and turned to find Dace standing behind him. The God of Thieves was grinning broadly, rather pleased with the effect of his dramatic entrance.

"What are *you* doing here?"

"You know, most people would prostrate themselves when confronted with a god," Dace pointed out, a little miffed at Tarja's less-than-enthusiastic reception.

"I'm not 'most people.' What happened to R'shiel?"

"That's a *god*?" Adrina asked. She looked awestruck, but then, she was a pagan. Being confronted with one of her gods probably meant a great deal more to her than it meant to him.

"Unfortunately, yes. This is Dacendaran. He's supposed to be the God of Thieves, I think. Personally, I think he's the God of Unreliable Fools."

"Don't be absurd, Tarja, there's no such entity. If you're going to be like that, then I won't help you."

"That's an empty threat under the circumstances," Brak remarked.

"But he can't be a god," Adrina scoffed. "I've seen him in the Defenders' camp. He was hanging around with Mikel."

"My newest and most fervent . . . no actually, he's more like a *reluctant* disciple."

"Brak, what the hell is going on?"

He held up his hand wearily to stay Tarja's avalanche of questions. "Look, I know I have a lot of explaining to do, and I will, I promise. But let's find Damin first. I don't want to have to go over this more than once."

chapter 60

Before I tell you where R'shiel is," Brak began, looking at each one of them in turn, "I have to explain a few things."

They had gathered around a brightly burning fire, safe in the knowledge that Brak's magic concealed them from prying eyes. Tarja was sceptical when he promised they would not be seen, and his men were decidedly edgy, but even Almodavar seemed satisfied with the Harshini's assurance that he was protecting them. The fire warmed them more than it should have, and he wondered if Brak's magic was responsible for that too. The half-Harshini's eyes were completely black, a sure sign he was drawing on his power. It reminded Tarja sharply how alien the Harshini really were.

"You'd better tell them the rules, too," Dace added.

"What rules?" Tarja asked warily.

"I'll get to that. There are other things you must understand first."

Tarja shifted restlessly. He knew from experience how futile it was to demand answers from Brak when he wasn't ready to give them. Damin sat on his left, with Adrina curled up beside him. On the other side of the fire sat Almodavar, Ghari and Dace, who seemed quite content to let Brak do the talking.

"As you've probably figured out by now," Brak continued, "the Kariens were waiting for us when we reached the Citadel."

"I tried to warn you," Dace interjected.

"You *knew* they were waiting for you? Why in the name of the Founders didn't you turn back?"

"Dace warned us Xaphista had believers in the Citadel, Tarja. Even he didn't know Terbolt and his priests were there."

"So much for the infallibility of the gods."

Dace glared at him, but let the comment pass.

"It wouldn't have mattered if Dace had given us the disposition of every Karien on the continent, there were forces at work that would have seen to it that we did not succeed."

"How could you fail with the gods on your side?" Adrina scoffed.

"That's just the point. The only side the gods care about is their own."

Dace snorted with disgust at the comment, but he seemed unusually reticent tonight and offered no other sign of his displeasure.

"Anyway, we reached the Citadel and everything went according to plan until Joyhinia appeared at the Gathering. The real Joyhinia that is, as lucid as she ever was."

"How? I destroyed her wit. Her mind was gone."

"The Karien priests found her another mind and transferred it into her body. Once Joyhinia appeared things fell apart fairly rapidly. The demon meld collapsed and R'shiel couldn't hold the coercion. She was discovered within minutes of Terbolt's appearance. Mahina was arrested. Draco's dead, by the way. So is Affiana."

"And just what were *you* doing while R'shiel was being arrested?" Tarja asked, his voice dangerous. The news that that man who fathered him was dead meant little to him. He was more concerned about Mahina. He was sick with worry about R'shiel.

"I was also being detained—by Zegarnald."

Damin sat bolt upright and stared at the Harshini in astonishment. "The God of War prevented you from going to the demon child's aid? That makes no sense. He delivered her to me for safekeeping. Why would he allow her to fall into the hands of his enemies?"

"The Kariens are *your* enemies, Damin, not Zegarnald's. Xaphista is *his* adversary and that's all he's interested in."

"I don't understand," Adrina said, giving voice to Tarja's own confusion.

"The only reason the gods allowed R'shiel to be created was their need to destroy Xaphista. They're not interested in anything else. The demon child has a job to do and they want to be damned sure she's capable of doing it."

"You mean they want to know if she can kill?"

"She can do that readily enough," Ghari warned her. "Ask anyone who knew her in the rebellion."

Brak nodded. "That's not what concerns them. They're more worried that Xaphista will win her over to his cause. She can kill a god. *Which* god she destroys is entirely up to her."

"So they let the Kariens capture her? Isn't that rather counterproductive?" Damin asked.

"Zegarnald's theory is that if she is going to succumb to Xaphista, he'd rather know now, before she fully realizes what she is capable of."

"He wants to find out while there's still a chance she can be killed," Tarja translated for the benefit of the others. "That's *your* job, isn't it, Brak?"

The Harshini dropped his eyes.

Adrina looked at Tarja in confusion before turning back to Brak. "But what happened to R'shiel?"

"She was taken prisoner."

"And then what?" Damin asked. He knew Brak, too; knew they had yet to hear the worst of it.

"You recall I said the Kariens transferred another mind into Joyhinia's body? Well, it wasn't just any mind." Brak looked straight at Tarja. "It was Loclon's mind."

Tarja experienced a moment of such blind, mindless rage that he thought he might explode from it. He didn't say a word. He just sat there, trembling, clenching his fists in helpless fury. The others looked at him curiously, sensing his mood but unaware of the reason for it. Nobody but Brak, Dace and Tarja knew of what Loclon had done to R'shiel in the past. They did not understand.

"I gather from the look on Tarja's face that this Loclon is not a very nice person?" Damin asked flippantly. Tarja turned on him with such fury that the Warlord leaned back, out of his reach. "Sorry . . . Just trying to lighten the mood. I'll shut up."

"That would be a very good idea," Adrina agreed sternly.

Brak resumed his narrative, looking almost as annoyed at Damin as Adrina was. "If you need details, I'll let Tarja fill you in if he wants to. Suffice to say that Loclon has harmed R'shiel in the past. Enough that he's probably the only thing in this world she truly fears. R'shiel's feelings for Joyhinia aren't much better. Being confronted by both of them in the one body was more than she could take."

"Did he kill her?" Tarja asked. His voice was colder than the night.

Brak shook his head. "He roughed her up a bit, but he couldn't risk killing her. But for a few cuts and bruises, physically she's fine."

"Physically?"

"You remember the night we escaped the Grimfield?"

"I'm not likely to forget it."

"Then you recall what happened to R'shiel after she tried to kill Loclon? How she retreated into herself?"

Tarja nodded. "She was like it for days."

"Well that's basically what's happened to her now. She's alive, she speaks, she eats; but R'shiel is not there."

"You mean she's in some sort of coma?" Adrina asked.

"Not exactly. Tarja knows what I mean. He's seen her like this before."

"Then how do we wake her?"

"We can't. She has to come back of her own accord."

"If she wants to come back," Dace reminded Brak.

"What do you mean?"

Brak sighed. "Wherever she is, it's more than likely Xaphista is there too."

"Then only the gods can reach her? Why don't you do something, Dacendaran?"

"I'm not allowed to, Damin," the young god replied. "Zeggie says she has to turn away from Xaphista of her own accord, or when it comes time to face him she'll simply give in." He looked around the fire-lit circle of faces, begging for understanding. "Look, I'm going to be in enough trouble for freeing Brak. I'd help if I could, but with all these wars going on, Zegarnald is as strong as he's ever been. Unless you can start some sort of worldwide crime wave, I haven't the strength to defy him."

"Then how can Xaphista get to her?" Tarja asked. He didn't have the benefit of a pagan education. He was floundering with all this talk of gods.

"Xaphista gains his strength from his believers and he's got millions of them. That's why the Primal gods fear him."

"But she's half-Harshini, isn't she?" Damin pointed out. "Why didn't she just call on her power and escape herself?"

"The priests have blocked her power. They're using some sort of collar I've never seen before. If she tries to touch the source of her power it burns. If she manages to get past that, the pain is intolerable. Not even the demons can reach her."

Tarja watched Brak, wondering how much of what he told them was conjecture and how much he knew to be fact.

"So what is Xaphista doing to her?" Adrina wondered aloud.

"I doubt if he's hurting her," Brak shrugged. "If anything he'll be trying to coax her to follow him. He doesn't need to kill R'shiel to remove the threat. He just needs her on his side."

"So if she defies him, he'll kill her and if she doesn't, you'll kill her anyway," Tarja concluded bleakly.

Brak didn't answer; he didn't have to.

"Where is she, Brak?"

"With the Defenders camped less than two leagues from here. Terbolt is escorting her back to Karien."

The stunned silence lasted only a moment.

"We have to rescue her," Almodavar announced.

"How?" Tarja demanded.

"We'll think of something," Damin said, with a nod to his captain. "You're surely not suggesting that we leave her there?"

"Why not? She's as safe there as anywhere. I'm not going to risk the life of every man here, just so that the moment we get her back Brak can kill her."

The Harshini stared at him with unreadable black eyes.

"Brakandaran would never . . ." Damin began, then saw the look on the Harshini's face. "Gods! You can't be serious!"

Adrina glanced around at the men angrily. "This is insane! You can't leave her there. You can't let them take her back to Karien. They would destroy her, and trust me, I know what I'm talking about! You have to rescue her!"

"It won't be easy," Ghari warned. "And if she has turned to Xaphista, she may not want to be rescued."

"Bollocks!" the Fardohnyan princess spat angrily. "You don't know what's happened to her. You have to give her a chance."

Tarja nodded in agreement. "Nobody wants to get her back more than I, Adrina, but she's being held in the middle of a thousand Defenders."

"But we have the Harshini on our side," Damin pointed out. "We could be in and out before anyone knew about it. That's assuming you'll help us, Brak."

"I'll help you as much as I can, but you must understand that I can't do anything for R'shiel. She has to make her own decisions." He turned to Dace. "I'm allowed to do that much aren't I, Divine One?"

Dace nodded miserably. "I suppose."

"And once we have rescued the demon child?" Ghari asked. "You forget the Karien force approaching from the north. Unless Lord Brakandaran can magically transport us away from here, we'll have little hope of escape. Cratyn is angry enough to hunt down his wife. I imagine losing the demon child will do nothing to improve his temper."

"We need something to distract him," Damin agreed.

"That's easy," Adrina said. "I'll surrender."

"No!" Damin cried.

"What else will turn him back, Damin? He seeks his wife. He doesn't know that the Defenders approach, or that they have the demon child. If you can get R'shiel out of the Defenders' camp, Terbolt will be furious certainly, but the Defenders will not pursue you with the same dedication that Cratyn will. With Brak's help you can get clear. If Cratyn joins the hunt, nothing will deter him."

Tarja could see the logic in her plan, but remained silent, as did the others. This was something they needed to decide among themselves. He wondered if Damin was beginning to realize just how hard he would find it to let Adrina go.

"I can't let you do it, Adrina. If Cratyn suspects for a minute—"

"I'm prepared to take that risk, Damin."

"Well, I'm not. You're not going back to him and that's final. We haven't come this far to quit now." He turned to Tarja, his face chiselled in determination. "We'll get R'shiel back, Tarja, then we'll run like hell. We'll split our forces and scatter them so wide, Cratyn and Terbolt won't even begin to know where to look. Brak can conceal us and—"

"And his priests will think I've lit a beacon for them," Brak warned.

"But you're shielding us now. Can't they feel it?"

"I'm helping," Dace admitted.

"Then you can help us when we flee."

The God of Thieves shook his head. "That would be interfering. If you take R'shiel and try to stop what's happening to her, and Zegarnald catches me helping you . . ." Dace left the sentence hanging ominously.

The gods could not destroy each other, Tarja knew that much, but he wondered what one god could do to another that would cause Dacendaran such concern. He had a feeling he didn't really want to know.

Damin thought for a moment, then shrugged. "What the hell. I wasn't planning to live forever anyway. What say we go and rescue the demon child anyway, and to hell with the risk?"

"You're mad!" Adrina declared, but she didn't offer any further protest, or repeat her offer to return to her husband.

One by one the others nodded their agreement, including Brak, until Damin turned to Tarja questioningly.

"Well?"

Tarja looked up and met Brak's unwavering, alien eyes. He wanted to rescue R'shiel more than he wanted to keep breathing, but he could not shake the feeling that saving her from her current predicament might be placing her in even more danger.

"Let's do it," he agreed, sounding far more certain than he felt.

It was too late by the time they finished their discussion to take any action that night, so they planned their rescue attempt for the following evening. The delay made Tarja nervous. The Kariens were already too close for comfort and the wait served only to bring them closer.

The Defenders had stopped for the night, so Damin sent out scouts to spy out the lay of their camp, as it was more than likely the camp would be set up in the same way each evening. Two Hythrun Raiders and two Defenders, hand-picked by Tarja for both their experience and their common sense, were dispatched to learn as much as they could before sunrise—specifically, where the occupants of the coach were camped. Tarja didn't need a spy to tell him they would be in the center of the camp, but it would simplify things considerably if he knew exactly which tent and the disposition of the guards.

He spent the rest of the night organizing the Defenders. Although they traveled in civilian clothing, every man had his uniform safely tucked away in his saddlebags. Sneaking into the Defender camp would be impossible, so Tarja planned to march through it openly. With luck, he could simply walk up to R'shiel's tent, order her brought out, and then escort her away without a question being asked.

If she was alone.

If the guards on the tent did not recognize him.

If the guards hadn't been given any orders to the contrary.

If she was guarded by Defenders, rather than Karien priests.

He forced himself to stop thinking about the ifs. There were too many of them for comfort.

Damin agreed with his plan, but was rather disappointed that he was not to be included in the rescue party. He consoled himself with the prospect of some useful sabotage. A small party of his Raiders would sneak into the camp and disable the coach, while the rest would attempt to scatter the horses. Pursuit was certain, once R'shiel was discovered missing, but they planned to make it as difficult as possible.

That left only Adrina, her slave and the thirty men left of her Guard. The question of what to do with them was rather hotly debated, mostly between Damin and the princess. She did not want to be left behind to wait, and Damin was understandably reluctant to lead her into the middle of the Defenders' camp. In they end they compromised. Adrina would stay with the horses on the edge of the camp, ready for a quick getaway. The Fardohnyans were more easily dealt with. With Damin as his interpreter, Tarja told the Fardohnyans they were free to go. He gave them maps to find their way home and enough supplies to see them to the Glass River. The young Lanceman accepted their release with quiet gratitude, following an assurance that the princess would be safe. The men would leave at dawn—one more scattered group in a landscape that would soon be crowded with them.

Their plans made, they settled down to rest until daylight. They would need to travel north tomorrow, shadowing the Defenders until they stopped again for the evening. Tarja hoped that Cratyn was far enough back that his troop would not run into the approaching Defenders. They had no real idea how far behind he was. Their estimates were based almost entirely on the assumption that Cratyn and his knights were probably armored, and therefore unable to maintain any sort of sustained speed. The chances were good that the Karien force would not meet up with the Defenders until the day after tomorrow. Tarja needed to be well away by then.

Sleep eluded him, and he finally gave up pretending that he was getting any rest, just as the first of the stars winked out of existence with the onset of daylight. He walked to the edge of the camp, climbing a small hill to look out over their route for the next day. The sound of following footsteps alerted him to the fact that he was not alone, but he did not turn. He had a feeling he knew who it was.

"Can't sleep?"

"Nor can you, I'd guess."

Brak stepped up beside him and followed Tarja's gaze.

"I don't need sleep the way you do. One of the advantages of being half Harshini."

They were silent for a time, each alone with his thoughts.

"How bad was it?" Tarja asked eventually.

"Bad enough," Brak admitted. "You might get a shock when you find her. He cut her hair."

Her glorious, dark-red hair. Tarja felt his ire rising, but forced it down. It would serve no purpose here.

"Tell me the rest of it."

"There's not much to tell. It took a while before I finally convinced Dace to release me—it was a good thing you sent him, by the way. Zegarnald was quite happy to let me rot. Anyway, Terbolt had already left the Citadel by then. Joyhinia, or rather Loclon, is still nominally in charge of the Sisterhood, but he's taking his orders from a Karien called Squire Mathen. I don't know who he is, but he's working to his own agenda. Loclon doesn't have much freedom of action."

"For as long as I live, I will regret not killing him when I had the chance."

"Accept it, Tarja. Being consumed by your regrets is a bad way to live."

Tarja was surprised by the bitterness in his voice. "You speak from experience?"

"Oh yes," the Harshini replied with feeling.

Tarja glanced at him curiously. Brak's eyes had returned to their normal faded blue, but they were full of pain.

"I killed R'shiel's father, Tarja. In doing so, not only did I destroy a good friend and my king, I saved her mother and allowed R'shiel to be born. Trust me, I have regrets that you couldn't begin to understand."

Tarja did understand though, more than Brak realized. "If R'shiel turns to Xaphista and the other gods want you to kill her, you'll have destroyed your king for nothing."

Brak nodded. "Nobody in this world wants her to succeed more than I do, Tarja." Then he added with a sour smile, "and nobody has as much to lose if she does."

"Will she succeed?"

"I wish I knew."

chapter 61

The Crown Prince of Karien was pious, noble and dedicated, but he was not stupid. He knew the Hythrun were better horsemen, knew that they could travel much farther and faster than he could. So he broke with tradition and traveled without armor. He left his dukes behind and took only his good friend Drendyn, the Earl of Tiler's Pass, and young Jannis, the Earl of Menthall. They were the only two men in his council he knew to be loyal to *him*, rather than to his father. The remainder of his force was made up of young knights who wanted to curry favor with the heir to the throne. Jasnoff would not reign forever, nor would the elder dukes. If he succeeded, these men would form the core of his personal support when he became king.

If he failed, none of them was so important or well connected that they would be missed.

Mikel learnt of all this the night before they left in pursuit of the princess. Cratyn was reluctant to let him out of his sight, so he lay in the corner of the prince's tent pretending sleep, listening to Cratyn make his plans. The prince seemed consumed by a cold determination that would brook no interference. Their force would travel light: no armor, no lances, no lackeys, he declared. They would travel from before sunrise until after sunset. They would eat on the run and each man would lead a spare horse so that they could change mounts frequently. They would catch the Hythrun before they reached the Glass River.

Mikel admired Cratyn's determination, but a small part of him was beginning to wonder what he had done. The prince was justifiably angry with Adrina. She had betrayed him most foully, but Mikel hadn't really thought about what Cratyn would actually do when he learnt of her treachery.

He had expected him to be angry, certainly, but he didn't think the prince would decide to hunt her down personally. His own anger at Adrina's betrayal had faded somewhat. He wanted her punished, but he wasn't sure he wanted to witness her murder, and there was no question about it—that was *exactly* what Cratyn had in mind.

The journey south proved a nightmare. Mikel clung to his saddle through long days of endless hard riding, cold rations and freezing nights. Cratyn made no allowance for his age or inexperience, and worse, when they did finally stop each night, he treated Mikel as his page and expected him to unsaddle his horse and fetch and carry for him, just as if they were back in Karien. Mikel's admiration was slowly turning into burning resentment.

On their fourth day out they finally stumbled across proof that they were on the right road. While looking for a campsite for the night, one of the knights discovered a small grove of trees with the remains of several fires scattered among the bare trunks. The ashes appeared to be quite fresh. Drendyn, the most experienced hunter among them, estimated that the Hythrun were only a day and a half ahead. The news invigorated Cratyn and the next day the pace he set was even harder. But, toward the evening of their fifth day on the road, they made a discovery that changed the whole nature of their mission.

Night had fallen, but the moon was bright. Cratyn judged it safe to continue, although he did slacken the pace a little and sent two knights out to ride in the van, a precaution he did not normally bother with. Mikel rode behind him, swaying in the saddle as fatigue threatened to unseat him. They had found no further sign of the Hythrun, but Cratyn's determination was becoming an obsession. He would ride all night if he thought the horses could take it.

The sound of galloping hooves jerked Mikel fully awake. One of the knights sent to ride point was thundering toward them. Cratyn called a halt and waited for the man to reach them. Mikel leaned forward anxiously, hoping to hear what was being said. *Had they found the Hythrun?*

"Sire! Lord Terbolt approaches!"

"Terbolt?" Cratyn repeated, sounding rather puzzled. "But he is supposed to be at the Citadel. My father dispatched him there at the same time we left for the border."

"There's nearly a thousand Defenders with him, your Highness. They are camped not more than two or three leagues from here."

Cratyn nodded, but his brow was furrowed. "You saw no sign of the Hythrun?"

"No, sire."

"Then we may have ridden past them. We'll have to turn back."

"But Cratyn, what about Terbolt?" Drendyn asked. The young earl rode at Cratyn's side and was probably the only man in camp who dared address him by name. "Shouldn't we at least pay our respects?"

"I've no time to stand on protocol," Cratyn snapped impatiently.

"Perhaps, but a thousand pairs of eyes are better than two hundred."

The prince thought about it for a moment then nodded. "Very well, we shall join Lord Terbolt. And then we'll look under every rock and every blade of grass between the border and the Glass River until we unearth the traitors."

There was a time when Cratyn's words would have thrilled Mikel, but now they simply left him cold.

Cratyn and Mikel rode ahead of the troop and into the Defenders' camp amid curious looks and sullen stares. Drendyn had been left in charge with orders to wait until Cratyn returned. Mikel was disillusioned enough to realize that his place beside Cratyn was earned through distrust, not honor.

As they moved past countless small fires surrounded by red-coated troopers, Mikel wondered what the Defenders thought about surrendering to Karien. In his experience, they were proud men—proud of both their reputation and their Corps. To be under the command of a Karien Duke must be galling. He was old enough to understand that it was only their discipline that kept them in line. The Hythrun had fled and Mikel suspected that the Kariens would have behaved no better, were the situation reversed. It seemed a tragedy that the very discipline that made the Defenders famous now placed them at the mercy of their enemies.

Lord Terbolt met them in the center of the camp, a little surprised to find his prince so far from the border. Cratyn dismounted but to Mikel's relief one of Lord Terbolt's men led his horse away. Mikel jumped to the ground wearily, somewhat pleased to find his own mount being catered for in a similar manner. Cratyn waved him forward and he followed the prince into Lord Terbolt's tent, wondering if the Duke would think to feed them as well.

"I must say, I didn't expect to find you out here, your Highness," Terbolt said as he poured two cups of wine. As an afterthought, he glanced at Mikel and jerked his head in the direction of a barrel in the corner of the tent. "There's water over there. Drink if you wish."

Mikel bowed and hurried over to the barrel, dipping the ladle into the chill water gratefully as Cratyn settled into Terbolt's only comfortable chair.

"I did not expect to find you either, my Lord."

"My work was done at the Citadel. I've left Mathen overseeing things."

Cratyn frowned. "A commoner?"

"He may be a commoner, your Highness, but he's about the smartest man I've ever met. And the most ruthless. I trust him completely. I believe you'll find him eminently qualified for the position."

"And the demon child?"

"She is here. I'll have her brought to you if you wish, although if she truly is destined for great things, I can't see it in her myself. But who are we to question our God, eh?"

"Send for her."

Terbolt nodded and went to the entrance. He pushed back the tent flap and issued the order, then returned to his wine.

"You've not told me what brings you out here, your Highness."

"Adrina has been kidnaped by the Hythrun. They left the border just before Jenga surrendered."

Terbolt looked genuinely horrified. "Gods! How did they get across the border? Wasn't she guarded?"

"I believe my wife may have . . . contributed . . . to her own capture," Cratyn said cautiously. He did not want to admit to Lord Terbolt that she had run away.

The duke frowned. "I was never happy with this arrangement, Cratyn. You know that. I would far rather you had married my daughter."

"And I would much rather have married Chastity, my Lord."

"There's not much we can do about it now, I suppose," Terbolt said with a sigh.

"Not much." Cratyn sipped his wine and studied the duke over the rim of his cup. "Unless of course, something were to happen to my wife."

"Your Highness?"

"She *has* been kidnaped by the Hythrun, after all. You know what barbarians they are. They might do anything. For that matter, they may even kill her." Mikel had heard Cratyn express the same sentiment to Drendyn, but never so coldly, so calmly.

"That would be a great shame," Terbolt agreed, with the same, bland expression. If Mikel had not heard it for himself, he would not have believed the duke could agree to such a thing so easily. "Are you sure they came this way? We've seen no sign of them."

Before Cratyn could answer the tent flap was thrown open and a Defender stepped inside. He saluted sharply before speaking.

"R'shiel is not in her tent, my Lord. If you would tell me where she has been moved, I will have her brought here immediately."

"What do you mean she's not in her tent?"

"She was moved a short time ago, sir. The captain who collected her said that it was at your request. I thought perhaps—"

"I gave no such orders! Who was the captain?"

"I don't know, sir. The troopers on duty didn't recognize him."

Cratyn leapt to his feet, knocking over the chair in his haste. "It was Tarja Tenragan! I'd stake my life on it!"

"I don't see how—"

"He was with them! Don't you see? That's why we've found no sign of the Hythrun. They've been hiding, waiting for their chance to rescue the demon child. Who else could it be?"

Terbolt thought about it for less then a minute. "How long ago did they take her, Captain?"

"A quarter of an hour, perhaps, my Lord, no more."

"Then they'll still be in the camp somewhere. Rouse your men, Captain! We have intruders among us. R'shiel must not be allowed to escape. And I want Tarja Tenragan. I don't particularly care whether he's dead or alive."

The Defender saluted sharply enough, but it was clear, even to

Mikel, that he did not care for his orders. Cratyn was pacing the tent impatiently. As soon as the Medalonian had left, he turned to Terbolt.

"If Tarja is here, then Wolfblade is out there somewhere too. And that means Adrina is with them."

Terbolt nodded and reached for his sword. "Then the hunting should be good tonight. Tarja Tenragan's head will make an excellent trophy."

"You can mount it over the gates of Yarnarrow Castle," Cratyn agreed with bloodthirsty enthusiasm. "Right next to that bitch Adrina's."

chapter 62

s R'shiel's days blurred into each other, she knew they were getting closer and closer to Karien. Every day took her nearer to the decision she realized she would soon have to make. The decision that might cost her her life.

Xaphista spoke to her often, coaxing one minute, taunting the next. As they neared the border his attempts to win her over developed an edge of desperation which R'shiel found inexplicable. They were nearing the place where he was strongest. If anything, she thought he might have begun to relax.

She was led to her tent once the camp was set up, and went inside without complaint. The priests left her alone now. Even Terbolt showed no interest in her. She was simply the package that he was escorting north. He had no interest in social intercourse, even assuming that R'shiel would have responded to it.

Loneliness can destroy the soul, R'shiel.

How can I be lonely with you filling my head, day and night?

I would be a good friend, demon child. I would never allow you to be lonely.

You need to study humans a bit more, Xaphista. Promising that you'll never leave me alone is hardly a pleasant thought.

Is it pleasure you seek? I can give you more pleasure than you could possibly imagine.

You don't understand pleasure.

Then you shall teach me to understand. Tell me what you want and I will learn.

Why are you so desperate?

Why are you so stubborn?

When R'shiel refused to answer, he went away.

Later that evening, after her barely touched meal had been removed by a silent priest, she lay on her pallet and pondered her fate consciously for the first time since her capture.

Her chances of rescue were remote. Brak would have come to her already if he could. The demons were linked to her power and she could not call them without invoking the pain of the collar. Tarja was on the border, probably already in the custody of the Kariens and awaiting execution. Damin Wolfblade was either a prisoner of the Kariens himself or fleeing for Hythria. The Harshini would not bestir themselves from Sanctuary with so many Karien priests abroad and the Primal gods . . . well, if Xaphista were to be believed, it was their fault she was in this mess in the first place.

As she ran through the list of those who might come to her aid, she realized that she was truly on her own. If she was to be saved—if she *wanted* to be saved—she was going to have to do something about it herself.

The Harshini power that made her what she was lurked tantalizingly out of reach. She knew it was there; could feel it beckoning, but the pain that barred her way was stronger than any wall. The only way to access it was to get rid of the collar, and Xaphista would not allow that to happen until he was certain that she was completely and utterly his. There was no point in pretending. He was a god. He could see into her soul. If he willingly removed the collar, it would be because he knew that she was no longer a threat to him.

Escape that way was no escape at all.

Or perhaps it was. Perhaps he was right. Why should she do the bidding of the Primal gods who had been responsible for so much of her suffering? Why shouldn't she join with Xaphista? A lifetime of comfort lay down that path. As the High Priestess of the Overlord, she would know unlimited power. She could have anything she wanted. Xaphista would destroy Loclon if she asked. He could spare Tarja if she demanded it.

Anything you want.

The idea was very, very tempting.

Come to me, demon child. Now!

R'shiel did not answer immediately. Besides the weighty nature of the decision she faced, there were voices outside that sounded vaguely familiar. She sat up, straining to hear the exchange. Then the tent flap opened and Tarja stepped through.

He stared at her wordlessly for a moment. The guttering candle by the pallet only served to highlight his shock at her appearance. Her bruises had faded, and her hair had grown out enough so that at least she didn't have bald patches any more, but she knew she looked terrible. She was thin and wasted and so deep into herself that she found herself unable to return.

"R'shiel?"

Do I look so bad that he doesn't recognize me?

Turn away from him, demon child. He cannot offer you the succor that I can. Come to me now, child. Everything you ever wanted rests with me.

But Xaphista was wrong. Everything she ever wanted stood before her, with a look of shock and despair on his face.

His presence seemed to give her an anchor. She clung to it, like a climber pulling himself hand over hand up a long rope, out of a hole so deep the top was merely a speck of light in the distance.

"R'shiel? Do you know who I am?"

She nodded. It was the best she could do.

A small relieved smile flickered over his lips, then he stepped closer and gently took her hand.

"I'm taking you out of here," he explained, as if he knew how hard she was trying to comprehend. "We have to walk away like nothing's wrong."

You will never know peace if you turn from me now!

She nodded again, not capable of speaking. Tarja held open the flap and she walked forward, her footsteps taking all her concentration.

He doesn't even love you! Not really. Kalianah forced it on him. Only I can love you like you want to be loved.

R'shiel fell in with the guard brought to escort her from the tent. Tarja walked by her side. He was so tense she could feel it radiating off him like light from the sun.

You will not defeat me, demon child.

She ignored him, understanding now that her responses gave him power over her. Acknowledging his presence was only a step away from worshipping him and it was worship that gave this elevated demon his strength.

You will find that all you believe in is a lie. Then, when you come to face me, I will not be so understanding. You will suffer for this.

Then the collar started to burn.

chapter 63

drina waited in the darkness with Tamylan, holding the six horses that would take Damin, her and Tamylan, Almo-davar and the two other Raiders Damin had chosen to accompany them to freedom. The entire band would split into similar small groups and scatter in every direction. The plan was to give the Defenders so many targets that they would not know which was the one they sought. She wasn't even sure which direction they would head, but it would be opposite to the one Tarja and Brak took with R'shiel. There was no point in making things any easier for their adversaries than it already was.

They had said their goodbyes earlier and Tarja had surprised her by seeking her out. As he had always maintained a distance between them, the specter of her brother's death preventing them from ever becoming close, she found his gesture quite out of character. He had led her away a short distance from the others as they were preparing to depart.

"If we succeed, we may never meet again, your Highness."

"I respect you, Tarja, but not enough to hope we fail on the off-chance we might become friends."

"Then can a would-be friend give you some parting advice?"

"If you think it will do any good. Listening to advice isn't one of my strong suits either."

He smiled for a moment, then his expression grew serious. "Decide what you plan to do about Damin, and sooner rather than later."

"What's to decide? I know he's your friend, Tarja, but don't mistake his actions for anything noble. He doesn't want a Karien heir to my father's throne. It's really that simple."

Tarja shook his head. "Kid yourself all you want, Adrina. He's in love with you. Probably almost as much as you are with him." He held up his hand to forestall her protest. "Don't bother to deny it. The only two people in Medalon who can't see what's going on are you and Damin."

"You're imagining things!" she scoffed.

"Am I?" he asked. "In that case, it doesn't matter where you go, simply that you stay free of Cratyn. I'll go and tell Damin you've decided to come with R'shiel and me instead, shall I? That way he's free to head back to Hythria and you can—"

"No!" Her panic at his suggestion had surprised her.

He smiled. "See? It's not really that simple at all, is it?"

Adrina was not willing to concede the unthinkable. "You're jumping to conclusions, Tarja. If I go with Damin, I'll be closer to home. The gods alone know where you and R'shiel are liable to wind up."

Tarja shook his head and smiled knowingly. "Have it your way, your Highness. But don't say I didn't warn you."

He leaned forward and kissed her cheek, then led her back to the others.

Have it your way. Adrina stamped her feet against the cold and replayed the conversation in her mind. It was her own fault, she knew. These Medalonians simply didn't understand. She'd had scores of lovers . . . well, that was an exaggeration, but she'd had several. They were fun for a while and then they left. Of course, they had all been *court'esa*, and in the employ of her father, but that didn't make them any less intimate . . . well . . . maybe it did. A *court'esa*'s livelihood depended on their ability to satisfy and entertain their employer. She was the king's daughter so she had only ever been provided with the very best.

Damin was her first—her only—lover who did not need her approval or her patronage. He did not need her wealth. He did not need her position to advance himself. He could not even marry her as she was already married to someone else. On the contrary, he courted danger by courting her.

Perhaps that was the attraction for him. It certainly wasn't love. The heir to the Hythrun throne did *not* fall in love with the King of Fardohnya's eldest daughter. That, along with lovers who rode all day and made love all night, belonged in a bard's tale. It was the sort of plot one could expect to find in a badly acted tragedy by a band of traveling minstrels. It simply didn't happen in real life.

She would not allow it to happen.

One of the horses snorted irritably. Adrina patted the gelding's neck, whispering soothing nothings to him, hoping nobody could hear them. *What in the name of the gods is taking them so long?* Adrina peered into the darkness, wishing she knew how long they had been waiting. It seemed to be forever, but she was not good at judging time. Others who took care of such mundane things had always regulated her life. She glanced at Tamylan, who was standing by the other horses. The day's rest had done her good, but she was still stiff and sore. She held the reins, standing close to the horses for warmth, her whole body listening for danger.

Perhaps I should ask Tam what she thinks?

Adrina knew that if asked for, Tamylan's opinion would be as honest as it was tactless.

I should do something for her when we get home. Free her, maybe, and gift her with some property. Enough that she need never work again. She really has been a tower of strength through all of this. I wonder what I ever did to deserve such loyalty?

Not much, that Adrina could recall.

How did I ever come to this? she wondered. *I am standing here in the dead of the night, freezing to death, a bare fifty paces from a camp full of Defenders, in the middle of nowhere and the only people I can count as my friends are a slave, a man wanted for murder and an enemy warlord.*

Which brought her back to wondering about Damin.

She was determined not to believe what Tarja told her, but when they had sneaked away into the darkness Damin had slipped back to kiss her goodbye. It was, short, hard and passionate. Not the kiss of a lover, but the kiss of a daredevil stealing a moment of pleasure in the midst of danger.

He wasn't in love with anyone but himself.

All thoughts of Damin Wolfblade's failings were suddenly forgotten as a high-pitched, agonized scream split the night. The horses reared at the sound, almost jerking Adrina's arm out of its socket. She and Tamylan struggled to keep the beasts under control as all hell broke loose in the Defenders' camp.

Torches flared brightly as the camp was roused, the sound of shouting, of orders issued then countermanded, overlaid the screams that tore into Adrina's soul.

The screams were female. Whoever it was, she sounded like she was dying.

"Mount up, Tam!" she whispered urgently. When Damin and the others made it out of the camp, every second would count. The shouting grew closer and the torches were so near that she could see the flames clearly, although the fold of the land still concealed their bearers. Tam scrambled into the saddle of the nearest horse, but dropped the reins of the other two. With a curse, Adrina kicked her mount forward and leaned down to reach for the reins of the nearest beast.

"*Go!* Get out of here! Now!"

She turned toward the shout and discovered Damin, Almodavar and one of the Raiders barrelling down the small slope behind them. On their heels were so many Defenders she could not begin to count them. She froze for a moment, torn between escape and assuring herself that Damin would win free of his pursuers.

"*Run!*" Damin screamed, seeing her hesitation.

The slope was swarming with Defenders now. Torches dotted their ranks, lighting their red coats in scattered patches along the ridge like drops of hot blood. Tam gave up trying to catch the other horse and looked to her mistress desperately.

"Adrina! Let's *go!*"

She wavered for another instant. Long enough to see first Almodavar and then the Raider overcome by the Defenders. But Damin still ran free.

Turning her horse savagely, she galloped toward him. Tam's desperate cry of protest was drowned out by the shouts of the Defenders and the tortured screams that tore relentlessly through the darkness. The gap between them narrowed as the distance between Damin and the Defenders closed even faster.

The arrow, when it hit her in the shoulder, took her completely by surprise. She toppled from the saddle just as Damin reached her and that was only seconds before the Defenders overcame them both.

She had time to notice that the screams had stopped, just before she fainted.

When Adrina came to she was in a tent, which was bare of anything but the center pole supporting the roof. She realized there was another body that lay groaning softly on the other side of the tent. She rolled over and cried out in pain. Her shoulder ached abominably and her fingers came away sticky with blood when she gently probed the source of her agony.

She tried to recall what had happened, but the details were sketchy. She remembered trying to help Damin. And the screams. Gods, she would never forget the screams. Something had hit her and she had fallen. Had Damin won free? She seemed to recall seeing his face, his eyes full of anger. *Why had he been angry? Because she had tried to come to his rescue? Typical.*

And what in the name of the gods had happened to Tam? Her last sight of the slave was her desperately calling Adrina back. *Had she been captured too? Why wasn't she here?* The fate of a female slave in a Fardohnyan war camp was a foregone conclusion, but the Defenders were better disciplined. The Sisterhood who ruled them would not countenance such behavior. Tamylan's absence meant she had escaped—or she was dead. Adrina prayed it was the former. She feared it was the latter.

The body groaned again and Adrina stopped thinking of her own troubles long enough to wonder who it was. She sat up carefully and moved across the small gap separating them on her knees. Her companion was a young woman with short-cropped red hair wearing dark, close-fitting leathers and a silver collar smeared with dried blood.

"*R'shiel?*"

It couldn't really be anyone else, but she was hardly what Adrina had envisioned. The girl was younger than she expected, and in her present condition she was far from the matchless beauty Damin had described.

What did one say to the fabled Harshini demon child?

"I'm Adrina," she said, unable to think of anything else.

R'shiel stared at her uncomprehendingly.

"We have a mutual friend," she added inanely. "Tarja Tenragan."

I sound like Lady Chastity.

The demon child blinked at the mention of Tarja's name, but that was the only reaction Adrina could get from her.

"R'shiel?"

She shook her shoulder, gently at first, and then quite roughly when that had no effect. Although R'shiel's eyes were open, there was no light of comprehension in them. Adrina shrugged and immediately regretted it. Her shoulder was pounding and there was no point speaking to someone who was so obviously not listening. Brak had said something about that. Something about R'shiel retreating so far into herself that she was almost comatose.

"Well, I hope you don't stay away for too much longer," she told R'shiel irritably. "Right now the only thing that's going to save either of us is a bloody miracle, so if you don't mind, get over whatever it is that's upsetting you girl, and come to your senses. There are people here who need you."

Her reprimand delivered, Adrina sat back on her heels and waited for them to come for her.

chapter 64

here are people here who need you.

The words filtered down through R'shiel's pain. She did not know who had voiced them, but they echoed through the emptiness like a reproach.

I warned you, demon child. If you will not come to me through love, you will come to me through fear. The end result is the same.

The memory of the pain was too fresh for R'shiel to deny Xaphista's claim. But if she could not face him, she could run from him.

There are people here who need you.

R'shiel clung to the thought, clawing her way back to sanity with every scrap of her remaining strength.

She blinked suddenly and looked around. Canvas walls surrounded her and the ground where she lay was cold and hard. She turned her head, ignoring the pain the movement caused as the square of bright light intruded. It was blocked a moment later by the figure of a man stepping through, followed by several others. They were Defenders, but that meant nothing. The Defenders were her enemies now.

Someone pulled her to her feet, along with another prisoner. R'shiel did not have time to wonder who she was before they were both hustled out of the tent and led through the camp to Lord Terbolt's tent.

Waiting inside was Lord Terbolt, a young man with brown hair and angry eyes, and in the corner, the young Karien boy who had been a prisoner in the Defenders' camp. She could not imagine how he came to be here.

"Your Highness," Terbolt said with a short bow.

R'shiel was a little surprised to hear her fellow prisoner being addressed so formally. It hurt too much to move her head so she tried to study her out of the corner of her eye.

She was shorter than R'shiel, but even her rough clothing and her dishevelled appearance could not conceal her innate beauty. She was foreign; her skin was dusky and her hair much darker than R'shiel's, and she had startling green eyes. Perhaps she was Fardohnyan. She certainly wasn't from Medalon and Karien never produced such exotic looks.

"And this is supposed to be the demon child?" the young man asked skeptically. "She doesn't look like much, does she?"

"I recall thinking the same thing when I met you, Cretin," the woman snapped with a surprising amount of venom.

The young man leapt to his feet angrily. "You will only speak when spoken to, whore!"

R'shiel fought to stay conscious, the argument between the angry young Karien and the beautiful Fardohnyan woman giving her something to focus on. She didn't know either of them, but their conflict kept the nothingness at bay. It kept away Xaphista's persistent attempts to coax her back down into the hole. If she went back now, she would never escape. She knew that with a certainty.

"Don't you dare speak to me in such a tone!" the Fardohnyan declared. "When my father hears about this—"

"When he hears about what, Adrina? Your treachery or your Hythrun lover?"

Adrina. Damin's floozy in the see-through dress. Hysterical laughter bubbled up inside her but she fought it down. The sobering process was helped considerably by the realization that this young man was probably Prince Cratyn. And the Hythrun lover? Even in her semi-conscious state, R'shiel could easily guess who that was.

"What lover?" Adrina scoffed. "Is this some pathetic story you've invented to provide an excuse to have me stoned? No one will believe you, Cretin. I am a loyal and dutiful wife. It is you who could never get the job done."

Cratyn smiled coldly. "I have a witness, Adrina."

R'shiel's eyes fixed on the Karien boy, who looked as if he would rather be any place but in this tent. He was so guilty he was trembling with it.

Adrina glanced at the boy also, then laughed. "*Mikel* is your witness? A boy who's spent as much time with the enemy as he has with you? He's not even a disciple of the Overlord. He follows Dacendaran, the God of Thieves, and I have *that* from the god himself."

"There are no other gods," Cratyn retorted.

Good, then you don't need me, R'shiel said to herself.

Terbolt turned to the boy who cowered under his gaze.

"Is this true, boy? Do you follow a false god?"

"No!" he cried. "I follow the Overlord."

"That's not what Dace says," Adrina said smugly.

"Dace?" The boy looked utterly confused. "But he's just a thief."

"Then you do know him?" Terbolt asked.

"Well, yes, but—"

Cratyn grabbed the boy and shook him savagely. "Is this true? You are an agent of the God of Thieves?"

"Pick on someone your own size, Cretin."

He threw the boy down and turned on the princess, slapping her with a vicious backhanded blow. "Shut up!"

Adrina stumbled backward but when she looked back at him, once she regained her balance and wiped the blood from the corner of her mouth, her eyes were full of defiance.

"It's not going to work, is it, Cretin. What was your plan? Hunt me down and kill me and claim the Hythrun did it? Only the Defenders found me first, so you had to fall back on your other plan, didn't you? Accuse me of adultery and have me stoned. But your star witness can't testify for you, can he? He isn't just a disciple of Dacendaran, he counts him as a friend! Now what are you going to do?" Cratyn hit her again. Adrina staggered backwards, then turned on R'shiel. "Hey! Demon child! If you're thinking of doing anything useful, now would be a pretty good time!"

Cratyn struck her again. His anger had slipped beyond reason.

"Leave the princess alone!" Mikel cried in protest but Lord Terbolt held him back.

Come to me, R'shiel. Through love or fear, the end result is the same.

The boy struggled against Terbolt as Adrina launched herself at Cratyn. She hit him with a clenched fist, almost knocking him off his feet. Princess she might be, but she fought like an alley cat, although she cried out as fresh blood seeped from the wound in her shoulder. But neither the pain nor the fact that Cratyn was bigger and stronger than she was seemed to deter her.

Cratyn managed to push Adrina off him and draw his sword. At the sight of the blade, Adrina knew she was done for, R'shiel could tell by the look in her eyes. Mikel was sobbing as he realized what Cratyn intended.

But not Adrina. She was defiant to the last.

"Go on, Cretin. Kill me. But before you do, I want you to know that I *did* take a lover. And do you know what? It was *wonderful*! He was strong and passionate and I made love to him every chance I could, anywhere I could. But the best part . . . the *best* part . . . was that he made me forget you and your evil, insidious Overlord."

Your evil, insidious Overlord.

Cratyn raised his sword at the same time that R'shiel reached into her boot and drew the small dagger that Garet Warner had given her. Her aim was unerring. It took Cratyn in the chest with a solid thunk.

The young prince looked down in astonishment at the blade that was buried up to the hilt in his tabard, before his eyes rolled back in his head and he dropped to the floor.

Adrina stared at R'shiel for a moment then smiled. "I'll give you one thing, demon child, your timing is impeccable."

She had no chance to reply. Terbolt threw the boy aside and opened his mouth to call the guards. R'shiel's eyes darkened as she drew on her power. The burning seared through her but she ignored it.

She understood now. The collar worked on fear as much as pain. Xaphista had told her that himself. *Come to me, R'shiel. Through love or fear, the end result is the same.* Fear, not pain. It was her fear of the pain the blocked her power, not the pain itself. If Adrina could stand fearlessly in the face of death, R'shiel could cope with a little burning agony.

She raised her arm and pointed at Terbolt. The duke dropped to the ground before he could utter a word, dead or unconscious—even R'shiel didn't know for certain. She turned her attention inward then and focused on the collar. It disintegrated with a thought, falling away from her neck like sparkles thrown at a children's party. With it went the pain. In the back of her mind she caught the echo of an anguished cry. Xaphista realizing she was lost to him.

For the first time in weeks, R'shiel felt whole again. The power coursing through her eased her pain and healed the burns. The feeling was the closest thing to pure ecstasy she had ever experienced.

R'shiel turned her black eyes on Adrina. She liked this fearless Fardohnyan princess. She reached out and touched her shoulder, felt the muscle and skin knit beneath her hand.

Adrina stared in wonder for a moment, flexing her healed shoulder, then she frowned at R'shiel. "Thank you. Now, are you just going to stand there looking majestic, or are we going to help the others?"

"Where are they?"

"How should I know? Mikel!"

The boy edged his way past the bodies of Lord Terbolt and Prince Cratyn. Adrina caught his sleeve as he neared the entrance and pulled him to her, squatting down so that she was eye to eye with the terrified child.

"Do you know where they're holding the others, Mikel?"

He nodded dumbly.

"Good. Then we shall go and rescue them. You needn't be afraid. R'shiel is Harshini and she'll protect us with her magic." The boy began to cry. Adrina rolled her eyes, but she put her arms around him and hugged him gently. "There, there, Mikel. Don't let it upset you."

"But I've betrayed the Overlord. And my prince."

"Yes, well, I wouldn't lose too much sleep over that, child. You have Dacendaran to pray to now and Cratyn isn't worth crying over. Now, are you going to help us or not?"

Mikel wiped his eyes and nodded.

"Good boy. Shall we go then?" She looked up at R'shiel questioningly.

"This could get messy," she warned. "The priests can feel me now and I'm really not very good at this."

Adrina looked around the tent and shrugged. "You seem to be doing just fine to me."

They stepped out of the tent and into chaos. The priests rushed toward Terbolt's tent clutching their magic-killing staffs, shouting conflicting orders to the Defenders. As R'shiel emerged into the sunlight with Adrina and Mikel, the priests halted their headlong rush. They stood before her cautiously, their lips moving silently as they prayed to their god.

Garanus stepped forward, holding his staff before him. The Defenders, for whom religion was a quaint foreign custom, stood back to give him room. They were curious, not alarmed. Two women and a child hardly warranted their attention and they had no idea what lay inside the Karien lord's tent. The priests' antics were more entertaining than threatening and they were reluctant allies at best.

"I call on the Overlord to strike you down, demon child!" Garanus chanted as he approached. He knew she was drawing on her power; his staff would have warned him, even if her eyes did not. "I call on Xaphista to vanquish your evil!"

"*Vanquish?*" Adrina muttered behind her. "Where do they come up with this nonsense? Do something about him, R'shiel. We haven't got time for this."

Brave she might be, but Adrina certainly wasn't blessed with patience in any great quantity.

Garanus was chanting loudly, in unison with the other priests. Her skin tingled as the magic they tried to raise washed over her. It was stronger than it should have been. Xaphista was lending them a hand.

Without warning a bolt of bright light exploded from the tip of Garanus's staff. R'shiel raised her arm and deflected the bolt with a thought. It landed with a crash amidst the tents a few paces away, sending Defenders scurrying for safety. Another bolt followed it and then another. Xaphista wanted to destroy her. There was no question about that now. She had chosen sides and in His mind, chosen the wrong one.

I am the demon child, she told herself, and Xaphista has only a smattering of believers here. *This battle, at least, I can win.*

R'shiel deflected another blinding bolt of lightning and then pointed at the staff Garanus carried. It exploded in a burst of shattered gems, sending the few Defenders left standing diving for cover. The staffs of the other three priests behind him exploded almost immediately after.

She looked past them and discovered Brak, his eyes as black as hers, standing behind the priests. He nodded as she caught his eye, but made no move to aid her. R'shiel smiled briefly, then focused her disconcerting eyes on the Kariens.

"If you leave now, I will let you live. If you choose to stay, you will meet Xaphista a lot sooner than you expected."

To his credit, Garanus hesitated. Without his staff he had no more power than any other mortal. He debated the issue for a moment or two then glanced over his shoulder at Brak. He might be brave enough to tackle one simple girl, but two Harshini filled with a power he was helpless to combat, were enough to sway him. He conceded defeat with ill grace.

"This is a temporary victory only, demon child. You cannot defeat the Overlord."

"We'll find that out some other day. Now go, before I change my mind."

The priests fled as the Defenders emerged from their cover. Their faces ranged from confused to completely stunned. Others hurried to put out the scattered fires that she had started as she deflected the lightning. For weeks they had ridden under the command of Terbolt and his priests. R'shiel's dismissal of them left them speechless. Brak walked toward her and treated her to a rare smile of approval.

"Where have you been?"

"I could ask you the same thing," he replied.

Not all the Defenders were at a loss for words, however. A captain stepped forward, blocking their path, his sword drawn. R'shiel recognized him as Denjon, one of Tarja's classmates when they were cadets.

"Where is Lord Terbolt, R'shiel?"

"In the tent with Cratyn," Adrina answered for her, rather more cheerfully than the situation warranted. "You might want to take command now, Captain. Lord Terbolt is indisposed and it seems I'm a widow."

The captain stared at them for a moment, then allowed himself a thin smile. "That's tragic news, your Highness. You have my condolences."

"Thank you, Captain, but don't worry, I'm sure I'll be able to deal with my grief."

"Where are Tarja and the others, Denjon?"

"The Hythrun and the Defenders who tried to free you are being held down near the picket line. Tarja's in the Infirmary tent."

R'shiel's heart skipped a beat. "Where? What happened?"

"What do you think happened, R'shiel? He doesn't believe in giving in gracefully. He took a sword in the belly trying to get you out of here."

There was a reprimand in his words that startled R'shiel. "You sound as if you think this is all my fault."

"Isn't it?" Denjon asked. He met her alien eyes for a moment then looked away. "Sergeant! Find Captain Dorak and tell him to go to Lord Terbolt's tent. And then go down to the picket line and. . . . who's in charge of the Hythrun?"

"Lord Wolfblade," Adrina told him.

"*The* Lord Wolfblade?" He had obviously not been aware of the importance of his prisoner. Adrina nodded, rather amused by his expression. Denjon turned back to the sergeant. "Bring Lord Wolfblade to me. And do it tactfully, Sergeant. The last I heard he was supposed to be on our side."

"Sir!" The man saluted and turned to go, but Denjon called him back before he had taken more than two steps.

"Send someone to fetch Captain Kilton and Captain Linst, too. I'll be in the Infirmary."

The sergeant left to carry out his orders and Denjon turned back to R'shiel.

"I have to warn you, he's in a bad way."

"Just take me to him, Denjon."

"As you wish."

The captain turned and led the way through the camp followed by R'shiel, Brak, Adrina, Mikel and the curious eyes of a thousand Defenders who sensed that something very significant had just occurred.

Just how significant it was would not be known until the officers had decided what to do now that they were effectively free of Karien control. They had two choices, R'shiel knew: obey their orders and continue on to the border, or defy them and choose a much more dangerous path.

She was certain the latter was what they wanted to do, but she was not at all certain that they would act on it. The Defenders took their duty very seriously. Of all the men she knew in the corps, only Tarja and Jenga had ever had the strength to defy their oath when faced with something they found they could not stomach.

As Denjon pushed back the flap to the large Infirmary tent and the sickening smell of blood and death washed over her, she could only hope that Tarja's brother captains, when it came to the crunch, were made of the same stuff.

chapter 65

The first thing that R'shiel noticed in the long tent was the absence of any physics. With an occupation almost entirely restricted to Sisters of the Blade, it did not seem possible that the Defenders would undertake such a journey without some of them in attendance. When she questioned Denjon about them, he shrugged.

"It was Lord Terbolt's decision. There are no sisters in the camp at all. I don't think he trusts them. Besides," he added. "We were simply escorting him to the border. We weren't expecting any trouble."

"Why would Terbolt want a thousand-man escort? That seems a bit excessive, even for a Karien."

"Because when the Fardohnyans cross the southern border, the Defenders will send for reinforcements," Damin remarked, pushing through the tent flap behind them. "If the troops are in the north, even if the Sisterhood wanted to, they couldn't send help. What the Kariens don't know is that Hablet is playing his own game. He's not coming to help the Kariens, he's heading for Hythria."

Adrina spun around at the sound of his voice and flew at him. Damin caught her in a brief hug, then held her at arm's length. "Are you alright?"

"I'm fine. R'shiel came through in the nick of time."

At the mention of her name, he looked up, unable to hide his shock. With her hair cut close and her eyes black with the power she refused to relinquish, she must look nothing like the girl he remembered.

"Where's Tarja?" he asked.

The sergeant must have told him what was happening, or what little he knew, at any rate.

R'shiel glanced at Denjon, who pointed to the narrow pallet at the far end of the tent. Only a few of the beds were occupied, and the men in them all looked seriously injured. The Defenders had a fairly generous definition of "walking wounded." If a man could stand, he wasn't sick enough to be confined to bed. These men were simply the worst of the night's casualties. There would be many more out in the camp suffering the effects of Tarja's abortive rescue attempt.

Afraid of what she would find, she pushed past Denjon and the medic in attendance and approached him cautiously. Her throat constricted as she neared him. He was paler than death and barely breathing.

"If you've anything important to say to him, make it quick," the medic suggested with cold practicality. "He's going fast. Lost so much blood it's a wonder he's still got anything for his heart to do."

R'shiel stared at the man in horror, then sought Brak out among those crowded into the tent. He had released his hold on the power and his faded eyes were clouded with doubt.

He knew what she wanted. She did not have to ask.

"I don't know, R'shiel."

Adrina still clung to Damin but she looked at them both with wide eyes, confused by their doubt.

"What do you mean, you don't know? You're Harshini. You can heal him, can't you? R'shiel fixed me up with just a touch."

R'shiel knelt beside the bed and placed her hand on Tarja's forehead. His skin was cold and clammy. He was deeply unconscious, a step away from death and heading in the wrong direction. The power seemed to both sharpen and deaden her senses at the same time. She could feel the life slipping away from him, but she was insulated from the grief somehow. Perhaps it would hit her later, once she let the power go.

"Get out," she ordered softly. When no one seemed inclined to heed her, she looked up, her eyes blazing. "Out! All of you!"

Startled by her tone, they did not argue. As they filed from the tent, she turned back to Tarja, wishing she knew where to start. Healing Adrina's fresh, uncomplicated arrow wound was one thing. Bringing someone back from the brink of death was quite another.

R'shiel waited until she knew she was alone, except for the one person she was certain would not leave her while she was drawing on this much power. She didn't know if it was loyalty or distrust that kept him there. Nor did she care.

"I can't do this, Brak. I don't know enough about healing."

"I'll not be much help to you, R'shiel. Like yours, my talent lies in the other direction."

She looked up sharply, wondering how he could be so callous.

"I have to try."

"Have you considered the possibility that this was meant to be?"

"What do you mean?" He could not meet her eye. "Brak! What do you mean?"

"Death decides when one's time is up, R'shiel, not you, or me, or anyone else for that matter."

"You're telling me Tarja's time is up?"

"I'm telling you Death doesn't negotiate."

She pushed the hair from Tarja's forehead gently. "What if I speak to Death? Can't I ask him not to take Tarja?"

"Not without offering a life of equal value in return."

"How do you know that?"

"Because that's what happened when the Harshini healed you, R'shiel. Death demanded a life in return."

"Whose life? Who could make that kind of decision?"

When he did not answer she looked up, her face drained of color. "It was you, wasn't it?" R'shiel looked down at Tarja for a moment then slowly climbed to her feet. "Was it Tarja, Brak? Is that why you want me to let him die? So you can fulfil your bargain with death?"

"R'shiel—"

"Tell me, Brak!" she cried, turning on him angrily. "Who is going to die? Whose life did you trade for mine? You bastard! How could you do such a thing?"

"I couldn't let you die, R'shiel."

"You think I want to live knowing some poor sod carries a death sentence so I can keep breathing? Who, Brak? Who did you condemn to death? It was Tarja, wasn't it? Tarja has to die, so I can live. A soul of equal value, you said . . ."

Brak grabbed her by the shoulders and shook her. Hard. She stopped her tirade and threw her arms around him, sobbing.

"It wasn't Tarja," he told her gently as he held her.

She pulled away from him and wiped her eyes. "Who was it, Brak?"

"You don't need to know."

"Yes I do."

"No, you don't. And I'm not going to tell you, at any rate. See to Tarja. Perhaps he's destined to die, perhaps he isn't. I don't know."

"I don't believe in destiny."

"Which accounts for most of the trouble you've found yourself in lately." He led her back to the pallet and knelt beside her, studying Tarja's unconscious form with a much more experienced eye. "He's close to death, R'shiel. Even Cheltaran would find it hard to bring him back."

"I have the power to flatten mountains, Brak, you said that yourself. If you could just show me . . ." She stroked Tarja's clammy forehead, her desperation almost severing her hold on the power. "Can't you do what Glenanaran did for me? Stop time?"

"And hold him on the edge of death to what purpose, R'shiel? The problem isn't the wound, it's the blood he's lost. You can knit bones and flesh easily enough, but not even the gods can manufacture blood out of thin air."

"But I can feel him dying!"

"I know."

"Then tell me what to do!" she cried. "Should I call Cheltaran? He's the God of Healing. He should—"

"He won't come, R'shiel," Dacendaran told her miserably, as he appeared at the foot of the bed. "Zegarnald won't let him."

Anger surged through R'shiel, its edge honed by the power she held. *How dare Zegarnald deny Tarja his only chance at life?* "What do you mean? He won't *let* him come?"

The young god shrugged uncomfortably. "He said something about you taking the easy way too often."

"You mean Tarja is dying as some sort of *test?*" she gasped furiously. "What sort of sick breed are you, Dace? That's inhuman!"

"*Now* you finally begin to understand," Brak said.

Dace tugged on a loose thread on his motley shirt, avoiding R'shiel's accusing eyes. "It's not my fault. I'm not even supposed to be here. But Kali likes Tarja, so she's keeping Zegarnald busy."

"What did Kalianah say, Dace?"

R'shiel looked at Brak, wondering at the question.

"She said to tell R'shiel that love will prevail."

"Oh, well that's a big help," R'shiel scoffed.

"Don't be like that. I'm just the messenger. She said to tell you that you have guardians that protect you and that protection will embrace all who love you truly. That's why she did what she did, I think. She knows things sometimes . . ." Dace trailed off with a sigh. "I'm sorry, R'shiel. I have to go. I wish you'd been a thief. I could have helped you a lot more."

R'shiel felt the god leave, but she was too concerned about Tarja to care much. She was terrified that he would slip away before she could intervene, and afraid of what would happen if she did. Living without him would be hard enough; contributing to his death would be intolerable.

"You should never ignore a message from the gods, R'shiel," Brak warned. "Particularly one as powerful as Kalianah."

"*Love will prevail*," she repeated caustically, in a fair imitation of Dace.

"She also said you have guardians that protect you, and that protection will embrace all who love you truly."

"What guardians?"

Brak did not answer. He merely waited for the answer to come to her. When it did, she could have cried, but whether from anger at her own stupidity, or sheer relief, she could not tell.

"The demons!"

She had barely framed the thought when Dranymire popped into existence at the foot of the bed. His appearance was followed by a high-pitched squeal, as the little demon who had grown so fond of sleeping in their bed scrambled thoughtlessly across Tarja and jumped into her arms. The little demon appeared to have recovered from her ordeal in the Citadel. R'shiel hugged the creature and turned to Dranymire.

"We were wondering when you would remember us," the demon said in his unnaturally deep voice.

"I'm sorry, Dranymire. But after the Gathering . . . so much has happened . . ."

The demon shrugged. "You have nothing to apologize for, except perhaps for not thinking of us sooner. What grieves you, demon child?"

"Can you show me how to heal Tarja?"

"Did you learn nothing at Sanctuary?"

"But he's lost so much blood!"

"Don't human bodies make their own blood?" Dranymire asked curiously. "They certainly spill enough of it to make one think it was readily replaced."

"He'll die before his body can replace what he's lost," Brak explained.

"Then you need blood to keep him alive, long enough for his own body to repair itself." He looked at R'shiel with his too-big eyes. They were filled with compassion. "This human's death would cause you much pain, I suspect."

"More than anything I have ever suffered."

Dranymire nodded solemnly. "We could do nothing to protect you from pain the gods imposed on you, but we can do something to prevent this."

"What can you do? I don't understand."

"We shall be his blood."

"*What?*" R'shiel began to wonder if she had slipped back into the realms of her living nightmare.

"We shall meld and become the blood that he requires."

"You can *do* that?" She looked at Brak for confirmation. The idea was too bizarre to comprehend.

Brak nodded. "Wounded Harshini have been saved by their bonded demons entering their bodies until they could reach help. It's not unheard of."

"It is, where *I* come from."

He smiled faintly. "You still have so much to learn, don't you?"

"Will this really work?"

Brak glanced at Dranymire, who shrugged. "Humans and Harshini are not so different."

"Then let's do it," she announced, reaching for the thin blanket that covered Tarja.

Brak laid a restraining hand on hers. "A word of caution, R'shiel. This will mean that until he's recovered enough to survive on his own, Tarja will be literally possessed by demons. Not even Dranymire knows what that will do to him if he survives. Are you prepared for that?"

She thought for a moment before replying.

"One problem at a time. I'll deal with the consequences later."

He shook his head. "Just so long as you understand that you could be making a big mistake."

R'shiel did not reply. Rather she pulled the blanket down, revealing the blood-soaked bandages that bound Tarja's midriff.

"I mean it, R'shiel."

She looked up at him and shrugged. "I don't make mistakes, Brak. Everything I've ever done in my life seemed like the right idea at the time."

chapter 66

enjon led Adrina and the others away from the Infirmary tent, obviously glad to be gone from such blatant proof of the continuing existence of the Harshini. R'shiel had obviously been acquainted with the captain and he seemed to know Tarja quite well, too. It was more than likely the reason he had not struck them down when they emerged from Terbolt's tent. On the other hand, if Jenga's reaction had been anything to go by, surrender was an alien concept to these men. Perhaps R'shiel had merely provided them with the excuse their training and their oath denied them.

Whatever the reason for their cautious cooperation, three other captains awaited them outside Terbolt's tent. Denjon introduced them as Dorak, Kilton, and Linst. The men all wore that same serious, wary expression that she had come to associate with the Defenders. Between that and their identical uniforms, she found it hard to tell them apart.

"The Karien Prince is dead," Dorak told Denjon, casting a wary eye over Adrina and Damin as they approached. "He was stabbed. Terbolt's dead too, although there's not a mark on him. It could have been poison."

"It wasn't poison," Denjon replied. "Are they still in there?"

Dorak nodded.

"Let's talk in the mess tent. I'd rather this wasn't overheard." He glanced at Mikel meaningfully.

The child followed Adrina like a faithful shadow, afraid to let her out of his sight.

"Mikel, why don't you go down and join Captain Almodavar and the others. I'm sure he'll look after you until we finish here."

"Am I a prisoner now?"

"No. Just go down and tell him everything will be sorted out soon," Damin added, with surprising gentleness. "Your brother's down there somewhere too. I'm sure he'll be happy to see you."

He nodded doubtfully. "Is he all right?"

"Why don't you go and find out?"

With one last cautious look, the boy turned and ran toward the picket lines.

The captains led the way to another long tent. The only difference between this one and the infirmary was the interior. The mess tent was lined with collapsible tables and benches rather than beds. The smell was marginally better, too. Once inside, Denjon dismissed the cooks and waited until he was certain they were gone before he turned to the others.

"We have a decision to make, gentlemen."

"Then perhaps you'd like to tell us what's going on?" one of the captains said. It was Linst or the other one. Adrina really couldn't remember which one was which.

"I would if I knew. Perhaps you could enlighten us, your Highness?"

After so long among the Kariens, who considered the input of a woman no input at all, Adrina wasn't really expecting to be included in the conversation. But these men served the Sisterhood. They suffered no illusions about the ability of women. She glanced at Damin, who squeezed her hand in encouragement.

"I want to know what happened to my slave, first."

"What slave?" Denjon asked.

"The young woman who was with me when we were captured."

The captains glanced at each other and shrugged. "There were no other women captured, your Highness. She probably escaped in the confusion."

"Could you send some men out to find her, Captain? She's alone in a foreign country and not equipped to survive on her wits. Not in the wilderness, at least." Denjon nodded to Linst, who left the tent to issue the order. That worrying detail taken care of, Adrina felt a lot more secure about her future among these men. "Thank you. Now what did you want to know?"

"Let's start with what you're doing here," Denjon suggested.

"I fled Karien. The Defenders offered me their protection and when the order for the surrender came from the Citadel, I decided to leave, rather than return to my husband. Lord Wolfblade kindly offered to escort me."

"Did you kill Cratyn?" Kilton asked curiously.

"No. R'shiel did."

"No offense, ma'am, but I can't say I'm sorry. He was an obnoxious little bastard."

Adrina immediately warmed to the captain. Cratyn must have made quite an impact in the short time he was in the Defender's camp.

"No need to apologize, Captain. You merely demonstrate that you are an excellent judge of character."

"Where are the rest of the Hythrun?" Denjon asked Damin, anxious to stick to the business at hand, although he did allow himself a small smile at Adrina's comment. None of these men seemed the least bit bothered by Cratyn's demise. "Rumors in the Citadel had it that you had near a thousand men on the border."

"I don't share the Lord Defender's enthusiasm for following orders, Captain. The bulk of my men left as soon as I realized Jenga intended to surrender. We were the last to leave."

"And Tarja?"

Damin smiled at the Captain's expression. "He was following Jenga's orders. I believe the plan was to make life as difficult as possible for your new masters. The Defenders he took with him were all he thought he could sneak out without the Kariens noticing."

Denjon nodded, looking rather relieved. "Following the Lord Defender's orders, you say? Well that makes our decision somewhat easier."

"Making life difficult for the Kariens does seem a rather noble cause," Kilton agreed with a grin.

Linst returned from arranging Tamylan's rescue party and looked at his brother captains with a shake of his head. "You can't seriously be considering joining him?"

"I doubt Tarja will live long enough to join anything," Dorak added. "But if the Lord Defender ordered him to undertake a special mission, aren't we duty-bound to pick up where he left off?"

"There's a thousand men in this camp! How many of them do you think will want to follow you on such a damned fool mission?"

"Most of them, I imagine," Kilton shrugged. "Bring me one man in the camp, from the lowliest kitchenhand to the highest ranked officer, who was pleased to be marching anywhere under Karien command."

Linst nodded in agreement, albeit reluctantly. "Aye. But if we follow the Lord Defender's orders, aren't we disobeying the Sisterhood?"

"Ah, but there are no Sisters of the Blade here. In the absence of orders to the contrary, we have no choice but to follow the orders of the Lord Defender."

Adrina smiled at Kilton's rather liberal interpretation of the law.

"That seems fairly cut and dried," Denjon agreed. "And what about you, Lord Wolfblade? Are you still allied with Medalon?"

"You're holding my men prisoner, Captain."

"Then you should consider your answer most carefully, my Lord."

Damin smiled faintly. "Much as I hate to turn down a good fight, I'm afraid I must return to Hythria. The Fardohnyans will be standing at my border come spring. I plan to discourage them from crossing."

"Pity," Kilton sighed. "Your Raiders are quite good in a fight."

Judging by the surprised look on Damin's face, such an admission was high praise indeed.

"You and your men are free to go, Lord Wolfblade. If you stay clear of the Citadel, you should be able to make it home by spring," Denjon told him. "You were right when you said the bulk of our forces are in the north. By the way, I heard that the Warlord of Elasapine withdrew from Bordertown as soon as he heard of the surrender."

"Narvell's no better at following orders than I am," Damin said. "It's a pity, though. He'll be too far into Hythria to call him back, by the time I get there."

"Then we have to stop my father attacking Hythria," Adrina said.

"How?"

"By offering him an alliance."

"He's already allied with Karien."

"The alliance was dependent on my marriage to Cratyn. As that is no longer the case, the treaty can reasonably be assumed to be null and void."

If Kilton could twist the law to suit the outcome he desired, there was no reason Adrina couldn't do the same thing.

"I doubt if Hablet will see things quite so clearly," Damin warned.

"Then we'll have to make him see."

"Marry her, Damin, then he won't have a choice." The demon child's unexpected entrance gave Adrina a chance to recover from the shock of her suggestion. R'shiel had finally shed the power she had used to destroy Terbolt and intimidate the Karien priests, and her eyes had returned to normal. They were an unusual shade of violet, wide set and clear. She was very tall—almost as tall as Damin—and she carried herself with an unconscious aura of power. The comatose, uncertain child who had been led into Terbolt's tent had emerged a woman, sure of her power and certain of her purpose.

"Is Tarja . . . ?" Denjon ventured cautiously.

"Dead? No. He'll live. Brak is with him. He's not to be moved, nor is anyone to approach him until I say so. Is that clear?"

Denjon and the others nodded their agreement. Adrina doubted anyone would deny her when she used that tone. She then turned to Damin and smiled. It was obvious R'shiel was fond of the Warlord and the thought sent an unexpected spear of jealousy through her.

"I wasn't kidding, Damin. If you marry Adrina, and Hablet still wants to attack Hythria, he'll have to go over the Sunrise Mountains. Fardohnyan law demands a peace treaty between both Houses in the marriage. It may not keep him out of the rest of Hythria, but at least he won't be able to take the easy road. He'll be unable to set foot in Krakandar Province until he figures a way around the marriage contract."

Damin nodded thoughtfully. He seemed to accept the suggestion with remarkable composure. "It would delay him, I suppose, assuming I was willing to go along with such a ludicrous plan. But he could just as easily deny the marriage had taken place and carry on regardless."

"I'll have Jelanna perform the ceremony herself, if that's what it takes."

Adrina gasped. Somehow the idea that this girl could command the Goddess of Fertility, the goddess her father worshipped with almost fanatical intensity, was more terrifying than anything else she had done this morning.

But things were moving a bit too fast and R'shiel had not even asked her what she thought about this rather hasty decision.

"Do *I* get a say in this?"

"Why?" R'shiel asked. "were you planning to object?"

"That's not the point. But as a matter of fact, I was planning to object. I've had all the arranged marriages I want, thank you. Besides, I've been a widow for just over an hour. It's indecent."

"Don't be such a hypocrite," R'shiel said bluntly. "You've been sleeping with Damin for ages and he obviously loves you, or he would never have been so stupid as to try to keep you from returning to Karien."

Adrina felt herself blushing, something she had not done since she was sixteen and was introduced to her first *court'esa*. She glanced at Damin, who actually looked embarrassed. The captains were fighting to maintain straight faces.

R'shiel did not seem to notice, or care, about their feelings.

"Denjon, if you truly mean to undermine the Karien occupation of Medalon, then the first useful thing you can do is give me a few experienced men and enough supplies to reach the Citadel."

"I'd have thought the Citadel was the last place you'd want to go."

"There is something that I have to take care of. Or rather, someone. I had it pointed out to me very recently that I take the easy way out, too often. That's about to change."

"I'll see to it," Denjon agreed. "Unless you want to wait until Tarja . . ."

"No. This can't wait and I've done all I can for him. Brak will watch over him until he regains consciousness. In the meantime, you'd better do something about those priests I let loose. You don't want them reaching the border and warning the Kariens about what's happened here."

"There's the rest of Cratyn's troop out there, too," Damin reminded them. "You'd be well advised to do something about them before the day is out."

"We can take care of a few hundred Kariens," Denjon assured him.

"As for you two," R'shiel said, turning on Damin and Adrina. "Get one of the captains to marry you; they can perform the ceremony at a pinch under Medalonian law. Once Tarja has recovered, Brak can go to Talabar to deliver the news to King Hablet. If one of the fabled Harshini walking his palace halls doesn't convince him, nothing will."

Damin was no more able to argue with her than Adrina was. This was not R'shiel speaking, this was the demon child finally come into her power. She had no intention of marrying Damin Wolfblade and was quite sure he did not want to marry her; but she would wait until R'shiel left for the Citadel before she announced it. Adrina was not foolish enough to defy R'shiel in her current mood.

"There's a vineyard just south of Testra, that we used as a headquarters during the rebellion," she continued, addressing the captains once more. "My guess is that Tarja sent his troops there. You'll need to get a message to them. Once I've taken care of what I have to do at the Citadel, I'll join you."

"And then what, R'shiel?" Damin asked cautiously.

She hesitated for a moment, as if some weighty decision hung in the balance.

"And then I'm going to put a stop to this insanity, Damin. I am going to kick the Kariens out of Medalon and make damned sure they never stick their noses over our border again."

"I don't know how you think you can manage that," Dorak scoffed.

"It's quite simple, Captain," the demon child replied. "I am going to bow to the inevitable and fulfil my destiny. I am going to destroy Xaphista."

chapter 67

'shiel rode far from the Defenders' camp under a leaden sky, her face flushed and tingling from the cold. She had told nobody the reason for her journey, just that she needed to be alone. She had especially avoided Brak. He may have guessed what she was planning and she did not want to give him the opportunity to object.

The Hythrun mare stretched her legs as the camp dwindled behind them. She had no particular destination in mind and in truth, for a good while she simply enjoyed the ride and the speed of the magnificent sorcerer-bred horse. It was the first time in a very long while she had done anything for the sheer joy of it, and she was reluctant to end it too soon.

Eventually, she came to a small rise on the undulating plain and looked back to discover the Defenders' camp was completely obscured by the fold of the land. She dismounted and stroked the lathered mare's neck, urging her to seek out what feed she could on the sparse winter plain. With a nicker of understanding the mare wandered off. When R'shiel was certain the horse was a safe distance from the knoll, she turned and looked up at the sky.

"Zegarnald!"

She received no answer other than the soughing wind rustling through the dried grass like a satin skirt brushing against a taffeta petticoat.

"Zegarnald!"

"Demon child."

She spun to find the War God standing on the knoll behind her. He was dressed in golden armor that glittered in the dull afternoon light. He was enormous. The battles that were tearing this world apart had made him as strong as he had ever been.

"You defied Xaphista, I see."

"No thanks to you."

"Brakandaran seems to have taught you disrespect, along with survival."

"Brak didn't teach me survival, and I don't need any lessons in being disrespectful from anyone," she retorted.

"Then why did you call me, demon child?"

"My name is R'shiel."

"You are the demon child."

"I am R'shiel!" she insisted. "The demon child is a creature you invented. It's not who I am!"

"Then you refuse your destiny?" The god sounded puzzled. Such fine distinctions were beyond his ability to comprehend.

"I'm not refusing it, Zegarnald. I'm accepting it. I will do as you ask. I will restore the balance and destroy the gods who have skewed things by becoming too strong."

"Gods? Surely you mean only one god?"

R'shiel smiled ingenuously. "You surely don't think I can just remove Xaphista without affecting any other gods, do you?"

Zegarnald pondered the problem for a moment and then nodded slowly. "Yes, I see. I had not considered that."

"Then you will leave me to fulfil my destiny as I see fit?"

The War God frowned. "You will go to Slarn and destroy Xaphista. What else is to be done?"

"Xaphista's power is drawn from his believers in Karien. I can't destroy him without destroying that too."

He thought on that and then nodded slowly. "Yes, I can see that."

"Then you'll leave me be? No more *tests*? No more *tempering*?"

"But..."

"Zegarnald, you have to trust me. I'm the only one who can do this. You have to let me do it my way. I'm half human. I know how humans think. I need you to promise that you will not interfere unless I ask you to."

"You ask a great deal of me, demon child."

"You're asking a great deal of me," she pointed out.

The God of War thought over the problem for a while before he nodded his agreement.

"Very well. I will do as you ask."

"Give me your oath."

"You doubt me?" He swelled at the implied insult.

"No. That's why I want your oath."

"Very well, I give you my solemn promise I will not interfere in your handling of this affair unless you ask it."

"No matter what happens?"

"No matter what happens," he agreed unhappily.

R'shiel smiled at him. "Thank you, Divine One. Now, just to prove that I will need your help from time to time, I have a job for you."

"A *job*?"

"Yes. I want you to find Damin's brother, Narvell, the Warlord of Elasapine and get him to turn back. Tell him he has to protect Krakandar from a Fardohnyan invasion."

"I AM *NOT* YOUR MESSENGER!" the god boomed, making the ground shake with his indignation.

"As you wish," she shrugged, turning away from him. "If Hablet crosses the Hythrun border too easily, there won't be a battle. On the other hand, if Narvell turns back, there should be a nice little bloodbath. But, if you'd rather not . . ."

"Perhaps I could consent to do this one favor for you," the god conceded with ill grace. "*But I am not your messenger*, demon child. Do not presume to use me in such a manner again."

"I wouldn't dream of it, Divine One."

It was nearly dark when R'shiel returned to the camp and she rode straight to the infirmary tent to check on Tarja.

Outwardly, his condition had not changed. He still lay as pale as death and barely breathing, but the fact that he still lived at all was a good sign. As she knelt beside the pallet, she was shocked to see his hands and feet bound to the bed with sturdy ropes.

Angrily, she turned on the medic who was changing the bandages of a man on the other side of the tent.

"Who did this?" she demanded.

"That man who came with you," the medic shrugged. "Jack, or Brak, or whatever his name is. He said things might get a bit rough and that tying him down was for his own protection."

R'shiel was horrified and fully intended to confront Brak about such a barbarous practice, but she was not so sure of herself that she untied the ropes. She sat with Tarja for a time, stroking his pallid forehead, trying to will him to live, before she left the Infirmary to seek Brak out.

It was fully dark when she emerged from the Infirmary and she looked about with a frown, realizing she had no idea where Brak would be. She was still pondering the problem when faint voices raised in anger reached her. One of the voices was unmistakably female and R'shiel could easily guess who it was.

Curiously, she followed the sound to a tent not far from the one where she and Adrina had been held prisoner. She could see Adrina's silhouette through the canvas wall as she paced in front of the lamp. They could probably *hear* her in Talabar.

"In case you're interested, the whole camp can hear you screeching," she announced as she pushed the flap back.

Adrina spun around angrily. Damin was sitting on a small campstool on the other side of the small table that held the flickering lamp, looking thoroughly miserable. A glowing brazier in the corner warmed the tent, almost as much as Adrina's anger.

"I DO *NOT* . . ." she began, then took a deep breath. "I do not screech."

"You do," R'shiel said. "I take it this . . . argument has to do with my declaration that you two should get married? So who's the dissenting party?"

"R'shiel, perhaps it's not such a good idea . . ." Damin began.

"Not a good idea! It's downright insane!" Adrina retorted. "Hablet will have a fit when he hears about it, and the first thing the Hythrun Warlords will do is hire an assassin to have me killed."

"You've both lived with the threat of assassins all your life—what difference will another make? As for Hablet, we'll just have to convince him there's a profit in it."

"And what about how I *feel*?" Adrina asked, unable to deny the truth of R'shiel's words. Anything that was profitable was fine by her father.

"How do you feel, then?"

"Used!" she snapped without hesitation.

"I need Hythria and Fardohnya at peace, Adrina. I can't face Xaphista any other way."

Adrina turned to Damin for support. "Even if this marriage stays my father's hand for a time, the Hythrun Warlords will never accept me as their High Princess."

"She has a point, R'shiel."

"The High Arrion will support you—she's your sister, isn't she? There are already Harshini in Greenharbour. With the Sorcerers' Collective backing you and once it's known that the demon child has sanctioned your union . . ."

"The demon child is still a legend in Hythria," Damin reminded her. "The only way this will work is if you return to Hythria with us. If you want to stop a civil war and want the other Warlords to believe in the demon child, then you're going to have to *show* them the demon child."

"I can't go to Hythria, Damin. I have to take care of something at the Citadel. Tarja will need my help when he's recovered and I still have to figure out how I'm going to deal with the Kariens."

"None of which you will be able to give your full attention to, until Fardohnya and Hythria are at peace," Damin pointed out, turning her own argument back on her. "What's the hurry, anyway? It'll take months before Tarja and the other captains can get the Defenders under their command organized enough to mount an effective resistance. The Citadel is under the control of the Kariens and you're not going to be able to do anything about *that* until you've destroyed Xaphista. The war in Medalon is over for now."

"I *have* to return to the Citadel. You don't understand . . ."

"No, you're the one who doesn't understand," Adrina cut in. "You want to change the whole world to suit your liking, then run off on some personal vendetta while the rest of us get killed trying to carry out your orders. Nobody wants to see the Kariens brought to their knees more than I, R'shiel, but Damin is right. If you want us to do this, then you're going to have to do it with us. Your mission to the Citadel will have to wait."

R'shiel glanced at the two of them and sighed. They were both such stubborn, strong-willed personalities and she needed this marriage to take place. She would have called on Kalianah to intervene, but Damin was one of Zegarnald's favorites. The War God would know she was up to something if another god interfered with Damin.

Frustration welling in her, she was forced to concede that they were right. Sending Damin back to Hythria with Adrina as his bride without proof of the demon child's existence would be akin to a death sentence.

"Very well, I'll come. But only long enough to convince the Warlords. After that, it's up to you two."

Damin glanced at Adrina, who nodded in agreement, although her scowl made it clear that she was less than enthusiastic about the whole idea.

"So, I'm to be the High Princess of Hythria."

"First a princess of Fardohnya, then Karien and now Hythria," Damin remarked. "You do get around, Adrina."

She turned on him angrily and R'shiel left the tent to continue her search for Brak, before she became even more embroiled in their argument.

Damn them, she though as she strode through the camp. *Damn them for being so obstinate. Damn them for being right.*

Brak had told her once that destiny had a way of catching up with you. Well, maybe it had. But just because it had caught her, didn't mean she couldn't make things happen her way. She would bring peace to the south, even if it meant delaying her inevitable confrontation with Loclon. That she would have to face him before this was over was as certain as her destiny was to destroy a god.

Any god . . . or all of them. It didn't really matter which . . .

The trick, R'shiel decided, as she moved through the firelit Defenders' camp, would be to manage affairs in such a way that nobody realized what was happening until it was too late to stop it.

GLOSSARY

Medalon

AFFIANA—Innkeeper in Testra. Brak's great-great grand niece.

B'THRIM SNOWBUILDER—Villager from Haven. Elder sister of J'nel.

BASEL—Sergeant of the Defenders stationed on the southern border.

BEK—Prisoner at the Grimfield. Sentenced to five years for arson.

BELDA—Sister of the Blade at the Grimfield.

BERETH—Former Sister of the Blade. Now a pagan.

CRISABELLE CORTANEN—Wife of Wilem Cortanen, Commandant of the Defenders.

DAVYDD TAILORSON—Lieutenant of the Defenders attached to the Intelligence Corps.

DAYAN JENGA—Quartermaster of the Defenders stationed in Bordertown. Younger brother of the Lord Defender.

DENJON—Captain of the Defenders.

DRACO—First Spear of the Sister and ceremonial bodyguard.

FOHLI—Corporal of the Defenders in the Grimfield.

FRANCIL ASHAREN—Sister of the Blade. Member of the Quorum. Longest standing member. Mistress of the Citadel.

GARET WARNER—Commandant of the Defenders. Head of Defender Intelligence and second most senior officer in the Defenders.

GAWN—Captain of the Defenders posted to the southern border.

GEORJ DRAKE—Captain of the Defenders. Tarja's best friend.

GHARI RODAK—Rebel Lieutenant. Brother of Mandah.

GWENELL—Physic. Sister of the Blade in charge of the Sisterhood's Infirmary at the Citadel.

HARITH NORTARN—Sister of the Blade. Member of the Quorum. Mistress of Sisterhood.

HEANER—Mistress of the most notorious brothel in the Citadel.

HELLA—Joyhinia's maid at the Citadel.

HERVE RODAK—A Rebel from Testra. Mandah and Ghari's cousin.

J'NEL SNOWBUILDER—Died in Haven from complications of childbirth without naming the father of her child.

JACOMINA LAROSSE—Sister of the Blade. Member of the Quorum. Mistress of Enlightenment.

JOYHINIA TENRAGAN—First Sister of the Sisters of the Blade following Mahina's impeachment.

JUNEE RIVERSON—Probate at the Citadel.

KHIRA—Pagan Rebel and Physic in the Grimfield.

KILENE—Probate at the Citadel.

KORGAN—Deceased. Former Lord Defender. Rumored to be Tarja's father.

LENK—Corporal of the Defenders at the Grimfield.

L'RIN—Innkeeper of the Inn of the Hopeless in the Grimfield.

LOCLON—Wain Loclon. Lieutenant of the Defenders and Champion of the Arena. Promoted to Captain following the Purge.

LOUHINA FARCRON—Sister of the Blade. Appointed to the Quorum following Joyhinia's elevation to First Sister.

LYCREN—Sergeant of the Defenders in the Grimfield.

MAHINA CORTANEN—First Sister. Mother of Wilem.

MANDAH RODAK—Formerly a novice and now a pagan rebel from Medalon. Elder sister of Ghari.

MARIELLE—Prisoner at the Grimfield, sentenced with R'shiel.

MARTA—Probate at the Citadel.

MYSEKIS—Captain of the Defenders stationed in the Grimfield.

NHEAL ALCARNEN—Captain of the Defenders.

PADRIC—Pagan rebel.

PALIN JENGA—Lord Defender. Commander in Chief of the Defenders. Brother of Dayan Jenga and rumored to be R'shiel's father.

PENY—*Court'esa* working for Mistress Heaner.

PROZLAN—Sister of the Blade stationed at the Grimfield, responsible for discipline among the female prisoners.

R'SHIEL—Probate. Daughter of the First Sister.

SUELAN—Sister of the Blade. The First Sister's Secretary and Harith's niece.

SUNNY—Sunflower Hopechild. *Court'esa* from the Citadel who befriends R'shiel on their journey to the Grimfield.

TARJA—Tarjanian Tenragan. Son of the First Sister, Joyhinia. Captain of the Defenders.

TEGGERT—Former convict. Works as a cook in the Commandant's household in the Grimfield.

UNWIN—Sister of the Blade at the Grimfield in charge of the Grimfield's Kitchens.

VERKIN—Kriath Verkin. Commandant of Bordetown.

WANDEAR—Probate at the Citadel.

WILEM—Commandant of the Grimfield. Son of Mahina and married to Crisabelle.

WYLBIR—A rebel. Former sergeant of the Defenders.

ZAC—Prisoner in the Grimfield.

Harshini

BRAK—Lord Brakandaran té Carn. Only other living half-breed Harshini.

DRANYMIRE—Prime Demon bonded to the house of té Ortyn.

GLENANARAN—Harshini sorcerer who leaves Sanctuary to help Brak.

KORANDELLAN TÉ ORTYN—King of the Harshini. Nephew of Lorandranek and brother of Shananara.

LORANDRANEK TÉ ORTYN—Deceased. Former king of the Harshini, driven mad by the task laid on him by the gods.

SHANANARA—Her Royal Highness, Shananara té Ortyn. Daughter of Rorandelan. Sister of Korandellan.

The Gods

BREHN—God of Storms.

CHELTARAN—God of Healing.

DACENDARAN—God of Thieves.

GIMLORIE—God of Music.

JASHIA—God of Fire.

JAKERLON—God of Liars.

JELANNA—Goddess of Fertility.

JONDALUP—God of Chance.

KAELARN—God of the Oceans.

KALIANAH—Goddess of Love.

LEYLANAN—Goddess of the Ironbrook River.

MAERA—Goddess of the Glass River.

PATANAN—God of Good Fortune.

VODEN—God of Green Life.

ZEGARNALD—God of War.

Hythria

ALMODAVAR—Hythrun Raider. Captain of Damin Wolfblade's Raiders.

CYRUS EAGLESPIKE—Hythrun. Warlord of Dregian Province. Damin Wolfblade's distant cousin.

DAMIN WOLFBLADE—Warlord of Krakandar and heir to the High Prince's throne. Son of Princess Marla and nephew of Lernen Wolfblade, High Prince of Hythria.

KALAN—High Arrion of the Sorcerers' Collective in Hythria. Damin Wolfblade's half sister, also known as Kalan of Elasapine. She has a twin brother, Narvell Hawksword.

LERNEN WOLFBLADE—High Prince of Hythria. Damin's uncle. A known pervert with no desire to produce an heir and rather exotic sexual appetites.

MARLA WOLFBLADE—Princess of Hythria. Sister of Lernen Wolfblade and mother of Damin. Married 5 times she is also the mother of Kalan and Narvell Hawksword of Elasapine.

RORIN—Seneschal to the High Arrion of the Sorcerers' Collective.

SOOTHAN—Captain of a Hythrun fishing boat.

Karien

ARINGARD—Queen of Karien. Married to Jasnoff and mother of Cratyn.

CHARITY—Karien noblewoman. Granddaughter of Baron Lodnan.

CHASTITY—Daughter of Terbolt. Adrina's Lady-In-Waiting. Formerly betrothed to Cratyn.

CRATYN—Crown Prince of Karien. Son of Jasnoff and Aringard.

DRENDYN—Karien. Earl of Tiler's Pass. Cratyn's cousin and nephew of King Jasnoff.

ELFRON—Karien priest sent to the Citadel with Lord Pieter to denounce the Sisterhood's handling of the pagans.

GARANUS—Karien Priest sent to the Citadel with Terbolt, the Duke of Setenton.

HOPE—Adrina's Lady-In-Waiting.

JASNOFF—King of Karien. Married to Aringard. Father of Cratyn and uncle to Drendyn.

JAYMES OF KIRKLAND—Karien page attached to Lord Laetho's retinue. Son of Lord Laetho's Third Steward, he cannot be knighted due to his common birth.

LORD PIETER—Karien Envoy to Medalon.

MIKEL OF KIRKLAND—Karien page attached to Lord Laetho's retinue. Jaymes' younger brother. Appointed as Adrina's page following his escape from Medalon.

OVERLORD—See Xaphista.

PACIFICA—Adrina's Lady-In-Waiting.

TERBOLT—Karien. Duke of Setenton and father of Chastity.

VONULUS—Karien Priest appointed as Confessor to Adrina.

XAPHISTA—The Overlord. God of the Kariens.

Fardohnya

ADRINA—Princess of Fardohnya. Eldest legitimate child of King Hablet and his first wife. Adrina's mother was beheaded for trying to assassinate her husband's mistress and her illegitimate son Tristan.

CASSANDRA—Princess of Fardohnya. Adrina's younger sister and second legitimate child of Hablet.

HABLET—King of the Fardohnyans. Has 14 illegitimate sons and thirteen legitimate daughters. He refuses to name his heir, hoping one of his wives will give him a legitimate son.

JAPINEL—Fardohnyan tailor, alchemist and con-man.

LECTER TURON—Chamberlain of the Fardohnyan Court. Lector is a eunuch who makes his fortune collecting bribes.

RAVEN—Head of the Assassins' Guild that operates in Hythria and Fardohnya.

TERIAHNA—The Raven. Head of the Assassins' Guild.

TAMYLAN—Fardohnyan slave raised to serve Adrina. Lover of Tristan on Adrina's orders.

TRISTAN—Bastard son of King Hablet of Fardohnya. Adrina's half-brother and Captain of her Guard sent to Karien.